PRINCE OF TRICKS

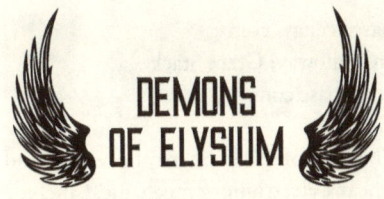

DEMONS
OF ELYSIUM

JANE KINDRED

RIPTIDE
PUBLISHING

Riptide Publishing
PO Box 1537
Burnsville, NC 28714
www.riptidepublishing.com

Prince of Tricks
Copyright © 2014, 2021 by Jane Kindred

Cover art: L.C. Chase, lcchase.com
Editors: Carole-ann Galloway; Grace Stack
Layout: L.C. Chase, lcchase.com

ISBN: 978-1-62649-946-1

Second edition
July, 2021

Also available in ebook:
ISBN: 978-1-62649-945-4

PRINCE OF TRICKS

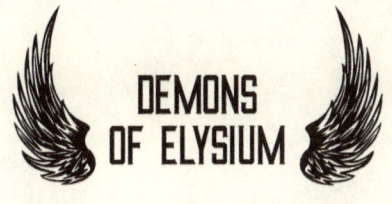

DEMONS
OF ELYSIUM

JANE KINDRED

RIPTIDE
PUBLISHING

For Pussy Riot.

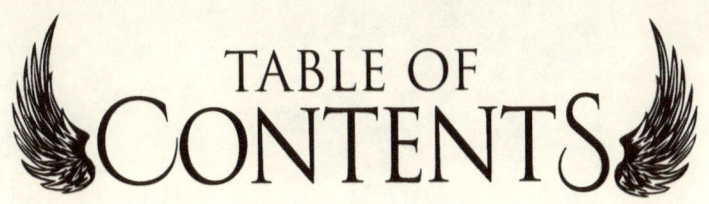

TABLE OF
CONTENTS

CHAPTER ONE

The demon in his bed had a spectacular ass. Belphagor let the sheet slide down as he shifted position beside Vasily on the narrow cot, baring the part in question. Light played against the marked flesh in stripes through the threadbare curtain—watermarks against fire.

It was this lovely bit of firespirit ass that had been Belphagor's undoing—though its form at the time had barely hinted at its present magnificence. For the reigning master of wingcasting—the preferred game of chance in this demonic little enclave of Heaven—reputation was everything. Having his purse cut by a scrawny, untrained street demon had warranted a swift and public response.

At a full hand above six feet, Vasily would have stood out in a crowd even without the flame-red hair that distinguished him. And yet of all the marks he might have chosen, he'd targeted Belphagor that evening at The Brimstone a year ago.

Ghosting his finger over the pleasing lines of his handiwork on Vasily's skin, Belphagor shook his head in amusement, the corner of his mouth turning up at the memory of that ill-advised attempt.

The firespirit scoundrel had been watching him all night. As usual, Belphagor had cleaned out nearly every player in the Raqia den of iniquity. He gathered his winnings and stretched as he stood, giving the obviously inexperienced cutpurse the chance to make his move. At the lightening of the weight at his hip, he turned and grabbed the thief by the collar as he tried to slip away. Without missing a beat, the next player slid into Belphagor's vacated seat, the kibitzers flowing around the pair like parts in a well-oiled machine. An altercation over facets or even a brawl was a minor inconvenience at The Brimstone.

The thief twisted in Belphagor's grip, hissing like a cornered alley cat, but Belphagor held fast. He took stock as he retrieved the purse. Lean and hungry looking, with hard eyes of a startling hazel hue that danced with the glittering flames of reflected lamplight, the young demon couldn't have seen more than eighteen summers. He wouldn't make it to nineteen if he continued such inept thieving.

Belphagor tucked his winnings away. "You'll have to be much faster than that if you expect to make a living."

"Fast enough for you, old-timer." His vocal chords grated like sandpaper, as if from years of smoke and drink.

"We'll see how fast your fingers are after the Ophanim have broken your knuckles." Belphagor turned him about and hauled him toward the stairs that led up to the street. The young finger-smith struggled to free himself, spitting in Belphagor's face when his efforts failed, a glint of feral terror in his eyes.

Belphagor wiped the warm spittle from his cheek. "Relax, little spitfire. I'm sure they'll leave you one good hand."

"I'm hardly little." That much was true; the closer Belphagor held him, the more obvious it became. "And I'm not afraid of the Ophanim Guard." That much was *not* true. "Or of you, you ponce."

Belphagor's mouth twitched as he tried to keep a straight face. "On second thought, a night in the supernal cellar probably wouldn't teach you a thing. What you need is to learn some manners. I've half a mind to give you a good strapping."

The threat elicited a derisive laugh. "I'd like to see you try!"

Belphagor let his eyebrow drift upward. "Is that a challenge?" He held up the purse. "I have a pound of crystal that says you won't last three strokes without begging for mercy."

The thief fixed his gaze on the offered prize like a starved dog with a cutlet dangling before him. "You're lying. You'd never give that up for such a sucker bet."

"I never go back on my word. And I never make a sucker bet." Belphagor let go of him, tossing the winnings lightly in his hand as he turned back into the club. "My room is in the rear." He made his way to the rented rooms without looking back. When he reached his door, he turned to find the would-be thief behind him, eyes glowing and changing in the light like fire opals. There was a pureblood in his line somewhere—and not far back.

Belphagor ushered him inside and locked the door, pocketing the key. "In case you have any ideas about snatching and running."

Defiant heat flashed in those opalescent eyes. "You want me to roll for you, you'll have to pay. Five facets. Ten if you want me to act like I like it."

Belphagor regarded him evenly. "The deal is you take three strokes without crying mercy, you get the money. You don't, you get nothing. It's a wager. I'm not renting you."

He reached for the hooks above the dressing table, fingers pausing to stroke the straight-edged razor before closing around the strop. Let the insolent pickpocket wonder just what he had coming.

With the strop folded into a loop, Belphagor turned and appraised his subject. The bones needed a little meat on them, but they were good ones.

He snapped the loop between his hands. "What's your name?" Judging by the startled blink, Belphagor had successfully unnerved him.

The growled answer came after a slight pause. "Vasily."

Belphagor stroked the leather against his palm. "Well, if five facets is all you're asking, young Vasily, you're selling yourself short. But I'm going to call you *mal'chik*." He grabbed the long tangles of Vasily's hair and twisted. "Because you're behaving like a spoiled little boy."

Vasily stumbled as Belphagor swung him around, grabbing at his own hair instead of aiming a blow that might have ended things then and there.

Belphagor pulled up the stool by the table and sat, tossing Vasily over his lap in one smooth motion and pinning him with a one-armed wrestler's hold.

"Let go of me, you bastard!" The panic in Vasily's voice said he was already too disarmed to fight.

Belphagor responded with unaffected calm. "You have a decision to make, Vasily. We made a bargain. The question now is whether you intend to honor it. Three strokes without crying out, and you win the purse. Are we agreed?"

Vasily's breathing was rapid as he seemed to consider, before finally growling, "Agreed."

"What was that? I didn't quite hear you." In the quiet, the pounding of firespirit blood was audible. "Understand that once we begin, there is no changing your mind."

"Agreed!"

Without giving him time to reconsider, Belphagor brought the strop down against Vasily's thighs, satisfaction curling the corners of his mouth at the strangled gasp this elicited. Vasily had obviously never had a proper beating. Of course, the beatings Belphagor gave went well beyond what could be considered proper.

Before Vasily could recover, Belphagor drew back and struck again, this time at the top of his buttocks—just a touch too high, designed to deliver a blinding sting. The threadbare pants tore as Vasily shuddered from head to toe.

Belphagor let him wait for the next stroke so the sting would build. "Had enough?"

"Was that supposed to hurt?" Vasily's voice was tight. "I barely felt it."

On the last word, Belphagor hauled back and struck, the tip of his strop curling around the exposed flesh on Vasily's hip as it landed.

Vasily cried out as though the sound had been wrung from him by surprise and jerked against his hold.

"Just as I thought," said Belphagor. "You forfeit."

The defeated thief struggled to catch his breath, clearly on the verge of tears, and Belphagor struck him again to see them spill. The teardrops almost sizzled as they hit the floor.

Vasily countered them with rage, his fury building until he radiated heat. "You said three strokes." The rough growl bordered on a sob.

"Three if you could take them without crying out. You forgot to ask what happened if you lost."

Belphagor struck him again, and Vasily snarled and swore, wasting his energy and magnifying the pain by thrashing and howling. Anger transformed into desperation as the strokes continued, until he broke down at last into incoherent begging and went limp, all resistance drained from him.

Belphagor let him cry. Instinct told him it was what Vasily needed, to be able to let go and express the emotion erupting as if it had been bottled inside him without leaving room for air.

When Belphagor released him, Vasily slipped onto his knees, still sobbing, his head hanging in defeat.

"There now, *mal'chik*." Belphagor brushed the damp hair away from Vasily's eyes. "I reckon you've learned your lesson." After a moment's hesitation, he kissed the fire-warm brow.

Vasily's breath drew in with a hitch, and he gazed up at Belphagor in confusion, as if kindness were foreign to him. "Do you want me to get you off now?"

Belphagor pushed away the hand reaching for his belt, annoyed at having considered the offer for an instant. "Really, *mal'chik*, I'm much too old for you."

Vasily continued to stare up at him with the unfocused gaze of one who had just experienced for the first time the ecstatic transport possible through extreme physical discipline. It would be a shame to put him out on the street in such a state.

Belphagor sighed. "I suppose you need somewhere to sleep."

The young demon nodded uncertainly, and Belphagor drew him to his feet and led him to the bed, where Vasily curled up in his arms as if he'd always belonged there.

Belphagor had only meant to hold him until Vasily drifted off, but sunlight was streaming through the leaded panes when he opened his eyes, making fire of the red hair sprawled across his chest.

He kissed the top of Vasily's head, and the demon stirred and stretched. "Come, *mal'chik*. Time to go."

Vasily paused midyawn. "Go?" He repeated the word as if it had no meaning.

"I have business to attend to." Belphagor rose and picked up the purse from the bureau. "You didn't win the wager. But you were a very good boy." He shook a pile of facets into his hand and held them out—enough to keep the firespirit belly full for a month.

Vasily's eyes flashed, the urge to knock the facets to the floor plain on his face. But living on the streets of Raqia had no doubt made him too wise for that, and he took his reward. Something in the volatile anger emanating from him as Vasily made for the door kindled a fire of Belphagor's own—deep inside, in a place he'd forgotten. It took everything he had not to call him back. Before he could do anything so foolhardy, Vasily was gone.

But the firespirit was impossible to get out of his head. Vasily returned to The Brimstone for the next several nights, ignoring Belphagor, playing errand boy to a pair of demons with questionable reputations. Belphagor considered taking him aside and cautioning him, but it would probably do more harm than good.

When the three of them arrived one evening with a large entourage in tow, already well in their cups, Belphagor kept a surreptitious eye on Vasily. The attention of one demon in particular raised Belphagor's hackles. Valac was a famously sore loser who'd met Belphagor on the street once after a game and attacked him with a knife. Belphagor had given him a serious thrashing, but he still bore a scar on his forearm as a memento.

Valac plied Vasily with drinks, laughing at his increasing state of inebriation as the younger demon quickly became too drunk to notice he was being made sport of.

Belphagor fumed, trying to keep his mind on his game, losing a round that ought to have been child's play. When the group departed, loudly proclaiming they were bent on more ribald adventure, and took Vasily with them, Belphagor folded, leaving his stunned opponent a sizable pot.

It didn't take a genius to guess where the group was bound—the less reputable venues in the quarter known as the Devil's Doorstep, where Belphagor spotted them in a drinking hall famous for rough trade. Several demons were gathered around Vasily as they challenged him to guzzle whole pints of ale. He swayed on his stool but gamely took their challenges—so far managing to stay upright.

Belphagor pulled up the hood of his cloak and sat nursing a cordial of wormwood in the corner, determined to step in if things got out of hand. Their disrespect for the naïve demon had raised his ire, but the sight of Valac groping him was almost insufferable.

When Valac tilted Vasily's head back for a kiss and emptied a mouthful of whiskey into him, Belphagor found himself on his feet, fists clenched against the table. But after a sputter of surprise, Vasily swallowed and grinned, and the party cheered him.

"Swallowed it all!" Valac slapped him on the back. "Our boy's a pro." He took the bottle in one hand and Vasily in the other. "Let's see what else he can swallow." The others rose with him, leading Vasily weaving between them out to the alley.

Belphagor choked the glass in his hand. It was none of his business. Vasily was old enough to consent and had gone willingly. Belphagor's interference wouldn't be welcome. He forced himself to finish his drink and set out for The Brimstone, but cheering from the alley as he passed gave him pause. After pushing his way through the gathered crowd, he found Vasily on his hands and knees in front of Valac, engaged in an act of which he seemed barely conscious. Tossing demons out of his way, Belphagor dragged Valac off and threw him against the wall.

Someone else grabbed Vasily by the hair to keep him upright.

Belphagor uttered a low growl. "Get your filthy hands off my boy."

Red-faced, Valac pulled himself together as he scrambled to his feet. "And who the fuck are you?"

He fixed Valac with a cold stare. "The name's Belphagor."

Recognition seemed to sober Valac up. He cleared his throat, looking sullen. "Nobody told me he was your boy."

"You knew well enough he was somebody's. But I doubt you gave a damn." The others backed away, and Belphagor caught Vasily as he slumped to the ground. "Spread the word," he warned darkly. "Anyone who touches Vasily will answer to me."

There were no objections as Belphagor led him away.

Vasily's demeanor was far from grateful when he woke with a hangover in Belphagor's bed. He squinted in the late-morning light, his expression surly and his glower deepening when he focused on Belphagor. "Who said you could bring me here? I suppose you want your facets' worth."

"You're not here to talk," Belphagor snapped. "You're here to listen."

Vasily managed to wince and widen his eyes in the same gesture.

"You're to stay away from that filth you've been carousing with."

"Who's going to stop me?" Vasily threw off the covers but stumbled when he tried to stand. Belphagor caught him around the waist and pulled him onto his lap. He could feel the ribs beneath the warm skin.

"I am." Belphagor wrapped an arm around him, murmuring against his ear. "Even if you decide to spit in my face and go back to the street when I let go of you. I'll be watching out for you. You want to sell yourself, that's your business. But you'll get what you're worth, from respectable sources."

Vasily stiffened against his hold. "What makes you think I want a pimp?"

Belphagor smoothed the hair away from his cheek. "I don't want to be your pimp, you stupid boy. I don't need the bother. But I will beat the living hell out of anyone who misuses you, whether you think you deserve it or not."

"Why?" He choked out the word, clearly fighting tears.

"I don't know. I just know that I will." Perhaps it was because Vasily reminded him of himself when he was young and naïve with no one to look out for him. Perhaps it was more than that. "From now on, you are my boy. My *mal'chik*."

Firespirit tears, it turned out, were extremely hot.

"Sweet boy," he murmured now against Vasily's shoulder, sculpting a hand around the firm slope at the thigh. In a year's time, he had filled out impressively. Vasily stirred, not yet awake but his muscles tensing beneath the flesh. "*Moi mal'chik.*" Belphagor breathed the word, an exhalation of essential rightness and desire. This was *his* boy, his *mal'chik*.

Vasily's pulse quickened, waking mind surging to the surface. Belphagor rested his cheek against a flexing biceps and watched Vasily's magnificent cock swell with blood.

"Good morning." He pressed his own hardness against the small of Vasily's back. "Any regrets?"

Vasily turned his head toward him, the rough nap of bearded cheek rubbing a pleasant irritation against Belphagor's skin. "Regrets?" The gravel in his voice was even more pronounced first thing in the morning. "*Nyet, ser.*"

The Russian response sent a rush of possessive fire through Belphagor's veins. It was the language he demanded during discipline, part of the ritual of obedience as well as a device to focus the subject's conscious mind on something other than physical sensation. Vasily had used it without prompting, a sign of his total surrender. It made Belphagor want to possess him fully. Immediately.

But he was also a bit of a masochist in his own right. He could wait. He'd waited a year just to have him the first time. And it had been mere hours since.

He tightened his hand against the bruised, beautiful ass, and Vasily made a slight noise of discomfort. "You'll have quite a reminder of my hand when you try to sit for the next few days."

"Not just your hand," said Vasily gruffly.

To keep from giving in to the desire for instant gratification, Belphagor had to bite Vasily's shoulder, drawing a lovely hiss of steamy breath from him. "Show me how that memory makes you feel." He sucked lightly at the place he'd bitten. "Put your cock in your fist."

Vasily didn't hesitate, his sizeable hand closing around the equally sizeable shaft. He stroked himself rapidly, enthusiastically, while Belphagor snaked an arm around his waist beneath the pumping forearm and played with Vasily's nipples.

"Good boy. That's it, my sweet boy."

"I'm not a boy," Vasily growled, his last word grunted in an almost surprised ejaculation of sound to match the efforts of his body. Hot firespirit fluid shot from the swollen head of his cock in a perfect trail up his abs and into the hollow below his throat.

Belphagor pushed him onto his back and straddled him, his own unfulfilled erection poised between them like an exclamation point. "I told you, you're *my* boy. Mine." He dipped his head and scooped his tongue into the warm stuff at Vasily's throat like a cat's into cream. "And don't you forget it."

A red glimmer threatened in the depths of Vasily's pupils, giving the irises an amber cast. This evidence of his defiance, despite the fact that Belphagor had finally given him what he wanted—or broken down and caved to his charms, more like—was a Pavlovian bell to Belphagor's hunger for him.

It had nearly driven him mad to keep Vasily at arm's length this long, telling himself he didn't deserve him, that Vasily couldn't possibly want him. He'd felt a duty to mentor him and see to his neglected education, putting aside the possibility of anything more. The past year had been a kind of delicious torture as he'd taken to the floor at night with a pile of blankets to give Vasily the bed—only to wake most nights to discover Vasily climbing under the covers to curl up in his arms. Sleep had been impossible, tangled in those long, sinewy limbs, enveloped in the uncanny warmth Vasily exuded without breaking a sweat—all the while resisting his growing desire.

Even now, after the consummation of it, his heart fluttered like a panicked bird caged in his chest, waiting for something terrible to happen. Waiting for Vasily to realize Belphagor wasn't as young as he appeared and to ridicule the helpless state to which he'd reduced him: hopelessly enamored of another demon, after the equivalent of a human lifetime of solitude.

For Belphagor, that solitude had been his strength. He hadn't needed anyone since the earliest betrayals of youthful love. But Vasily had brought him to his knees. Never mind that it was *Vasily* on his knees that had done it to him.

"What's got your fire up, *mal'chik*?" He kissed the spot he'd cleaned with his tongue beneath Vasily's Adam's apple. "I thought you wanted to be mine."

"I hate it when you treat me like a child."

Belphagor raised an eyebrow. "I'm fairly certain I treated you as rather the opposite last night. Was it not satisfactory?"

The natural pink of Vasily's cheeks reddened more obviously. "Of course it was. I mean, it was more than satisfactory. *Way* more. Damn it, Beli." He crooked his arm across his face as if looking up into Belphagor's eyes during such talk embarrassed him. He was utterly charming. As was the little endearment that had slipped out, though Belphagor might have decked another demon for it.

He kissed Vasily's sullen mouth. "It was also far more for me." It was almost a whisper. "You've absolutely spoiled me for anyone else."

"*Good.*" The word was delivered with a sudden sharpness. So that was what was bothering him. It sparked a bit of defiance of his own. He wasn't used to having anyone put restraints on him. That was Belphagor's specialty.

"Don't seek to possess me, *mal'chik*. I'm an airspirit."

Vasily moved his arm away from his eyes, and they were glowing with furious heat. "So that's how it is. You own me, you tell me what I can and can't do, but you can do as you like." The roiling anger in that gaze warmed Belphagor like combustion from the inside out. The thought of putting Vasily over his knee once more made him almost painfully hard. Without equivocation, he was a slave to this brutally beautiful young demon. Which was all the more reason to play it cool.

"Yes, Vasya. That's how it is."

The violent rebuff wasn't unexpected, but Belphagor had nonetheless failed to brace for it. He found himself forcefully ejected from the cot and sprawled on the cold wooden floor with Vasily standing over him, magnificent in his literal naked anger.

"Then maybe you should skip the foreplay and go fuck yourself!" Vasily delivered the Germanic hardness of the lovely verb *fuck* as if he were demonstrating it. As Vasily jerked his jeans onto his legs like he was punishing the fabric, Belphagor watched with unabashed admiration of the musculature being hidden away. Hooray at least for his lazy laundering habits that had resulted in this morning's "commando" mode.

Belphagor picked himself up, along with the black T-shirt on the floor beside him, which he held out to Vasily as if he couldn't care less whether the demon walked out on him. He'd learned better than to show his hand in matters of the heart.

Vasily snatched the shirt from his grip and yanked it on over the tangled red locks he'd been cultivating. The shirt had once been Belphagor's. It had stretched to its limits and was now much too small on the firespirit's frame. Belphagor wished there were cameras in Heaven. He could just about die from gazing at the image Vasily struck.

Vasily was waiting for him to apologize or take back what he'd said, to placate him into staying. Belphagor had no intention of doing so. He had simply stated a fact. Vasily was his. It was indisputable. When he finished pouting over being consigned to the role he'd chosen himself, he'd be back.

The younger demon yanked open the rickety door—now in danger of coming right off the hinges in his grip—cast one last furious, fiery glare in Belphagor's direction, and left with a fierce slam. The bottom hinge bent.

Belphagor glanced down at his relentless state of arousal with a sigh of resignation. His masochistic streak might be at an all-time high.

CHAPTER TWO

Belphagor had expected Vasily to be gone no longer than a day. Tooting his own horn though it might be—and the exquisite whipping he'd delivered aside—he'd fucked Vasily to the point of blissed-out insensibility. It was difficult to imagine anyone not coming back for more, let alone his *mal'chik*, who'd been begging for the physical consummation of their intense attraction for nigh on a year.

But Belphagor had underestimated Vasily's own masochism. Blessed with the most stubborn, bull-headed personality Belphagor had ever encountered, Vasily might deny himself what he wanted most, even after having had a taste of it, just to get back at Belphagor for his apparent indifference.

It was an essential part of the game they were engaged in. As that first whipping a year ago had demonstrated, the power dynamic the younger demon craved required the added element of emotional betrayal. He needed to feel wronged, to reach a fever pitch of indignation, in order to let go and fully surrender himself to Belphagor's control. Unless he was driven to a hopeless resignation, no amount of physical dominance or eroticized pain would satisfy him.

Bringing Vasily to the brink of despondency and then enveloping him in the comfort and tenderness he despaired of—knowing nothing else in the world could make him feel loved—was in turn the most emotionally fulfilling experience Belphagor had ever had. To be loved himself by the one who felt utterly abandoned by him pierced Belphagor in a deep, internal place—went to the very marrow of his bones.

He knew what it was to love desperately and to be abandoned. The one he'd loved would never come to redeem him, but he could be for Vasily what he himself had once longed for so hopelessly.

In the gaming room of The Brimstone for the next several evenings, Belphagor kept an eye out for Vasily's entrance without appearing to do so. He hadn't become the best wingcasting player in Raqia by telegraphing his moves. He played exceptionally well, in fact, by maintaining an external awareness beyond the boundaries of the marble-rimmed table while projecting an air of inattentiveness to anything but his own cards. The false inward focus was contagious and tended to make his opponent forget to take note of the broader actions of the game.

When he cast the die or called his opponent's cast, he let his attention encompass the entire establishment. This part of the game was only chance. Willing the die to land on the elemental creature one had called as the twelve-sided game piece struck the table's rim had no effect on the outcome. Shifting the air around the table might—with a flick of the wrist in casting or the breath of a bored sigh—but most demons were woefully ignorant of their own elemental power. That Belphagor's cardinal element responded more readily to his influence was no coincidence.

He'd devoted years of his life—and the number was considerable for a demon who, in truth, had fallen to the world of Man more times than he liked to admit—to understanding how to master the dominant element in his blood. The number of Fallen who literally fell was small in comparison to the demonic population, and the average demon had never experienced terrestrial magic.

In Heaven, a demon—or even an angel, though they were generally too uptight to try—might manipulate his element for simple tricks and folk magic, but in the world of Man, every celestial possessed a power that manifested as elemental wings.

Belphagor had first fallen when he was only fifteen. He hadn't known about earthly radiance, and the Fallen he'd encountered there, in the city of Petrograd, hadn't told him. It was only in fleeing the law some months after his arrival that he'd inadvertently found his wings.

Leaping from a bridge to escape, he'd expected to swim for the riverbank and found himself instead soaring far above it. Elemental magic had burst from his shoulder blades as wings of solid air, perceivable only as an absence of light, as if they absorbed its visible range.

"Ptarmigan," he said absently as the die tumbled from his opponent's fingers and struck the rim. The other demon scowled as the die landed with the aforementioned fowl faceup. Sometimes Belphagor's luck was better when he put no effort into the game at all.

"It's a loaded die," the player accused. The demon had clearly had too much to drink.

Belphagor narrowed his gaze on the pallid waterspirit. "I beg your pardon?"

"Loaded die!" He stood and delivered the accusation loudly enough for the house to hear. Any such accusation had to be taken seriously. The game was immediately halted and the pot forfeited to the house while the deck and die were confiscated for examination.

It took every ounce of Belphagor's restraint to keep from leaping on the little worm and delivering a very unerotic beating. He'd turned up the cuffs of his shirt in preparation for it without being aware he'd done so, showing his ink like an animal might show its teeth in warning.

The bluish-black tattoos that decorated his fingers and the backs of his hands were the badges of his incarceration in the Russian prison system. They marked him as *vor*, a thief, and announced in no uncertain terms that he was not to be trifled with.

Among the right people, the association commanded a certain level of respect in the world of Man that he might never have been afforded due to his less-than-impressive physical stature. But in Raqia, it had the added intimidation factor of making it clear that he had not only dealt with the harsh prison system of the *Zona* but with the Seraph bounty hunters who exploited it with their own terrestrial magic.

Just as the game inspector pocketed Belphagor's favorite wingcasting set, the street door opened, ushering in a blast of wet winter wind and a party of young angelic toughs.

One of them had his arm over the shoulder of a demon smartly dressed in a black velvet frock coat and tailored slacks. Despite his impressive size, had it not been for the shock of red matted locks done up in a knot just below the demon's crown, Belphagor might actually have missed him.

The player still glaring across the table at him ceased to matter.

Angels were touching his boy.

Belphagor's brain dropped into his testicles. Charging across the bar like a bull sporting bloody banderillas, he struck the angelic prick right in the kisser.

The angel went down in stunned surprise. Time seemed to freeze for a moment before the rest of his entourage sprang forward and descended on Belphagor, dragging him upstairs to the street. Despite his size, he was more than a match for a pair of the little bastards, or even three; prison had taught him a number of valuable skills. But Belphagor had angered a pack of them.

"Learn your fucking place, you piece of Fallen trash."

While he struggled, snarling, with the ones who had his arms, a fist landed in his gut, and another slammed into his cheek. As Belphagor spat blood into the snow, the angel about to pummel him suddenly howled with pain. Vasily was behind him, twisting the angel's arm into an unnatural pose.

Belphagor's odds had just improved.

The howling one went sprawling across the slush-dirty cobblestone while the pair holding Belphagor let go of him to converge on Vasily. Belphagor slammed his elbow into the throat of another on his left, simultaneously kicking sidelong against the knee of the one on his right, dislocating it with a loud pop drowned out by the angel's shriek as he hopped backward. While the choking one on Belphagor's left swung wildly at him, Belphagor grasped the wide-swiping arm and knocked him face-first into the brick wall of The Brimstone, punching him in the kidney for good measure.

He turned and saw the two who'd attacked Vasily scrambling away, badly bloodied. The one who'd been sprawled on the ground dragged himself across the street with his arm at an alarming angle, wailing like a child. The rest wisely took off running, shouting racial slurs over their shoulders in cowardice.

Belphagor wiped his fist across his bloody lip and met Vasily's eyes. Flame sparked dangerously in them.

"*Sukin syn*," Vasily snarled. This was not the Russian Belphagor had taught him. "You think you own me, you son of a bitch? You think you can just march up and mark your property the moment someone else takes a fancy to me?"

Belphagor's stance was casual, but the set of his jaw was hard. "I told you." He spoke calmly. Dangerously. "Angels are not to touch you."

Vasily had just dispatched a handful of angels in seconds, the same angels who'd been beating the snot out of Belphagor a moment before, yet his angry expression was now tinged with fear.

Knowing he could strike that fear into Vasily despite his superior physical strength made Belphagor hungry to make good on the unspoken promise. "Did I not make myself clear, *mal'chik*?"

"No— I mean, yes, you—" Vasily stopped and swallowed, clearly trying to pull his defiance back on. "Why?"

"Why?"

"Why can't I take facets from angels if they want to spend them on me?" He brushed at the velvet coat a bit proudly. The gesture reminded Belphagor of a fine gray velvet frock coat he'd received from a patron on his first fall. He ignored the long-buried ache in his chest.

"What did you do to get it?"

Vasily eyed him warily. Snow had begun to dust his broad shoulders. "Same as always."

Belphagor took a step closer. "When I took you off the street, you weren't making enough to keep your belly full. Now you're earning expensive gifts."

Vasily's cheeks reddened. "You don't think I'm good enough to earn them?"

Belphagor's fierce mien slipped a little. "Of course I do. It's the angels who aren't good enough. I've never met one who wasn't five times as tight with his purse as a demon with only a handful of facets to his name." Stepping even closer, he grabbed the satin-backed lapel. "What did you do?"

Vasily glared. "The duke wanted to show off for his friends. I let them all watch."

Belphagor took several slow breaths without showing it outwardly, willing down the anger licking over him like his own seraphic fire. "Did he keep you well fed?" He realized as soon as the words left his mouth that this could be taken in more than one way, but Vasily didn't seem to recognize the potential double entendre.

The younger demon shrugged. "There's a whole staff of demons at the place—the duke keeps a villa on the Left Bank for parties—and there's a buffet constantly filled for his guests. He let me have as much as I liked."

"I see." The scene sounded all too familiar, though the parties at which Belphagor had been the star attraction had been in Petrograd more than half a century ago. "This duke can obviously offer you finer dress and fare than I can. Maybe you're better off with him."

Vasily's stunned expression made his heart ache. "You're throwing me out?"

"You left, Vasya."

The normally gruff, burly demon looked as though he was about to break down in tears. "I was mad at you. I wasn't going to . . ." His gravelly voice trailed off, and he glanced down the dimly lit street. "I beat them all up." He'd blown his only meal ticket. Vasily took a step back into the lamplight, standing in the snow that was now falling steadily. A group of revelers being kept warm by the spirits they were drinking spilled out of the tavern across the street.

"*Mal'chik.*" The sharp, quiet utterance did the trick. Vasily turned his bewildered focus on him.

Belphagor moved in and took hold of Vasily's lapel once more. "If you intend to be mine, get your ass back in that room." He yanked on the fancy coat and shoved Vasily toward the door of the familiar den of iniquity. The demon went without a word.

Inside their room, however, the firespirit defiance showed once more. "So I can't sell my favors to angels, but you can have whoever you desire."

Belphagor allowed himself a little smile. "That is precisely whom I have." He leaned back against the door, arms folded across his chest. "Give me the coat."

Vasily's eyes flared, but after a moment's hesitation, he complied, throwing the garment at him.

Belphagor caught it smoothly, an eyebrow raised at the attitude. He pulled on the coat, though it hung on his smaller frame, and busied himself with rolling up the cuffs. "Take off the shirt. I want your back bared."

Vasily stiffened at the implication that a flogging was in order but silently did as he was told, taking the time to fold the shirt and set it aside, though his demeanor was far from obedient. He stared Belphagor down in nothing but the formal slacks.

Belphagor shook his head in disapproval. "Get rid of the pants. They're dreadful. What did you do with your blue jeans?"

"They're at the villa." Vasily dropped the pants and worked them with sharp jerks over the boots he still wore. Commando, Belphagor noted, and properly saluting. He stroked his answering salute through his leather pants.

"That's unfortunate, as those are going in the trash." Belphagor frowned. "Do you have any idea what I had to do to get those jeans? They're fairly common in the world of Man, except in the land of our mother tongue, where they go for a pretty kopek. There's been another revolution, you see—much like the ones the Fallen are constantly threatening and never following through on. The jeans are a symbol of the freedom enjoyed in the lands beyond the wall that has recently been torn down, and everyone your age wants to wear them.

"Before the revolution, they were much scarcer, but the demand has outpaced the new availability. I gambled for them with the equivalent of a rather large sum of crystal facets, won them, and then had to resort to fisticuffs when the loser decided he didn't want to part with them after all."

He'd been coming closer to Vasily while he spoke, his expression stone hard to match his cock, though the words seemed trivial. He wrapped his hand around the back of Vasily's neck and bore down on his shoulders. "Show me exactly what it was you did for your pretty duke and his audience of angels."

Vasily resisted the pressure on his shoulders but allowed Belphagor to push him onto his knees nonetheless. Eyes red with anger and unshed tears, Vasily opened his mouth without question when Belphagor unbuttoned and released himself.

Belphagor kept his hand at the back of Vasily's neck, letting out his breath in a soft sigh of pleasure as Vasily stroked his warm tongue along Belphagor's rigid cock from base to tip and swallowed him.

Vasily's celestial ability with his element was superbly controlled. He could vary his internal heat, and he used this skill now to mind-numbing effect. Belphagor clutched Vasily's locks at his nape to steady himself as the demon took him in deep, tongue and throat working in tandem around the cock he'd swallowed without the slightest sign of discomfort.

The low answering moans to Belphagor's groans of pleasure nearly did him in, and he had to take control. He used Vasily's mouth like a passive vessel as he thrust into him, pulling the eager demon forward by his tangled locks. Belphagor closed his eyes, a shiver building in his spine as he contemplated letting go and spilling into the hot throat. But when he opened his eyes again, Vasily's were leaking tears.

He stopped and drew himself out in alarm. "What is it? What's wrong?" He cursed himself mentally, realizing they hadn't established a safeword. He'd let himself get carried away at Vasily's expense. "I'm sorry, *mal'chik*—"

"No." Vasily shook his head forcefully, hazel eyes no longer full of heat as he looked up at Belphagor. "*Mne zhal.* I disappointed you. *Prostite menya.*"

"Sweet boy." Belphagor cupped the bearded cheek. "No. Why do you think you've disappointed me?"

"I let the angels have me, I lost the jeans—"

"*Mal'chik.*" Belphagor slipped out of the coat. "Stand up."

Vasily obeyed, his tearstained face bewildered as Belphagor put the garment on him.

Belphagor straightened the velvet collar, brushing at Vasily's shoulders as he considered how to handle this. He *had* gone too far, but not the way he'd feared. He'd gotten so carried away with the erotic give and take of cruelty and anger that he hadn't considered that Vasily would begin to take his chastisement to heart. In his enjoyment of Vasily's submission, Belphagor had stopped paying attention to his state of mind. Given half a minute to consider his actions, Vasily had internalized Belphagor's correction. He'd have to be careful to watch for the signs in the future. Using Vasily passively, as satisfying as it was, had given his boy time to think and to doubt his own worth—as if a pair of jeans could be more valuable to Belphagor than he was.

He drew Vasily's head down gently to kiss him, the heat of his mouth making Belphagor's cock twitch as his tongue usurped its place. "You could never disappoint me," he said when he'd let him go at last. "Everything you do—every scowl, every burst of temper, every act of defiance against me—it gives me pleasure, do you understand that?"

Vasily shook his head, his expression baffled.

"You give me an excuse to punish you," he admitted with a wry smile. "The only way you could truly disappoint me is if you behaved. I'd hate it if you didn't constantly infuriate me."

Vasily's nervous laugh said he wasn't convinced. "But the jeans. I cost you crystal."

"The jeans, you silly boy, were an evening's winnings."

Vasily's eyes narrowed. "But you said they were scarce and costly."

"Naturally, they're costly. To anyone else. You do realize I'm rather good at this game." He winked and then pushed Vasily backward onto the cot, taking him by surprise as he climbed over him. He bit his lip at the picture of Vasily beneath him wearing nothing but the coat. "Your pretty prize is worth far more. But I'm afraid it may end up a bit the worse for wear, my dear *mal'chik*, because I'm about to give you what-for."

With his knees pinning Vasily's arms, Belphagor lowered his cock, and Vasily moaned as he took it in. Belphagor teased the eager mouth until his cock was slick before sitting back with his leather-clad thighs resting over Vasily's bare ones. Just enough room to slide his damp cock beneath Vasily's, stroke it along the cleft of the firm buttocks, and open him. Vasily arched up with a gasp as Belphagor stopped just inside the tight rim.

He leaned close. "If you want a proper lubricant, lovely boy, tell me now."

"Fuck me," Vasily begged, and Belphagor obliged.

Buried deep inside him, he took Vasily's flagging cock in his hand and stroked it like it was his own—fucking him slowly all the while—until it was at full mast. While it bobbed between them, Belphagor slipped his belt from its loops, fastened the leather around Vasily's wrists, and stretched them back over the firespirit's head to thread the belt through the frame of the cot and buckle it in place.

"Are you mine?" He began to fuck him in time with the stroke of his hand around the base of Vasily's stiff cock.

"*Da, ser*," Vasily gasped. "*Pozhaluista*." *Please*. This was better than obedience. He wanted to be Belphagor's.

Belphagor worked his hand faster over the generous shaft, groaning with pleasure as he pumped his hips, almost forgetting the cock in his hand wasn't his own. Vasily tilted his head back, bearing a striking resemblance to a painting of the martyred St. Sebastian with his eyes on the divine. The image of Vasily as Regnier's tortured saint nearly pushed Belphagor over the edge, but he wanted to watch Vasily's climax before he had his own.

He didn't have long to wait. The muscles in Vasily's thighs tightened, and he moaned loudly before letting out a deep, guttural sound as he jerked against the belt at his wrists and shot straight into the air like a geyser. And like a geyser, the fluid bursting out of him was *hot*.

Belphagor sucked in a surprised breath, having pointed the cock at himself to keep from soiling the handsome coat. The semen spilled down his shirt to his exposed lower abs and into his groin like melted wax.

"*Mne zhal*!" Vasily gasped. "I'm sorry!" Though another groan of pleasure followed this exclamation of regret. He could hardly be expected to stop mideruption.

"No matter." Belphagor bit the words out through gritted teeth. It wasn't as if this was the first time he'd taken his pleasure with a little pain.

Vasily shook his head. "It matters. You promised to punish me," he reminded Belphagor breathlessly.

"So I did. For my mistakes as well as your own." Belphagor braced his hands against the cot on either side of Vasily's upstretched arms and dug his knees into the mattress. "In that case, we need a word for you to say if the punishment exceeds what you can bear. A word that won't be difficult for you to think of even if you're a bit dazed but one you're not likely to say on accident either."

Vasily squirmed beneath him and let out a soft sound of protest as Belphagor reminded him of his vulnerable position with a sharp thrust.

The heat inside Vasily gave him an idea. "How about Seraphim?"

Vasily nodded, looking up at him with a mixture of anticipation and misgiving on his face.

"Say it, so you'll remember."

"Seraphim," said Vasily and then let out a yelp as Belphagor yanked his head back by the hair at his forehead.

"Good boy." Belphagor gave him one more slow but sharp thrust. "You can make as much noise as you like. You can swear at me or plead for mercy or resist if you wish to. I will only stop if you use the word."

"*Da, ser,*" Vasily managed as Belphagor let go of all restraint and fucked him like a battering ram.

Belphagor tested his limits, holding nothing back, and Vasily in turn held nothing back in his vocalizations, yet the agreed-upon safeword never passed his lips.

No one had ever taken this much from Belphagor. There had been negotiations with many over the years who'd chosen to be Belphagor's "boys," some true masochists among them who had reveled in punishment, but they'd been nothing like Vasily, who took what Belphagor dished out like the brutality it was and yet desired it even as he railed against it.

Belphagor would have to be careful not to push Vasily too far. At some point in the near future, he'd have to test him to make sure Vasily would use the safeword. But not today.

Belphagor roared out his release, his final thrust drawing a loud cry from Vasily. He watched Vasily's face as the last of the ecstatic pleasure shuddered through him, hoping his boy hadn't allowed him to exceed his comfort level once more out of some misguided notion that using his safeword would be yet another infraction.

Just as Belphagor was about to open his mouth to ask if he was all right, Vasily gasped out, "I love you, Beli."

Belphagor laid his head against Vasily's heaving chest, wondering what he'd done to get so lucky. Whether he deserved such love and devotion or not, it was terrifying how much he'd begun to need this demon. He'd let himself become more vulnerable with Vasily than he'd been with anyone in his life.

They both had similar backgrounds, growing up on the streets of Raqia—on their own since early childhood—and neither with any qualms about selling what they had. But Belphagor had built a careful wall around himself, brick by brick, to ensure that no one could hurt him. Vasily, however, was raw and full of need, eager to lay himself bare for the love he craved.

"Don't ever leave me," Belphagor whispered.

It never occurred to him that someone might take him.

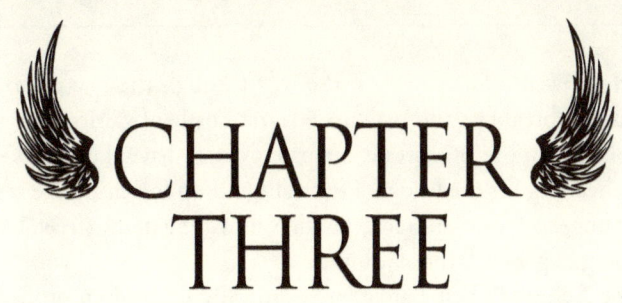

CHAPTER THREE

Vasily stifled a yelp. Belphagor's feet were like ice. He'd peeled out of his clothes and taken off both their boots before falling asleep with his arms wrapped around Vasily. It might have been just to absorb his firespirit heat—and it might have been wholly unavoidable given the size of the bed—but Vasily didn't mind. It made him feel safe and desired, no matter the reason.

He'd never experienced the feeling before, and he reveled in it. But the blanket on Belphagor's cot was inadequate coverage for two grown men, and Belphagor was no firespirit. His circulation could stand to be improved.

In the early morning dark, Vasily quietly extricated himself and slipped out of the velvet coat, laying it over Belphagor's sleeping form to replace the warmth he'd withdrawn from the bed. Belphagor was always doing nice things for him, incongruous with his fierce reputation—and his equally fierce possession of Vasily. It was Vasily's turn to treat Belphagor.

In addition to the fine threads the duke had dressed him in, he'd paid Vasily handsomely. Despite Belphagor's overprotective fears, Vasily hadn't been taken advantage of by the angels. No one had forced him to do anything, and the duke had been very appreciative of Vasily's willingness to indulge his fancies.

Careful not to wake Belphagor, he pulled on the other clothes the duke had given him—he had nothing else—and made sure the purse of crystal was still in his pocket. Then he let himself out into the hallway.

It had been foolish to leave his regular clothes at the angel's villa— foolish and faithless to go off on his own in a fit of pique and not let Belphagor know where he was or even whether he was safe.

Vasily used a few facets on the way through the market to buy Belphagor's breakfast and pick up a dearer bottle of spirits than what he could get at The Brimstone. He paid extra to have them delivered, before heading for the bridge. He might end up forfeiting the rest of his earnings to the duke after last night's thrashing in the street, but he was going to get back those jeans.

The Acheron's Left Bank was technically in Elysium proper, on the other side of the river from the Demon District. But it was so named because the area attracted the bohemian faction of the current generation of angels.

What had once been a district of abandoned warehouses and dilapidated factories had been taken over by artists and revolutionaries. Recent angelic graduates—or dropouts—from the universities at Zevul, or the military academies in Ma'on, took up residence here to sow their wild oats and debate philosophy and politics, imagining they were a better breed of angel than their forebears.

It was, however, still Elysium, and no one was likely to mistake Vasily for an angel. Coming here on his own in daylight without his angelic benefactor was perhaps not the smartest idea he'd ever had. The fact that it was winter might be his saving grace. Otherwise, the doors of the street cafés would be wide open, angels taking their tea in the fresh air with a copy of the morning's *Verity*. Instead, they scowled at him through half-parted curtains at the windows.

The disapproval of angels mattered little to him. He ignored it as he ignored the slurs shouted at him from those who happened to be out at such an early hour.

It was the Ophanim Guard he had to watch out for. They were pure firespirits of the angelic Second Choir, not diluted by other elements like Vasily's kind; it was the mixed blood that marked the Fallen as less than angels and made them the peasant class.

The Ophanim served the supernal House of Arkhangel'sk that ruled the Heavens. Nominally the palace guard, they were also the local gendarmes, and with the recent proliferation of revolutionary groups, they patrolled the less savory streets of Elysium to keep an eye out for trouble. Or a dozen eyes out, as the case might be. Ophanim either had eyes on all sides or were able to pivot their heads a full 360 degrees—and do it so swiftly that one could never be certain whether it was a single unnerving pair that had moved.

They were also known for their painful, electrified touch. Vasily had thus far managed to steer clear of angelic law—it tended not to bother with what happened on the other side of the river—and he had no desire to run afoul of them. Luckily, they gave off a cold, blue-white luminescence, and it was easy enough to dart around the side of a building and take a side alley at the first sign of the distinctive glow.

He reached Duke Elyon's villa suffering nothing more than a bit of verbal abuse—and that from a distance. Angels who'd once made sport of him seemed to find his maturing physique a bit intimidating, he was pleased to note. But when Elyon received him, it was not with pleasure.

Vasily hadn't exactly expected a warm welcome after the altercation outside The Brimstone, but he hadn't raised his hand to the duke himself. He'd imagined an awkward encounter at best and cold politeness at worst. Instead he was greeted with open hostility.

"What the fuck do you think you're doing here?" The handsome duke—golden haired and blue eyed like all Fourth Choir angels but with the fine, chiseled features and pointed chin that marked him as an aristocrat—leveled a look of scorn at Vasily through two black-rimmed eyes above a swollen, broken nose. Belphagor had certainly decked him good.

"I came to get my things." Vasily took the purse from his pocket. "I can't return the coat, but if you want your facets back—"

Elyon snatched the purse from him and tossed it to a waiting servant. "You're a very stupid demon, boy." Elyon was no older than he was, and the way he said *boy* was nothing like the term of endearment Belphagor used. Vasily's face burned. "If you had any brains at all, you'd have counted yourself lucky not to have been taught a lesson for your insolence and gone back to sucking back-alley demon dross for a lump of coal." The duke gave him an unfriendly smile. "But since you're here, I have a job for you."

Vasily bristled. He didn't relish servicing the duke now that he'd shown him such naked contempt. "I didn't come to do business. I just want my clothes."

"It's not a job for you to perform; it's a job for you to be."

He wasn't sure what that meant, but he didn't like the duke's tone. "I'm afraid I have to decline."

Before he'd met Belphagor, he'd never once refused a potential patron, thinking he didn't have the right. Belphagor had taught him this phrase to use in undesirable situations, insisting that his skills were a valuable commodity and his body didn't belong to those who paid him. What he provided was in high demand, and he could choose to take someone as a "client"—as Belphagor called it—or not, as he pleased.

Elyon sneered. "It's not an invitation." He jerked his head at a pair of large demons—bodyguards, it seemed—who'd come through the door on the other side of the room. "See that he doesn't leave."

Vasily tensed for a fight as the demons moved to block the way he'd entered. The only other exit was to a dining room beyond, where several of the angels from the night before appeared to be assembled for breakfast. He wasn't sure he'd be able to fight this many of them, and there was nowhere to run.

He thought of all the advice he'd gotten on the streets growing up. *"If you're caught by a gang, just do what they ask and count yourself lucky if they don't mess you up permanently."* Perhaps that was sound advice for a youth with no defense, but he couldn't see himself passively submitting to an assault. Things were going to get ugly.

Vasily cursed his stupidity. Duke Elyon was right. He was incredibly foolish to have come here.

But the duke's next words weren't what he expected. "I'm going to give you an honor you don't deserve, boy." Elyon smiled. "You're going to start a revolution."

Belphagor wasn't worried when he woke to find Vasily no longer in his bed. After the intimacy they'd shared last night, there was no way his *mal'chik* would have left him again. He'd probably gone to use the public outhouse; Vasily hated using the chamber pot.

Belphagor had no such qualms, and he stood pissing into it, smiling to himself at the memory of Vasily in nothing but boots and the velvet coat, wrists lashed to the bedframe. Perhaps not the wisest thing to think about at that moment, as a partial erection made the job difficult.

When someone knocked on the door, he laughed, thinking it must be Vasily. "You don't have to knock, *mal'chik*. You live here. Come in."

"Delivery for you." Not Vasily after all.

Belphagor pulled on a dressing gown and opened the door as he tied it off. A boy from the market stood in the hallway bearing a basket of sweet buns and cooked sausage, with a tin of fine black-market Russian tea. In his other hand was a jug of rather expensive earthly vodka.

"What's this? I didn't send for it."

"Tall firespirit with a gritty voice bought it," said the boy. "Told me to bring it here."

The unexpected treat made Belphagor feel generous, and he gave the boy a good-sized facet for his trouble. Setting the kettle on the iron brazier he used to heat the room and the occasional pot of water or broth, Belphagor wondered what else Vasily must be up to. He waited for him to return after the tea had brewed but drank a cup in annoyance when it began to get cold. He'd just begun to nibble on a bite of sausage when another knock came at the door.

He opened it this time without calling to Vasily and found a messenger bearing a letter—which was odd, because he hardly knew anyone who could write. When he'd sent the messenger away with a considerably smaller facet, he opened the letter and scowled.

I don't think things are going to work out, it read. *I've had a better offer. No hard feelings.*

Not only did it sound nothing like his *mal'chik*, but it was written in angelic script—which few demons could read. Belphagor was teaching Vasily to write, but he had so far learned only the Cyrillic alphabet.

The note did, however, tell him something. An angel was most likely the author. And whoever had written it had coerced Vasily's cooperation. Raqia demons might be well aware of Vasily's importance to Belphagor, but angels would not have troubled to learn whom a demon mattered to. That knowledge must have come from Vasily himself. Which meant someone had taken his boy.

Belphagor sat on the cot for a moment to calm his breathing and the sick feeling in his gut. He couldn't afford to act out of panic or blind rage.

He would have to use the same skills that made him a master at the game of wingcasting—his ability to read an opponent like a cheap paperback and to get players to reveal what he wanted to know without them even realizing they were being read. He would find out who had taken Vasily and take him back—and then punish the one who had taken him.

The obvious and most likely culprit was the pretty duke Belphagor had punched in the snout. He took some grim satisfaction in the certainty that the angel wouldn't be so pretty today. Of course, Belphagor's impulsive act of jealousy had most likely put Vasily in harm's way, so it was nothing to be proud of.

So what did he know about his enemy? He was a duke, fresh out of university if his youth and arrogance were any indication, and he kept a play pad on the Left Bank. Belphagor's fury nearly choked him at the thought of Vasily being entertainment for the privileged angel bastards. He forced the images out of his head. He had to concentrate on the game—he had to *think* of it as a game, as abhorrent as it was to him, and he had to win it.

What else did he know? The duke was not an Arkhangel'sk. There were any number of supernal nobles with the title—cousins and uncles of the young principality—but there were no other direct descendants in the House of Arkhangel'sk except the principality himself and a younger brother—and Grand Duke Lebes would be far too closely attended to be able to play in Raqia.

If the angel was not an Arkhangel'sk and was a duke but not a *grand* duke—assuming Vasily had known the distinction and hadn't just used the term generically—yet had a villa in Elysium, Left Bank or otherwise, he was someone of considerable wealth and importance.

The most likely familial connection to the supernal family that would afford such privilege and freedom was a relative of the queen. Sefira Huzievna had been a grand duchess of the House of Arcadia, the ruling house of the Princedom of Vilon.

In any case, the number of newly independent dukes with villas on the Left Bank was certainly not infinite.

But there might be an easier way to determine the duke's identity. Someone who'd been at The Brimstone the night before might have heard his name.

Belphagor made himself eat before he dressed, even though Vasily's thoughtful gift had lost its appeal. It was never wise to play hungry. He hung up the frock coat, smoothing the velvet he'd crushed beneath Vasily, and suppressed the extra heartbeat the memory engendered.

Vasily had gone out into the cold without it, draping it over Belphagor while he slept. His boy had been thinking of him with every action he'd taken this morning, and he clearly hadn't intended to be gone long.

Belphagor had to hold on to that knowledge and not allow himself to succumb to the train of thought that tried to convince him that even if Vasily hadn't written the note, he might have dictated it. Such thinking would drive him mad, and his heart knew it wasn't so even if his head wanted to mock him.

He pulled on his leather duster and billed leather cap to keep warm and to project an air of appropriate gravity. He might be less imposing than the average demon, but he'd built a reputation for being someone few demons would dare to mess with.

The right costume helped to maintain the persona. The tattoos that remained visible on his hands beneath the cuffs didn't hurt either. And the fact that they were currently marred by scraped knuckles wouldn't go unnoticed. If anyone in the den knew the name of the duke, they also knew Belphagor had been the one to bloody him.

A stop at the bar for a shot of hot coffee liqueur to warm himself up did not disappoint.

The bartender grinned at the bruises on Belphagor's face as he downed the drink. "I imagine the prince you taught a lesson last night is looking a bit less pretty this morning."

"I should hope so, Oza." Belphagor set the glass down on the bar decisively. "I don't suppose the prince dropped his name." He winked. "I'd like to send him flowers."

Oza laughed. "Not a clue. I don't ask for names. Besides, you never let that one get close enough to sample my fine brew."

Belphagor slid a pair of facets across the bar. "Alas, I did cost you more than one customer, I'm afraid."

Oza pocketed the facets. "You might ask over at The Cat."

Belphagor smirked. "Not really my kind of place." The Cat was a local brothel trading in the more traditional variety of ass than the kind Belphagor was partial to.

"But from what I hear, it's that prince's kind of place. Seems he and his comrades like to sample all the local wares. To hear some of the girls tell it, a group of angelic nobles has been spending facets over there the past few nights like they piss diamonds." Oza shrugged. "Hell, maybe they do. What do I know?"

Belphagor shook his head with a wry smile. "Allow me to ruin the mystique for you. They don't."

"I'm not going to ask how you know that, my friend." Oza snapped the bar towel at him, and Belphagor tipped his hat with a grin.

"Many thanks, Oza." He made his way through the game room—busy as always, regardless of the time of day or year—and headed out into the cold.

He'd never seen so many breasts in his life. The parlor of The Cat—protected from the curious eyes of passersby by a second set of doors inside the entryway and a layer of heavy curtains through which he had to pass—was unseasonably warm. Covering not only the entrance but draping every inch of the walls, the curtains kept in the heat generated by a massive fireplace on either end of the room.

Fancy ladies, providing pre-entertainment to prospective clients, lounged about the cushioned seats in little more than petticoats and corsets—and not the sort that covered the bust. Those few wearing a chemise beneath the lacings had the fabric off their shoulders to expose at least one breast, but most were simply displayed in all their glory.

Two unoccupied ladies approached him at the same time, vying for his business. While they cooed over him, a younger demoness wearing slightly more clothing offered him a tray of complimentary spirits. He took a drink to give his hands something to do, feeling bad for the girl who seemed far too young to be apprenticing at a brothel. He hadn't been much older when he'd made his first facet, but he'd have done it for free at the time. She merely seemed resigned to it.

The women steered him toward a seat on a narrow couch, and he fell into it, slightly alarmed at their aggressiveness. One of them slid her hand into his coat, heading for his crotch. He grabbed her with his free hand in time to dissuade her, but the other demoness had taken advantage of the opportunity. Belphagor let out a strangled yelp as the small hand slipped through the buttons at his fly and grabbed him.

"Don't be shy," she said. "I'll warm you up, on the house."

Belphagor squirmed away from her and set the drink on the floor, realizing he'd need both hands free. "Not necessary." He held her off. "I prefer to watch."

"Ooh." The other gave him a wink, tossing dark curls striped with candy-apple red—the sort of unnatural color a human woman might buy at an *apteka* in the world of Man but which could only be gotten in Raqia from a glamour of ruby oil. "Why didn't you say so? Sefi and I are very good friends."

She stretched across him to tangle her hands in the other's sapphire blue tresses, her breasts so close to his face he could have bitten one. Though it would probably be ill-advised. The two women put on a show of exaggerated kissing that was obviously solely for his benefit.

He wasn't going to learn anything this way. Belphagor amended the thought: he was learning quite a bit, but nothing he wanted to. "Perhaps we could go somewhere more private."

Sefi winked as they separated. "That's more like it, sweetmeat." She slid off the couch and took his hand. "Come on. Tabris and I will take good care of you."

Belphagor allowed them to lead him down the corridor into a room that was little more than a closet with a mat thrown on the floor. Thinking he'd have a moment to explain, Belphagor was mortified to find himself dropped unceremoniously onto his ass while Sefi straddled him backward, lifted her petticoat, and used two fingers to give him a view straight up inside her.

Belphagor covered his eyes. "Wait. Wait a minute. I was hoping we could talk." When he peered between his fingers, Tabris was balanced on Sefi's back, legs—and the rest, *bozhe moi*—spread wide. She wrinkled her nose at him in confusion.

"Please." Belphagor addressed his comment to an indistinct spot on the wall above them. "Just . . . put yourselves back together."

Sefi dropped her skirt and turned with a black look as Tabris slid onto the floor. "Conversation isn't free. Course if there's a facet in it, I'll talk your dick off."

Belphagor shuddered at the thought. He was rather fond of his dick. "Obviously, I'll pay you." Relieved to be able to get down to business, he opened his purse, but before he could offer any facets, both women had dipped their fingers in and taken nearly a night's winnings. He supposed they worked harder for their money than he did, so he didn't argue the point, but he tied the purse shut. When he glanced up, the crystal was nowhere to be seen. He didn't dare ask where it had gone.

Sefi curled up on the mat, resting on her hip, with an arm around Tabris, fingers playing idly in the other woman's hair. Perhaps they were indeed very good friends. "So what is it you want to know, sweetmeat? If it's how to pleasure a woman, it's far easier to show than tell."

"Actually, I'm looking for a man."

"Ha!" Tabris elbowed Sefi. "Pay up. Told you he didn't like girls."

Belphagor suppressed a smile. "You're not wrong. But I meant information. I understand a group of angels has been hanging about recently. A duke and his retinue, perhaps."

"Duke Elyon?" Sefi shrugged. "That's no secret. His tastes run both ways. Brought his own firespirit rentboy with him the last time. Poor sweet thing didn't even know tastes *could* run both ways until we showed him."

Belphagor's mouth dropped open, but he quickly closed it. He couldn't imagine Vasily with a girl. The idea didn't punch him in the gut like the thought of the angel manhandling him, but it made him feel odd. What if Vasily discovered he preferred a more conventional pairing? What if he'd only been with Belphagor because he didn't know any better? His only experiences on the street, after all, had been with men.

Belphagor gnawed at his thumb. He was being ridiculous. Last night had *not* been about not knowing better. And if Vasily had just come from his first sexual encounter with a girl, he'd certainly shown no sign of disappointment in Belphagor's sex. Even if he did prefer women, that wasn't important right now. What mattered was finding him and keeping him from being some bastard angel's slave.

"This Duke Elyon, he has a villa on the Left Bank, does he not?"

Tabris started to answer, but Sefi interrupted. "Maybe he does and maybe he doesn't." She glanced pointedly at his purse, tucked behind his hip.

Belphagor narrowed his eyes. "You've taken half my wages already."

"*Wages.*" Sefi lifted his hand from his knee, startling him. "I heard about you." She held up his tattooed fingers. "You're the Prince of Tricks."

Tabris laughed, taking his other hand and examining it. "Well, that explains a lot. Where'd you get these? Did they hurt?"

Belphagor pulled his hands away. "I got them in the world of Man. And anything worth doing hurts at first."

Tabris's eyes widened. "You've fallen? What's it like?"

Sefi hushed her. "Never mind that, Tabi. He's the Prince of Tricks, and he can afford to pay if he wants anything more out of us."

"I think you've told me just about everything I needed to know." Belphagor moved to stand, but Sefi climbed over him so that he'd have to push her roughly if he wanted to get up.

She moved her hand up his thigh toward his purse, closing her fingers over his when he grabbed it. "Give us the rest, and I'll tell you where Duke Elyon's little palace is."

"I'm sure I can find it myself."

"You're the one who jumped him at The Brimstone last night." Sefi smiled knowingly. "It was about his rentboy, wasn't it? I saw your face when I mentioned him. What was his name, Tabi? Valentin?" She licked her lips. "You might be interested to know that I had the pleasure of being his first. He was absolutely adorable. Didn't last very long, but Tabi helped work him up again, and I let him have another go when he was ready. Took to it like a pro."

Tabris grinned at him, making a lewd gesture with her tongue. Belphagor had no idea how to react. He certainly wasn't going to come to blows with a woman for touching his boy, and he wasn't sure he was even upset about it. As long as the angel hadn't coerced Vasily into it, Belphagor had agreed he could do what he liked with demons. It had simply never occurred to him that he might like . . . this.

He pushed the demoness aside as firmly as he could without manhandling her. "That's all very interesting but not really anything I need to know."

As he rose, Tabris scooted out of the way, but Sefi stood with him. "Perhaps you'd be interested in what else I know about your Valentin."

"Not likely."

"For instance, where I saw him headed this morning."

Belphagor paused at the door of the cupboard-like room. "And where was that?"

The demoness threw another pointed glance at his purse.

He sighed and untied it but held it away as she reached for it. "This is all I have, so why don't you tell me what you know first, and then I'll give it to you."

She tucked her arms under her bare breasts, almost fluffing them upward in a huff. "Fine. I saw him cross the Acheron and head for the Left Bank in the direction of Duke Elyon's villa. He was wearing his fancy duds from last night but not the coat." Her eyelids lowered in a provocative smile. "With the heat *he* puts off, I guess he didn't need it."

Her account confirmed she'd actually seen him, but it was troubling news that he'd been headed for the villa. Belphagor had assumed the angel and his cronies must have accosted Vasily when he'd gone to the market. Why would he have gone voluntarily?

"Was anyone with him?"

"Nope. All by his lonesome. I offered him some company from the window, and he thanked me, all polite with that demure little growl of his. Said he had business to attend to."

Belphagor's jaw tightened. Vasily definitely hadn't been taken against his will, at least not up to that point. "Anything else you recall?"

"That's the last I saw of him. If you want to know where the villa is, it's about a mile north of the Palace Bridge, just past the cafés and galleries."

Belphagor hung on to the purse, suspecting she knew more than she was telling.

"There is one other thing." She kept her eyes on the purse. "Those angels were all full of anarchy talk when they were here, saying they were demon-sympathizers and thought the principality should be overthrown and the power given to the people. Full of horse shit, of course. All of 'em are. But I'd wager my snatch they're planning something up there at that fancy villa. Elyon's no fan of the House of Arkhangel'sk."

This last bit confirmed what he'd been thinking about the duke. Belphagor had simply stopped short of considering what a young, ambitious supernal might be up to in spending his days among Left Bank poets and his nights renting whores in Raqia.

This wasn't merely about slumming in the Demon District. Duke Elyon, whether truly interested in demons' rights or not—and Belphagor guessed not—wasn't just sowing wild oats, he was sowing discord.

Elysium, of course, was no stranger to unrest. As long as there had been a celestial seat, one faction or another had been vying for it. The current principality had come to power after the assassination of the previous ruler by an avowed anarchist.

Principality Rifion had been the patriarch of the House of Arkhangel'sk for over a century, and the throne had come to his grandson Helison only because Helison's father had died an untimely death in a hunting accident.

A suspicious type might surmise that Helison himself was the author of both deaths, but there had never been a less ambitious principality in Heaven. He was, in fact, remarkably like the last emperor of Russia in the world of Man. In mannerisms as well as in appearance, Helison could have been taken for Tsar Nikolai II himself. Belphagor ought to know. He'd met the man.

During the tsar's final days in Petrograd, Belphagor had been the darling of the party circuit among imperial hangers-on. Afterward, when madness overtook his adopted country and the imperial family was imprisoned by Bolshevik thugs, Belphagor found himself face-to-face with the disgraced tsar only weeks before his death.

Like many in Russia then and afterward, Belphagor did whatever was necessary to survive. A temporary impersonation of a guard at the

Governor's Mansion in Tobol'sk got him a warm bed for the night and a full belly, something that was in scarce supply.

Because his own name was too conspicuous, he'd been using the one earthly name that meant something to him then—*Feliks*—and as fate would have it, a young Bolshevik soldier of the same name had been murdered that evening for a handful of rubles coming back from the local bar. Hiding in an alleyway, Belphagor saw the boy fall, but the *muzhik* who'd knifed him didn't see Belphagor.

There had been a time when he would have rushed to help—but not then. By then, he knew that no one in any sphere looked out for anyone else, and he wasn't about to die for a stranger.

He waited until the young soldier was staring glassy-eyed into the dark Siberian night, and then he scrambled out of hiding to take the clothes before someone else did. The name *Feliks* on the uniform gave Belphagor pause. He knew these letters of the earthly alphabet intimately. He'd practiced writing them out, waiting foolishly for a man who would never come. Feliks must have been the soldier's family name, unusual, but it seemed at that moment to be a sign.

The heavy coat and scarf that were part of the uniform were a welcome find, but even better, the body was warm still. The clothes took some of the chill out of Belphagor's bones as soon as he put them on.

Hurrying down the lane afterward to find a better hiding place to sleep, he was caught by another soldier. He felt for Feliks's gun—prepared to kill before he'd go back to a Russian jail—but the soldier didn't know Feliks well enough to realize Belphagor wasn't him. And so Belphagor went to work for the night, guarding the fallen imperial family.

The health of the young Alexei had taken a bad turn, and Belphagor was stationed outside his room. The imperial family was of no interest to Belphagor. Princes and grand dukes, he'd learned, were liars and cheats. But that night, he heard Alexei's suffering, cries of genuine pain that brought to mind similar sounds he'd heard in a prison cell—sounds he'd only later realized were his own.

Their lives were utterly different—they were from literally different worlds—but Alexei was only three years younger than Belphagor. Though the cause of his suffering was as different as the two of them, Belphagor felt an inexplicable kinship with the boy. Agony was universal.

The former empress stayed with her son through the night until at last he slept, and she, too, dozed, in a chair beside his bed. She moaned in her sleep, shifting uncomfortably, as if her bond with her son was so strong that she felt his pain physically.

He tried to imagine what having a mother was like. He didn't remember his. She'd left him before he reached six summers. Whether voluntarily or through some harm that had come to her, he would never know. He'd simply woken one morning to find her gone.

She'd belonged to the same profession he would later take up, so it could easily have been either. But he wondered, as he watched the anguished empress, if his own mother had felt his pain, wherever she was. The thought wasn't comforting, and he found himself hoping for the first time that she was dead after all, just to spare her any such awareness. Even if she'd abandoned him, she didn't deserve *that*.

He was startled by a hand on his shoulder. Tsar Nikolai himself—though that was no longer his title—stood in the doorway, accompanied by a flank of guards who seemed reluctant to treat him as a prisoner. Belphagor and the tsar were of a similar height, and he met Nikolai's eyes within the haggard face, surprised at their gentleness.

The tsar nodded to him. "How is my son? Has there been much pain?"

"He's sleeping now," was all Belphagor could think to say.

Nikolai gave his shoulder a squeeze. "You're a kind boy." He turned away, allowing his escorts to lead him back to his room.

Shortly afterward, the other guard inside the door shook the empress awake—unkindly, Belphagor thought—and insisted she return to her bed. She had to rely on a cane and moved with difficulty, her haunted eyes on her son as she was led away.

Belphagor was momentarily alone with Alexei Nikolaevich. Curiosity got the better of him, and he slipped into the room to peer closer at the sleeping prince. He had a beautiful face, though it seemed as drawn and thin as Belphagor's, as if the prince were starving too. Perhaps everyone in this country was starving.

When Alexei stirred and cried out in his sleep, Belphagor sat and took his hand to keep him from drawing the attention of the soldiers. At least, it was what he told himself.

The sleeping boy squeezed his hand, perhaps believing it to be his mother's, and tears streamed down Belphagor's face inexplicably. They were nothing like each other, the son of an empress and the son of a demon whore—and yet they were the same.

Belphagor moved on after a few days, never wanting to risk staying in the same place for long. Less than a month later, he saw the news. It had taken more than twenty minutes under a hail of bullets in a Yekaterinburg basement for all of them to die.

For years afterward, he would see the beautiful, suffering boy in his dreams and wake up crying.

Sefi let out an impatient sigh. "That's all I know. Do I get the purse or not?"

Belphagor shook himself, annoyed that he'd become absorbed in a past too distant to matter. Except, in recent days, he'd begun to think increasingly that it did.

He started to hand her the purse but paused and closed his fist around it once more, to her audible consternation. "There might be one other thing I'd like to buy. Let me think a moment." He was formulating a plan.

Heaven had become uncannily reminiscent of that other place and time, as if locked in an inexorable march forward to repeat terrestrial history. The principality, like Nikolai, was out of touch—not, it seemed, unconcerned with the plight of the least of his princedom but unaware of how perception mattered.

The Ophanim Guard dealt swiftly and harshly with dissent, while the principality gave speeches in Palace Square about how he wanted to listen to the voices of the common angel—and demon, one had to assume. Voices he believed were being suppressed by shiftless upstarts using incendiary language to incite unrest. Either the principality was simply obtuse or his advisors had him too misinformed to see what was right in front of him.

Belphagor was sure it was something few demons gave any thought. His was a unique perspective given that most who fell remained in the world of Man. Thus, his contemporaries from that bygone earthly era who had aged at the pace of Men were no more. Only his fondness for the unique culture of Raqia—and the money to be made here—had kept him from living out a human lifespan in the lower sphere.

He'd stayed long enough each time to age a bit more than he cared to. Where most celestials succumbed to the frailty and fading of age only at the end, Belphagor had amassed enough time in the world of Man after he'd reached adulthood to resemble a human in his late twenties. Perhaps a year or two more, but he liked to think not.

He'd seen the two worlds on remarkably parallel paths of self-destruction over the span of almost a century. It remained to be seen whether Heaven's supernal ruler would recognize the handwriting on the wall in time to prevent a similar disintegration.

Belphagor was tempted to send him an anonymous gift of a volume of Russian history of the late-nineteenth and early-twentieth centuries. But whether anyone but he was aware of the striking similarities or not, aristocratic malcontents and opportunists like Elyon could certainly perceive that Heaven was ripe for revolution.

"I'd like to buy your services as escorts to a party," he said at last.

"You already promised the purse for what I gave you," Sefi protested. "I'll call in Masha if you're trying to renege."

"I'll do it." Tabris had jumped to her feet, sensing an opportunity, no doubt, to undercut her good friend's business.

"I'm not reneging." Belphagor held out the purse, and Sefi snatched it with a glare at Tabris, stuffing it into her corset beneath her ample tits. "But I'd like to hire you both this evening."

In light of the report of Vasily's willing return to the villa, and the inclinations of the group of angels, Elyon's interest in Vasily had become more complicated. In any event, he couldn't simply march into the villa and demand that the duke return his boy. Belphagor wouldn't get a toe inside the door before the angels beat the tar out of him and tossed him in the river.

Sefi eyed him with suspicion. "What party? I thought you said this was all the money you had."

Shrewd businesswoman, this one.

Belphagor smiled. "It's all I have *on* me. You don't think I'd give you my last facet for such scant information? I'll give each of you a ten-carat purse for your parts. What I need is to get into Duke Elyon's villa without a big fuss. While he's in residence, there must be some kind of nightly merrymaking. At least before they hit the brothels and dens of iniquity in our fair quarter. And I expect anyone from The Cat is a perpetual favorite on the guest list. Do I assume correctly?"

"I suppose," said Sefi. "But what do we have to do?"

"Whatever you'd normally do—just not with me. All I need is an in."

"Done." Tabris held out her hand to shake on the deal.

But Sefi still looked dubious. "You better not be making trouble for us. We have reputations to protect."

"I assure you, any trouble I make will be well away from your lovely selves." He took Tabris's hand and kissed it, making her giggle, though Sefi merely rolled her eyes when he reached for hers. "And now, if you don't mind, I have some other business to attend to. I'll return at dusk. I trust you know how to dress for the occasion."

Sefi waggled her breasts at him as he reached for the door. "Born dressed for it, sweetmeat."

He let himself out of the brothel while Sefi and Tabris found another victim—a willing one, no doubt. Belphagor shrugged. To each his own. He drew a breath of relief in the cold—and titless—air. Aesthetically, he appreciated a good tit as much as the next cocksucker, but these had been a bit too close for comfort.

In the meantime, he had to scrounge up something to wear that wouldn't immediately mark him as out of place, in addition to gathering an entourage of his own. It wouldn't be wise to walk into Elyon's territory without a little backup, and there were plenty of players at The Brimstone who owed him a favor. It was time to call in a marker or two.

CHAPTER FOUR

Showing off for the angels had been Vasily's mistake. After one of Duke Elyon's companions had engaged Vasily for a quick suck and then bragged about his unique abilities, the duke had offered to hire him for the weekend—for more crystal than Vasily had ever seen. Still nursing his outrage at Belphagor's double standard, he'd happily accepted.

When the duke had given his inner circle a brief sample of Vasily's oral skills—respectfully inquiring as to whether Vasily minded and assuring him that he needn't fully service them all—the angels had wanted to know what else he could do with his element.

Vasily had demonstrated his cigar-lighting trick—concentrating the heat of his fire into the tip of his tongue—had smoldered kindling for them with his hands, and after untold tankards of mead, had even given them a display of his most crass and useless firespirit talent: melting a candle in his ass.

When Elyon had undertaken to hold Vasily against his will, he'd employed a Cherub to subdue him. Vasily was familiar with the other two orders of their elemental choir, but he'd never seen one of these before. They were as unlike the other firespirits as he was.

The creature's size was not as imposing as a Seraph's, and it didn't glow with the intensity of the Ophanim, instead emitting a bright, white radiance with a hint of phosphorescence. But its form was far more corporeal than those of its majestic cousins—though the countenance itself was almost nauseatingly mutable. It shifted at will from that of an imposing man into several other aspects: one leonine, another ox-like, and a third akin to a large and dangerous bird of prey.

After demonstrating its considerable superiority in both strength and element—which it used like bolts of lightning from its hands—the Cherub had chained Vasily's wrists behind his back to ensure he couldn't use his own fire against the duke.

Vasily was sulking now in the duke's scullery, where the bastard had put him on ice. The chain at his wrists was bound to an iron ring on the wall intended to hold a hook for hanging meat. At least he'd gotten his clothing back after all, but it was little comfort. He was surrounded by blocks chiseled from the frozen river to keep the perishables in the duke's pantry cool.

He still had no idea what the duke wanted of him. He'd told Elyon that Belphagor would come looking for him when he didn't return.

"Don't trouble yourself about your mackerel," Elyon had sneered. "You've already sent word to him that you no longer require his protection."

The angel had gotten in his face to say it, and Vasily, after determining that he'd just called Belphagor his pimp, had cracked Elyon's broken nose with a furious headbutt. It had earned him a stomp to the groin from the duke after the Cherub had yanked Vasily onto his back, but seeing the blood pouring from Elyon's nose had been worth it.

There'd been plenty of time, however, for Vasily to sit and curse himself for getting into this predicament. He wasn't terribly worried for his own sake. Whatever the duke had planned for him, Vasily could take care of himself. But he couldn't stand the thought that Belphagor might believe the note even for a minute.

The way he'd possessed Vasily last night was what he'd dreamed of, what he'd yearned for since Belphagor had taken the strop to him for trying to steal his purse. Before the last strike of the leather, Vasily had belonged to him. The unrelenting fall of the strop in Belphagor's hand against his ass had transported him from fury to fear to abject misery. And then somewhere beyond.

Belphagor's unwavering control had drawn something from him more powerful than any climax, as if his spirit had soared from his body on invisible wings. He'd been able to let go of himself, of the fearful restraint he felt he had to maintain that kept him from careening over the edge of civility into the domain of some ungoverned beast.

Belphagor had given him that, all the while keeping him safe from whatever it was Vasily feared might happen if the terrifying emotion inside him were released. And then, more shocking than what had come before, he'd held Vasily while all that emotion poured out of him, held him like he was something to be cherished and told him he was a good boy.

That had been the moment Vasily had fallen helplessly and hopelessly in love with him. He hadn't known precisely what his own age was—it was only later that Belphagor had helped him pin down the year of his birth by recalling various celestial events—but he knew he was no longer a boy.

For several years already he'd been earning his way by selling what he chose to sell, and his body had long since changed from a child's to a man's. Yet when Belphagor had called him "boy," and not just *a* boy, but a *good* boy, his heart had nearly burst.

He still couldn't explain why those words were like magic to him. And something about hearing it said in the earthly tongue made that magic stronger: *mal'chik*. In that single utterance from Belphagor's lips, he heard, *I love you. You belong to me. You're safe. You are mine.* He was Belphagor's. And that was all that mattered.

It hadn't stopped him, of course, from being a complete prat. Even after Belphagor had finally admitted his desire for him, finally touched him as he'd been longing to be touched, Vasily had stormed off like a child because Belphagor hadn't given enough.

When Vasily had gone back to him last night, he'd feared Belphagor might decide he wasn't mature enough to handle their intimacy after all. And then Belphagor, as he'd put it, had given him "what-for." The first time they'd been together had been the best fuck of Vasily's life, but this time—this had been like having every cell in his body undone, fucked, and then put back together and fucked again. He hadn't wanted it to end and had thought he might have happily died of it if it hadn't.

If Belphagor believed that after everything—after *that*—Vasily had chosen to walk away from him for the favors of an angelic noble...

He jerked against the chain, raging at himself and at Elyon, but the iron ring didn't budge. "Let me the fuck out of here, you son of a succubus!" The sound fell flat against the thick walls. Even his voice wasn't escaping this room.

Dusk, thankfully, came early this time of year, with the winter solstice only days away, and enclaves of debauchery such as the Demon District and the Left Bank became even livelier.

Tabris and Sefira—Sefi had named herself after Helison's queen—were eagerly awaiting him, as if Belphagor were local nobility himself. Perhaps he was. He smiled to himself. Prince of Tricks. He had a number of them up his sleeve tonight.

He'd dressed conservatively in a three-piece suit and top hat, with a heavy woolen overcoat and white gloves to cover his tattoos. Aristocratic fashion had made this much of his disguise easier for him.

In addition to the quest for clothes, he'd spent a few hours at the Demon Market, where he'd procured a glamour that lightened his hair and skin, with a dash of sapphire oil in his eyes to turn the dark irises blue. He might not be able to pass for an angel, but he could easily pass for an angel's bastard.

His fancy ladies, however, weren't the least bit taken in, which worried him slightly. "What gave me away?" he asked as they cooed over him. "I thought I'd done a rather nice job of impersonating a pompous ass."

"It's not how you look, sweetmeat," said Sefi wryly. "It's how you *don't* look. Your eyes haven't stopped on these once." She fluffed her now more conservatively corseted breasts, pushed up and nearly strangling her, it seemed to him. He had to concede the point.

With a demoness on each arm, he headed in the direction of The Brimstone.

Tabris drew her cheap fur collar close. "I thought we were going to Duke Elyon's palace."

"We are. I'm picking up some company who will likely be more to your taste." He'd recruited half a dozen respectable demons—or as respectable as one might find gambling in a Raqia den of iniquity—who were indebted to him in one way or another. When he'd explained the majority of their duties during the evening's venture, to the last demon, they'd vowed to sacrifice themselves to the cause.

"We like your company just fine." Tabris pressed against him playfully. "Easiest date ever."

No doubt. Nevertheless, his ladies seemed to shine in the more appreciative company of his entourage. They made a lively group as they bypassed the nearby Palace Bridge in favor of a walk along the embankment past the bustling Demon Market.

At this time of evening, things were starting to get interesting. Street performers vied for facets, while the daytime games of dice played by boys along the cobblestone walks made way for more serious games and rounds of cards.

Cart vendors switched from hawking trinkets and sweets in favor of hearty meat pies and sausages, interspersed with peasant "remedies," including black-market whiskey and vodka from the world of Man. And elderly demonesses who sold fortunes and baubles were usurped by much younger ones promising more certain favor.

At the market's terminus, they took the bridge the locals called Hell's Gate across the Acheron to where the Left Bank began. The difference between the two sides, Belphagor noted, seemed to be only in the discretion of the activities and the ratio of angels to demons participating in them.

As they continued up the embankment, however, the bohemian neighborhood grew markedly more moneyed, and more of the debauchery presumably moved inside, behind the high walls of the fancy riverbank villas.

Sefi pointed out the duke's domicile, though Belphagor would have guessed had she not. It was indeed more of a palace, as Tabris had called it, its gaudy fountains and façade of gilded columns reminiscent of the Arkhangel'sk Summer Palace.

The festivities were well underway, and Belphagor's party blended in without difficulty. Sefi and Tabris made a smooth entrance for them by drawing the attention of the guests already in attendance. The assets that had failed to elicit the proper response from Belphagor were now given their due.

Duke Elyon was easy to spot with a bandage taped over his nose. It gave Belphagor some measure of gratification to see the bloom of blood pooled beneath the skin under his eyes. With the duke's attention turned on the ladies, Belphagor wandered unnoticed from the group to explore the villa.

A more intimate party was underway in the drawing room beyond the main parlor, where Elyon's angelic peers were engaged in various acts of carnal pleasure with demons in the gender of their choice. Though he didn't really expect to find him here, Belphagor scanned the room for Vasily's wild locks among the heads bobbing in laps and the backsides being happily plundered, but there was no sign of him.

Belphagor continued through the dimly lit passages, finding a few guest rooms similarly occupied, but much of the place was not in use.

He checked every closed door he came upon, using his airspirit skill to turn the knob soundlessly and slowly enough to open it a crack. If it was empty, he slipped inside. If it turned out to be occupied by those with a preference for less public pleasure, he retreated with equal stealth.

He found only one door locked, which seemed promising. There wasn't a lock made he couldn't open, and in a moment, he was in, his heart pounding with hopeful anxiety that he would find Vasily. But it was nothing more than a storage room full of papers.

Upon closer examination, the papers turned out to be pamphlets advocating a workers' revolt against the principality, with demons and angelic sympathizers called upon to occupy Council Square. Freshly printed, they advertised tomorrow evening as the intended date. Which meant someone would be distributing these tonight.

"What the hell are you doing in here?"

Belphagor turned to find Elyon standing behind him. "I was looking for the water closet."

The angel eyed him with mistrust. "This room was supposed to be locked."

Belphagor shrugged as he let the pamphlet he was holding drop from his fingers. "Someone evidently forgot. I'm one hundred percent behind your cause, so there's no need to worry."

"Who are you?" Elyon demanded.

"Semyon Xomoyovich of the House of Ea." Belphagor gave him a polite bow. "I'm visiting from Iriy and heard this was the place to be." He let the comment hang there for Elyon to decide whether he meant it in terms of the festivities or the political dissent.

Elyon studied him with narrowed eyes—an expression, Belphagor was pleased to note, that appeared to hurt. "Have we met before?"

Hoping the glamour was still holding, he smoothed his gloved hand across the slick hair at his forehead, neatly oiled and combed away from a severe side part in the manner of the aristocratic set. "I don't believe I've had the pleasure."

Elyon frowned, obviously sensing something but unable to make the connection. The glamour must be doing its job. The duke stepped in toward the door and put the key in the lock, waiting for Belphagor to come out past him.

"These aren't ready for general distribution." He closed the door firmly.

"But the call is for tomorrow, is it not?"

"It's not certain that the public demonstration will be going ahead as planned. I'd appreciate if you wouldn't mention it until the word is out."

Belphagor raised an eyebrow. "Seems like a rather large expense to go to and not follow through."

"There may be other actions taking place." Elyon clearly had no intention of giving an inch. "Timing is everything. In the meantime, please enjoy my hospitality. We have entertainment of every flavor here this evening."

Belphagor accompanied him back toward the party. "Indeed. I brought one flavor of my own—a succulent pair of succubi from The Cat—but I may be in the mood to sample another." He winked as Elyon glanced over at him. "I hear you've tamed that firespirit brute that always hangs about The Brimstone. I'd love to get a taste of that."

Elyon's expression was instantly guarded. "Firespirit brute? I'm sure I don't know who you mean, but there are treats of all sorts to sample in the salon that may take your fancy."

"The ladies at The Cat bragged about you bringing in some red-haired wild boy the other night. That wasn't the firespirit I've heard about? With the steamy mouth?" He winked again and gave Elyon a friendly elbow in the ribs.

The duke regarded him for a moment. "Oh, him. He was a bit of a slumming novelty. Haven't seen him since. Probably gone back to bending over in back alleys for drunks."

Belphagor clenched his fist at his side, but kept his face neutral. "Ah, well. There was a half-Virtue in the salon who seemed quite eager to entertain me. I suppose I'll head back that way."

"I thought you were in search of the water closet."

Belphagor laughed. "So I was. I'd almost forgotten."

"Just down the hallway from the salon." The angel gestured in the direction from which Belphagor had come.

"Excellent. Thank you." He excused himself and found the room Elyon had indicated. Once inside, he punched the wall, stifling a groan as he flexed his bruised fingers. *Idiot.* Duke Elyon had been deliberately goading him. Belphagor had obviously tipped his hand.

He waited for a few minutes before stepping into the hallway, thinking he could slip out quietly, but Elyon had apparently hired muscle since the night before. Two earthspirit bruisers who made Vasily look petite were waiting for him.

He might have tried to fight them anyway, but the ferocious glare of a Cherub at the end of the corridor made him think twice. He'd had the misfortune of running afoul of their rare breed before. He submitted with a sigh as they escorted him out through the servants' entrance off the kitchen and watched him until he'd left the property.

Belphagor circled around to the front, but there were more demon bouncers on duty there as well. He'd put Elyon on his guard. There was no way he was sneaking back into the villa, glamour or no glamour. He hadn't even had the opportunity to mobilize his backup. They were probably enjoying themselves inside with Sefi and Tabris, none the wiser that he'd been ejected from the duke's domicile. He'd have to formulate a plan B.

Inside the pantry, Vasily couldn't believe his ears. Someone had entered the kitchen, making a fuss about being thrown out of the villa, and the voice was unmistakably Belphagor's. Vasily had stood and strained at the end of his bonds, shouting to Belphagor that he was here, but there was no indication that anyone heard him. Elyon must have acquired a spell from the Demon Market that hid the scullery from outside perception.

It gave Vasily some comfort as he huddled among the ice that Belphagor had come looking for him. He hadn't believed that stupid note Elyon had sent—or if he had, he'd come anyway to take back what was his.

Vasily had to admit, the idea of Belphagor coming to drag him away from anyone else to whom he might stray gave him a thrill of pleasure. He ought to be outraged, he supposed, knowing Belphagor treated him as a possession, but it was one more facet of the inexplicable rightness he felt in the dynamic of their relationship. What he'd never have tolerated in anyone else raised both his ire and his cock when it came from Belphagor.

The door opened unexpectedly, and Vasily jumped to his feet, thinking Belphagor had found his way past the duke's men. But it was Duke Elyon himself, his expression smug. Vasily wanted to put his hands around the bastard's throat and squeeze until he smelled angelic flesh burning. The duke had been wise to restrain him.

Elyon regarded him with a smirk. "Seems our timetable has moved up. Arzal will prepare you for your role in bringing about a glorious new Heaven."

That didn't sound at *all* ominous.

"Just what is this role I'm supposed to play?" Vasily demanded as the Cherub stepped forward from where he lurked in a radiance-concealing cloak.

Arzal seized Vasily's throat in a crushing grip and lifted him off his feet, sending a paralyzing jolt through him. It wasn't the electrified pain described by those who'd been accosted by Ophanim but something beyond it that scrambled every impulse in his brain and obliterated coherent thought.

The Cherub seemed to be in a different plane from the rest of Heaven, shifting through the space it occupied as though a different reality existed for each metamorphosis of its aspect.

Before Vasily's senses ceased to function entirely, he heard Duke Elyon as if from a great distance.

"You're going to be famous," he said. "You're going to be the demon who assassinates the principality of the Firmament of Shehaqim and sets the Fallen free."

Belphagor killed time in the gaming room of The Brimstone while waiting for his hired entourage to return. As far as he was concerned, they still owed him, since all they'd done so far was enjoy the delightful company he'd paid for and the entertainment of a swanky angelic affair. He hadn't fully formulated plan B, but what he was contemplating would take all the demons he could gather.

He'd just about given up waiting when a commotion rose at the door to the den.

"Leave her be!" one of the barmaids yelled. "Can't you see she's had a fright?"

Belphagor raised his head and saw Tabris being harassed by the dregs of the clientele, too drunk by this hour to keep their jackassery in check. He pushed his way through, stunned to see her lovely clothes torn and face bruised. Her hair was a tangled mess, with a bit of blood matted in it.

"Tabris!" Out of fear for her, his voice dropped into the harsh tone he used during discipline, projecting loudly. The demons who were taunting and grabbing at her started at the sound and parted to make way for him automatically.

Tabris burst into tears and fell into his arms as he reached her.

He glared at the rowdy group. "I think you've all drunk your fill. I suggest you head back to your beds and sleep it off before I take each of you out separately and teach you a lesson about respecting a lady."

"She's no lady," said one. "So I guess the lady must be you."

The laughter this spawned died down swiftly as Belphagor pressed Tabris into the barmaid's arms.

"I beg your pardon?"

The culprit looked uncomfortable, glancing about at his companions as if to see whether anyone would defend him. Apparently deciding they wouldn't, he shrugged and lowered his head to his drink. "Must've been mistaken."

Belphagor eyed him a moment longer before putting an arm around Tabris's shoulder once more and leading her back to his room.

"Well, that's a fucking first," someone muttered under his breath to a rumble of nervous laughter.

Belphagor sat her down on his cot and closed the door, bringing a damp cloth from the basin as he came to sit beside her. "What happened?" He dabbed gently at the smeared blood on her face while she continued to weep. "Who did this to you?"

"Angels," she sobbed. "They've got Ouestucati."

"Ouestucati?"

"Sefi!" she burst out miserably. "They've got Sefi. We decided to head back to The Cat when we couldn't find you. She was nervous about something she'd overheard, and she said you'd want to know. Your friends were occupied, and she didn't want to wait, so we left." Tabris tried to dry her eyes on her torn sleeve. "We were crossing the bridge when they came out of nowhere—a group of angels from the villa." She started to sob harder, the sleeve useless against the onslaught of tears. "They grabbed her, and I tried to fight them, but they knocked me to the ground and took her."

Belphagor pulled her against his shoulder and let her cry, fairly certain that whatever had befallen Sefi was his fault. "We'll get her back."

She nodded against him after a moment and sat up, sniffling and wiping at her eyes with her dirty gloves. "You're very sweet, Prince of Tricks. But this isn't your problem. I shouldn't have bothered you with it. I—I was shaken up, and I wasn't thinking. We have people at The Cat who take care of us."

He shook his head. "Listen, Tabris. This *is* my problem. I got you and Sefi into this, and I'm going to figure something out. The duke has my boy."

"Your boy," Tabris repeated. "You mean the fire demon. He . . . belongs to you?"

"That's right." It made him feel warm inside to hear it said. "And I don't tolerate angels taking what's mine."

She studied his face. "But it's more than that, isn't it?"

Belphagor's mouth turned up in a wry smile. "It's always more than that, my dear. But that's enough."

"It's more than that with me and Ouestucati too. That's her real name. She uses Sefira for work." She cast him a sidelong look, almost embarrassed. "We're sisters."

Belphagor tried to keep his eyes from widening comically, recalling how little modesty there had been between them earlier in the day.

Tabris shrugged. "We do what we need to—short of each other. And we try not to let on we're related. You'd be surprised how many men try to get us to put on a show for them if they get wind of it."

He'd been surprised at the disclosure that they were sisters, but nothing surprised him about men's desires. He'd been paid to do all kinds of things in his time and—mostly—didn't judge another's predilections.

"Well, we're going to get Ouestucati and Vasily back, but we'll have to act quickly. I think they took your sister because of whatever she overheard, and I'd be willing to bet good facets it was about the act of sedition the duke is encouraging against the crown tomorrow."

"So you don't think they took her to—to hurt her."

"I don't. I think they're keeping her quiet." Not that they wouldn't hurt her as well if it struck their fancy, but Belphagor considered it best not to speculate—for either of them.

What worried him more, however, was how important it might be to keep Sefi quiet and to what lengths the duke would go to do it. Hopefully, they only intended to keep her out of the way until their plans came to fruition.

He took the pamphlet from his pocket that he'd managed to pilfer from Elyon's storeroom in plain view of the angel with the simple misdirection of a hand smoothing the hair at his forehead. "I found this—hundreds of them, actually, waiting to be distributed—in the villa."

When he tried to hand it to her, Tabris pushed it back at him with an embarrassed shrug. "My eyes are terrible. Read it to me?"

He chastised himself mentally. Illiteracy was widespread among the Fallen population, particularly so among those in his former profession, many of whom, like himself, had grown up on the streets.

It wasn't as if they had governesses who taught them letters in the nursery or were eligible to attend the celestial halls of learning. He'd been lucky enough to learn to read and write in the language of Men—the only benefit that had come of his youthful incarceration—and then had taught himself the angelic alphabet when he'd returned to Raqia.

He read her the notice about the demonstration in Council Square, noting that tomorrow's date—now today's—featured on it prominently. "Elyon caught me in the storeroom reading one of these. Before he tossed me out on my ass, he claimed the action wasn't certain to happen, but I find it doubtful they'd go to the trouble and expense of printing them only to change their minds."

What he hadn't figured out was what Vasily had to do with it, or what Sefi and Vasily might have learned that had gotten them into trouble. Belphagor's knowledge of the existence of the pamphlets and their connection to the duke hadn't been enough to warrant trying to keep him quiet.

Tabris looked puzzled. "But there's always talk like that about. And everyone knows there are angels who support it. Even if the rest of the angels don't know, who'd believe a demon if they told?"

"Precisely my thought. Which is why I believe Ouestucati must have learned something more. Just as my boy must have." He put the pamphlet away. "Since it advertises the event at dusk, I think whatever else is going on will coincide with it, which gives us perhaps twelve hours to figure out what the duke is up to and where he's holding Ouestucati and Vasily. And to round up enough demons to get my back when I spoil the duke's fun."

Tabris's anxious look said she was losing faith in his offer to help. "How do you intend to do that? Who's going to go up against a duke and risk being executed for treason just to rescue a couple of whores?" She swallowed nervously. "I mean . . . no offense . . . but your Vasily—"

Belphagor waved away her concern. "That isn't a term that offends me. Both Vasily and I have done our share of whoring. Vasily just happens to be damned good at it." He smiled at her surprised expression. "As for whether any demon would be willing to risk an assault on an angelic villa, let's just say I make a better gambler than a whore. There's hardly a demon in Raqia who hasn't lost to me at the wingcasting table, and half of them still owe me." The corner of his mouth turned up. "The rest I have other things on."

He walked Tabris home and told her to get some rest, promising to let her know as soon as he'd amassed recruits and formulated a plan. What he needed more than muscle, however, was information. He needed to ferret out Duke Elyon's true plan. The action had to be a cover for something else.

If Elyon was fomenting a demon rebellion, what exactly would it get him? As a duke, he wasn't in line for the throne himself, and even if a rebellion managed to topple the current rule, it was unlikely to be replaced by another monarchy. What did he have to gain by either unrest or a complete replacement of the old guard? It had to be something that would put the angel in a position of power. Perhaps by betraying the very demons he was professing to support.

The first order of business was to determine whether anyone else knew of the call to assembly. While Belphagor wasn't big on politics himself, he sometimes did business on the periphery of it. Where there was money to be made off the zeal of others, he was happy to make it.

Back at The Brimstone, Belphagor found Oza on duty once more, just arrived for his pre-dawn shift. Some hours at The Brimstone were slower than others, but downtime wasn't really a concept. Those who gambled at all hours wanted drink at all hours. Gambling was thirsty business.

"Weren't you awake *yesterday* morning?" Oza eyed him suspiciously as Belphagor sat at the bar. "I don't know what the Heavens are coming to if you're starting to make a habit of being up before noon."

Belphagor laughed. "Don't start questioning the nature of reality yet. I'm not 'up' before noon. I just haven't gone to bed."

"Well, that's a relief. What can I get for you on this fine winter morning? I don't imagine you need a hot toddy." Oza grinned. "I expect you've got one in your bed."

"Vasily and I aren't—" Belphagor stopped himself midprotest. He'd been somewhat defensively making a point of letting people know he wasn't having sex with Vasily, worried it might seem he was taking advantage of the firespirit's youth. But the protest was no longer true.

Oza raised his brows. "Finally remembered what it is you demons get up to in that room, have you? It's not the palace, you know. Walls aren't made of oak."

"*Bozhe moi.*" Though the earthly invocation of the Orthodox God might seem incongruous, Russian language permeated Raqia culture. After centuries of demons falling to and returning from that nearest of earthly realms, it had become like a second language to the Fallen.

Oza laughed. "I picked 'one year' in the pool. Thank you, my friend. That's going to pay off nicely."

Belphagor gaped at him. "There's been a betting pool over when I'd finally—" He stopped and buried his head in his crossed arms on the bar. "*Bozhe moi.* I'd like an absinthe."

"Coming right up." Oza sounded eminently pleased with himself.

Belphagor lifted his head. "Since you're obviously going to be sharing this juicy tidbit—"

"For those who didn't already hear it themselves." Oza gave him a wicked grin as he set up the glass to pour.

"Yes, I'm delighted to have provided so much entertainment for so many. But I'm wondering if you have any other juicy tidbits you'd care to throw my way. Seeing as I've made you a rich man."

Oza poured water over the sugar on the slotted spoon and pushed the glass toward him. "What sort of juicy tidbits?"

Belphagor took the pamphlet from his pocket and set it on the bar. "Heard anything about this?"

Oza perused it and gave him a somewhat ambiguous nod. Though Belphagor settled the tab for his drinks monthly like everyone else who roomed at The Brimstone, he set a facet on the bar.

Oza tucked it into his pocket. "Heard some drunken boasting about it."

"Any demons I might know?"

The bartender shook his head. "Not demons. Angels." He glanced about the relatively empty bar. At this hour, most of the patrons were doggedly gambling their last facets at the tables in the vain hope, no doubt, that this was the game that would turn their fortunes. "Military."

"Military?" Belphagor kept his voice low. "A rebellion among the ranks?" When Oza busied himself with wiping down the bar, Belphagor dropped another facet.

"Officers." Oza swept up the facet. "Some secret society bent on liberating the Fallen. That's all I can tell you. They don't confide in me, they just brag to one another." Most of the information Belphagor got from Oza, he seemed happy to give. The facets he earned for it were mere perks. But this time, Belphagor detected a note of genuine concern that someone might retaliate if they found out he'd talked about them.

This was much bigger than Belphagor had thought. Just rounding up a few demons to take on the angels at Elyon's villa wasn't going to be enough. But he was running out of time.

"Thank you, *tovarishch.*" He hoped the Russian word would have the desired effect. Meaning *comrade*, it had associations in the world of Man with violent revolution and repressive regimes. It was also a reminder that he and Oza had spent time together in that world, in the most repressive regime of all: the Russian prison system known as the *Zona.* "I don't suppose you recall who any of these angels were?"

Oza frowned, as though the reminder had crossed a line. "How would I know angels' names?" He turned to wash out some glasses behind the bar in a basin of gray water.

When Belphagor finished his drink and got up to leave, Oza murmured one other bit of information before turning away to his stockroom. "The Union of Liberation."

This was a term Belphagor had never heard before, but he gathered it was the name the angelic officers were using for their secret society. He'd have to find one of them and work his influence to get the information he needed, and he would have to do it fast. It seemed, for the morning at least, Belphagor would have to go back to turning tricks.

CHAPTER FIVE

Apparently, the Cherub hadn't killed Vasily, but it had given him one hell of a headache. He wasn't in the scullery icebox. He wasn't sure where he was, but his arms were no longer bound behind his back, thank the Heavens, and there was someone with him.

He kindled the fire in his eyes to see across the dark little room. Propped unconscious against the wall in the opposite corner was a demoness with sapphire hair. Vasily blushed. It was the working girl Duke Elyon had bought for him at The Cat.

He'd gone with the duke and his friends, feeling a bit awkward in a brothel full of women but not expecting that he would take part in any of the activities. At first, he'd thought Elyon was joking when he'd brought the pretty demoness to him in the parlor, and he'd reddened at the sight of her uncovered breasts.

"All yours," the duke had said with a grin. "At least for the next hour."

The demoness Sefira had hooked her arms around his shoulders and run her tongue down the side of his neck. All of a sudden, Vasily hadn't been so sure he wanted to decline.

"I like men," he'd tried to explain as Sefira drew him to a pile of cushions.

Sefira had merely grinned. "Don't we all, sweetie?"

In the end, he'd discovered to his surprise that liking one thing didn't automatically mean one couldn't also like another.

The demoness stirred, breaking his reverie, and he started guiltily.

"Sefira." He kept his voice low as he crawled over to her, not knowing if anyone was listening outside the door. "It's me. Vasily. The fire demon from the other night at The Cat."

She focused on him, and he saw with dismay that her eye had been blackened and her lip was swollen and cut. "Well, of course you are." Sefira put a hand to her head with a groan. "Oh, sweetie." She closed her eyes. "I think we're in trouble."

Belphagor knew the spots the angels frequented while trolling for demon cock. That much hadn't changed in all the years he'd been alive. They liked to stay close to the river but not so close that they might be seen. Just outside the Demon Market was where he'd done the most business.

Though he'd been off the market for quite some time, he did his best to entice whenever a group of officers strolled—or staggered—by, taking advantage of his size to look somewhat innocent and passive. They were drunk enough that they wouldn't notice he wasn't quite as youthful as the rest of the boys.

It wasn't long before a group of three young officers took a fancy to him. Belphagor had been hoping to get one alone, but he might be able to make this work. He requested a modest handful of facets for his services. They each paid up, and the deal was struck.

They'd had the foresight to rent a room for the night in the Devil's Doorstep, where it soon became apparent that at least two of his patrons were no novices to taking their pleasure with the coarser sex. The third, wide-eyed and quiet, seemed to be there largely to please his superior who'd done the negotiation.

After pleasuring the angels and testing their responses, Belphagor wound up his performance with a jerkoff for show, rising up on his knees when he finished to lift his shirt and stroke his sticky hand over his abs.

They hadn't asked about his tattoos until then—and of course hadn't seen the large cross on his chest that marked him as a "king of thieves" in the world of Man. It was impressive. No one who saw it could ever resist asking about it. He gave them a vague story about magical symbols that protected him, and they seemed to buy it. They certainly wouldn't have known the earthly significance. Most angels, despite dubbing demons "Fallen," only half believed there was another sphere to fall to.

Phaleg, the youngest of the three and a freshly minted officer whose enthusiasm in their activities had seemed the most genuine, let his eyes linger on the cross a moment long. "Well, on behalf of angelkind, may I say you've done your race proud."

Belphagor smiled, realizing this was his chance, before they got nervous and showed him the door. "On behalf of demonkind, I sincerely appreciate your patronage. The House of Arkhangel'sk may not be a friend to the Fallen, but the supernal army has always been good to us."

That was a lie, of course. He'd had the shit kicked out of him by drunken soldiers on more than one occasion, but the illusion of goodwill was all he was interested in.

The angel who seemed to be in a position of command gave him a stern look. "Careful what you say about the principality. We *are* His Supernal Majesty's right arm."

Phaleg took a bottle of mead from the table and uncorked it. "Please, Phanuel. It's no secret that the principality neglected to sign the Liberation Decree when he was crowned. Some of us—" he took a swig with a nod to Belphagor "—favor a representative government. Even the Fallen ought to have a voice."

"I hear there's some kind of protest in Elysium later today," Belphagor offered casually.

Phaleg put an arm around his shoulder and turned him toward the door. "You should stick to what you're so clearly called to, boy."

Belphagor was sure none of them still imagined him to be youthful. This was obviously meant to put him in his place. He lingered at the door after Phaleg opened it. Dawn would be here in an hour or two, and he was still no closer to finding out what the Union of Liberation might be up to.

The others were pulling on their coats.

"Have you paid for the room for the whole night?" Belphagor put on an engaging smile. "I'll happily polish you off in the morning for nothing extra. I wouldn't mind a place to sleep until sunup. I've been on my feet for hours, and it's awfully chilly out there."

Phaleg hesitated, obviously intrigued by the idea. "Well, we *did* pay for the room."

Phanuel rolled his eyes and went past him into the hallway. "I prefer to sleep in a *clean* bed. I believe this one's seen a bit too much action." The junior officer, who hadn't spoken once, followed Phanuel out. "You coming, Phaleg?"

"I may be." Phaleg grinned. "A bit later."

"Suit yourself." Phanuel and his silent companion disappeared into the dark hallway as Phaleg closed the door. Belphagor had the distinct impression the other two had come along on this venture for the perverse thrill of it, whereas Phaleg seemed to express an actual desire for his own sex.

There couldn't be many angels who would admit to such a preference among their peers. Trolling for rentboys was one thing, an expected thing, but actually desiring the companionship of a man over a woman was viewed as deviant among the Host.

Phaleg studied him with interest. "What's your name, demon?"

"Ivan." Best not to take a chance he'd heard of the Prince of Tricks. "Sorry if I overstepped my place by speaking of the rally."

Phaleg ignored this. "May I kiss you on the mouth?"

Belphagor hesitated. Mutual cock-play was one thing, but it felt wrong to engage in romantic behavior with someone else while Vasily was in trouble—or perhaps even at all. The unexpected conviction made his skin prickle. He'd never had to consider someone else's feelings before, and he wasn't sure he cared for it.

"Never mind." Phaleg looked somewhat crestfallen. "Let's just catch a few winks for now." He sat on the bed and observed it with a grimace. "I'm not sure we dare look under the covers. But I suspect you and I can keep each other warm on top of them."

Belphagor considered the young officer: little older than Vasily, yet already out of the academy and awarded a command. Belphagor had a hunch about him. The game would be risky, but he was running out of options.

He dropped his voice into a more comfortable register. "I get the feeling you've played at this before. But never as the one at anyone's mercy."

Phaleg looked up at him, and the moment's hesitation combined with the little jump of the pulse at his throat confirmed that Belphagor's instincts were right. "Mercy? I'm not sure what you mean."

"You've always held the purse, set the terms, made polite little bargains to have your prick sucked." He took a step toward the bed. "Never the one on his knees swallowing a thick knob and gobbling hot spunk with abandon. Never the one bent over a schoolboy's bench being buggered senseless while others line up to have a turn on you, all the while showing your eagerness for more with a raging erection begging to be relieved."

Phaleg swallowed, and the slow movement in his throat was all the answer Belphagor needed.

"Is that what you picture when you stroke yourself in the dead of night?" He stepped close to the angel as he spoke, so close that he might have unfastened his pants and slid his cock into the pristine thing's mouth. And if he had, he was certain Phaleg wouldn't have stopped him.

When he received no other answer than the rapid breathing and the pounding of Phaleg's heart, he clenched his fist in the pale hair at the angel's forehead. "I asked you a question." His tone was now the steely one he reserved for professional power play.

Phaleg nodded, his effort impeded by Belphagor's grip.

"I've no interest in assaulting a frightened *boy* who can't even voice his own desires. Do you want to be at the mercy of a demon? Speak clearly."

"Yes," Phaleg managed, barely audible.

Belphagor dragged him onto the floor on his knees, and Phaleg did nothing to stop him, looking up with eyes wide and a face as white as Elysium's summer night sky. Through the tight elkskin of his uniform, the hard curve of his erection was unmistakable.

"You're straining your leathers. That's bound to leave an impression in them your superiors will notice." He held Phaleg's frightened gaze. "Let it out."

A tiny gasp escaped Phaleg's mouth, and after only an instant's delay, he hastily unbuttoned and drew his swollen cock from his breeches.

Belphagor nodded his approval and tilted Phaleg's head back, making him moan. There was nothing like angels for pretty, boyish charm, and Phaleg, with his cock in his hand and eyes glistening with fear and anticipation, was a prime example.

"Do you want to come, boy?" Belphagor brushed his calf against the swollen prick.

Phaleg groaned and gasped, "Please." He was riper for the plucking than Belphagor had hoped.

He released his grip abruptly and clapped his hands together with a sharp retort. "On your feet. Drop your pants."

Trembling, Phaleg scrambled to obey, and Belphagor turned him toward the grimy window and pushed his feet wider apart, the pants still around his ankles. He stood behind Phaleg and spoke at his ear as he reached around to unbutton the dress shirt.

"Think about the other angels who may be passing by below with no idea that you're standing here in the dark doing a demon's bidding, at a demon's mercy of your own volition."

Phaleg moaned, swaying back against him.

Belphagor slipped the fabric down over Phaleg's arms and let the crisply starched shirt of the uniform fall in the dust. "Is this what you want? Is this who you want to be?" He cupped Phaleg's balls through his legs. "A pretty toy for a demon cockwhore?"

"Yes," Phaleg moaned.

Belphagor took him by the shoulders, turning Phaleg to face him once more, and pushed him back against the glass. The angel's cock was like the oversized stamen of a flower sprouting gloriously from among its pale golden bed.

"Masturbate for me," Belphagor ordered.

Phaleg stroked himself with a groan of gratitude, his eyes closing as he leaned his head back.

"Stop."

The blue eyes shot open, and Phaleg dropped his hand from his swollen prick. For a novice, he was quite good at obedience. Thank Heaven for military academies.

Belphagor braced both hands flat on the glass beside the angel's head, leaning just close enough to him that Phaleg's cock pressed lightly against Belphagor's abs where his shirt was still partly unbuttoned.

"Before I let you come, you have to do something for me." Phaleg blinked at him warily. Belphagor tightened his abs against the part he pressed, and Phaleg bit his lip. "Will you answer my questions without questioning me in return?"

Phaleg nodded.

"Good boy. Put your hand around your cock and hold it there." When Phaleg had eagerly complied, Belphagor put his lips to the angel's ear. "What do you know about the Union of Liberation?"

"Fuck." Phaleg tried to move away, but Belphagor shoved him back.

"Did I tell you to stop touching yourself?"

"You tricked me!"

Belphagor inclined his head. "Nevertheless. Hand to cock. Or will you deny that you're deep in the grip of the most fulfilling sexual experience of your life and forgo the orgasm I'm about to grant you?"

Phaleg's eyes were furious, his face pink with humiliation and his breathing rapid. "You're mocking me. This is a joke to you." He blinked angrily as the rims of his eyes reddened and welled with tears.

"Not at all, dear boy. I am deeply honored that you've put such trust in me. Your blossoming desire"—he flicked his eyes to the still-raging erection between them—"is something beautiful to behold. I want to give you what you need, what you've been longing for, what you feared you'd never find."

Phaleg closed his eyes, a tear escaping down his cheek. "I put my trust in you foolishly."

"You're afraid I'll expose you because you've let yourself be more vulnerable with me than you've ever been with anyone else, given me all of your power, even your pride."

More tears were falling, and Phaleg turned his head aside.

"It's a tremendous gift. I accept it with the grave responsibility attendant such an honor." He dragged a knuckle over the damp cheek, and Phaleg made a miserable sound in his throat. "But your fear is holding you back from having what you want more than anything. Let go and give it all to me, and I promise I will cherish it like precious porcelain." He licked a salty tear from the pure celestial skin. "Cock in hand."

With a gasp of anguish as if Belphagor had buried a knife in his gut, Phaleg obeyed.

"Good boy." He moved back, hands still against the glass. "Will you answer my questions? Will you be utterly debased?"

Phaleg gasped out his answer, tears flowing freely. "Yes."

"Tell me about the Union of Liberation."

When he answered, it was with a tone of such defeat that Belphagor almost felt bad about what he was doing to him. But this was for his Vasily.

"It's a secret society among the Supernal Army."

"Stroke yourself. Slowly."

Phaleg obeyed with a soft sigh.

"What are the aims of the society?"

"To replace the supernal dynasty with a constitutional monarchy." Phaleg kept stroking, his hand sliding slowly up and down the rigid length. "And to liberate the Fallen."

"You may stroke harder. Is Duke Elyon of the House of Arcadia a member of the Union of Liberation?"

The vigorous movements of Phaleg's hand were loud in the quiet room. "Yes. He's in the upper echelon."

Belphagor let him work at himself, watching the angel's face as his climax built, listening to his soft grunts and groans of pleasure. He was a stroke away from shooting hot semen over his hand, his breathing at a fever pitch.

"Stop."

Phaleg moaned as if he'd been kicked but dropped his hand instantly, his body twisting as he strove to control himself.

"You're not to come until I say, do you understand me?"

"Yes, sir." Ah, now that was lovely. Spontaneous deference.

"*Da, ser*," Belphagor snapped. "You will answer in the peasant tongue."

"*Da, ser*," Phaleg repeated in his flat angelic accent.

Belphagor's cock twitched wistfully, tamped down by his conscience. He was not here for himself. "Begin again." He smiled at Phaleg's desperate groan as the slender fingers practically choked the end of his prick. "Stroke slowly. That's it. A little faster."

Phaleg let out a soft, unconscious string of expletives as he struggled not to come. "Fuck. Oh fuck me. Oh shit."

"What is the Union of Liberation planning for tonight?"

Phaleg's legs were trembling uncontrollably. "To assassinate the principality. Please," he moaned. "Oh fuck, please."

Belphagor knew the angel couldn't hold back a second longer. "Open your eyes."

Gasping and whimpering, Phaleg opened them and looked into Belphagor's. He was completely bereft of his own free will, eyes shining with the knowledge of it as if he'd taken the purest hit of firedust in the Heavens.

"Come for me," said Belphagor.

Phaleg erupted in a beautiful stream of white, nearly wailing with relief, jerking out more of it in spurts and pearls of release until his knees buckled and Belphagor caught him and slid with him to the floor of the dirty, hourly rent room.

Phaleg began to shudder and sob, curling into a fetal cocoon, and Belphagor sat quietly beside him, rubbing his shoulder, and let him sob it all out.

When his weeping slowed, Phaleg wiped his eyes and glanced up hopelessly. "What are you going to do? Will you expose the Union of Liberation? I'll take the fall for them. I'm sworn to die for the cause. I won't give you names."

"You'll give me names if I ask for them." Belphagor's tone was matter-of-fact, and Phaleg's face radiated shame when he couldn't deny it. "But I don't need any names. I have no intention of exposing anyone. I couldn't care less about the principality or your revolution."

"Then why—" He shook his head, utterly baffled.

"Why did I make you betray everything you believed in for the best orgasm you've ever had in your life?"

Phaleg closed his mouth and swallowed as he nodded.

Belphagor gave him a gentle but reproachful smile. "Come now, we both know there was more to it than that. You didn't do it for an orgasm. You did it because you needed to surrender everything to me to feel for a few minutes of your life what it was to be authentic and free. And understood. And I understand you very well. I promised you could trust me, and I never go back on my word. I will never expose you to anyone. In any way. If we meet again on the street, I'll walk past you without a glance unless you choose to acknowledge me for the benefit of those you're with as the whore you purchased for a night. And I will graciously play the part I played earlier this morning with your comrades at arms—not that I'll be selling anything again," he added. "I've retired. This was a special return engagement for one night only."

Phaleg relaxed, resting his head against Belphagor's hip. "Thank you." He sighed as if a great weight had been lifted from him.

"But I hope you'll trust me a little further. I need to know more. I would have asked the rest of my questions earlier, but you'd put such trust in me already, I couldn't let you fail at the impossible task I'd set before you. That would be cruel."

Phaleg laughed softly. "You gave me permission to do what you knew I couldn't stop."

One corner of Belphagor's mouth tugged upward. "Of course."

"So what is it you need to know?" The angel would tell him anything now.

"Duke Elyon has taken someone very important to me, and it has something to do with this mission of your Union of Liberation."

"Taken someone? A demon?"

"Naturally."

"Elyon talked about recruiting a demon to kill the principality. In case the revolt failed, the demon would go down as a martyr to the cause." Phaleg gave him an apologetic look. "I have no control at my level to affect these decisions."

Belphagor frowned. Vasily wasn't likely to kill for the duke, even to earn his freedom, and certainly hadn't volunteered to be executed for some foolish cause. "So how is that to be carried out? While the larger assembly is there for a protest, members of the Union of Liberation infiltrate and stir up the crowd to revolt? And then this demon somehow gets past the Ophanim Guard to make the attempt on the principality's life?"

Phaleg nodded. "Essentially, yes. The Union of Liberation would provide a distraction, allowing him to get close. And in the aftermath, we arise with our solution to end the chaos of the principality dying without an heir. Little Grand Duchess Omeliea would never be put forth as a viable option, and the principality's younger cousin would be suspect after such an event, particularly with the assassination of the previous principality still fresh in everyone's minds."

"That sounds foolish. Destined to fail." But perhaps the upper echelon didn't intend for it to succeed.

Phaleg began to shiver, the heat of his exertion no longer sufficient against the unheated room.

"You should put on your trousers before you freeze to death."

Phaleg sat up, looking embarrassed, as if he'd been waiting for permission and realized now the game was over. While the angel struggled to work the elkskin back over his legs, Belphagor picked up the shirt and dusted it off, setting it over Phaleg's shoulders. Phaleg glanced up as Belphagor crouched behind him.

"I want you to know that I meant what I said. I'm deeply honored by what you gave me, and I will cherish it. And if you ever find yourself again in need of someone who understands you—for a price—you can find me at The Brimstone. Ask for Belphagor."

"Belphagor?" Phaleg looked puzzled before realization dawned on him. "You're that wingcasting champion who—"

"Who takes every angel who plays against him for every last facet he has." Belphagor winked mischievously. He helped Phaleg up and waited while he pulled himself together before brushing at the dusty shoulders of the woolen jacket. "May I kiss you?"

Phaleg blushed liked a schoolgirl. "Of course."

Belphagor pulled the angel close, but instead of kissing him on the mouth, he pressed his lips to the smooth cheek. "You were breathtaking in your willing surrender. Never forget that."

CHAPTER SIX

Belphagor turned one last trick outside the market before dawn and left the satisfied patron sleeping. And naked. He tucked the blankets around the officer, who would be just a bit wiser when he woke to discover his state of undress. Belphagor might not be able to pass for an angelic officer under close examination, but the uniform and cap he'd stolen would let him move through the assembly at the square without being noticed.

He headed back to The Brimstone after sunup, wired from being awake since the previous morning. Even if there had been time to sleep, he doubted he could have without Vasily by his side. He drank a full pot of black Russian tea, with a vodka chaser from the bottle Vasily had procured, hoping for a second wind.

The reminder that his boy had been up early and thinking of him after their intense night together made Belphagor ache in the expected places but also in others that had nothing to do with sex.

His hands ached for the lack of Vasily's smooth, flushed skin; his lungs, from breathing in too deep, trying to catch the lingering smoky scent. And his breastbone hurt. Or somewhere close to it. Somewhere just to the left. *Oh, hell.*

He had to do something else to keep from going mad. There had to be more information he could gather before tonight, something he could use to put a stop to the events that had been set in motion—and to get his boy back before it was too late. Regardless, he couldn't sleep, and he couldn't sit in this room and wait for dark.

Before he headed out, Belphagor reluctantly smothered the glowing coals in the small brazier that vented through the roof of The Brimstone. The morning was bitterly cold. Sooty smoke from dozens of the stoves had already been rising from the den when he'd returned.

He hadn't had to use his much since Vasily had come to stay with him. He warmed his hands against the dwindling heat before he closed the brazier door. He was wearing a pair of fingerless gloves—something he also hadn't needed in ages—and still the warmth didn't penetrate. He'd grown dangerously accustomed to all the tiny, daily ways Vasily had changed his life.

There was no way for Vasily to tell what time of day or night it was inside the windowless room or how much time had passed since they'd woken up here. He sat behind Sefira with his knees drawn up and his arms wrapped around her for warmth. She didn't look good. He kept having to shake her gently to keep her from dozing off, worried that if she slept again, she wouldn't wake up. She'd taken a bad blow to the head.

He tried to keep her talking, figuring she couldn't slip into unconsciousness if she had to concentrate. "So how high up do you suppose this thing goes? Is Elyon the top?"

Sefira sighed as if talking were an effort, her head against his chest. "Sounded to me like he was giving orders. 'Make sure the demon is close to the principality before it goes down.' Not 'We need to make sure.'"

"Before it goes down." Vasily shook his head. "Do you think they really mean to assassinate him? Right there in plain sight?"

"He was giving rather specific instructions on how to get the knife just under the ribs. Any whore knows that advice; if you're in trouble, you don't want to miss. Nothing's worse than making some rapist son of a bitch angrier because you wounded him. You stick him hard in the soft organs, and you run like hell."

Vasily nodded against the top of her head. Working the street had been dangerous for him, but it had scared the hell out of him to see the young girls on their own dealing with some of the worst of demon nature—and as often as not, angel nature. It was why situations at houses like The Cat were so coveted: warm beds, companionship, protection, and the safety of lights and numbers. There were no such establishments for men, but it seemed only fair. Men, after all, were the ones the women had to worry about.

Sefira's shoulder slumped against him, and he shook her. "Stay awake, Sefi. Keep me company."

She pushed his hand away. "Go 'way, Tabi. 'M sleepy."

"*Sefira.*"

At the sharp sound, Sefira jolted awake and began to weep tears of exhaustion. "I'm so tired, sweetie. My head hurts."

"I know." He rocked her gently. "I'm sorry. But you have to stay awake until I can get you help."

"Won't be any." Her tone was resigned. "I heard them talking while they had me tied in the back of the cart under the blankets. They want it to look like you strangled me. That's the only reason they didn't finish me themselves."

Vasily shook his head vehemently. "That is *not* going to happen. I won't let it. Belphagor won't."

Sefira sighed. "You really are too adorable. I'm very glad I got to be your first. Wouldn't've missed that for the worlds." Her body went slack against him, and this time he couldn't rouse her. He felt for her pulse at her throat, relieved that it was still strong, and then eased her carefully onto the wood floor, his hand beneath her head.

It was infuriating that he couldn't do a damned thing to help her. She didn't deserve to be in here with him, caught in the middle of whatever foul scheme Duke Elyon had planned. He straightened and crossed to the door, punching it with his fists like he was boxing, swearing at the top of his lungs until his throat was sore and his hands were bloody. How the hell could he have been so stupid as to get involved with these fucking angels?

He'd only been inside for an hour, but when Belphagor hit the street again, Raqia was bustling despite the cold. The news of the planned action at Council Square was out; the pamphlets had been distributed. Those who could read were passing the information along to those who couldn't—amid cynical speculation as to what difference it could possibly make and dire predictions that something terrible would happen.

A conspiracy theory was already afloat that the supernal army had orchestrated the event to round up demons so they could slaughter them. It was eerily close to the truth. If the principality was assassinated and a demon blamed for it, the bricks of Council Square would run red with the blood of the Fallen before the next dawn.

Belphagor did his best to stoke the flames of that particular theory among the general populace. He also circulated more practical information among those who were in his debt. By noon, he'd made as many connections as he could, passing the word that any demon who owed him something should assemble in The Brimstone's private meeting room in an hour.

He arrived back at the den just as Oza was getting off duty. What the bartender owed him—in exchange for information Belphagor had kept quiet—was the meeting room itself, no questions asked. Oza opened the room and bid him good afternoon, wanting to know nothing more about the purpose of Belphagor's gathering.

The number of demons who quietly made their way from the gaming tables into the room over the next half hour was heartening. There was something to be said for beating the pants off half the population of Raqia—whether figuratively or literally.

The five who'd gone with him to Duke Elyon's villa were among the first to arrive, curious what he might have in mind after the pleasant evening they'd apparently spent.

"If you want us to bed more whores for free," one of them offered, "we're all for it."

Belphagor cut the laughter short. "If you'd been paying attention to the whores, they wouldn't have been jumped while walking home and beaten by angels. They'd both be happily back at work at The Cat right now. Instead, one is recuperating, and the other has been abducted."

The room went silent.

Belphagor glanced around at the guilty-looking faces. "Any of you have any information?"

Paimon, one of the more trustworthy, spoke up sheepishly. "I'm afraid we all must have been out cold by then. The duke was serving some rather fancy liquor, and I guess it went to our heads. Don't remember a thing until some angelic servant gave us the boot this morning."

Belphagor looked at the others. "You all passed out? At the same time?"

Paimon frowned. "Do you suppose the duke had us spelled?"

"Or drugged." Belphagor inclined his head. "It's a distinct possibility. Sefira, the one who's missing, told her sister she'd overheard something troubling and wanted to leave right away. I think whoever abducted Sefira wanted to keep her quiet, and it seems they'd already taken measures to ensure no one else heard anything either. It so happens, however, that I was able to obtain certain information this morning that may be part of it."

Belphagor paused and closed the door. "You've all heard already about the action planned at Council Square tonight. What you don't know is that Duke Elyon and a secret society of angelic officers are behind it, and they intend to overthrow the current government. They also intend to use my Vasily to do it."

"Your Vasily?" A paunchy demon who looked like he'd rather be at the bar gave him a quizzical scowl. "You mean that firespirit rentboy who's always on your heels?"

Belphagor took a menacing step toward him. "Do you have some objection to my choice of companion, Jeqon?"

Jeqon reddened. "None of my business, I'm sure."

"If anyone else has a problem with my relationship, you may as well leave now. I assure you, however, that we *will* be settling accounts." He glanced around, noting a few pairs of eyes that wouldn't quite meet his, but no one moved.

"No? All right, then. Elyon's group will be stirring up the demons in the square—perhaps disguised as demons themselves, so trust no one who is not in this room with us now—during which time they plan to assassinate the principality and blame it on the Fallen. My understanding is that Vasily, specifically, is to be their scapegoat. What I want each of you to do is be ready when Vasily shows up. I believe you're all familiar with what he looks like?"

"Trouble," muttered one of them, followed by a nervous ripple of laughter through the room.

"I'll take that as a yes," said Belphagor dryly. "When Vasily arrives, he may be drugged, or perhaps bespelled in some way. He is likely to be accompanied by Elyon's men and closely guarded. Your job is to see that he doesn't get near the principality—that *no* demon gets near enough to assassinate the principality, as counter as that may be to your own instincts—and that no harm comes to Vasily in the process. I'll be disguised as a supernal officer, and I'll need a few of you to assist me in distracting whomever Vasily's with so I can get him safely away."

"And what do we get in exchange?" asked Paimon.

Belphagor smiled. "You mean, besides the satisfaction of serving your principality?" He paused for the cursing and guffaws. "Absolution of any debt you owe me. In full. Whether that debt is monetary or something less tangible. But that is *only* if Vasily gets away safely and the principality is also unharmed. I don't think anyone needs me to explain the consequences to all of the Fallen should any of us end up being used as the supernal opposition's scapegoat."

"And how will you know we've actually participated in this venture?" Jeqon asked. "You're just going to absolve everyone's debt without question?"

"I will assign each of you one demon to pass information to. I will find mine before Vasily and I leave the square and give him a word. I will then ask each of you later what that word is. If you are at the square close enough to receive the word, it will be clear to me that you've fulfilled our agreement. If you give me the word but failed to pass it on to your assigned demon, I will assume that you and you alone betrayed me, and everyone below you in the chain of contact will be absolved. Trust me—that is not a position you want to be in."

"That doesn't seem fair," Jeqon objected. "What if whoever I'm assigned doesn't show?"

"Then I suppose it would behoove you to make sure that he does." Belphagor gave him the sort of smile he delivered right before the killing blow at the wingcasting table. "But be forewarned: The word you receive may not be the same as the word you *per*ceive." Like a game of telephone in the world of Man, the word would change with the telling—thanks to a simple spell Belphagor had purchased in the market before he'd returned. Only by completing the chain of assignments would the word return to its natural form. Thus, whatever the final demon gave him would tell him instantly if—and where— the chain had been broken.

One of the others spoke up while the rest murmured among themselves. "What's that supposed to mean?"

"It means," said Belphagor, "that the final task for each of you before your debt is canceled will be a quick round of cards. Just an informal match, no crystal exchanged, wherein you will tell me the word. And you do not want to be the demon who's gotten it out of sequence."

Jeqon, always loath to admit when he'd been beaten, made a scoffing sound in his throat. "What's to stop me from just finding the last demon and pounding the word out of him?"

Belphagor stared at him until Jeqon began to sweat. "If you think you can sit across the wingcasting table from me and lie without me knowing, think again. Do you really want to test me to find out?" Jeqon evidently didn't. "All right, that's it, boys. I thank you. I'll leave the list of assigned names at the bar, so stop by to get yours before you head out this evening."

There were now less than four hours until dusk. Belphagor's final task was to find out what he could about what had happened to Sefira.

When Vasily heard the key in the lock, he jumped up and pressed his back against the wall beside the door, ready to leap on whoever was on the other side. But as the door swung open, he was met by a jolt of pain. As fast as lightning, the Cherub had struck him in the chest with an outstretched wing. It stung like nothing Vasily had ever experienced and took the wind from him completely, knocking him to the ground.

A pair of boots appeared before him as the floor seemed to reel beneath his cheek. "It's best not to provoke a Cherub." Duke Elyon was the owner of the boots. "They can be rather unpredictable." The angel paused, and one of the boots turned toward the opposite wall. "I see our pretty whore isn't doing so well."

"Needs a doctor," Vasily gritted between his teeth, though his head was vibrating like a broadsword that had struck an iron post.

"I thought you might feel some concern for her after she plucked your poppy. A performance which, I must reiterate, the rest of us enjoyed a great deal."

Vasily let out a low, snarling growl, in part because he was too furious for words, but more so because he could barely form any.

"I'd be happy to get her the medical attention she needs, but I need you to do something for me in exchange."

Vasily clenched his fists against the floor. "What?"

"Accompany a few friends of mine to the square when the principality arrives to address our little gathering."

"What square? What gathering?"

"We're presently inside the Conciliary on Council Square. This evening, a few thousand demons will join a cadre of officers of the Supernal Army to protest the ascendancy of Principality Helison to the throne of Heaven. After we've publicly refused to swear allegiance, the principality himself will feel compelled to make an appearance to quell the rebellion. And that is when I need *you*, dear boy."

It irked him to hear the words that ought to be Belphagor's on Elyon's tongue. Vasily gripped the wall beside him and managed to pull himself up. "I'm not killing anyone for you."

"Who said anything about killing anyone?"

"You did. You said I'd assassinate the principality. And Sefira told me you wanted to make it look like I'd killed her too."

"The blow to her head has clearly left her a bit addled. As for what I said, it was that you'd be famous for it, not that you'd do it. I would never leave a detail like that to a demon."

"So what the hell do you want me to do?"

"Merely to stand about and look menacing."

"And take the fall for the assassination."

Elyon flashed his handsome angelic smile, though it was marred somewhat by his bruised and swollen nose. "Something like that. In return, I'll see to it that the whore is well taken care of."

"How about you bring her a doctor and take care of her first. Then I'll see about doing you any favors."

Elyon frowned and gave a nod to the Cherub in the doorway. "Arzal."

The Cherub crossed to where Sefira lay motionless on the stone and lifted her, eliciting an unconscious moan.

"Snap her neck," said Elyon.

"No!" Vasily tried to scramble up, making it as far as his knees. "Please!"

Arzal paused and looked to Elyon with his eagle aspect.

The duke sighed. "A typical demon who responds only to threats. So be it. Forget the fair bargain I offered you. You'll do as I bid you, firespirit, or the whore dies."

Where Belphagor's gift of influence failed, liquor and bribery took up the slack. He had ingested the "angelic bastard" glamour once more and donned the stolen uniform before heading to the Left Bank to see what he could learn. No one, it seemed, had witnessed the attack on the demonesses, but when Belphagor claimed he had, he began to get results.

A few academy dropouts who'd been partying at the villa recalled seeing Sefira return without her sister—voluntarily, they claimed, but in the company of Elyon's most trusted companions. It had struck them as odd, not only for the lack of Tabris, who had apparently never been absent from her side at any gathering of the duke's, but because her escorts had not been smiling. No one spent any amount of time around Sefira that did not include pleasure.

Belphagor managed to find out which angels had been with her by boasting of being in the inner circle and dropping random names over drink. His drinking mates were eager to correct him to show him up.

Armed with the information, he moved on to what passed for gaming houses in the Left Bank and played the celestial equivalent of backgammon with a group of artists and musicians. He dropped the story that he'd been commissioned to paint the duke with his three companions but hadn't been paid. The outrage was immediate, and in solidarity, the painters in the group agreed to help him sneak into the villa to steal back his painting.

It was little more than an hour until sundown by the time he'd gained access to the companions' quarters in the duke's villa and had left his new friends to create a diversion while he searched the rooms. Unsurprisingly, he came up empty; it would have been quite a piece of luck to have found Vasily and Sefira tied to a pair of armchairs, waiting to be rescued.

But an opportunity presented itself when an angel who'd managed to bypass the diversion surprised Belphagor emerging from a particularly large closet he'd been investigating.

The angel gaped at him, still holding the doorknob. "What do you think you're doing?"

Belphagor resisted the urge to state the obvious and took a chance on one of the names. "You must be Haglon. Do you have any idea how you've messed this thing up?"

The angel took a step backward with a look of consternation. "You mistake me, sir. My name is Praxil."

"That's hardly likely to matter to the duke. I suppose Haglon and Ormas have left you to take the blame for this fuckup with the whore?"

Praxil's look of annoyance shifted to one of mild alarm. "What in Heaven are you on about? I did exactly what Elyon asked. He seemed perfectly pleased when we delivered the demoness to him this morning."

"And was she breathing at the time?"

"Of course she was. Elyon said he wanted her alive." Praxil narrowed his eyes. "What do you mean 'at the time'? Isn't she now?"

Belphagor folded his arms and didn't answer, hoping his grim expression would be interpreted in whatever way would get him the most information.

"Shit. Look, I told Haglon to be careful, but would he listen to me? He never listens to anyone when Elyon's not there to rein him in. She tried to run for it when we were getting her out of the back of the cart, and he belted her. All the idiot had to do was grab her. With her hands tied, she lost her balance and hit the flagstone."

Flagstone. There wasn't any at the villa—or in this part of Elysium—so far as Belphagor had seen. The only flagstone he knew of was at Palace Square. And the nearby Council Square.

"I thought he'd killed her then and there." Praxil shook his head. "But she came to after he slapped her cheeks a bit, and she seemed all right." He ran his fingers through his hair, clutching it anxiously. "Does Elyon know yet?"

"No, and I suppose we should keep it that way as long as possible. He'll have all our heads if his plan is botched."

Praxil narrowed his eyes again. "Who did you say you were?"

"I didn't. Semyon Xomoyovich. I just arrived from Zevul this morning. Elyon told me to keep an eye on the demoness until things were ready to move forward."

"An eye on her? Isn't that Cherub, Arzal, taking care of the demons? He's supposed to make sure the firespirit does his job. Why else would Elyon want the whore?"

Belphagor's concentration was momentarily rattled by the mention of Vasily. "The firespirit? What does he have to do with her?"

Praxil had finally become suspicious. "You seem to be missing a fair amount of critical information. And for someone who just arrived this morning, the duke seems to have placed a great deal of trust in you. Exactly when did the academy start accepting half-breeds anyway?"

Belphagor shrugged. "I never said I was at the academy. I was one of Elyon's kept boys."

"Bullshit. I'd have seen you about. Who the hell are you?"

Belphagor had worn out his influence with this one. He started for the door, but Praxil caught his jacket sleeve as he tried to pass.

"Not so fast. I'm taking you straight to Elyon to explain yourself."

"Fine. While you're at it, you want to tell him how the whore ended up dead? It's your funeral."

"How do I know you're telling the truth about that?" It had certainly taken him long enough to have this genius thought. Praxil smirked as if he were clever. "Why don't we take a look for ourselves?"

Belphagor had to fight the urge to laugh aloud. "That's exactly why I headed back here, to find one of you to take a look before I had to tell Elyon. I sure as hell don't want to be the messenger who gets shot."

The angel gave him a peculiar look, and Belphagor realized he'd mixed his metaphors with his spheres. Gunpowder was strictly of the world of Man—as was the saying. One could be shot by an arrow in Heaven, of course, but beheading would be the more efficient means of dispatching the bearer of bad news. "Shot through at the end of Elyon's sword."

Praxil frowned but let it drop, and Belphagor kept his mouth shut as they headed up Palace Avenue. He'd been running out of time anyway. If they'd stayed a minute longer at the villa, the protest at the square would have been in full swing by the time they arrived.

As it was, dusk was upon them before they drew near. Belphagor had hoped his luck would continue to hold and his escort might take him straight to where Vasily and Sefira were being confined, but there was no chance of that now. The square had begun to fill with demons who'd gotten the word.

"You got lucky," Praxil grumbled as they headed into the crowd.

Not lucky enough.

He tried to stay close to Praxil, but the scene was fast becoming chaotic, and he lost him before long. The last he'd seen, the angel had been heading for the platform someone had erected in front of the Conciliary, from which demons were currently taking to the podium, enumerating the crimes of the supernacy and leading the crowd in chants of "Liberation now!" and "End the dominion of the Host!"

The latter was a play on words. The Order of Dominions—Heaven's philosophers and scholars by whom all angels were educated at Zevul's universities—were the ones who promulgated the doctrine of the Host's natural rule over the Fallen. As well as the belief that the supernal House of Arkhangel'sk was destined to represent that rule as surely as Divine Right had been fostered for centuries in the world of Man.

Belphagor made his way through the crowd toward the platform and spotted Paimon, the demon he'd designated to receive the word from him. Paimon nodded discreetly. Other officers' uniforms had begun to appear in the crowd, and the agitating that Phaleg had warned him about was soon evident. But Belphagor saw no sign of Duke Elyon himself—or any others from the party at the villa or the afternoon at the Left Bank.

He did, however, see Phaleg himself, not a few feet away. Phaleg didn't recognize him, which he supposed was a good thing. It meant

Belphagor's glamour still held. Of course, he'd promised not to let on that he knew Phaleg if they were ever to meet again, but he felt a mild pang of disappointment nonetheless as the angel's eyes passed over him without reaction.

There was nothing like that little glint of recognition when a "boy" he'd disciplined or trained found himself face-to-face with Belphagor once more. They always had the instinct to immediately lower their eyes in deference to him, which he found immensely gratifying, like a tutor seeing a former pupil and taking pride in the knowledge that his lessons had gone deep. Not to mention his cock.

Little by little, however, he noticed the officers of the Supernal Army moving out of the crowd and gathering on either side of the square as if falling into formation. He moved closer to the perimeter to avoid being conspicuous but not wanting to get too far from where the principality was likely to be if he arrived to address the uprising—and not wanting to lose sight of Paimon.

As darkness settled in, the Winter Palace began to blaze with candlelight that glittered on the snow-covered skeletal trees between the two squares. It was as picturesque and enchanting as its earthly counterpart, even if the lights there were now electric. Its illuminated presence seemed to rile the demons. Council Square was lit more ruggedly with their torches, which they began to raise in the direction of the palace with their shouts, as though they might advance on it and set it on fire.

In response, a full regiment of the Ophanim Palace Guard filed out along the boulevard that lined the embankment, their ominous glow in eerie contrast to the hot, angry sputter of the torches. Their action seemed to signal Duke Elyon's appearance at last. He emerged from the Conciliary to make his way to the raised platform amid an entourage of fellow supernal officers who ousted the demons from the podium.

Instead of Elyon, however, one of his entourage stepped up.

"We stand today with these citizens of the Firmament of Shehaqim," the angel shouted over the crowd. "Three thousand officers of the Supernal Army who reject the legitimacy of Principality Helison Alimielovich as supernal ruler."

A hush came over the square as the Fallen protestors looked around at each other in shock.

"But we do not stand with anarchy," he continued. "We call upon the principality to meet with us in this place and hear the people's demands. But we will not condone lawlessness. We call upon our brothers in the Supernal Army to take this stand with us, to stand against tyranny, to stand for freedom, and to stand for a new Heaven belonging to all its citizens."

The demons had recovered from their surprise, and a great shout of support went up from the crowd, along with renewed chants. Elyon's man waited patiently for the noise to die down and then resumed his grand words in the same series of pledges of support juxtaposed with warnings that did not seem to penetrate the excited mood of the crowd. It was clear, however, to anyone paying attention that the Union of Liberation had no intention of engaging in an actual revolt and every intention of putting one down should it erupt.

None of this mattered to Belphagor. He waited for any sign that the principality was actually going to be goaded out of his palace to address the uprising, and he kept his eyes on the Conciliary, certain Vasily would be emerging from the same place Elyon had if the principality indeed were to arrive.

Belphagor had no idea how Elyon meant for his plan to come off, since there was no way Vasily could have been induced to do his bidding, but the duke's demeanor was supremely confident. Whatever he had in mind, there was no sign that he feared it might fail.

As the speechmaking and hollow promises went on without an appearance from the principality, Belphagor began to think Elyon would be disappointed. It was certainly Helison's style to avoid dealing with controversy.

But at last there was movement from the palace. A protective cordon of Ophanim began to advance along the embankment, and in their midst was the principality himself, flanked by his personal Seraphim Guard.

The noise of the crowd exploded for a moment and then died down into hushed tones as they waited to see what their principality would do. As a sign of goodwill, perhaps, Helison hadn't come with any officers of the Supernal Army. Those to the left of the stage moved away at the sight of the Seraphim, and Helison passed through the gap in their ranks and mounted the platform.

All eyes were on him and the almost blinding brilliance of the firespirits beside him. Thus, the battalion who followed from Palace Square some ninety seconds later—blocked from view by the white glare of the Ophanim—went unnoticed. Except by Belphagor, who'd made a career of noticing things without appearing to.

He also noticed the door of the Conciliary quietly opening at the principality's back.

Belphagor nodded to Paimon and made his move toward the platform as Vasily was ushered out between a pair of officers.

"The actions of anyone now assembled in this square this evening shall be considered treasonous," Helison proclaimed. "For those who are not officers of the Supernal Army, your sedition will be forgiven if you clear out immediately." This was far more decisive than Belphagor had given him credit for.

The Ophanim along Celestial Boulevard parted to reveal the approaching infantry battalion marching forward with swords drawn. Rows of mounted angels were now visible behind them.

Demons scattered into the dark, though a fair number held their ground, chanting their slogans once more. The mutinying ranks drew their swords as well and congregated to the right of the platform, where Belphagor was positioned, and a phalanx loyal to the principality lined up along the left. The mutineers looked to Elyon, but upon Helison's arrival, the duke had fallen back and might easily be mistaken for one of the loyal troops. He'd been wise not to do the speaking.

The demons who had failed to sneak away at the first opportunity were trapped between the Liberation forces amassing on this side of the square and the loyal ranks advancing. The chaos of jostling demons and white-faced young angels trying to remain in position was making it difficult for Belphagor to get close to Vasily. He even lost sight of him for a moment among the press of bodies, which wasn't easy to do.

"Any member of the Supernal Army here present," Helison continued, "who will not swear allegiance to me now, publicly, as their principality and the justly crowned heir to the throne of the

Firmament of Shehaqim and All the Heavens, shall be treated as enemies of the state. They will be apprehended and taken into custody by the Supernal Army and tried for crimes against the firmament."

Some of the mutinying officers were now clearly ready to abandon their cause, scrambling for the periphery to slip through into the bordering garden park. Belphagor was moving against the flow when several events occurred at once.

Just out of his reach, Vasily emerged from the chaos and sprang onto the platform as if pushed. At the same moment, the attention of the Seraphim was drawn to a group of drunken demons trying futilely to storm the platform from the front.

Converging with these two opposing motions, a tangle of angels broke ranks, scrambling toward Vasily as if to stop him, but Belphagor caught the flash of steel from one of their coats as a knife darted out. The principality fell forward against the podium with a soft gasp of surprise as if he wasn't quite sure what had happened.

"Assassin!" This, at last, was Duke Elyon, leaping onto the platform and drawing his sword. "Stop that demon before he gets away! He's stabbed the principality!"

Belphagor watched in horror as Elyon's blade cut an arc through the air with a clear trajectory toward Vasily's neck, bared as the officers who'd grabbed him thrust him forward onto his knees.

But Elyon's swing fell short when a Seraph tackled him and dropped him smoothly to the ground.

"Not me, you fools!" Elyon protested as he hit the platform with a thud. "The demon!"

The brilliance of the Seraphim did not extend to their intellect. The Seraph, trained to stop anyone brandishing a weapon who approached within the vicinity of the principality, pinned the duke with a bright, blazing foot to the back of his neck. Belphagor caught the gaze of one of the officers holding Vasily. It was Phaleg, and the recognition in his eyes was clear. Belphagor's glamour must have worn off.

"You there!" barked Phaleg, and Belphagor jumped. "Get his other arm." He turned to the angel at Vasily's other side. "Move out of the way! If you can't do your job, make room so someone else can."

Belphagor took hold of Vasily's arm at his back, and the two of them hauled Vasily from the platform. Vasily's eyes lit up at the sight of Belphagor, but he wisely kept his mouth shut.

Phaleg yanked him backward, addressing Elyon, who was struggling uselessly beneath the Seraph's foot. "We'll get him into the holding cell inside the Conciliary where he can't do any more harm."

Likely too distracted to register Belphagor's presence, Elyon gave Phaleg a sharp nod.

Paimon was hovering nearby as Belphagor and Phaleg dragged Vasily toward the stone edifice. Belphagor wasn't sure whether he'd managed a successful rescue yet or not, but it seemed best to let the demons clear out.

"Palaver," he said to Paimon as he passed him. It took the demon a moment to register what this meant before he nodded and scurried away to find his contact and repeat what he'd heard.

Phaleg led Belphagor into the Conciliary, where a Cherub stood guard at one of the interior doors.

Phaleg addressed the Cherub. "Things have gone a bit south. Elyon wants us to keep the demon here until the square settles." He held out his hand. "You'd better give me the key and make yourself scarce."

The Cherub's head swiveled about disturbingly on its shoulders, showing the face of an ox, but it dropped the key in Phaleg's palm and then unfurled and flapped its wings. With a deafening crack like a sonic boom, the Cherub was gone.

Phaleg let go of Vasily and nodded to Belphagor. "There's another door to the outside on the far end of the corridor. I'll tell the duke you overpowered me." There was a bit of a flush to his cheeks as he said it.

"I'm so sorry, Beli." Vasily was seemingly oblivious to the angel. "This is all my fault."

Belphagor let his grip slide down Vasily's arm to his hand. "Hush, *mal'chik*. We'll worry about which of us is to blame later." He made a subtle motion with his eyebrow that lent more significance to the words. "Right now we need to get you out of here."

Vasily resisted the tug on his hand as Belphagor moved for the rear door. "Sefira. She's inside."

Phaleg turned the key in the lock and opened the door, and Belphagor followed Vasily in, relieved that he could keep his promise to Tabris and return her sister to her, but he stopped as soon as he saw the girl lying on the floor. Her neck was twisted at an odd angle, and it was clear the body was lifeless.

"*No.*" Vasily knelt before her. "Sefi . . ." He lifted her head onto his lap, dangling from a broken neck. "That son of a bitch." His voice was especially gravelly and harsh with emotion. "He said he'd kill her if I didn't follow his orders. But he had the damned Cherub snap her neck the minute I did."

Belphagor laid a soft hand on his shoulder. "We can't linger, sweet boy. There's nothing we can do for her."

"I'm not fucking leaving her here!"

Vasily's vehemence took Belphagor aback. He stepped out of the way as Vasily stood, hoisting Sefira's limp body in his arms, and swept past him through the door, not waiting for Belphagor as he headed down the corridor.

Belphagor pressed Phaleg's arm as he stepped past him. "Thank you."

Phaleg shrugged and gave him a wistful smile. "Least I could do. Sir."

CHAPTER
SEVEN

They hurried through the dark streets of Elysium without speaking, spurred forward by an icy wind. Vasily was afraid to open his mouth. He was sure something stupid would come out, if not outright sobbing, like a sniveling angelic schoolboy who'd been punched in the junk.

He couldn't tell Belphagor what Sefira had meant to him. He wasn't sure *what* she'd meant to him exactly, but he couldn't very well explain how they'd met. But far worse than his complicated feelings was the knowledge that she'd died because of him. And specifically because he'd been a fucking idiot, letting the duke pick him up in the first place just because he was mad at Belphagor—and then going back to the villa alone.

He skidded on the ice as they crossed the frozen Acheron and almost lost his balance, nearly dropping Sefira. *Sefira's corpse.*

Belphagor reached out a hand to steady him. "Why don't you let me take her the rest of the way?"

Vasily shook his head stubbornly. "She weighs almost as much as you do." It was a bit of an exaggeration, but Belphagor didn't correct him. "Besides, we're almost there."

What he would do with her when they reached Raqia, he hadn't considered. He supposed they'd have to take her back to The Cat and let Tabris make what arrangements she needed. The thought of facing Tabris made him bite down on his tongue hard to keep from blubbering. Then a sobering thought struck him. He was only assuming Tabris hadn't been taken. What if they had her somewhere? What if they'd killed her too? How the hell was he going to explain all of this to Belphagor without exposing himself as a terrible rakehell?

The bright lights of the Demon Market in their colored globes cheered him somewhat as they reached the Demon District. He hated the sterility of Elysium's pristine torcheres.

"We'll go in the back way with her," said Belphagor, steering him toward the alley behind The Brimstone. "You wait by the door, and I'll go around front and let you in."

Vasily couldn't think of a way to broach the idea of taking her "home" to The Cat without revealing too much, so he nodded and went along with it, standing in the icy slush of the alley.

Belphagor appeared at the back door shortly with a heavy woolen blanket. They wrapped her in it and slipped inside, Vasily keeping his head down in hopes that no one at the bar would take notice if he wasn't looking at them.

Inside their room, Belphagor helped him lay Sefira gently on the cot and position her in a natural pose out of respect. It warmed his heart a bit that Belphagor seemed to know this was important to him.

"I'll fetch Tabris," said Belphagor, and Vasily didn't think to ask him how he knew about Tabris until after he'd gone. He sat beside Sefira's body on the bed, her expression now almost peaceful with her head straightened out as well as they'd been able, and let his tears fall in silence.

Belphagor could barely put one foot in front of the other as he crossed the Demon District toward The Cat. He'd never felt so tired in his life. It dawned on him that he hadn't slept in almost forty-eight hours, but exhaustion alone couldn't account for how his feet dragged as he neared the brothel. He'd promised Tabris he would find her sister and that everything would be okay. He'd only made good on one of those promises.

Tabris knew as soon she saw him. She wasn't working, of course—still nursing bruises on her face that might put clients off—so an apprentice was sent to fetch her for him while he waited in the parlor. When she arrived, he stood and took his cap from his head, and Tabris let out a horrible wail, sinking to the ground and clinging to the frame of the doorway.

The procuress bustled forth like a generously proportioned streak of lightning and took Tabris in hand. Belphagor followed them into the private quarters. The girl was a heartbreaking mess, sobbing and howling, with intermittent shrieks that seemed to reinforce the name of the house.

"Who are you?" The procuress glared up at him as she sat with Tabris collapsed in her arms like a sack of howling grain that wouldn't hold its shape. "You've come with news?"

"The name's Belphagor." He shifted awkwardly. "I found . . . the body." Another horrible sound of grief from Tabris followed this admission.

The demon matron gave him a look of dark appraisal. "The Prince of Tricks himself comes to deliver news of a dead whore?"

"I believe I may be somewhat to blame." He shifted uncomfortably under her gaze. "I hired Ouestucati and Tabris to accompany me to a party on the Left Bank, and it was upon returning from that engagement by themselves, after I'd been . . . forcibly ejected earlier in the evening, that they were attacked."

"Angels," wailed Tabris. "They took her, Masha. They took her away from me."

Belphagor twisted his cap in his hands. "Tabris, I'm so sorry—"

"Where is she now?" Masha interrupted.

"In my room at The Brimstone."

The procuress's eyes fixed on him with menace. "You *found* a dead girl in your own room. That seems a most unlikely circumstance."

"I didn't find her there, I took her there—Vasily and I—after we discovered she'd been murdered. I didn't think it appropriate to bring a corpse to the door of The Cat." Belphagor bit his tongue at the renewed sounds of misery from Tabris.

Masha's eyes widened with recognition. "Vasily? You don't mean that precious firespirit boy Ouestucati initiated the other night?"

Belphagor felt his brow go white with annoyance. Just how many people had watched Vasily's "initiation"? "He's my companion. He'd gone missing the day after his visit here with a group of angels, and I came to find out more about them."

Masha shook her head. "You're the only demon in Raqia who'd visit The Cat to find out more about the sexual habits of angelic males."

Belphagor snorted. "I know plenty about the sexual habits of angelic males."

A knock sounded on the door, saving him from making more of a jackass of himself.

"Masha?"

Masha barked her answer at the door. "This had better be extremely important, *dyevushka*."

The door opened, and the apprentice he'd seen earlier popped her head around it. The young girl's face was white. "There are Ophanim at the door demanding entrance." She glanced at Belphagor. "I think they're looking for him."

Masha extricated herself from Tabris and stood, eyes burning into Belphagor's. "You've brought Ophanim to my door?"

"I doubt they'd be looking for me here," he replied dryly. "Or me at all. I hardly think I warrant the notice of the palace guard."

Masha glanced at the girl. "Whom did they ask after, Anzhela?"

"It's hard to understand them," she admitted. "They want 'the demon assassin.'"

"Shit." Belphagor rubbed the stubble at his chin. "They want Vasily."

"Explain," said Masha. "Quickly."

"Duke Elyon of the House of Arcadia blackmailed Vasily into putting himself in position to take the fall for assassinating the principality."

Masha regarded him. "Blackmailed how?"

"Elyon employed a Cherub to do his dirty work, and apparently he threatened to . . ." Belphagor glanced at Tabris. "To kill the girl if Vasily didn't follow his orders. Vasily made himself a target, visually, in Council Square, but I was there. He wasn't the assassin. It was one of the angelic officers of the Supernal Army."

"And Ouestucati?"

Belphagor answered grimly. "The Cherub killed her anyway." On the bed, Tabris's anguish had given way to quiet tears.

Sounds of surprised demons were coming from the parlor as the Ophanim had apparently gained entrance and were searching the little alcoves for their quarry.

Masha nodded brusquely to the apprentice. "Get him out the back way, Anzhela."

Belphagor paused as Anzhela held the door for him. "I expect there will be more Ophanim at The Brimstone, if not now, very shortly. Vasily and I may have to make a quick escape."

"What about Ouesti?" Tabris sat up, the tears still pouring. Looking into her grieving face made him feel he'd murdered her sister himself.

"I'm afraid we may take the fall for her death as well. There's no way for you to collect her now with the Ophanim about. If Vasily and I flee, she'll be found soon enough." He stepped toward her and gave her hand a brief, inadequate squeeze before he followed Anzhela out the door. From the shouts of dismay and alarm down the hall as demons protested the unpleasant contact with the Ophanim, it wasn't a moment too soon.

Anzhela led him to a back stairway that descended into a cellar. The exit was a window that opened onto a sunken well with a set of rough-hewn stone footholds leading to the surface. Belphagor climbed up to the street and hurried to the alley behind The Brimstone, keeping an eye out for ophanic radiance. He pounded on the back door, locked as usual from inside, but it opened almost immediately as demons began to flee through it. The Ophanim had obviously arrived.

"You don't want to go in there," one of the demons warned him. "Palace guard swarming all over the place."

"Thanks, friend. Just need to get my goods." He slipped in through the exodus and made a hasty dash through the back of the bar to the rented rooms, afraid Vasily might have been caught already. But he was waiting, anxious, at the dead demoness's side.

Belphagor locked the door at the sound of tables being overturned in the gaming room and the shrieking of the unfortunate demons who hadn't made a run for it in time.

Vasily jumped up. "What the hell's going on?"

"Hell's a good word for it. We're heading down." Belphagor whipped aside the tattered rug that hid his most valuable asset.

"Down?" Vasily looked baffled.

"Meant to tell you about this. Didn't get around to it." Belphagor moved his hand over the wood slats of the floor, murmuring the words of his revealing spell. An iron ring appeared in the center of a hinged square that had been invisible a moment before.

A loud banging came at the door, followed by the most unpleasant, grating voice he'd ever heard in his life, like nails being hammered outward through his eardrums and the backs of his eyes.

"Open in the name of Principality Helison Alimielovich of the House of Arkhangel'sk!"

"Belphagor!" Vasily hissed.

Belphagor yanked up on the ring and opened the trap door. "In. Now."

Vasily's mouth dropped open. The door to their room began to splinter. He scrambled down and disappeared into the darkness, and Belphagor followed, pulling the trapdoor over their heads and whispering the spell that would conceal it once more.

Like the vapor of an ordinary demon that might hang in the air on a cold day, Vasily's breath was visible in the dark. The pale ruby glow of his exhalations made the blackness of the hole bearable while they waited for the Ophanim in the room overhead to move on. At last it seemed safe to speak.

"Why didn't you tell me about this hiding place?" Vasily could just make out Belphagor's smirk in the gloom through the illumination of his exhalations and the help of a little heat in his eyes.

"It's not exactly a hiding place." Belphagor came close to him. "Why didn't you tell me you glowed in the dark?"

Vasily made a face. "I don't glow in the dark. It's my fire."

"I like it."

Vasily gave him a sideways smile. "Glad to hear it." His smile turned quizzical. "What do you mean, it's not a hiding place?"

"It's more of an . . . other place. Point your breath behind you."

Vasily turned and exhaled, revealing a stone staircase that wound down into the darkness. "What is this?"

"A portal." Belphagor stepped down in front of him. "To the world of Man."

"Seriously?" Vasily's eyes widened as he followed close behind to keep the path illuminated. "How did you manage to get a room that sat on top of a portal?"

"By being a damned good wingcasting player. I won it in a game. The poor fellow was so devastated, he asked to use it one last time so he could get out of Raqia for good and not have to see me gloating at him over the tables." Belphagor chuckled over his shoulder. "Not that I gloat."

"So we're falling?" Vasily had always wanted to, but the idea made him anxious.

"Indeed we are, *mal'chik*. It appears you're a wanted demon. I hope you remember the language lessons I've been teaching you."

"*Da, ser*," Vasily replied automatically. He hadn't meant it in a sexual context, though of course that was the only context in which he'd used it before.

Belphagor stopped on the stairs and looked up at him, a hard glint in his dark eyes visible in the soft ruby haze. "Come down here." Not quite an order, but not a suggestion. He pointed to the steps below him.

Vasily descended until Belphagor stopped him. He turned and looked up. They were at a level height.

Belphagor tucked his hand around the back of Vasily's neck, his grip firm but gentle. "I told you not to leave me." The soft admonition didn't quite have the icy tone Vasily had expected.

"I didn't leave you."

"You weren't in my bed when I woke up."

"And I belong always in your bed?"

"Yes." The brusque certainty of this answer made Vasily's heart beat faster. Belphagor stroked his thumb against the side of Vasily's neck. "I got your gifts. The duke must have paid you well."

Vasily swallowed, thinking of the extra facets he'd received for the pleasure he'd gotten from Sefira and Tabris, and how he'd have to be careful never to mention the trip to The Cat.

"You deserve to be paid well." Belphagor studied him in the glow of Vasily's own exhalations. "You're extraordinary."

"Bel . . ." He stopped, realizing he was on the verge of confessing just from the sweetness in Belphagor's voice. Vasily swallowed. "I was going to tell you about the facets. I'd have given them to you. I just wanted you to have something nice first."

"Given them to me?" Belphagor's eyes hardened, as did his grip on the back of Vasily's neck. "Do you think I'm your pimp?"

"No . . . *Ow.*" He put his hand up defensively when Belphagor dug his fingers into the hair at his nape, but he dropped it, dismayed by the impulse.

Belphagor tugged his head back. "Were you going to fight me?"

"*Nyet, ser.*"

Unexpectedly, Belphagor kissed him, his mouth insistent, even hungry, yet his lips soft and sensuous. Vasily let out a moan as Belphagor tasted him.

Just as suddenly, Belphagor pulled away, still gripping his hair. "You don't give me money, understand? If you earn money, it's yours." A wicked gleam flashed in his eyes. "Unless I sell you myself." Belphagor raised his eyebrow at Vasily's sharp intake of breath. "Does that upset you? The idea that I might sell you?"

Vasily's eyes burned with hot tears he wasn't about to shed. He was only able to nod.

"You're my property, *mal'chik*. If I choose to sell you, I will sell you. Unless you've changed your mind about belonging to me."

"*Nyet, ser.*" The damned tears got out anyway, and Vasily lowered his eyes, staring down at Belphagor's feet.

Belphagor whispered at his ear. "Why are you crying, *mal'chik*?"

Vasily sought the words but couldn't find them. He shrugged helplessly. "*Ya ne znayu.* I don't know the words."

"I don't expect you to be fluent in the language of Men. You may tell me in angelic."

"I don't want to belong to anyone else." Vasily's breath caught in his throat. "Please don't sell me."

"Vasya. *Mal'chik.* Look at me."

Vasily raised his eyes. Tears landed on the stone step in front of him with a soft sizzle.

"You misunderstood me, sweet boy. I would never give you away, for any amount of money. And you are not my slave. That isn't what it means for you to belong to me. You're a permanent part of me. I'd just as soon sell my own heart."

Belphagor's hand at his nape softened, and he brought it down the side of Vasily's neck to stroke his thumb along the bearded jaw. "What I meant was that I might, at some unspecified future date, take a fancy to watching another demon *fuck your ass*." His voice went hard on the final three words, and Vasily went hard at the same time. "If you'd allow complete strangers to be an audience to such an intimate act, you should certainly have no objection to my enjoying the same privilege. Preferably with you draped over my lap so I can get a good view of the cock drilling your hole while I make you come."

"Fuck," Vasily whispered unbidden. He'd completely forgotten about crying.

"Indeed. The future date may have just moved up." Belphagor adjusted himself, and Vasily's eyes were riveted on the motion. The borrowed garments of the Supernal Army left absolutely nothing to the imagination. "So, you were saying?"

Vasily blinked at him. "What?"

"You didn't leave me. What, then, did you do?"

"I . . ." Vasily could barely form a coherent thought. "The angels . . . my pants."

Belphagor tilted his head. "Come again?"

He hadn't come once yet, but the invitation nearly undid him. "My jeans. The ones you gave me. I went back to the villa to get them."

Belphagor looked thoroughly taken aback. "You what?"

"You said you'd gone to a lot of trouble to get them, and they were the only ones I had. I didn't want to wear that fucking angel suit forever."

A reluctant smile crept over Belphagor's features. "*Bozhe moi.* You are absolutely . . ." Vasily felt his face grow hot, thinking Belphagor was about to call him stupid. Belphagor shook his head. "The sweetest damned demon I've ever laid eyes on."

"But it was stupid," said Vasily, filling in the word he couldn't have stood to hear on Belphagor's tongue. "I walked right into Elyon's hands."

"Your heart was in the right place. And today you're a little bit wiser. But don't you worry, *mal'chik.*" Belphagor smoothed his thumb over Vasily's damp cheek and kissed him once more. "I'll get you all the jeans you want when we get to the world of Man." He turned Vasily about, pointing him down the staircase. "Now breathe, sweet boy, so we can see where we're going."

Vasily let his exhalations guide them once more, experimenting with smoke rings as they descended. "How far is it?"

"Never the same distance twice," said Belphagor. "We're not literally descending; it's just the effect of the portal magic that makes it feel as if we are. When we've passed fully through the spheres, it will seem as though we've reached the bottom."

"And then what?"

"We take a train."

"A what?"

"You'll see."

Belphagor was quiet as they continued down the stairs, and Vasily didn't ask any more questions. He figured he'd see it all soon enough, and the thought of an entirely different world appearing before them made him forget for a while that they were on the run.

He'd long wanted to see the places Belphagor had been. The tattoos on Belphagor's skin secretly thrilled him, though Belphagor didn't like to talk about them. Vasily knew they were marks of his time "below," and he'd traced them with awe whenever Belphagor had let him get that close. Of course, now they'd crossed the barrier of intimacy Belphagor had resisted for so long, he'd be able to look and touch all he wanted.

Stepping out of the cleft in the rock tunnel by the railroad tracks at Lake Baikal had become banal to Belphagor over the many journeys he'd made. He'd forgotten how extraordinary the experience was until he saw it through Vasily's eyes. Watching him gaze in astonishment at the world of Man was worth the fall.

The Siberian landscape was wild and heartbreakingly beautiful in a way nothing could be in the celestial sphere. Around the great frozen lake, ice draped everything. Like the slow drip of mineral deposits on the walls of a cave, it cascaded in sheets against the rugged stone where it had melted under the lonely winter sun and refrozen after the early dusk. And it armed the ends of pine branches with long, sharp, glittering needles.

The train itself, of course, was a kind of magic specific to this world. Heaven still lingered in the genteel age of horse-drawn carriages and hansom cabs—not that any demon would have had the experience of riding in one of those either.

Belphagor had never been sure why the portal came out here, though the story went that the first Fallen—angels known as Grigori who'd been cast out of Heaven for mixing their blood with the inferior blood of Man—had fallen literally from the sky, creating the deepest lake in the world with the force of their impact.

Whatever the truth of it was, it made for as gentle a transition as possible into the fantastic realm of Man. Even the first train they took on the Circumbaikal Railway was smaller and less overwhelming than the next they'd take when they reached the Trans-Siberian. And the four days it took to cross the continent provided a gradual introduction to the post-industrial-revolution world before depositing them at the end of the line: the bustling metropolis of Moscow.

Another benefit of the lower sphere that Belphagor had forgotten was the ease with which his airspirit abilities could be employed. Most humans were extremely susceptible to influence, and without spending a facet—which in the world of Man was a considerable sum; they were known as diamonds here—he managed to obtain a private compartment for them.

As Vasily's punishment for breaking the rules Belphagor had set for him, he would be allowed no release until Belphagor gave him leave. This gave Belphagor the opportunity to torment the firespirit in myriad ways.

As satisfying as it was to have his own cock sucked while Vasily crouched naked on the floor in front of him, afraid the *provodnik* or *provodnitsa* would knock on the door at any moment, he particularly enjoyed performing fellatio on Vasily himself while the firespirit cursed him and squirmed, white-knuckled, struggling not to come.

When he finally released Vasily on the verge of losing control, he sat back on his heels and jerked off onto the flaming-red erection, letting the pearly drops rain down on the throbbing head and leaving Vasily nearly weeping with frustration. With no showers on the train, he was coated in dried layers of what he termed Belphagor's "selfish enjoyment."

By their last night on the train, Vasily was so incensed that his skin flickered continually with a wave of ruby light. Having never experienced his own radiance in Heaven—the lower-order angels and demons generally couldn't—he was briefly distracted from his discomfort by the wonder of it. That is, until Belphagor made him drape himself over the tiny compartment table so he could fuck him from his bunk and then curled up and slept the blissful sleep of satisfaction while Vasily lay dripping with him, without permission to move.

When Belphagor woke in the morning to find Vasily still in position—though angry enough to burn him with his skin if Belphagor wasn't careful—he lost his resolve and fucked him again, pulling him onto his lap to lie back on the bunk as his own climax neared and whispering in his ear, "Touch yourself, *mal'chik*. I want to see you come while I come inside you."

He'd timed it perfectly since Vasily was ready to burst at the very suggestion. Belphagor jolted into him moments later with a growl of pleasure while a copious amount of semen streamed out of Vasily's tormented cock and bathed his abs. Vasily made the most satisfied sound Belphagor had ever heard emitting from a demon: a full-throated groan of relief that was surely audible in the adjacent compartments, if not throughout the entire car.

"*Khoroshiy mal'chik.*" Belphagor nuzzled his temple. "Good boy."

"*Spasibo, ser,*" Vasily moaned, sounding utterly content.

Belphagor ran his fingers through the hot jism and painted it over Vasily's skin. Like Vasily, it had the vague scent of a sweet charred wood. "*Bozhe moi*, but you're beautiful." A mournful whistle and the slowing motion of the train brought him back down to earth. "You should probably put some clothes on. We've just pulled into the station where we get off."

In punctuation of this remark, the *provodnik* rapped at their door. Vasily scrambled off and searched the floor frantically for his clothes while Belphagor took his time lacing his pants up.

"*Eto poslednyaya ostanovka,*" the *provodnik* barked, rattling the door Belphagor had thankfully latched from inside.

"*Miy prosto konchayu,*" Belphagor called.

"What does that mean?" Vasily was working on his jeans with some difficulty over the sticky layers of spunk.

"He says this is the last stop." Belphagor grinned. "I told him we were coming."

Vasily glared as he pulled his tight T-shirt over the spunk that hadn't dried. "You're a bit of a bastard, you know that?"

"*Ublyudok.*" Belphagor winked at Vasily's puzzled expression. "We're in Russia, *mal'chik*. Get it right."

He stood and tugged Vasily's bundle of locks to bring his head low enough for a kiss, savoring the smoky taste of him, and held on to the hair a bit longer once he'd pulled his mouth away. "You know I wasn't a fan of this mess you've been making of your hair, but I think it's growing on me. Makes it really easy to get a good handful." He yanked for good measure and then popped the latch on the door, leaving Vasily to follow him out.

Outside the station, Vasily might have gone in the opposite direction just to spite Belphagor if he hadn't been in the largest city he'd ever seen in his life, surrounded by people who weren't even his own species, with all manner of horseless conveyances rushing through the gray, icy streets at speeds that made him dizzy. He stuck close to Belphagor, a bit lightheaded and sweaty despite the cold. He attributed it to the strangeness of everything.

Belphagor glanced at him as they wove through people who were warmly bundled in furs and hats, heads down against the wind. "We need to get you a coat."

"I'm not cold."

"Nevertheless, we don't want to draw any more attention than we already will. I also need rubles."

"Rubles?"

"Local currency. They don't take facets here, and they're far too valuable in this world anyway. I need to pawn a few."

Vasily watched in awe as Belphagor conversed with passersby in fluent Russian and ascertained the location of the nearest pawnshop. He'd heard snatches of the language in Raqia all his life, but flowing effortlessly from Belphagor's tongue, it seemed surprisingly lovely. He supposed most of what he'd heard had been ribaldry, as most demons fell back on the tongue of Men to be able to speak as they pleased in a rather prudish Heaven.

Belphagor soon found the shop he wanted, where he not only pawned a handful of facets for a seemingly vast sum of coin and paper currency, but found a woolen coat that fit Vasily perfectly. Belphagor even managed to pawn his angelic army uniform for a change of more ordinary clothing.

"Where did you come by the uniform, anyway?" Vasily asked as they were heading back into the cold.

"Well, that's an interesting story," Belphagor replied vaguely. "I'll tell you about it later."

Something about his reticence triggered Vasily's suspicions, and he stopped on the street with one arm still half in the coat. "Did you fuck an angel?"

Belphagor's silence was answer enough.

"You're unbelievable. You completely lose your mind over me whoring with angels, and then you go off and fuck one at the villa while I'm being held prisoner by that piece-of-shit duke?"

Belphagor stopped. "How do you know I was at the villa?"

"I heard you when they were throwing you out. I was chained up in the scullery icebox."

"Son of a bitch. I can't believe I was that close. No wonder the little prick was smirking." He reached a hand up to Vasily's cheek, but Vasily jerked away. "I'm going to make him pay for that. Did he hurt you?"

"No, he didn't hurt me. Quit changing the subject. You fucked one of those angels while you were so damned concerned about me running out on you. Just say it."

Belphagor sighed. "Vasya—"

"*Poshel tiy na khui!*"

Belphagor's mouth twitched. "Well, your Russian is improving."

"I mean it. Fuck you." Feeling smothered by the warm coat, Vasily turned on his heel, forgetting he was in a strange place. He slipped on the icy surface of the hard walkway and nearly tumbled into the traffic of fast-moving vehicles.

Belphagor darted forward to pull him back, and they both fell on their asses. Without hesitation, two passing Russians stopped to help them up, both older and one a matronly female. Vasily was stunned by the kindness from total strangers on the street, and he'd certainly never encountered a woman of any age in Raqia who would stop to help a grown man, particularly one who looked as gruff as he did.

"*Spasibo*," he said as Belphagor thanked them with more eloquence.

The woman who'd grabbed hold of his arm suddenly put the back of her hand up to Vasily's forehead.

"*U vas yest likhoradka.*" She shook her head with a frown. "*Vam nuzhno k vrachu.*"

Vasily glanced at Belphagor for translation.

"She says you have a fever and we should get you to a doctor." Belphagor thanked her again, telling the woman that was precisely where they were headed. She nodded and went on her way. He turned to Vasily, unsmiling. "She's right, Vasya."

"That I have a fever?" Vasily scoffed. "You ought to be used to my temperature by now."

"No, you're warmer than usual. You're sweating. It's below freezing out here."

Vasily frowned. "I do feel a little stuffy. But this coat—"

"The coat isn't even lined." Belphagor shook his head. "I'm sorry, *mal'chik*. I should have realized this might happen."

"What might happen?" Vasily was growing alarmed. He really didn't feel well at all, and he'd been trying to ignore it. "Is the terrestrial air dangerous for firespirits?"

"No, it isn't that." Belphagor put an arm around him and began walking with purpose. "At least, not precisely. Firespirits do just fine down here. The Seraphim, in fact, seem to thrive."

"There are Seraphim in the world of Man?"

"Not that you'd notice. They can jump directly in and out of the spheres, and they only show up to hunt demons. But what *is* dangerous is the diseases humans spread. They're unknown in Heaven, because the aether nullifies it, but demons who fall are susceptible while they're breathing terrestrial air. I've built up an immunity over the years, but you've never been exposed to them before. Someone could have coughed near you on the train and passed an airborne virus to you."

Vasily didn't like the sound of that. "What's a virus?"

"It's an invisible thing that will make you feel quite unpleasant for a little while. We have to get you someplace where you can stay in bed and ride it out. It's like a hangover, only it lasts for days."

Vasily shivered at the thought of some invisible creature inside him. He wasn't so sure he liked this world after all. The people seemed nice, but he hadn't expected tiny evil beings that could inhabit him and make him sick.

Belphagor had steered them down a flight of stairs into some kind of underground market. He stopped and perused a heavy book chained to a metal box and then began dropping ruble coins into the front of the box. Vasily leaned against the wall beside him, too dizzy to puzzle out what Belphagor was doing, and closed his eyes.

"*Alo. Dmitri doma*? Belphagor. Bel. *Ot* Raqia."

Vasily opened his eyes, which surprisingly hurt to do. "Who are you talking to?"

Belphagor put his hand over the metal object he was holding, connected to the box by a coil of wire. "I'm on the phone." He moved his hand away. "Dmitri? *Blagodarit Nebo.* It's Belphagor. I'm in Moscow. I'm here with a friend, and we need a safe house. *On bolen.*" He paused a moment, seeming for all the world to be having a conversation with someone.

"How would I know?" Belphagor snapped. "The flu, if I have to guess. He's never been below before." The rest of the conversation with the box was in Russian, and Vasily gave up trying to understand.

"Vasya. *Mal'chik.*" Belphagor was shaking him. He must have fallen asleep standing up. "Come on."

"Where are we going?"

"My friend Dmitri's going to put us up." Belphagor put an arm around him once more and slung Vasily's arm over his shoulders, turning him toward another set of stairs. "We're taking the metro. It's an underground train."

Vasily nodded, trying to keep his eyes open, though it felt like he had ground pepper inside his lids. He let Belphagor lead him, barely aware of the train they boarded. He kept looking out the windows and seeing nothing, then remembered the train was underground. Why in the world would an underground train need windows?

Before he knew it, they were up on the street again, where the cool air felt much better on his face. He tried to take the coat off. It was roasting him. But Belphagor wouldn't let him.

Then they were climbing the stairs into an apartment building, and someone else was helping him through the door. Belphagor was crouching in front of him, tugging at his boots for some reason, and Vasily grasped the person beside him for balance as Belphagor took them off and then put some kind of soft shoes on his feet.

"What are you doing?" asked Vasily, or at least he tried to ask it, but he'd begun to shake violently. Suddenly, he was as cold as a block of ice in Elyon's scullery, even though they were inside and he was still wearing the coat.

"We don't have an extra bedroom," someone said. "I've closed off the dining room and moved the daybed into it. It's kind of small, though."

"You should see the bed we have at home."

Vasily caught the interested look the Russian demon gave Belphagor at that before another fit of shivering took him. The demon steered him into a bed and peeled the coat from his shoulders despite his protests.

Belphagor piled blankets on top of him, which helped the shivering somewhat.

"You're k-kind of an *ublyudok*," Vasily murmured, trying to keep his eyes open.

Belphagor kissed him on the forehead. "I know."

CHAPTER EIGHT

Belphagor held the hot cup up to his nose, savoring the smell of real black Russian tea. "You're a lifesaver, Dmitri." He took a grateful swallow.

Dmitri shrugged. "He'd just better not get us all sick. Where did you find this one anyway? He looks like an American punk rocker."

Belphagor smiled into his tea. "*I* look like a punk rocker. Vasily looks like a heavy metal god."

"*O, bozhe moi.*" Dmitri shook his head as he brought his cup of tea to the table, letting the deep brown hair that spoke of his purebred earthspirit heritage fall into his angelic baby blues. "You're in love."

"Shut up. Who's this Lev who answered the phone?"

Dmitri grinned. "Oh, just a hot Grigori piece of ass I picked up at an underground disco."

"You did not."

"I absolutely did. He didn't even know what he was; can you believe it?"

"How could he not know?"

"His mother was a common demon. She never told him who his father was."

Belphagor shook his head, stirring more sugar into his tea. "So where is this hot piece of ass?"

Dmitri's face went bright red as he stared over Belphagor's head.

"He's standing right behind me, isn't he?" said Belphagor in a stage whisper.

"*Khrystos*, Belphagor. Shut up."

Belphagor turned and smiled at the young man leaning against the doorpost, eyes narrowed at them. His smile widened as he took in the lithe, sensuous frame. *Damn.*

He held out his hand. "I'm Belphagor."

Instead of shaking it, Lev took the offered hand and gave it a kiss. "Lev. Pleased to meet you." He reached across Dmitri to take a sweet bun from the plate. "So what's your story, Belphagor?"

"You can call me Bel." He tried not to smile at the evil look Dmitri was giving him. "And my story's a bit complicated."

Dmitri snorted. "When is it not?"

"I suppose you should know whom you're harboring." Belphagor sighed. "Vasily's wanted for the assassination of the principality."

"He's *what*?" Dmitri nearly jumped out of his seat.

"At least I think it was an assassination. We didn't stick around to find out."

Dmitri frowned. "Since when do you take up with revolutionaries, hot or otherwise?"

"He's not a revolutionary. He was framed by angels so they could get rid of the new principality without taking any responsibility for it or for starting a civil war."

"And so you made a beeline for my apartment."

"I wasn't looking for your apartment. You offered. I was going to use the usual underground contacts, but then Vasily got sick and I needed to get him off the street."

"I'm telling you right now, Belphagor. I will not get in the middle of celestial politics. If Seraphim show up at my door, I'll be handing your boy over wrapped in a bow."

"Not in my home, you won't." Lev whirled to face Dmitri, leaving Belphagor with a prime view of the aforementioned hot Grigori ass. He wasn't sure he'd ever seen Dmitri speechless before. Belphagor was beginning to like this Lev.

Though it wasn't common knowledge, Dmitri was the Grigori chieftain, which was akin to saying he was the tsar of all the Fallen in the world. Or at least the most powerful Fallen: the Grigori, who were directly descended from the Order of Powers, and their Nephilim kin born of human liaisons. The "ordinary" Fallen could pledge loyalty to the Grigori or not.

Technically, the Grigori Duma, assembled ad hoc when important decisions had to be made, were the ultimate authority, but demons across the globe would do the chieftain's bidding at a word. Nevertheless, Dmitri preferred to live humbly, not wanting to draw attention to himself. But most demons thought twice before crossing him.

"I beg your pardon?" Dmitri finally managed.

"No demon who takes sanctuary in this apartment is going to be turned over to a Seraph bounty hunter. I don't care if you *are* the chieftain. You taught me the Grigori were all about protecting the Fallen."

"This is celestial—" Dmitri began, but Lev cut him off.

"Everything is celestial! Where the hell do we fall from? And everything is political. The angels think they have the right to treat us like chattel. One of us strays from the herd and they send their fire hounds to round him up. I don't care what Vasily's been accused of. The underground doesn't turn demons over to Seraphim. Since when did we become subjects of the principality of Heaven?" Lev turned and swept through the kitchen door, slamming it behind him.

"Wow," said Belphagor. "He must be one hell of a lay."

Dmitri expelled the breath he'd been holding. "Do you ever say anything that isn't wildly inappropriate?"

Belphagor smiled. "Not if I can help it."

Dmitri sighed and got to his feet. "I assume that unlike dear, literal Lev, you're aware that threat was hyperbolic. I might throw you out on your ass to find a less conspicuous safe house, but I wouldn't actually turn Vasily over to a Seraph."

Belphagor poured himself another cup of tea from the samovar. "Certainly not wrapped in a bow."

Dmitri tried not to smile. "I guess I'd better go unruffle his feathers."

"Whatever you want to call it, Dima. Give me a holler if you want me to join in."

Dmitri's laugh was just a touch nervous.

When the bedroom door closed and it seemed clear Dmitri wouldn't be coming out for a while, Belphagor helped himself to a shower. The shower shared a wall with the bedroom, however, and with the thin Soviet-era walls, he could hear some vigorous "unruffling" going on. He found himself reluctantly soaping up and unruffling himself after a bit, knowing Vasily was in no condition to bring him any relief.

He leaned his forehead against the common wall, letting the hot water pound on his back while he pounded on his front, listening to the soft grunts of effort and the rhythmic thump of a headboard against the ubiquitous wood paneling until he couldn't stand it any longer. He shot the shower wall, with just enough of a groan that the noise from the bedroom ceased immediately.

He smiled to himself as he toweled off, picturing Dmitri gripping the headboard to keep it still, every muscle in his compact but powerful form held tight while he finished. Dmitri had done well for himself.

He and Belphagor had spent some time together a few years back with mutual enjoyment in one another's company but never quite fitting together. Dmitri was happy to bottom, but he was no submissive, and any attempt on Belphagor's part to make things interesting had merely annoyed him. It was good to hear Dmitri enjoying himself—and clearly topping Lev, which was an interesting development. He wondered what it would be like to watch Dmitri fuck Vasily.

Belphagor groaned inwardly. The firespirit heat had clearly bedeviled him. He was becoming obsessed. Everything made him think of fucking Vasily or of having Vasily fucked. He gathered his secondhand clothes and headed for the converted dining room without putting them on, knowing Vasily would be uncomfortably warm.

Vasily was sound asleep, looking almost, dare he say it, angelic. Belphagor slipped under the covers beside him and spooned him. Sure enough, it was like hugging hot coals.

Vasily stirred, and Belphagor regretted waking him for his own selfish need to cuddle, but Vasily tugged Belphagor's arms tighter around him. "You smell like tea biscuits," he murmured. Dmitri—or Lev—had vanilla-scented soap.

Belphagor nuzzled his warm neck. "And you smell like a campfire." He paused and stifled a laugh. "And about a pint of semen."

There was a brief pause before Vasily muttered, "*Ublyudok.*"

Belphagor kissed his nape. "*Eto moi mal'chik.*" *That's my boy.*

Belphagor drifted off and had no idea how long he'd slept when he woke to the smell of blini frying in the adjacent kitchen. He climbed out of bed and tucked the covers around Vasily before shuffling out to investigate. Lev stood at the stove with Dmitri behind him nibbling his ear.

"I hope I get to eat some," said Belphagor, enjoying the double entendre.

Dmitri turned and gaped at him standing naked in the doorway. "*Bozhe moi.* Put something on, for the love of Heaven."

Belphagor put his hands on his hips and wiggled his toes in his slippers. "I'm wearing my *tapochki.*"

"Very funny."

Belphagor shrugged. "If you have something I can borrow, I'd appreciate it. I got my clothes at the pawnshop, and I'd rather wash them before I put them on again. You never know what's crawling around in human clothing."

Dmitri sighed and took the spatula from Lev. "Would you run and get him your robe, *lyubimaya*? Mine would swim on him."

Lev scuttled off, casting a significant glance at Belphagor as he passed him.

"Love, eh?" Belphagor commented after he'd gone.

Dmitri smiled without looking up from the blin he was flipping. "Seems that way. From the way you were cuddled up in there with your firespirit, I suspect it's going around."

"Who, him? He followed me home from the metro station." Belphagor sat at the table with a sigh. "I have to admit, it scares me a bit how much I—"

"*Bozhe MOI!*" Dmitri dropped the blin he was flipping onto the floor as he turned and saw Belphagor at the table. "Get your naked ass off my kitchen chair!"

Belphagor crossed his legs at the knees, bobbing one *tapochka* in the air. "It's a clean ass. You certainly didn't have any objections to putting your t—"

"Belphagor!"

"Oh, let him finish," said Lev from the door. He tossed the robe to Belphagor. "It was just getting interesting. Putting your . . . toe? *Tapochka*?"

Belphagor stood, slipping his arms smoothly into the robe as he slung it around his shoulders. "I never get kissed and tell."

Lev saw the blin on the floor and went to clean it up while Dmitri stood aside, glaring daggers at Belphagor.

"You never kiss me that way," Lev said to Dmitri with a smirk when he straightened.

"You want to go? Let's go." He tugged on Lev's arm as if he'd drag him to the bedroom, looking deadly serious. "I'll do it right now. I'll kiss you till you can't sit down."

"No need to leave the room for that on my account," said Belphagor. "Just pretend I'm not here."

Lev burst out laughing at the look on Dmitri's face. "Damn. You're totally ready to give me a tongue-lashing. What else have you done to Belphagor that I can get in on?"

Belphagor helpfully opened his mouth to offer up some more examples, but Dmitri pointed the spatula at him like he was wielding a weapon.

"Put a sock in it, Bel."

Belphagor raised an eyebrow. "We definitely didn't do that one."

Lev took the spatula out of Dmitri's hand and kissed him. "I like this demon, sweetie. Let's keep him."

As Lev took over the blin-making, Dmitri stepped out of the way and threw his hands in the air in surrender. "Well, you win, Belphagor. You've corrupted my boyfriend without even laying a finger on him."

Belphagor took a mock bow. "If you'd like me to corrupt him by laying anything else on him—or in him—you just let me know."

Dmitri sat on the other side of the table. "Jesus. You're exhausting."

Lev glanced over and winked at Belphagor. "He says that to all the boys." His eyes lingered on the tattooed stars on Belphagor's knees showing beneath the hem of the robe. "So what do those mean? If you don't mind me asking."

Belphagor stiffened reflexively, though these particular tattoos weren't ones he was ashamed of. Inevitably, when someone asked about one, they'd go on to ask about others.

"That's a bit personal, Lyova," Dmitri said quietly, and Lev looked abashed.

"No, it's all right," said Belphagor. "The stars mean I will kneel to no one."

"Gangster tattoos?" Lev ignored Dmitri's scowl and the sharp shake of his head.

"Prison. It's the Thieves' Code."

"*Vory v zakone.*" Lev nodded. "Gangsters."

"*Lev.*" Dmitri looked appalled.

Belphagor shrugged. "I suppose you're not wrong."

He had a complicated history with the *vory*, having served time first when he was still a pretty youth. If you didn't fight back in the *Zona*—or didn't know how to—it would eat you alive. He'd nearly been devoured. And most of the ink he wore on his back was testimony to that, stitched into him by force to announce his place to everyone who saw him.

It was only later, during subsequent incarcerations for one petty crime or another, that Belphagor had toughened up. He'd not only fought back but fought viciously, until he'd earned the series of tattoos that decorated his front, and others on his back to cover earlier shame. Unfortunately, rather than merely advancing him to a position of power, this had meant he was always on guard, always fighting to prove he deserved his ink.

And the longer he'd lived, the worse it had become. It was increasingly difficult to explain how he could have a legitimate right to wear such tattoos at his apparent young age. The last time he'd fallen, just before the Berlin wall came down, he'd done a short stint that convinced him he wouldn't survive another. He'd managed to come out on top in the inevitable fight with a *vor* who had the advantage of youthful vigor on his side, but he'd been forced to hurt the challenger badly, which he no longer relished. He just wanted to be left in peace.

"Sorry," said Lev, watching him. "Sometimes I don't know when to shut my mouth."

Belphagor resisted the urge to suggest putting something in it. He'd probably pushed Dmitri's buttons as far as he could get away with for the moment. "Don't worry about it." He grinned. "My fault for coming out naked."

"So what do you say we actually eat these blini before Lev ends up filling the room with them?" Dmitri smiled at Lev. "I think you've made plenty."

Lev glanced at the tall stack on the plate on the counter and laughed. "You have a point."

"What meal is this, anyway?" Belphagor glanced at the clock on the wall over the table as he retook his seat. "Is it six o'clock in the evening or six o'clock in the morning?" Moscow winter made it difficult to tell. Both looked like the middle of the night.

Dmitri laughed. "It's six in the morning. You slept for fourteen hours."

Belphagor yawned. "Transcontinental train lag is a bitch. Not to mention trans-sphere." He loaded his blin with jam and sour cream, relishing one of the many treats he couldn't get in Raqia.

There were definitely things about the world of Man that made it appealing, despite the short life a demon would have here. Dmitri already looked as old as Belphagor did, and he'd only been a few years older than Vasily was now the last time Belphagor had seen him. But he'd lived in the lesser sphere his entire life.

After making a serious dent in the stack of blini, Belphagor took a plain blin and a mug of tea into the makeshift guest room and woke Vasily. If Belphagor had slept fourteen hours, Vasily had slept even longer without replenishing any fluids he was sweating out with the fever.

Vasily sat up groggily and drank the tea, at least no longer shaking with chills, though he was still warmer than normal. He picked at the blin, definitely not yet on the mend.

"Where are we?" he asked. "I don't remember much about how we got here."

"A friend's place in Moscow. Dmitri and his partner Lev. They're Grigori."

Vasily's eyes widened a bit. "Grigori are real? I thought that was only a story."

"Very real. So are the Nephilim. And television. Want to see some?"

"Nephilim?"

"Television." Belphagor switched on the little set on the dining table, found a news station, and turned the TV toward him. "You can get some practice listening to Russian."

Vasily stared at the screen in amazement. "How the hell do they do that?"

"Tiny little people live in the box."

"*Seriously?*"

Belphagor laughed. "Sorry. I shouldn't tease you. Invisible signals are broadcast through the air to form moving pictures."

Vasily made a groggy attempt to glare fire at him. "You're hilarious."

Belphagor smiled and kissed him.

"What was that for?"

"For being adorable."

The weak fire in his eyes blazed a little stronger. "You're just full of mean this morning." Vasily settled back into his blankets, bleary eyes on the television for a few minutes until they fluttered closed.

By the following morning, Vasily's fever had finally broken. He woke alert, hungry, and only a few degrees warmer than an average demon. After eating the bowl of kasha Belphagor brought him, he demonstrated his other renewed appetites with an enthusiastic erection while he watched Belphagor dress in a pair of Russian army fatigues and a long thermal undershirt Lev had lent him.

"I see you're feeling better." Belphagor eyed the conspicuous bulge in Vasily's jeans as he tugged the snug undershirt over his abs and zipped the loose pants. Lev's build was the reverse of Belphagor's, with a slimmer torso but a rounder ass.

"Much," Vasily agreed, slipping his hand inside the waistband of his jeans.

"I hate to tell you this, sweet boy, but at the moment, you are anything but sweet." Belphagor gave him an apologetic smile. "To put it bluntly, you're absolutely filthy."

Vasily colored. "Well, whose fault is that?"

"I take full responsibility for drenching you repeatedly in my 'selfish enjoyment.'" Belphagor winked. "And I fully intend to punish myself by proxy by taking it out on your sweet self—once it's sweet again." He tossed Lev's robe at him. "Shower's that way."

Vasily growled and followed where he'd pointed down the hallway. After a few minutes, a loud curse came from the bathroom. "How do you use this damn thing?"

Belphagor had forgotten he'd never seen modern earthly plumbing and went in to turn the water on for him. "I probably should have showed you the water closet first. It's at the other end of the hall."

Vasily widened his stance as he stood under the warm water. "Too late." He aimed at the drain.

Belphagor watched with amusement as Vasily pissed in awkward spurts through the inconvenient erection. "I suppose I could help you wash up. You're probably weak from the fever." He closed the door and undressed, watching the remains of his own dried fluids wash from Vasily's skin down the drain. The firm ass still bore a faint hint of black and blue from where he'd marked him a week ago.

As Belphagor climbed in and closed the curtain, Vasily turned around, rubbing soap over his chest and smoothing his soapy hand down to his cock. "Are you going to help me with this?"

"No." Belphagor gave him a dark smile and stroked his own. "You're going to help me with this. Kneel."

Vasily was indignant. "In the water?"

"Don't make me drop you to your knees myself, *mal'chik*. I don't want you to slip and crack your skull."

Vasily stared at him for a few seconds as if he were daring him to do it but seemed to think better of it and sank to his knees. Water beaded in his hair and rolled onto his face.

Belphagor stepped forward and tapped the head of his cock against Vasily's lips. "Open, boy. Are you going to make me direct you every step of the way?"

Vasily glared up at him defiantly and opened his mouth but did nothing more when Belphagor's cock filled it. Belphagor sighed. Vasily was definitely feeling better. He gripped the roots of Vasily's hair above his forehead, tilted him back, and began to fuck him, watching Vasily blink and gasp for air a bit under the water hitting his face.

"You're a very stubborn boy," Belphagor said as he thrust. "You seem to need constant reminders that you belong to me and I'll do what I like with you." His lip curled at the sight of Vasily's large firespirit cock bobbing against his abs in response to this statement. "I suppose I'll have to make it clearer to you. After I'm done with you here, you'll return to the room naked and give your ass to whomever you find waiting."

Vasily's eyes widened as he sucked automatically, clearly forgetting he was playing the role of the uncooperative brat.

"You didn't think I'd do it, did you?" Belphagor breathed in deeply to keep from coming too soon. "You thought I was speaking idly of having you fucked while I watch." He let out a soft groan of excitement as Vasily moaned around his cock, now sucking in earnest. "We discussed it while you were sleeping, and both Dmitri and Lev expressed the desire to fuck your ass. And you're going to take it, as many times as they like."

Belphagor hissed out a breath, pulling back when Vasily swallowed hard against him in anticipation of what he could tell was coming. "Not in your mouth, *mal'chik.*" He fucked him shallowly, barely holding on, and turned off the water. "Don't want you *too* clean." As he pulled out, coming a touch sooner than he'd meant to, he shot the side of Vasily's mouth before aiming lower and jerking out the rest in a thick line that dripped down Vasily's chest and settled in the soft rusty curls at the root of his untended erection.

Vasily stared openmouthed and furious, and Belphagor bent down and licked the bit from his face, kissing him forcibly before he climbed out of the tub and dried off. "You leave the rest of that there. Get out of the tub and go wait on the dining room carpet until we want to use you."

Vasily's face blazed red as he rose, jism dripping down his clean abs. He stepped out and stood in front of Belphagor as if to menace him with his height before he opened the door and walked to the bedroom soaking wet.

Belphagor dressed and went to the kitchen to pour himself a cup of tea, where he sat and drank it at his leisure. Dmitri and Lev had gone out. When he decided Vasily must be sufficiently furious and humiliated, he returned to the guest room.

Belphagor bit his lip at the sight of his boy on hands and knees in the center of the carpet, his naked ass to the door. He almost wished he hadn't come yet so he could fuck him there after all, but the look on Vasily's face when he'd soiled him again with spunk had been worth forgoing more vigorous enjoyment.

"Stand up," he ordered.

Vasily turned his head, his eyes full of rage and red, both deep within and around the rims. He looked past Belphagor to the open door, his gaze flicking about as if in search of the two Grigori. He rose slowly and turned to face Belphagor, his cock raging more furiously than he was.

"They weren't interested." Belphagor managed to keep a neutral expression as Vasily's face fell before his mouth flattened into a thin line of resentment. Belphagor stood in front of him and then dropped to his knees and began licking him clean.

Vasily made a full-bodied jolt of surprise, his head jerking up toward the door once more and then down, in a kind of baffled double take, while Belphagor sucked the spunk from his curly hair and slid his tongue slowly over the red cock to the head.

"What are you doing?" Vasily finally managed in a hoarse whisper of astonishment.

Belphagor glanced up at him. "If you can't tell, dear boy, I'm not doing it very well." He winked and swallowed Vasily to the root.

Vasily groaned loudly as Belphagor worked his way up and down the shaft, taking his considerable length deep. Vasily's legs were shaking already. Belphagor had probably put him through too much too quickly after finding him feeling so much better.

Sucking him vigorously, he fingered the rim of Vasily's ass for an instant before slipping his thumb inside. Vasily jerked forward in surprise—nearly fell over him as his locked knees almost gave way—and ejaculated copiously into the back of Belphagor's throat with a shout. It stung a bit going down. He hadn't given the boy enough warning, and it was near boiling.

When he'd emptied him, he caught the trembling demon around the waist as Vasily practically melted to the ground. Belphagor buried his face in Vasily's lap for good measure and sucked any last remnants from his skin. He raised his head and winked. "Squeaky clean." And then he tilted Vasily back in his arms and kissed the hell out of him.

CHAPTER NINE

There was the awkward problem of having no clothes. Vasily wasn't about to put on the come-stained jeans and shirt he'd been wearing, and apparently there was no washerwoman who collected the laundry. They had to wash their own clothes in the sink or tub and then hang them on a line outside the kitchen window to dry. Belphagor had considerately washed both Vasily's garments and his own while Vasily was resting, but at this time of year, it could take days for the clothes to dry.

Dmitri was the only person in the apartment close enough to Vasily's size for a dressing gown, at least, to fit over his broad shoulders. Markedly uncomfortable, Vasily finally consented to come out and meet Belphagor's friends, wrapped in the borrowed garment.

Belphagor insisted that he wear the house shoes they'd provided upon his arrival, telling him that walking in his bare feet would make him sick. He'd always gone about their room in bare feet at home. The world of Man must be full of invisible dangers.

Dmitri seemed nice enough, if a little standoffish, but the angel-faced, dusty-haired Lev, he took an instant dislike to. It wasn't that there was anything wrong with the demon. He was friendly and charming. Too charming. Belphagor's attraction to him was immediately evident.

After they'd been introduced, Vasily sat at the kitchen table and tried not to scowl too obviously as he watched the interaction between Belphagor and the sexually provocative Grigori. Belphagor claimed to have only just met him, but while Vasily had been tossing with fever for the past forty-eight hours, they had apparently become fast friends. He wondered that Dmitri didn't take issue with their flirtatious banter. But perhaps that was why he seemed a bit cold.

Lev, evidently the cook of the house, stirred up a dinner of sausage and dilled potatoes while the others talked and smoked. Belphagor's enthusiasm over the meal was a little much. It was filling and palatable, but anyone would have thought it was a gourmet meal in an angelic bistro the way he was going on about it.

Russia, it seemed, had the best everything—things that had apparently been lacking in Raqia, though Belphagor had never complained—and Lev was like Russia personified.

"You missed out on Lev's blini," said Belphagor as he sat back with a cigar Dmitri had provided after dinner. "We'll have to see if we can get him to make them again tomorrow. Maybe blini for dinner?"

Vasily had no idea what blini was, but he began to imagine it was the thin demon's cock by the way Belphagor was sucking up to him about it.

Then the vodka was brought out, and Vasily tried to drown his annoyance and jealousy, taking pleasure in the competitive nature of their drinking ritual. After the second bottle was opened, he was feeling nicely numb, and it had loosened his tongue a bit until he was competing with Lev for clever flirtation. At least, he thought it was clever at the time. Alcohol always made him think he was much more entertaining than he actually was.

Belphagor had gotten him to show off his cigar-lighting trick, with his heat concentrated into the tip of his tongue, and had made a suggestive comment about what else he could do with it.

Lev asked whether he wasn't being a bit tongue-in-cheek, which the three of them seemed to find hilarious—apparently a reference to some earlier amusement they'd shared while he was sick. Vasily hated being on the outside of a joke.

"And what tricks do you do?" he'd asked Lev.

"Oh, nothing that clever," said Lev, which Vasily took to mean his trick had been anything but.

"Oh, come on," said Vasily. "I've shown you mine. Let's see yours."

Belphagor laughed, chewing on his cigar. "I don't think you've quite shown them yours yet, dear boy. I'm sure it's entirely too early in the evening for our hosts to engage in a game of show-and-tell."

"Not too early for me." Lev borrowed Dmitri's cigar instead of lighting one of his own, taking a sensuous puff on it as if it were more than a cigar.

"Maybe we could start with a game of wingcasting," Belphagor suggested, looking amused. "Dmitri, do you still have that deck and die I gave you?"

Dmitri smiled. "I do, in fact. Excellent idea." He got up and went down the hall to dig through a wooden secretary in the foyer.

"What's wingcasting?" asked Lev.

Belphagor raised a devilish eyebrow. "Oh, you're in for a treat."

Dmitri returned to the kitchen with the set. "You'll soon find out why they call him Prince of Tricks."

Belphagor winked. "That's not the only reason they call me that."

"Yes, well, maybe you'll show us the other reason later." Dmitri was smiling back at him as if they were both aware of the subtext.

Vasily suddenly recognized the less obvious flirting that had been going on between the two of them all evening. It had been a subdued, comfortable undertone of knowing looks and slightly caustic yet affectionate banter that Vasily hadn't consciously been aware of while concentrating on Lev's shameless behavior.

Lev and Belphagor's exchange had been the kind of hopeful, teasing escalation between two men who were interested in finding out what it would be like to fuck each other but not sure they'd get the chance. A sort of unspoken, mutual reassurance that each was hot enough to attract someone they found hot in return.

But Belphagor had fucked Dmitri before.

Vasily helped himself to another drink while Belphagor dealt the cards and explained the rules of the game to Lev. He was doing it too intimately for Vasily's taste, leaning over to show him a practice hand and demonstrating what he could do with various combinations of cards.

"The real skill in the game is in keeping an eye on what your opponent does," said Belphagor, "without letting on you're watching." He tossed the practice cards in the center of the table, picked up the die, and cast.

"Salamander," Dmitri called out casually, apparently perusing his hand while the die flew from Belphagor's fingers into the cake pan

Dmitri had set on the table to simulate the marble-sided wingcasting surface.

The die landed on Toad. Dmitri glanced at it briefly and tossed a Virtue of Facets on the discard pile.

"Wait," said Lev. "What was that?"

"Casting wing," said Belphagor. "Ptarmigan." Dmitri had already cast, and it landed on Phoenix, but Belphagor had taken up the discarded Virtue and tossed a Power of Knives onto the table.

"Slow down. I'm confused." Lev was glancing from his cards to the one in the center, while Vasily cast.

"You're supposed to call it," said Belphagor with a friendly nudge to Lev.

"What?"

The die had already landed.

"Sorry, no 'What' on the die, so you lose the cast. Toss down a card."

Lev looked flustered. "Which card?"

"Some more vodka, doll?" asked Dmitri sweetly, filling Lev's glass.

"Any card," said Belphagor. "And you can take my Power before you do it if you need that one, but you have to do it before you discard."

"Too late," said Vasily, slipping the Power of Knives into his hand.

"Oh, and I need this one." Dmitri snatched the top of the practice hand that had started the discard pile and tucked it into his own.

"Wait, *what* are you all doing?"

"Thrashing your ass pink," said Belphagor as he swept up the card beneath it and laid out a Full Choir and a Sphere of Archangels.

"And there he goes." Dmitri tossed in his cards. "Meet the Prince."

Vasily had nothing either, and he pushed his cards to the center of the table. Dmitri poured him a shot of vodka and another for himself. Belphagor picked up the one he hadn't touched yet and winked at Vasily with a *"Budem zdorovy!"* before they tossed their drinks back. Vasily snorted a bit at the sentiment. *Be healthy*, indeed.

Dmitri took Lev's cards out of his hand and passed them to Belphagor, who was counting the small pile of coins he'd won. They'd decided to play for kopeks, the minuscule division of rubles—a far cry from the high-stakes games at which Vasily was used to watching Belphagor clean up.

Lev pouted, pushing his next bet into the pot. "I don't think I like you demons very much."

"Don't worry." Belphagor tossed in his kopeks and shuffled. "The loser gets a consolation prize."

Lev glanced up. "Oh?"

"Vasily will do his other tongue trick," said Belphagor with a wink.

"Ha!" Vasily poured himself another drink. "And if I'm the loser?"

"Vasily will do his other tongue trick." Belphagor repeated the words with exaggerated emphasis. He smiled, dealing the cards. "For all of us."

"I see." Vasily was beginning to feel a pleasant buzz from the vodka that was almost as nice as smoking firedust. "So if one of you plays the poorest," he growled, his voice even rougher than usual with the burn of alcohol, "I suck your cock. And if I play the poorest, I suck all the cocks."

Belphagor smiled at Dmitri across the table. "He has a wonderfully subtle way with words, doesn't he?"

"I didn't realize that was the other tongue trick," said Lev. "Cow, dog, monkey, mountain lion, moose."

"What on earth was that?" Dmitri asked with a laugh.

Lev grinned. "That's my next five calls on the die."

"None of those animals is on the die." Belphagor tossed it to him with a smirk.

"I was rather hoping not." Lev tossed the die into the pan and called his own cast as it landed. His grin broadened. "I just suck at this game, don't I?"

Dmitri laughed and leaned over to kiss him, making it slow and sensuous, clearly putting on a show.

And just like that, the game had escalated. Belphagor reached under the table and spread open Vasily's robe, stroking his erection as if he'd known it would be there, and called, "Dragon" as Dmitri cast. The casual way he and Dmitri continued to play, with Belphagor's hand slowly milking Vasily's cock, made it impossible for Vasily to concentrate. Lev was watching him, not even trying to play, and

Belphagor pushed Vasily's chair back a bit from the table with his boot, exposing him.

"*Bozhe moi.*" Lev let out a low whistle.

Vasily's cock bounced slightly at the praise, and he was glad Belphagor hadn't started by touching the other demon to make him jealous. He didn't mind so much being the center of attention.

Lev scooted his chair back and opened his pants, letting his cock spring out amid its nest of dark hair—a perfectly fine, serviceable prick, but in no way competition for Vasily's. Dmitri reached over, giving this one its due attention, yet both he and Belphagor continued to play, moving their hands from the stiff cocks just long enough to cast, and not even missing a call.

Belphagor won another round and collected his winnings, leaving Vasily to play with himself a moment while he gathered the cards and shuffled. "You should take that robe off," he said without looking up. "It doesn't really suit you."

The room was a bit cold, but with Vasily's body heat, it was easy to ignore. He peeled off the robe and stood briefly to move it from under him, but Belphagor reached over to take his cock in hand so he couldn't sit down again. Across the table, a shiny pearl of pre-come emerged at the tip of Lev's cock as he watched Vasily.

Belphagor called Dmitri's cast and took the card he put down. "Which one of them do you think will go off first?" He cast the die.

"Damselfly." It landed on Toad, and Dmitri clucked his tongue. "Yours looks ready to blow, honestly. Bit of a Vesuvius waiting to happen."

Belphagor snorted. "Not if I tell him not to."

"You expect me to believe you can just order him not to come, and he won't?"

"Damn straight."

Vasily was starting to get annoyed at being talked about in the third person, but Belphagor had picked up the pace of his stroking, drawing a groan from him.

"Phoenix," said Belphagor, as if he were casually perusing his cards.

Across the table, Lev squirmed and gripped the edge of his seat as Dmitri's hand tightened around the tip of his cock.

Belphagor seemed to see Lev's imminent ejaculation as a challenge, despite having bragged of his control. Vasily had to grab onto the edge of the table and bite his lip during the next round of play at the way Belphagor was stroking him.

With a pause to tap the ash off his cigar, Belphagor cast the die again, ignoring Vasily and watching Lev, who'd let out a shaky groan with his gaze locked on Vasily. "What's the matter, Lev? Feeling the heat?" Belphagor pumped Vasily harder, tossing down a card. "I promise you, it's nothing to what you'd be feeling if he was doing his other tongue trick on you." Belphagor glanced at Dmitri. "Maybe we should have him do that now."

Lev broke out in a sweat, panting as if Vasily's mouth were already on him, and the thought made it very difficult for Vasily to concentrate.

"Let that sweet firespirit mouth slide down your cock and get you truly hot," Belphagor continued.

Vasily let out a hiss of steam to take the pressure off the other release that wanted out, and Lev whimpered.

"No fair verbally wanking the competition," Dmitri protested.

Belphagor set down his cards to cast the die again. "I don't remember anyone stipulating any rules."

"So that's how it's going to be."

Belphagor, perversely, had picked up speed, though he was still watching Lev. "Imagine that mouth taking you in, swallowing everything you've got."

"Fuck," Lev breathed.

Dmitri's grip inadvertently tightened around Lev's cock, and the game was over as the pretty Grigori ejaculated forcefully into his lover's hand with a stuttering moan.

Belphagor murmured, "Come" almost inaudibly, and Vasily let go with a groan of relief, his ejaculate spurting in a perfect arc onto the table.

"Full Choir," said Belphagor, dropping his hand faceup beside it.

Dmitri sighed and shook his head as he put down his cards. "You *are* a master player, Belphagor."

Belphagor grinned. "As I said, it's all in keeping an eye on the other players without seeming to." His grin faded a bit as Vasily swayed back on his heels—absurdly, still wearing the house shoes, though he was standing naked in the kitchen. Belphagor stood and put his hand on Vasily's cheek. "You look a bit pale, love. Too much fun too soon?"

Vasily shook his head, though he was feeling a little weak now that the adrenaline rush was fading. All he could concentrate on was the sound of the word *love* on Belphagor's tongue. He'd told Belphagor that he loved him a few times now, but Belphagor hadn't said it back. Maybe it was only a slip of the tongue or a meaningless endearment. He didn't want to call attention to it, but it made his heart beat faster. Belphagor was staring at him.

"Maybe too much vodka," Vasily admitted.

Belphagor's expression of worry relaxed, and he took Vasily's hand. "I'd better put this poor boy to bed."

Dmitri rose and picked up his neglected cigar and the lighter. "Good game." He winked with the stogie in his mouth as Belphagor turned Vasily toward the door to lead him away.

"Oh sure." Lev's voice trailed after them with mock petulance. "Leave me to clean up after everyone, as usual."

Belphagor kissed him as soon as he closed the door, and Vasily leaned back against the wood, melting into Belphagor, finally his alone.

"Did you have a good time?" Belphagor whispered, kissing his neck.

Vasily laughed. "Oh, it was *horrible*. The worst."

Belphagor raised his head from kissing Vasily's collarbone and gave him a sheepish smile. "All right, so that was a stupid question. But I want to make sure you didn't feel pressured, that you felt okay with being on display." He studied Vasily seriously. "You're jealous of Lev."

"So what if I am?"

"You don't have anything to worry about."

But the energy between the two of them had been obvious. And Belphagor had made it perfectly clear that while Vasily belonged to him and could only be with someone else if Belphagor wanted him to be, Belphagor himself was free to do whatever or whomever he liked.

"Who's worried?" Vasily shrugged. "I can be jealous without being worried." He shivered involuntarily, just a slight movement, but he was sure Belphagor would see it as his "tell." Instead, Belphagor rubbed his arms and turned him toward the bed.

"Under the covers. You may be a firespirit, but it's too cold in here for you to be standing about naked." He winked as Vasily climbed into the bed. "Even if it is how I prefer you." He undressed, revealing his tattoos part by part—as well as his erection.

Wrapping himself around Vasily beneath the covers, he made no attempt to engage him in more intimate contact except for the press of his hard cock against Vasily's back.

"Want me to do something about that?" asked Vasily in a soft growl.

Belphagor breathed in against his shoulder as if smelling him. "Yes, I do. But I'm going to engage in a bit of delicious masochism for a change and just lie here instead."

"Suit yourself," said Vasily, thinking Belphagor was a little peculiar, but enjoying the physical sensation of his unsatisfied desire. "I love you, Beli," he said quietly after a moment.

Belphagor squeezed him tight and kissed his cheek.

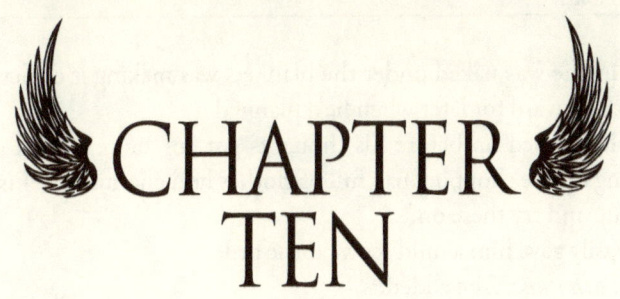

CHAPTER
TEN

I n the morning, Belphagor went out early to shop and returned while Vasily was still curled under the covers. With nothing to wear and Dmitri's robe still on the floor of the kitchen, it wasn't really surprising that he hadn't gotten up. Belphagor climbed on top of the covers, straddling Vasily on all fours.

"Wake up, *mal'chik*. See what I've bought."

Vasily stirred and looked up at him with a puzzled expression. "What are you doing?"

Belphagor waggled his eyebrows at him. "Notice anything?"

"I notice you've gone mad. What's wrong with you?"

Belphagor collapsed his weight onto him and dropped his chin on Vasily's chest. "You're no fun."

"I'd be more fun without these blankets between us."

"Lord, you're insatiable," he groaned. As if Belphagor wasn't. He couldn't remember the last time he'd been so consumed with wanting someone—a specific someone—at every possible opportunity. Going to sleep with a hard-on had been a test to see if he had any self-control left at all. He'd spent enough nights hiding a frustrated erection before they'd become intimate that it shouldn't have been such a hardship. But fantasizing about what it was like to fuck Vasily versus *knowing* what it was like made the same condition two very different experiences.

He'd gone out to buy himself a reward for not waking Vasily in the middle of the night to punish him for his own lust, though he was sure Vasily would have relished it. The sweet boy had been so good last night, and he needed rest to recover. Belphagor had come back with a reward for both of them. Feeling Vasily's warm body beneath him and knowing he was naked under the blankets was making it difficult to keep the reward for later when he'd planned.

He jumped up before his thoughts got any more carried away, holding up the shopping bag full of clothes he'd charmed for his boy. "Get up and try these on."

Vasily gave him a mild scowl at the order.

"*Pozhaluista*," he added.

"*Bozhe moi.* You said 'Please.' Don't tell me *you've* gotten a virus." Vasily took the bag from him and sat up, letting the covers fall. Just his chest bared to the coppery brush of hair beneath his navel made Belphagor feel warm. He turned and peeled off his coat and scarf.

"Put them on," he said as Vasily looked dubiously at the garments he was pulling out. "I want to see how they fit."

"What is this?" Vasily held up a knit shirt.

"It's a turtleneck. Keeps you warm."

Vasily rolled his eyes. "Like I need to keep warm."

"As you've demonstrated, you are not immune to this world's climate. Just humor me and try it on."

Vasily shrugged and pulled it over his head, struggling to get through the tight neck. "It's like fucking an uptight ass," he complained, finally coming up for air. "Who would wear this?" He straightened the dark crimson sweater that displayed his pecs marvelously. Belphagor was glad he'd gotten another in black.

"It's what all the supernal assassins are wearing this season."

Vasily laughed and climbed out of bed to try on a pair of pants, and Belphagor bit down on his tongue and drew blood to will his erection down. Vasily seemed oblivious to the effect he was having on Belphagor as he leaned over the bed and shuffled through the bag.

"You bought me underwear." He turned, depriving Belphagor of the view of his ass, and held the jockeys up to his crotch. "How . . . weird."

"Better than chafing, sweetheart."

"Maybe I like chafing."

Belphagor smiled darkly. "You would."

Vasily tossed the underwear aside and continued digging in the bag.

"*Mal'chik.* If you don't put one of those garments on this instant, I'm going to give you such a vicious thrashing you won't be able to sit."

Vasily turned toward him. "Are you trying to get me to put something on or not?"

"I'm trying to hold on to my sanity and not fuck you twenty-four hours a day until my dick falls off."

Vasily grinned. "Except for the dick-falling-off part, I don't see the problem."

"That's a pretty big 'except.' You forget, I'm not as youthful as you are. I'm liable to hurt myself."

Vasily burst out laughing. "Yes, you're positively ancient. How old are you, twenty-eight?"

Belphagor narrowed his eyes. "Do I look twenty-eight?" In truth, he was at least three multiples of twenty-eight. He tried not to count back that far. He had a vain hope that his stints in the world of Man hadn't aged him much more than he ought to appear.

"I have no idea what twenty-eight looks like, Belphagor. I'm just taking a random guess."

"Well, you're close enough. Now please, for the love of Heaven, cover that sweet ass before I go mad."

Shaking his head, Vasily picked up the white cotton underwear and stepped into them, sliding them up over his generous cock and glancing in over the waistband like he was trying to see if it would fit inside. Belphagor observed him standing by the bed in the tighty-whities and turtleneck and concluded he was hopelessly smitten. He gave his rising cock a stern mental warning.

Vasily pulled on a pair of American jeans that were apparently washed with acid. It seemed a strange thing to advertise, but they looked quite nice on Vasily. Belphagor had remembered his dimensions well.

"Thanks." Vasily tucked his hands into the pockets. "I was getting a little tired of being Naked Boy."

Belphagor raised his eyebrow, enjoying the slightly painful tug of his new adornment. "And you say *I'm* weird."

Vasily caught the glint of it. "What is that?" He stepped forward and ran his finger over Belphagor's eyebrow to the spiked barbell protruding from it.

"Do you like it?"

"I don't know. Did it hurt?"

"A bit."

Vasily brushed his thumb along one of the spikes, letting it linger, but said nothing more. Belphagor was pleased with the reaction.

Vasily was reserved with Dmitri and Lev when they got home from what Lev called "the day jobs." Belphagor asked him with amusement what his evening job was, and Lev smirked, teasing him with the first blin of the batch he was making—the "ugly blin," he called it, as the first always was—popping a piece of it into Belphagor's mouth with a wink.

Belphagor could feel Vasily's glare boring into him from across the room, but he continued flirting with Lev at the counter, annoyed that Vasily was taking it so seriously. He was used to giving attention to pretty young men and enjoying the way they responded to him. It was nothing more than that, and he wasn't about to change who he was just because Vasily imagined it meant something.

Vasily was even more reserved after that.

Dmitri seemed awkward in the face of Vasily's reticence. He was probably wondering if they had taken advantage of Vasily's high spirits and he was now regretting the game, but Belphagor knew that wasn't the case. What Vasily was doing was sulking.

He deliberately ignored Vasily during the dinner conversation, irritated that Dmitri was being made to feel as if he'd participated in something unseemly that Vasily hadn't enjoyed. Belphagor had negotiated the scene with Dmitri and Lev extensively while Vasily had been recuperating, making sure everyone would be comfortable with whatever happened and that no one felt pressured to do anything. The tension Vasily was stirring up with his behavior was tearing all of that careful and considerate planning down.

By the end of the evening, Belphagor was so livid that when Vasily made a flippant comment about going to bed alone, he snapped at him and told him to do it. Vasily stared at him wordlessly and then rose and retreated to the guest room.

Belphagor sighed and apologized to his hosts. "Sorry. I thought he could handle it. I know he enjoyed being shown off, but he can be a bit self-absorbed."

"Don't worry about it," said Lev with his usual amiability.

But Dmitri frowned. "Maybe we owe him an apology for putting him on the spot. We all knew what was going to happen, and he didn't."

Belphagor scowled, taking a cigar tin from his pocket and lighting one in the conventional manner. "He doesn't need to know everything I have planned. He needs to trust me."

"Don't you think you're being a little controlling?"

Belphagor smiled, offering a cigar to each of them. "I know my kind of sexual power play isn't to your taste, Dmitri, but believe me, it is to Vasily's."

"Did he say anything this morning about feeling uncomfortable about it?"

"Not a word. He was in a great mood until you two came home, and then he clammed up."

"Maybe he's shy," said Lev.

"Shy?" Belphagor blew out a puff of smoke with a laugh. "That's the last word I would apply to him. He's been working the street since he was too young to be doing it, and I've seen him with all kinds of demons—and angels—preening as the center of attention. He's probably sulking because he wasn't any longer."

Lev smiled. "Just because he's good at putting on a show for men who are paying him doesn't mean he isn't shy. That's the sense I was getting: he felt awkward with our conversation, not with what happened last night. You and Dmitri are old friends and know the world of Man intimately, and you and I . . ." He grinned. "Well, we kind of naturally hit it off. He probably feels like an outsider. He's never fallen before, and the only person he knows in the world is you."

Belphagor rolled his cigar between his fingers, disliking the feeling that he might have gotten things wrong. "I suppose I hadn't thought of it that way. I don't know why he can't simply be friendly, though. You're both being perfectly welcoming to him—and you were *extremely* welcoming to him last night." He gave Lev a mischievous smile. "I can't think of a better way to break the ice and get to know a demon than to strip down and have a semicircle jerk. And more, if there's time to get to know each other better."

Dmitri laughed. "You have a unique way of looking at things, Belphagor. It's not actually *entirely* necessary to fuck a demon to get to know him."

Belphagor gave him a mock look of dismay. "How in the world else would you?"

"I'm with Bel." Lev winked at him. "I'm not even sure we've been properly introduced. Who are you again?"

"It's only polite," said Belphagor with a grin. "You meet someone for the first time, you say hello, and then you drop trou, bend him over, and give him a nice 'Pleased to meet you' with a considerate reach-around."

Lev laughed. "Yes, the considerate reach-around is key. It's the 'How do you do?'" The three of them dissolved into laughter, but Lev went on after a moment more seriously. "But to be fair, Bel, I don't know if you understand what being introverted is if you think all Vasily has to do is be friendly to feel comfortable. You wouldn't know it from our interactions, but I'm not exactly wildly extroverted myself. Growing up as the only demon in your neighborhood and not even knowing another demon makes for a bit of an awkward adolescence. I don't normally get on with anyone I've just met the way I do with you. There's nothing that makes me feel more of an outcast than being around people I don't know who are all getting along, while I try to think of something conversational to say. Don't be too hard on Vasily for being quiet."

"As long as that's really all it is," added Dmitri. "Ease my mind a bit, if you would, Bel. Ask him if he was okay with our part in last night's festivities. And tell him we really enjoyed . . . getting to know him."

Lev snickered.

Belphagor stubbed out his cigar on his plate. "I promise you, he's only being sullen to get my attention. But I'll talk to him and make sure it's nothing else." He sighed and pushed away from the table. "Thank you for another wonderful meal, Lev. Your blini are, if I may say, Heavenly."

Lev batted his eyelashes. "Why, you flatterer."

Belphagor blew them both a kiss and said good night.

Vasily pretended to be asleep when Belphagor finally deigned to join him, lying on his side beneath the blankets, turned toward the wall.

Belphagor spoke from inside the doorway, obviously not falling for the ruse. "I got you something else at the market today, but if you're determined to be rude, maybe I'll just take it back."

"*I'm* rude?" Vasily turned on him, eyes hot with fire. "You didn't say a word to me all night, and you practically fucked Lev right in front of me on the dinner table."

"Don't be absurd. If I had wanted to fuck Lev on the dinner table, I'd have gone ahead and done it."

"Is that why you want to watch someone fuck me? So I won't be able to object while you fuck the entire world of Man?"

Belphagor sighed, his crossed arms rising over his chest. "Your penchant for hyperbole is becoming a tad tiresome." His deliberate use of angelic words Vasily didn't know—coupled with his blithe conversations with Dmitri and Lev in Russian that left Vasily scrambling to understand—had reached a point where Belphagor had to be doing it on purpose to humiliate him.

"You might as well keep on talking over my head in your precious *russkiy yazyk*, because I didn't understand *one fucking word* of that sentence!" The words burst out of him, and to his horror, hot tears burst out with them.

Belphagor frowned at him. "Come over here."

He was tempted to tell Belphagor to go fuck himself. But then they'd fight, and a fight with Belphagor only ended one of two ways: with Vasily on his knees—surrendering to his fearsome need to let Belphagor prove that he owned him, body and soul—or on his feet as they carried him as fast and as far away as possible, so that Belphagor couldn't. And Vasily had nowhere to go.

He forced himself to control his emotions and got out of bed to stand in front of Belphagor. Despite his resolve, he flinched when

Belphagor reached to grab hold of his hair as he so often did to bring Vasily down to his height. Unexpectedly, Belphagor gripped the back of his neck instead and drew him into his arms.

"*Mal'chik*." His voice was soft. "Have I made you feel stupid?"

Vasily stood stiffly in Belphagor's arms, uncertain how to respond. He wasn't used to Belphagor admitting he was wrong.

"It wasn't my intention. I never want you to feel that way. I forget you don't know Russian fluently—and I forget I'm speaking it when I'm here. And I'm used to having a different level of discourse—conversation—when I'm here than in Raqia."

"So you dumb it down for me," snapped Vasily, still resisting him. "And I know what 'discourse' is, you bastard."

Belphagor held him away so he had to look him in the eye. "I don't dumb it down for you. Okay, maybe I did just now, because I was self-conscious of my word choice. But it's the difference between the spheres. Raqia is in a different age. Its concerns are different. The only opportunities most Raqia demons have for education are serving in an angelic household and trying their damnedest to pick up what they can. That doesn't make Raqians stupid. But it makes my interactions in the celestial sphere literally a world away from this." He stroked his hand down the side of Vasily's face and held it there. "I didn't mean to leave you out of the conversation. I'm sorry."

Vasily wanted to jerk his head away, but instead he found himself nuzzling against Belphagor's hand, eyes closed to keep from seeing the tender look in Belphagor's that threatened to loose more tears from his.

As soon as Vasily relaxed into his touch, he realized he'd fallen into Belphagor's trap when Belphagor moved his hands to the sides of Vasily's head and pressed him down to his knees in a viselike grip. So it was option one after all. If he was being honest, it was the option he preferred.

"Keep your eyes closed." Belphagor's breath tickled against the curve beneath his jawline. "I have something for you."

Vasily's cock stiffened, and his breath quickened along with his heartbeat. Anger and desire tangled together inside his veins in a chemical reaction that only Belphagor could inspire, forming an altogether new element that Vasily had never known he needed as much as the air he breathed until Belphagor had ignited it in him.

Belphagor's thumb brushed against Vasily's lips, and he opened his mouth reflexively. He let the thumb slip inside, teeth grazing Belphagor's skin as he sucked, anticipating its replacement.

But when Belphagor withdrew the thumb, instead of the predictable escalation of the usual game, he took a step back. "Are you my boy?" His voice was soft, with a dangerous edge.

Vasily waited a breath, still nursing his anger. But there could only ever be one answer to that question. "*Da, ser.*"

"Are you mine to do with as I please?"

"*Da, ser.*" He'd let that come out too quickly. His cock was beginning to ache.

"You remember the word I gave you?"

Vasily was growing impatient. A little steam escaped with his answer. "Da, *ser.*"

Belphagor was no doubt mulling whether to punish Vasily for the attitude in that exasperated "*da.*" But he spoke again after a pause. "Good. *Khorosho.*" He stepped in close. "There's a little something I mean to do to you. Because it suits me. It may draw blood."

Vasily swallowed a sound that threatened to rise up with the heat in his cock—a sharp intake of breath mixed with a groan of desire.

"If you object, say the word now."

He was beginning to think option two might have been the wiser course of action, but he held his tongue. His erection wasn't getting any less hard.

Evidently taking his silence for ascent, Belphagor stroked his hand along the side of Vasily's neck and pinched a bit of skin between his fingers. "Don't move."

Something sharp stabbed swiftly through the flesh Belphagor held, and an equally sharp hiss of pain escaped Vasily unbidden.

"Hush, *mal'chik.* Trust me. Hold still." Belphagor's fingers tugged on the sharp thing still piercing Vasily's skin. "It's only a needle," he added, as if he thought that would calm him. "Aether-infused steel, impervious to any earthly contamination. Nothing to worry about."

More tugging ensued while Belphagor fiddled with the needle, and Vasily let out an involuntary moan.

Belphagor stroked the toe of his house shoe against Vasily's obvious erection. "I'm not sure if that was pain or arousal. Either way, it pleases me."

"Beli." Vasily's breath caught in his throat as he realized he'd let Belphagor do anything to him. Anything at all.

With a final twist against the stinging flesh, Belphagor released him. "All done, sweet boy. You can look now." He drew Vasily to his feet, pivoting him toward the mirror on the opposite wall as Vasily opened his eyes.

Something glinted in the glass—a piece of metal at the side of his neck.

Vasily put his hand to the odd, sharp thing penetrating his skin. "What?" He stepped toward the mirror, forgetting to ask permission, and peered closer. Like the one in Belphagor's eyebrow, a bar of steel capped with sharp spikes decorated his flesh.

Belphagor came up behind him and kissed his nape, careful around the jewelry. "Do you want to know what this is, my lovely boy?"

Vasily nodded, eyes on him in the mirror.

"This is my mark. It says you're mine, that I own you so completely you'll submit to whatever whim takes me."

Vasily bit his lip. It was exactly what he'd been thinking. Belphagor's words sent a shiver down his spine as Vasily brushed his fingers over the metal. Beneath his rough beard, it seemed to make him look older. And a bit dangerous.

"*Spasibo, ser.*"

Belphagor turned him about and brought his head down for a kiss, pausing with his lips brushing Vasily's. "Did I hurt you?"

Vasily bit his lip and nodded. "*Da, ser.*"

"Did you want me to?"

It took a moment for Vasily to find his voice. "*Da, ser.*"

"And last night, while I ordered you to strip and submit to being jerked off in front of near strangers . . . did you want that?"

Vasily closed his eyes. "*Da, ser.*"

Belphagor was silent for a moment, and then his arms tightened around Vasily's waist. "Do you want my cock in your ass now so you remember who owns you?"

"*Da, ser,*" Vasily rasped. "*Pozhaluista.*"

Belphagor turned him swiftly toward the bed, unfastening Vasily's pants and pulling them down along with his new white underwear before he pushed Vasily onto his knees. Vasily shivered at the jangle of the belt buckle snapping open as Belphagor thrust him facedown against the mattress with his other hand.

From somewhere, Belphagor had palmed his favorite oil. He entered Vasily, cock prodding insistently into the tight hole, and filled him as deeply as he could. Vasily groaned and shuddered under the rapid pumping of Belphagor's hips, nails gripping the sheet, trying not to come as his cock rubbed against the edge of the bed with the force of Belphagor's thrusts.

It was no use. The ritual piercing had already brought him to the brink. He cried out against the blankets to muffle the sound as his cock jerked and spurted into the sheets while Belphagor fucked him even harder.

When Vasily's hips stopped jerking and his cock relaxed, Belphagor dropped his weight against him, continuing to fuck him with slow and steady strokes. "Will you keep the gift? Will you be my sweet boy always?"

"Yes," Vasily gasped and then remembered, muddy-headed with the glow of release, to say, "*Da, ser,*" just as Belphagor began to pound him hard, grunting loudly, and shot into Vasily's ass.

Belphagor relaxed against him with a sigh as his orgasm died down, arms encircling him. "*Moi milyy mal'chik.*" This meant "sweet boy of mine," but to Vasily it sounded like "I love you"—or at least as close to it as he was likely to get.

CHAPTER ELEVEN

Belphagor was excited to show Vasily Moscow. It wasn't his usual stomping grounds when he came to the world of Man; he'd spent far more time in Leningrad, and it was where he'd intended to go before Vasily's illness had necessitated more immediate lodging. But where Leningrad was uncannily familiar in its resemblance to Elysium, Moscow was completely otherworldly.

He had to warn Vasily against physical affection—or even closeness—on the streets. Raqia wasn't exactly accepting of relations between two men, but such behavior wasn't considered shocking or immoral, merely looked down upon as somewhat seedy and indulgent, like frequenting prostitutes. In this corner of the world of Man, at least, it was not only illegal, it could get you killed.

Vasily was baffled. "You can't even do it for pay?"

"Oh, the trade exists here," Belphagor assured him. "But outside the law. All prostitution is illegal."

"That makes no sense." Vasily's eyes sparked with indignation. "How do you make compensating someone for their skills and services illegal? Everybody has to give it up for free to any jackass who wants it?"

Belphagor smiled as he helped Vasily put on his new coat. "The law doesn't say you have to give it up, dear boy. You just can't get paid if you do."

"Well, I hate that law. And the other one too."

He took Vasily to see Red Square, telling him how the country had changed since the beginning of the century—careful not to let on that he'd actually been around at the time—and how drastically it had been changing recently with the dissolution of the Soviet Union.

"The old government had a very tight control over everything and everyone. It's almost as though all of Russia were treated like Raqia." The names even sounded alike: Raqia and *Rossiya*—only a single sibilant differentiating the pronunciation of the two.

They walked around the walls of the Kremlin with its towers and spires that had always reminded Belphagor of New Year's *yolka* trees, their peaks topped with stars of gold-framed ruby glass. He told Vasily how the stars on the towers had replaced the two-headed eagle that was the symbol of the imperial rulers.

"Two-headed eagle?" Vasily glanced at him. "Sounds like the two-headed Seraph of the House of Arkhangel'sk."

"Exactly so," said Belphagor. "One of many similarities you'll find in the world of Man. When we have a chance, I want to take you to Leningrad and show you the Winter Palace there. It's as if the city's designers and architects must have been Fallen. You won't believe it."

"Leningrad." Vasily's brows drew together. "How long are you thinking we'll be in the world of Man?"

Belphagor shrugged. "You're rather conspicuous in Raqia. I'm not sure whether it will ever be safe to go back."

"*Ever*?" Vasily stared at him. "I don't want to stay here forever, Bel. It isn't home. How would I earn a living? You just told me practically everything about me is illegal."

"It's not that black-and-white."

"Black-and-white?" Vasily's eyes kindled as if colloidal gold had seeped into them like the glass in the ruby stars. "I think being the lowest of the low is pretty black-and-fucking-white."

Belphagor grabbed his elbow to turn away from the view of a passing guard. "Watch the brimstone."

"Brimstone?" Vasily looked at him as if he'd lost his mind.

"It's what the Fallen here call demonic radiance. Your eyes are glowing. We don't want to draw attention—from Men or from Malakim."

Vasily's eyes cooled. "Malakim? You mean that story is true about the archangelic messengers who fell to the world of Man to tell them of the wonders of Heaven?"

"As true as the Grigori and Nephilim. They've made a whole religion out of it, giving the short-lived humans the hope that when they die, they'll go there to live forever."

Vasily's mouth dropped open. "That's absurd! Who would believe that?"

"Millions," said Belphagor with a sigh. "And if they knew there were demons among them— Well, you think we have it bad in Heaven, you should see what they think of us here."

"You're not making me want to stay."

"Sorry." Belphagor almost reached to put an arm around him and pull him close, jerking back his hand before doing exactly what he'd warned Vasily not to. "Come on. Let me show you some more sights. Maybe the place will grow on you. There's one in particular I want you to see."

Hands in his pockets so he wouldn't be tempted to touch him, Belphagor led Vasily to the far side of the Kremlin, where the fantastic sculpted onion domes of a cathedral rose beyond the walls like dollops of confection. Instead of stars, each of these was topped with a golden cross, the symbol of the religion the Malakim had fostered, sparkling under the winter sun.

Vasily gazed up at it. "What's that?"

"It's a cathedral, a place of reverence for the faith co-opted by the Malakim." He paused. "The Cathedral of St. Vasily."

Vasily's expression said he thought Belphagor was teasing him, but when Belphagor didn't wink or say anything further, he looked back at the church. "A cathedral in the world of Man has my name?"

"A fair number of them do, I would guess. He's a popular saint." He smiled at Vasily's wrinkled brow. "A lot of demon names come from the names of earthly saints. Which is pretty funny if you think about it. Saints are the holiest of humans in the cult of Heaven, and demons are considered the greatest enemies of the faith."

Vasily was studying the cathedral with an odd look. "I don't even know who gave me my name. Do you think my mother chose it before she abandoned me?" His voice was gravelly with emotion.

"I don't know, *mal'chik*." He slipped his hand out of his pocket and gave Vasily's fingers a quick squeeze, their warmth making him wish they could hold hands and weave their fingers together as they walked. "Let's go home. Or as home as we're going to get for the time being. It's freezing out here."

As they crossed the snow-covered bricks of the square, a male and female couple walking arm in arm glanced over at them, and the man tipped his hat in their direction. A sort of blue-green aura seemed to travel from his hand to his hat and linger there a moment as he passed by. Belphagor nodded to him.

"*S Novym Godom!*" the young man called, and Belphagor returned the greeting. He hadn't been paying attention to the time of year. They must have arrived in Moscow right after New Year's Day.

Vasily caught his sleeve. "Did you see that?"

"Radiance," said Belphagor. "Fellow Fallen. He must have recognized ours."

"I thought you said that was dangerous."

"Most humans can't see that sort of radiance, or if they do, they deny it as a trick of the light. The fire in your eyes on the other hand, or wings—"

"*Wings?*" Vasily's eyes lit up, demonstrating a hint of what Belphagor had been warning against.

Belphagor smiled knowingly. "I forgot to tell you about wings, did I? Yet another detail you may have thought was merely legend. The same element in celestial air that keeps us from aging as swiftly as Men apparently dampens the radiance of the lower orders. Including demons. Not so here."

"You mean we all have them?"

"Every one of us, so far as I know. If we stay awhile, perhaps we can find a safe place for you to try yours."

Vasily shook his head in amazement. "That might be an actual reason to stay."

"It's one of the reasons most demons fall. They say the Grigori flew straight out of Heaven when they were cast out, and as Powers, when they struck the earth, they landed with such force they created Lake Baikal." He grinned. "That much, I'd venture to guess, is actually legend."

It was dark by the time they arrived back at the apartment, and Dmitri and Lev were already home. Lev had cabbage soup on the stove and black bread baking in the oven. Determining that dinner would be in an hour, Belphagor steered Vasily back to their room and closed the door.

"Get your clothes off," he ordered. "I'm freezing and I want your heat."

Vasily scowled a bit at the order, but revealed a burgeoning erection as he undid his jeans. Nothing made Belphagor harder than seeing how he affected Vasily with a terse word. He stroked himself through his pants as Vasily took off everything, the thick firespirit cock standing like a challenge between them. It was a challenge Belphagor was happy to accept.

He undressed casually while Vasily watched him with fire-opal eyes, Belphagor's stone-hard erection the only thing giving the lie to his affected disinterest. When he'd finished undressing, he stroked his hand down the warm firespirit body, steam practically rising from it in the chilly air of the apartment, and followed the motion with his tongue, relishing the smoky taste of Vasily's skin. He wanted to keep being cruel to him, to give Vasily the release of that firespirit rage he so desperately needed, but he couldn't stand it any longer, gazing up at the wild, furious thing awaiting his command.

"You're fucking beautiful. Come here." He took Vasily by the hand and led him to the bed, wrapping him in his arms, and Vasily climbed over him, melting into them with a sigh.

Belphagor kissed the warm skin at Vasily's throat, and every bit he could reach, making his way down one ginger-haired, muscled arm. "I'm going to ruin myself on you if I keep fucking you every time you make me hard. I'll run dry or break my cock in two."

Vasily laughed, the deep baritone rumble vibrating against him, and Belphagor smacked the pert ass bared to the air.

"Don't laugh at the old man, boy."

"*Nyet, ser*," Vasily promised. "Never."

When they emerged from the room later, Belphagor tried to be nonchalant, and if their Grigori hosts had heard anything, they gave no sign during dinner. Vasily seemed a little more relaxed and less insecure, and they had a pleasant chat while they ate.

Afterward, while Belphagor helped Lev with the dishes, Dmitri and Vasily actually had a conversation of sorts. Though Vasily's grunted answers couldn't have been putting Dmitri's mind much at ease, this, at least, was Vasily's usual demeanor and not the uncomfortable quiet of the previous night.

The dishes done, Lev made tea and artfully arranged a plate of chocolate biscuits but set them on a tray as if he meant to take them somewhere. He looked Belphagor straight in the eye and said, "If the daybed isn't soaked with come, there's an American television program on that we'd like to watch."

Belphagor burst out laughing, and Vasily turned an entertainingly ruby shade that was almost radiant.

Dmitri leaned against the doorframe, looking amused at Lev's frankness. "I'm sure it isn't *soaked*, love. If I recall correctly, I think what Bel said was 'make sure you don't let all that hot spunk dribble off onto the bed, I'm going to use it as lube.'" He grinned at Belphagor, who was now turning a bit red himself. "The walls, my friend, are extremely thin."

Lev marched into the dining room and set the tray on the table. "I'll get another bedspread for good measure." He went to the bedroom and returned with a somewhat worn but thick and comfortable blanket and tossed it onto the daybed, propping up the extra cushions against the wall. "*Voila*. Good as new."

While Belphagor and Vasily sat with chagrin, Dmitri brought the electric samovar to the dining table. After plugging it in to keep the water and the concentrated *zavarka* warm, he switched on the television while Lev poured the tea.

"They're showing an old holiday film that's been translated from English," said Dmitri. "First time anything American has been on Russian TV. The world of Man is changing."

Vasily dunked a biscuit in his tea. "What's 'American'?"

"America is another princedom," said Belphagor. "Russia's nemesis across the great sea, *Atlantika*. They've been involved in a covert war for nearly half a century until the recent change of power."

"Across the Quiet Sea on the other side, as well," Dmitri reminded him.

Vasily chewed his biscuit. "How can it be on both sides of two different seas?"

"The world of Man is a sphere—literally." Belphagor stirred sugar into his tea. "Keep going in one direction, and eventually you come right back around to where you started."

Vasily's eyes widened. "Are you putting me on?"

Belphagor smiled. "Not at all."

"Don't people fall off if they aren't on top of the sphere?"

"Gravity keeps everything in place, and the world is so big that it never feels like you're on a curved surface at all." He could see Vasily didn't quite know whether to believe him. "Never mind about the vast earthly globe." He put his arm around him and drew him against his side, settling back to watch the show as Lev sat beside Dmitri on his right. "It's getting smaller all the time."

The film, *Eta Zamechatel'naya Zhizn*, turned out to be the most charming thing Belphagor had ever seen, and he had to pretend to have a coughing fit near the end to cover his sniffling when the American banker George Bailey was saved from the brink of ruin by the love of his family and friends.

They all had a big laugh at the angel, Clarence, assigned as a guardian from Heaven to save George Bailey from killing himself and show him what life would have been like if he'd never been born. It was the kindly old angel's final chance to earn his wings through a good deed. Apparently, the Americans believed that Men became angels when they died. The hand of the Malakim was definitely in the mix of this lore.

They laughed again at the very end when George Bailey's youngest daughter, Zuzu, proudly told her father that every time a bell rang, it meant an angel had gotten his wings. Vasily seemed quiet as they talked about it afterward, his mind no doubt returning to what Belphagor had told him about his wings earlier. He had to find a place to let Vasily experience them.

He pulled Vasily closer and kissed his warm throat while Lev leaned over to Dmitri and whispered something.

Belphagor raised his eyebrow, enjoying the pinch of the bar that decorated it. "Telling secrets?"

Dmitri smiled. "Lev is curious to know what it would be like to be fucked by the two of you while I watch."

Lev pushed his shoulder. "Dimka! I didn't say that!"

Belphagor was amused by the flush that scattered over the Grigori's pale cheeks. "What did you say?"

"I said I bet the two of you could fuck a demon blind." Lev grinned sheepishly.

"I'm sure there's no need to fuck you *blind*," Belphagor replied with a wink. He glanced at Vasily to see that he was watching him warily, but beneath the tight pants, he was becoming noticeably engorged. "What do you think, Vasya? Should we satisfy our friend Lev's curiosity?" He unbuttoned the new jeans and let the white underwear swell through the fly.

Vasily didn't answer, but he didn't stop him.

Belphagor dipped his hand inside the elastic band and released Vasily, stroking him while he watched Dmitri unbutton Lev's shirt from behind him and kiss his bared shoulder. With a glance toward his generous handful, Belphagor drew Lev's attention. "Do you think you can take all of this?"

Lev nodded, seeming also to have gone shy and quiet. Dmitri reached around and undid Lev's fly as well, and the fine, hard cock sprang out in answer.

"Such a pretty cock," Belphagor murmured, wrapping his hand around it, now holding one in each hand. He looked up at Dmitri. "Let's get him naked." He said it just sharply enough that he felt both demons shiver and pulse in his hands. Dmitri stripped off Lev's shirt and long undershirt while Belphagor quickly relieved him of his pants, peeling his underwear down to his thighs. He glanced back at Vasily, who was looking a bit neglected. "Why don't you take these off him, *mal'chik*?"

Vasily leaned over him, letting his erection press into Belphagor's lap, and slowly slid the underwear off, depositing them on the floor. Belphagor took advantage of his position to pull Vasily's pants down as well, just enough to give him some freedom of movement. He moved aside and got the almond oil, but when he turned back, Vasily was sitting back on his heels on the daybed, looking uncomfortable.

Belphagor set the lube down, trying to hide his disappointment. "Let's talk privately for a minute." He led Vasily out of the room with his pants still hanging open, the enthusiasm of that magnificent erection not at all dampened, and shut the door. "You don't have to do this if you don't want to."

"It's not that." The awkward growl said Vasily was embarrassed.

"What is it? You don't want me to fuck him?"

"No. I mean, yes. But . . . no."

Belphagor tried to be patient. "No, you don't want me to fuck him? Or no, that's not it either?"

"That's not what— I mean, I suppose I'd rather you not…" Vasily's face went red. Belphagor had never seen him this flustered. "I've never fucked anyone before," he finally blurted in a harsh whisper.

Belphagor's eyebrows lifted in unison. "Never?"

"It's not what most patrons are interested in."

While this was certainly true, Belphagor couldn't imagine growing up on the streets of Raqia without experimenting happily with other rentboys as he'd done when he was young. "But you want to."

Vasily's gaze flitted toward the door as if he was still trying to make up his mind.

Belphagor stepped closer to him, stroking the pennant cock. "Will you trust me to handle this?"

Vasily nodded, though his face didn't quite seem to agree.

"That's my boy." Belphagor tilted his head, looking up at Vasily. "Anyway, there's nothing to it." His eyes flashed darkly. "Imagine it's pussy." He turned and went back into the room, leaving Vasily to follow him, knowing he would, and knowing he'd floored the boy. He hadn't told Vasily he knew about his initiation at The Cat.

The memory of why they'd come and of poor Ouestucati threatened to surface, but he pushed the sadness down. This wasn't the time or place for it.

Inside their room, they found Lev perched awkwardly on the edge of the daybed, Dmitri behind him with his arms around him and his chin on Lev's head.

"Don't worry about it." Lev put on an unconvincing smile. "It was only an idle thought."

Belphagor made a dismissive noise. "Nothing to be worried about. It seems Vasily's concerned that his size combined with the unpredictability of his element in the earthly sphere may be a bit much for you." Beside him, Vasily cleared his throat. "And I'm inclined to agree." He winked at the Grigori. "We wouldn't want the 'nice to meet you' moment to end up lighting a fire in your ass in all the wrong ways."

Lev laughed nervously, his eyes almost comically large. "No, indeed."

"I'd like to try something." Belphagor nodded to Dmitri. "Let's turn this bed perpendicular to the wall for better access."

Lev scrambled up, staring as Dmitri and Belphagor picked up the bed and swung it about.

"Stretch him over it." They stepped in as one, Belphagor bending to grab Lev's ankles and Dmitri taking his arms as Belphagor raised him off the ground. "On his back."

Dmitri nodded, and they swung Lev between them, tossing him lightly into the center, legs over one side.

Belphagor unbuttoned his shirt and slipped it off, grasping both arms of the garment to whip it into a thick rope, and handed the shirt to Dmitri. "Tie this over his eyes."

Dmitri gave him a slow smile, catching the game, and blindfolded Lev, tying an efficient knot behind his lover's head and laying him gently but firmly back against the mattress.

"*Mal'chik*, over here." Belphagor pointed toward the floor between Lev's spread thighs. "Kneel."

With a look of trepidation, Vasily obeyed, but Belphagor held his finger in front of his mouth for him to keep silent before indicating with a motion of his hand that Vasily should scoot back. When he did, Dmitri slid deftly and silently to the ground where Vasily had been. Vasily looked puzzled.

Belphagor bent to whisper in his ear. "Give Dmitri a kiss. Make it as warm as you can."

Vasily narrowed his eyes before a look of understanding dawned on him. When Dmitri turned his head toward him, Vasily leaned in and gave the Grigori a deep kiss that Belphagor felt to his toes. Lucky bastard. Dmitri's eyes watered with the heat he was absorbing, but he soldiered on.

Lev squirmed at the silence. "What's going on?"

"Quiet," said Belphagor in a calm voice that no rational demon ever disobeyed. "We'll deal with you when we're ready." While the words were leaving his mouth, Dmitri pulled away from Vasily's kiss and lowered his head into Lev's lap, sliding the fire-warmed tongue down the waiting erection as he swallowed it all.

Lev dug his fingers into the bedspread with a shaky gasp. "Oh my God."

Belphagor smiled, watching Lev buck almost involuntarily into his own lover's mouth. "Talented boy, isn't he?"

"God, yes." Several insensate moans followed while Dmitri gave Lev a thorough slathering in firespirit essence. The sound of his mouth riding up and down the slick flesh drove Belphagor to distraction until he dropped to a crouch beside Vasily and channeled his pent up arousal into stroking the firespirit's neglected cock.

As Lev's breathing quickened and his moans got louder, Belphagor took Vasily's hands and slid them up the demon's thighs. That final, unexpected stroke of heat sent Lev over the edge, and Dmitri sucked greedily as Lev came with a stuttering shout. When he'd finished, Dmitri let go and slipped silently out of the spot to stand as if he'd been observing the whole time.

"How are you feeling, love?" His throat was hoarse with Vasily's heat.

Lev put a hand to the blindfold. "Oh Jesus."

Dmitri's voice warmed with amusement. "Did you just get religion?"

"I think so. A little bit."

For the rest of the game to play out as Belphagor had planned, he had to disarm Lev once more before he wondered why Dmitri wasn't moving closer and taking off the blindfold.

He got to his feet. "Time to flip him."

Lev made a high-pitched sound of surprise as Dmitri took hold of his legs and Belphagor moved around the bed and took his arms to lift him once more. He gave Dmitri a nod, inclining his head to the left, and with one neat motion, they flipped Lev like a well-set blin and tossed him facedown.

Lev whimpered softly, anticipating what was coming next—as far as he knew.

Belphagor stroked his hand down the demon's back, letting his touch linger at the nicely rounded buttocks still radiating heat from the impressions left by Vasily's hot palms. Vasily's wary gaze was on him. Belphagor nodded once more toward Dmitri and waggled his tongue—perhaps a bit more salaciously than he'd intended, judging by the sharp bob of Vasily's ponderous cock. They'd never be able to pull off a substitute for his size, even if he could transfer its heat, but the trick had worked once. It ought to do as well a second time.

As Dmitri accepted another toe-curling kiss from the firespirit, Belphagor determined it would be his last. Not that Belphagor was jealous.

Dmitri knelt behind Lev, and Belphagor made a gesture with his thumbs to Vasily that was unmistakable. Vasily crouched behind Dmitri and stroked his hands up the backs of Lev's thighs, cupped the pert cheeks, and used his thumbs to spread them open.

"That other tongue trick," said Belphagor as Lev gasped. "It's not cocksucking."

Dmitri dove in between Vasily's hands, stuck out his tongue narrowed to a point, and thrust the superheated flesh into the opening Vasily was helpfully holding wide for him.

Lev was already howling with pleasure before Dmitri had made a single stroke.

Belphagor had watched long enough. He unbuttoned his fly and stepped over one of Vasily's arms, turning the firespirit's head toward him. No words or gestures necessary, Vasily swallowed him aggressively, as if he'd watched long enough too.

It only took a few moments to reach climax after so much excitement, and with the heat of Vasily's tongue washing over him— and Lev almost sobbing with pleasure behind him at the effects of the same borrowed heat—Belphagor came with a loud, satisfied shout to drown out the sound of Vasily happily humming around his mouthful.

Lev's moaning had reached a crescendo that said he'd managed to come again himself, and Dmitri was grunting into Lev's ass as he stroked himself. In a moment, all three of them were sighing happy little moans of satisfaction. Only Vasily's impressive hard-on remained unsatisfied.

Belphagor took Vasily's hands and helped him to his feet, while Dmitri rose and moved around to the other side of the bed to give his lover a kiss.

Lev sighed into his mouth, curling his arms around Dmitri's neck, and then pulled back in surprise. "Wait. Why do you taste like . . ."

Dmitri laughed and reached for the blindfold.

Belphagor put a hand on top of his. "Before you take that off, Dmitri, there's one more little treat Vasily has for Lev." He kissed Vasily and murmured against his lips, "Show him what the real deal feels like."

Vasily didn't have to ask what he meant. Without hesitation, he widened his stance and moved up closer to Lev's behind, stroking his generous handful with a look of relief.

Belphagor slipped an arm around his waist as he watched the rapid motions of Vasily's hand and let his breath tickle Vasily's neck. "Don't get carried away, *mal'chik*."

Vasily gave him a low growl. "I'm not an idiot."

"We'll have a talk about your insolence later," Belphagor promised. It was precisely the incentive Vasily needed to let go. An instant later, a sizeable load of hot firespirit come was splattering onto the handprints still gracing Lev's cheeks.

Lev gasped, his buttocks clenching under the unexpected sensation. "Holy fuck."

Belphagor smiled, remembering it well. "Imagine that shooting up your ass after taking a pounding from the cock it came from. And count your blessings."

Dmitri shook his head with a smile, loosening the blindfold while Vasily squeezed out the last of it. "I'm counting yours, my friend." He kissed Lev again as the blindfold came away, and Lev gave him a reproachful look.

Dmitri grinned. "Be careful what you ask for, sweetheart. With Belphagor around, you're likely to get more than you bargained for." He hitched up his pants with a rueful smile and glanced over at Vasily. "Thank you for humoring him."

Vasily let out a sound that was half nervous laugh, half satisfied growl.

"I hope you don't mind if I throw you out of our come-soaked bed now." Belphagor gave Dmitri a wicked grin as he buttoned his jeans. "That is, if Lev can walk."

Lev made a somewhat inarticulate sound, and Dmitri swept him up into his arms as he stood.

"He'll walk later. Enjoy the bed, and thank you both for a lovely evening."

When Dmitri had gone, Belphagor scooted the bed back against the wall and turned to Vasily. "So. Which would you like to be punished for first? Giving me attitude while whacking off on Lev's ass or not telling me about your adventure at The Cat?"

The crestfallen look on Vasily's face made him wish he'd left that for another time. There was too much heartache attached to the experience.

Belphagor sat on the bed and softened his tone. "Come here."

With a puzzled, miserable look, Vasily came to the bed, and Belphagor drew him down to sit on his lap.

"I'm too heavy for you," Vasily grumbled.

"I don't care." Belphagor wrapped his arms around him. "I'm sorry about Ouestucati."

Vasily turned in his arms. "Who?"

"That was Sefira's real name. Tabris told me after she'd been taken. Is it true she was your first?"

Vasily looked away, his cheeks reddening. "Elyon wanted to watch."

"And did you want to do it?" He planted a kiss beside the spiked adornment at Vasily's neck. "It's okay if you did, *mal'chik*."

"Yes, I wanted to."

"And you enjoyed it."

"Bel, please. I don't want to talk about this. Just beat me or whatever you're going to do. I'll take my punishment."

Belphagor sighed. "Just beat you? Is that all it is to you?"

"That isn't what I meant."

"Because I don't do these things with you merely to get myself off. And I have no intention of punishing you for simply enjoying something. Even if it's something I can't fathom enjoying. I only want to know what's going through your head."

"Yes, I enjoyed it!" His voice was a harsh growl, but instead of fire in his eyes, he'd begun to cry.

Belphagor held him and let him weep. "I'm sorry, *mal'chik*. I'm sorry for what happened to her, and I'm sorry to have prodded such a wound because of my jealousy. And, frankly, my curiosity got the better of me. Maybe when it isn't such a painful topic, you'll tell me about it."

Vasily nodded against him, letting the hot tears fall against his shoulder.

Belphagor's arms tightened around him. "But for now, what I intend to punish you for is not trusting me enough to share an experience with me that was clearly very important to you."

He listened quietly to the hitch of surprise in Vasily's breathing that stopped his tears. It was these endearing little things about his responses that had hopelessly ensnared Belphagor. "You'll receive that punishment when I've decided on how best to discipline you. Tonight, we will deal with the more immediate issue of speaking to me disrespectfully with your dick aimed at another demon's ass. And since I'm too tired to give you what you deserve in that respect, you can sleep on top of the covers with your ass exposed so it's ready for me to do what I want with it when I wake up in the morning."

Vasily pulled away from him, his tears utterly forgotten. "Are you fucking serious?"

"I am always fucking serious about discipline, my dear boy. Pants down, on top of the covers. *Now.* You're a firespirit; it shouldn't be that much of a hardship for you to sleep bare-assed."

Vasily stood with a look of absolute indignation and yanked his pants down, climbed past Belphagor onto the bed to lie down, and turned toward the wall.

Belphagor smoothed his hand across the beautiful ass, and Vasily's muscles tightened with resistance against him. Without another word, Belphagor undressed and got under the covers, turning the opposite way toward the room. The heat from that ass beside him and the thought of what he'd do to it when he'd gotten some rest made it almost impossible to sleep.

In the morning, he woke before Vasily and rolled over, remembering as he did so how he'd made the other demon sleep. He admired the ass for a while, rubbing his cock, and then decided the cruelest thing would be to deny Vasily the fucking he'd be expecting. Of course, it was also an exercise in self-denial, but there would be other moments.

He jerked himself off, making sure to be loud and vigorous enough about it that Vasily woke before he was finished. The look on Vasily's face as he turned and saw the fruit of Belphagor's efforts shoot up over his hand was priceless. Belphagor groaned with pleasure.

"What are you doing?" Vasily demanded.

"What does it look like I'm doing?" He finished up with a satisfied exhalation.

"You made me lie here all night with my ass out!"

"I certainly did. And what a lovely ass it is. I enjoyed it visually while pleasuring myself." He reached his sticky hand around and grabbed hold of the erection he knew would be there. "Should I do the same for you or let you walk around with this in your pants all morning? Or maybe out of your pants? I could make you keep your ass and cock out as long as I like, let Dmitri and Lev see how completely I own you." He began to stroke him. "You'd look lovely, if a bit silly, sitting there at breakfast eating kasha with this big, beautiful dick poking over the edge of the table."

"*Bozhe moi.* It's not *that* big." His voice was low with arousal despite his anger.

"You underestimate yourself in many respects, dear boy. I could have you kneel on the chair and put your cock right on your plate. Maybe see if Dmitri or Lev wanted to play with it. I'd have to give them instructions not to allow you to come, of course."

Vasily groaned softly, pushing into his hand.

"You like that idea. We could make you our toy for the day, something to stroke and tease and torment. I loved driving you mad on the train. You wanted to come so badly." He lifted his hand from the cock he was stroking and Vasily moaned. "Like you do now."

"Please, Beli," he gasped, squirming. "I'm sorry I was rude to you last night. Please don't do it again."

"So you want me to let you come." Belphagor began to stroke him again, deciding to ignore the breach of etiquette in the familiar use of his name.

Vasily groaned with relief. "*Pozhaluista.*"

"Were you thinking about me fucking you while you lay here all night displaying your ass?"

"*Da, ser.*"

"Perhaps later I'll fuck you and not let you come." He bore down hard with his hand at the word *come* and made him do it.

Vasily groaned into his pillow, spilling hot firespirit spunk onto the bed. "*Spasibo, ser,*" he gasped when he was done.

"That's my sweet boy." Belphagor gazed down at him as Vasily rolled onto his back, the ruddy cheeks flushed with pleasure and the hazel eyes bright. The realization that Vasily was his overwhelmed him suddenly, and he kissed him, nipping softly at the full lips and tracing the line of his jaw with its brace of rugged red sideburns. "I love the way you look," he whispered, shocked at what had almost come out of his mouth. He'd caught himself in time from making a foolish romantic declaration. "I love that you belong to me." He couldn't seem to stop himself from flirting around the words that wanted out.

Vasily lay looking up at him, a mixture of something hopeful and frightened in his eyes. He knew what Belphagor was trying not to say. Belphagor shut himself up by kissing him roughly, tasting the smoky heat, his thumb brushing the spiked tip of the piercing he'd given him as he moved his hand down Vasily's throat. The little piece of metal sticking through the tender flesh said *I love you* as certainly as any words he could utter. Why did it scare him to death to say it out loud?

He rose up on his elbow, tracing the damp lips with his fingers, and opened his mouth, his heart beating against the walls of his chest like the wings of a caged bird and his throat dry. He was saved by a knock on the door.

"Belphagor? Are you awake?" The door opened without a pause for him to answer, and he turned with a glare to see Dmitri peering around it. Dmitri jerked his eyes away from Vasily's damp, exposed cock and back to Belphagor's face. "Sorry to bother you so early, but I've received some news on the underground. Lev's got breakfast on. Can you join us in the kitchen?"

"We'll be there in a moment."

Belphagor sighed when the door was closed. It seemed the fun was over. Time to find out what had been going on in Heaven.

CHAPTER TWELVE

The news wasn't what Belphagor had been expecting.

Dmitri sat across from him while Lev served them *blinchiki*. "I got a call last night that someone was looking for you."

"Seraphim don't generally make phone calls," Belphagor noted, spooning jam onto his little pancakes.

"Not a Seraph, a girl."

Belphagor paused with a fork full of pancake in the air. "A girl?"

"She told my contact her name was Anzhela." Dmitri smirked. "I suppose that's her clever idea of a code name."

"Anzhela." Belphagor set his fork down. "There was an Anzhela at The Cat."

"The Cat?"

"It's a whorehouse in Raqia. One of our female colleagues there was murdered by Duke Elyon's hired Cherub while Vasily was being framed for the principality's assassination."

Dmitri shook his head. "Hired Cherub? What an odd place Heaven is. I don't know how you can stand all the intrigue."

"Right. Because there's none at all in the world of Man." Belphagor laughed and ate his neglected bite of *blinchiki*. "So your contact is saying this Anzhela is here? She's fallen?"

"It appears so. I don't know how she even found the underground, but she knew enough to ask the right people about you that it got to me. She was in St. Petersburg, and I told my contact he could send her to Moscow to meet with you. She'll be arriving at Yaroslavsky Station this morning."

St. Petersburg. So they'd renamed Leningrad again. It had been Petrograd when he'd first fallen.

Belphagor advised Vasily to stay at the apartment. There was no telling whether Anzhela had been followed, or whether the Seraphim themselves might have arranged this meeting as a trap. Vasily was extremely unhappy following these orders.

Anzhela was easy enough to find. Dressed in a celestial style that amounted to early-twentieth-century Earth, she was particularly conspicuous, and the male attention she was getting from fellow passengers as she made her way from the train didn't help.

Belphagor approached her as if he were a relative, angrily rebuking the young men harassing her, and Anzhela gave him a grateful smile as he took her arm.

"What are you doing here?" he asked in angelic. "What's going on?"

"Masha sent me. The Ophanim have arrested Tabris."

"They what?" Belphagor came to a sudden halt on the platform. "What for?"

"They found Ouestucati's body in your room at The Brimstone while they were looking for your boy. They think he was involved in a conspiracy with her against the principality and killed her over it. Tabris showed up while they were there. She wanted to see her sister. The Ophanim accused her of being an accomplice and arrested her, and now the entire Demon District is under suspicion. Masha fears they'll clean out all the brothels and round up the street whores. The principality wants to make a public example of anyone involved in the attempt on his life."

"So he's not dead." That was one good thing at least.

Anzhela shook her head. "Only wounded. The new Supernal Lord Chancellor is the acting principality while he recovers."

"And who would that be?" Belphagor asked, despite being certain of the answer.

"Duke Elyon of the House of Arcadia."

Belphagor walked swiftly with the young demoness as they began to draw attention once more. He had to get her some less-conspicuous clothes. "Do you have someone to stay with? Do you know anyone here?"

Anzhela shook her head. "Masha used to live in Leningrad— St. Petersburg. She knew some demons there, but they've gone. I found a safe house and asked about you."

"And why in Heaven's name would she send you alone to the world of Man? Have you fallen before?"

"I haven't. But she didn't trust anyone else."

"But she trusted you."

Anzhela nodded. "I'm her granddaughter."

Belphagor appraised her. At least that explained why such a young girl was working in a cathouse. "How old are you, Anzhela?"

"What difference does that make?"

"Humor me."

"I'm fifteen."

Belphagor drew up sharply without realizing he'd done it until Anzhela looked at him oddly. He'd been fifteen the first time he'd fallen to the world of Man. "You shouldn't be here," he said sternly. "This is no place for a demoness your age." He turned her about toward Dmitri's. He couldn't leave her defenseless on the street.

"She could have Seraphim on her tail," Dmitri argued later in private after Belphagor had brought her back to the apartment and explained the situation.

"She's just a kid. What was I supposed to do?"

Dmitri sighed. "You're right. Of course you're right. But this is getting dangerous for everyone involved."

"I know. I'm sorry. I never meant to bring any of this to your door." From the foyer where they'd gone to talk, Belphagor glanced into the kitchen at the others having tea. "I'm going to take her back to Raqia and try to clear Vasily's name."

"And exactly how do you intend to do that?"

"With the help of an officer of the Supernal Army whom I may or may not have sodomized."

"Jesus, Bel." Dmitri laughed despite himself. "Have you ever left a single ass unfucked?"

Belphagor grinned. "Not if I can help it. Though to be fair, the sodomy in this case was of the oral variety."

Dmitri's expression grew serious again. "You know Vasily's in love with you."

"Of course I know that."

"And that you're in love with him."

Belphagor folded his arms without answering.

The Grigori smiled and shook his head. "Don't look so miserable, my friend. It's not the end of the worlds." He glanced at Lev and smiled. "I can't say I entirely get the two of you. He seems a bit . . . volatile. And I don't know if you've noticed, but he's deeply jealous of the attention you've been giving Lev."

Belphagor laughed. "No, it had totally escaped me. And what about you?"

"Me? I've been over you for a while." He grinned when Belphagor punched his arm. "I won't say it doesn't give me a twinge to see how well Lev gets along with you, but I'm quite secure in the knowledge that he loves me. I have no fear of him leaving me—even with his fantasies about getting his mind fucked out by you and your firespirit." Dmitri grinned. "I just don't know if your Vasily has that sense of security."

"It's part of what he needs from me," Belphagor said defensively. "Security would send him running in the opposite direction."

"Keep telling yourself that. No projection going on there."

"Dmitri—"

"All right. I won't say another word. Tell me what you need from me to get your plan rolling. Do you need an escort back to the portal?"

"I need to get Anzhela some earthly clothes, and I think we can travel unnoticed."

"I'll take care of it."

"And I need Vasily to stay here."

Dmitri stared at him. "Are you out of your mind?"

"He's wanted for treason. The minute I take him back there, he'll be executed in the public square. I can't protect him from that until I get to the bottom of things with this Elyon and expose him for the real traitor."

"So you expect me to babysit your half-feral firespirit."

"I'm sure you and Lev can find some way to keep him entertained."

"Belphagor. Do you really see that happening without you here? After last night, it was clear that you were right—he wasn't doing anything against his will and he very much enjoyed playing with Lev.

But he was enjoying the fact that he was doing it on your orders, just as he enjoyed kissing me because you wanted to watch him heat me up."

"Don't sell yourself short."

"Belphagor. Seriously."

Belphagor sighed. "I know, Dmitri. But you never know. He's certainly had fun without me. The Cat being a perfect case in point."

"The Cat? Isn't that a brothel full of women?" Dmitri's eyes widened at the significant lift of Belphagor's pierced eyebrow. "Wow." He glanced at Vasily, who was looking uncomfortable between the young demoness and Lev chatting across him. "He's blushing."

"Probably because Anzhela was there when he lost his girl-virginity to the whore who was murdered."

"*Bozhe moi.*"

"Apparently, it was quite the show. There was a sibling tag-team thing going on between the two who initiated him. They even tried to do me when I went in to question them."

Dmitri shook his head. "You lead the most interesting life."

Belphagor shrugged. Telling Vasily he was leaving him here was going to be the interesting part.

"What the hell do you mean, *you're leaving me here*?" Vasily didn't care who heard him in the other room. Everyone else obviously already knew what Belphagor had in mind for him but himself.

"I'm trying to save your life, *mal'chik.*"

"Well, who asked you to?"

"If you show up in Raqia, you'll be hanged, no questions asked."

"And what the hell do you think you can do about it?"

Belphagor was being infuriatingly calm. He'd made up his mind and was completely unfazed by Vasily's objections. "I have a contact in the supernal army that I'm going to try to exploit to expose Elyon."

"What contact?"

"The angel who helped us get out of the square that night."

Vasily pressed his lips together, trying not to think of the night they'd fled, of Sefira's lifeless body on the floor of the storeroom at the Conciliary. And then he remembered the handsome young angelic officer who had inexplicably helped Belphagor hustle him out of the crowd and who'd gotten rid of the Cherub so they could make their escape.

"You fucked him."

Belphagor said nothing. Which was everything. Vasily remembered the argument they'd been having right before he'd fallen ill—the clothes Belphagor had been wearing.

"Was that the angel who gave you the uniform?"

"No." No problem answering that question.

"Well, who the fuck was that, then?"

Belphagor stared at him silently, wearing his "wingcasting" face, hiding everything he wished to hide, giving nothing to Vasily unless he chose to for his own purposes, as if Vasily were nothing but another opponent at the tables.

"*Who the fuck was that?*" Vasily shouted. The chandelier actually rattled.

Belphagor folded his arms. "The clothes belonged to another angel. I took them while he was passed out in postcoital bliss. Phaleg was part of a group of angels who picked me up at the market. They were novelty shopping; he was hungry for domination. We found the situation mutually beneficial."

Vasily groaned involuntarily as if he'd been stabbed. He could feel the knife grinding and twisting in his gut without mercy. "When?" His voice was hoarse, and he cleared it angrily. "When did this happen with 'Phaleg' and all these other angels?"

Belphagor took a breath as if Vasily were an annoying child pestering him with questions. "While you were sitting in Elyon's cell."

The knife jerked to the side, disemboweling him. He even looked down to see if his intestines were spilling out onto the floor. "At Elyon's villa?"

"No, I told you. They picked me up in the market."

"I don't know what you're talking about. What the hell does that mean? Why would angels pick you up at the fucking market?"

Belphagor did his annoying little eyebrow raise, like he thought he was cute. "Why do angels pick *you* up at the fucking market?"

Vasily's face went hot, and his mouth dropped open. He thought he might burst into tears, except he wasn't sad. He was furious. And humiliated. "You were turning tricks? With angels? *Why?*"

Belphagor's eyes flashed with cruelty, only it wasn't in the least bit like the cruelty he usually reserved for Vasily. There was nothing erotic about it. "Because you gave yourself to me and then had a tantrum, traipsing off to sell your ass to a group of angel bastards who wanted to watch you fuck pussy. And then you let me fuck you again, promising you were mine, without telling me you'd given yourself to a demoness whore you'd never even met before—a gift you gave to the fucking angel bastard who's used you to damn near start a celestial revolution. Who, I might add, is currently working to cement his own power in Elysium while the Ophanim Supernal Guard are out for your fucking head. So don't lecture me about who I may or may not have fucked."

Vasily's head was throbbing, and his eyes hurt, as if his element were boiling him alive from the inside. It was like the fever he'd had when they'd first arrived, only he wasn't in a dreamy, peculiar fog, and Belphagor wasn't holding him, telling him everything would be okay. Belphagor was throwing oil on him while he burned.

"Go ahead and go to Raqia, Belphagor," he managed. "And then go straight to hell."

The frozen Russian countryside that had been magical and fantastic on the way to Moscow was a bleak, icy heap of ash. Belphagor tried to tell himself he'd done what was necessary. Vasily would never have stayed if he hadn't kicked him to the ground like a proverbial dog. He'd done what he had to that night in Elysium to find his boy, and he would not apologize for it. But twisting the truth to make Vasily believe he'd done it out of spite to indulge his own pleasure made his chest hurt as if he'd somehow kicked himself. Repeatedly. With cleats. He was finding it hard to breathe.

"Are you all right?" Anzhela sat across from him with a look of concern. A fifteen-year-old girl whose livelihood was now at stake was concerned for him.

"Just a bit worried about things in Raqia. I'm going to need to get a message to an officer in the Supernal Army as soon as we arrive. Do you suppose your grandmother can spare you for another day?"

"She's not expecting me back. She thought I might find my father's people and stay in the world of Man. I don't think she remembered how fast things change here. He was sixty when I was born. Nothing, of course, in terms of celestial years, but his family who'd fallen when he was a youth is long gone."

"And where is he? Still in Raqia?"

"He was killed in a duel when I was a girl. He quarreled with another patron over my mother."

"I'm sorry to hear that."

Anzhela shrugged. "I didn't really know him."

"But your mother still works at The Cat?"

"No. The other patron won her."

"Won her?"

"My father owned her, though he'd let her go back to Masha when she had me. This other demon challenged him, and when he won the duel, he won my mother. He has her working at another brothel in the Devil's Doorstep. That's why Masha saved up to buy The Cat, so she could hire free girls and no one could sell them off."

Belphagor wasn't quite sure what to say to this. "So . . . you're an apprentice by choice?"

"I'm not an apprentice. I'm Masha's successor. She's grooming me to be the madam of The Cat when she's gone. Or she was, anyway." Anzhela smiled at his confusion. "I keep an eye on the girls when Masha isn't around, and the patrons ignore me, thinking I'm just a servant—or they try to buy my services if they're drunk enough. And if I see any of them getting rough with a girl or taking liberties she hasn't agreed to, I fetch the muscle to deal with them."

"So I guess you were there when Duke Elyon and his boys patronized the place."

"Yes. They were mostly respectful. A bit sloppy with drink. Ouestucati and Tabris were entertaining them when Elyon said your boy was a virgin. Ouesti wanted to take him on for free."

Belphagor smiled at the idea of Vasily as a virgin. "He was also respectful, I hope."

Anzhela laughed. "Oh, indeed. He was all 'Yes, ma'am' and 'No, ma'am' and 'Thank you, ma'am.' I'd never seen the like. After she'd done him, she took him aside and said he was to ask for her whenever he wanted, and she'd give him her special price."

"What did he say to that?"

"He thanked her and said he'd had a lovely time, but he was in love with a demon, and he didn't expect to be back."

Belphagor felt one of those cleats grinding against his sternum again.

Anzhela put her hand on his knee. "He won't stay mad at you, I promise. I've seen a lot of demons who've claimed to be in love with one of our girls, and only once or twice I've seen one with a look like your Vasily had when he said it. That look'll forgive anything."

Belphagor smiled and squeezed her hand. "You're a sweet girl, Anzhela."

The demoness shook her head without smiling. "I'm not a sweet girl. I'm a very smart one whose business it is to read men. And to listen and observe when men are at their most unguarded, with their pricks out of their pockets and their pants around their ankles. I can tell you what Duke Elyon aims to do."

Belphagor was startled by her frankness and astuteness. "I see. What would that be?"

"He plans to make the principality afraid of his people so that he alone is trusted. He also plans to marry the little Grand Duchess Omeliea so Principality Helison will make him his heir."

"Omeliea?" Belphagor was amazed that she'd discerned this much. "But the child is barely five years old."

"She's four and a half," Anzhela confirmed. "He doesn't care. His plan requires patience. It's understood that as the oldest daughter, she's unofficially been promised to the principality's cousin, but both of them are children, so Duke Elyon need only bide his time and prove his loyalty to the House of Arkhangel'sk."

"And hope Queen Sefira doesn't bear Helison a son."

"She's given birth to three girls in a row," Anzhela reminded him. "It's believed she can't bring a boy child to term."

Belphagor shrugged. The same had been thought of queens before. The bride of Tsar Nikolai II had borne him four girls before at last presenting him with an heir. It was never wise to underestimate the caprice of nature.

When they'd reached Lake Baikal and ascended the Hell Staircase, Anzhela directed Belphagor to the portal through which she'd fallen. His room at The Brimstone was being carefully watched and wouldn't be safe to enter through.

"How did you know about this portal?"

They'd come up through a storm drain at the somewhat respectable end of Raqia, where there were more homes than houses of ill repute.

"Masha found it when she was a girl. After falling and living among Men for a while, she came back and used it to smuggle out girls in trouble."

So he had competition. Belphagor had been known to charge a pretty facet to smuggle demons through his portal. Of course, such demons were almost exclusively male, so perhaps it wasn't competition after all but filling a niche for a service he'd been failing to provide.

His first order of business was to obtain another glamour and then find a place to stay. Anzhela offered to get him the glamour at the market and told him she knew a place where he could rent a room. She was turning out to be a remarkable resource. When she returned with the glamour, he offered her extra facets for her help, but she frowned and pushed them back.

"You're the one who's helping us. Masha wouldn't be pleased if I took crystal from you for merely facilitating what we can't do ourselves. She only wanted me to let you know what had happened here and that it wasn't safe for your boy to come home. I'm sure she never expected you'd risk returning to set things right."

Belphagor swallowed the glamour and shuddered at the taste. It was stronger than the usual elixir. He'd asked her for one that would last indefinitely, which had required a prick of blood from his finger to create an antidote to restore him.

"To be fair, I'm trying to set things right for Vasily, but if I can prevent the rest of the Demon District from being caught up in Elyon's campaign against him, I'm happy to do it. Besides, as you said, Masha didn't expect you to risk returning either, so I feel a bit responsible for you."

Belphagor took a swig from the vodka chaser she'd brought him. "For what it's worth, despite the turn things have taken in Raqia, I think you're safer here at present. Things are in even greater turmoil in the world of Man." He glanced down at his hands, waiting for the tattoos to disappear into the illusion. His skin was beginning to feel clammy. "Where's this room? As soon as I get settled there, I'll have a message for you to deliver to my angel friend—a task for which I *will* compensate you."

Anzhela was regarding him from within the hood of the earthly coat Dmitri had acquired for her. "It's at The Cat."

"The Cat? But you said it was under surveillance. How could I come and go without attracting attention?" His stomach cramped, and Belphagor grabbed for the wall of the building beside them in the alley. His hands had smoothed. The glamour was doing its work. But his entire body felt awkward, like his organs were shifting. "What the hell did you give me?" His voice had an odd, high quality. Belphagor clutched his chest and nearly shrieked out loud.

Anzhela smiled, nodding at his transformation. "It's perfect."

"*Bozhe moi,*" he squealed. "You've turned me into a girl!"

"It was your size that gave me the idea." She tucked her arm into his as though they were girlfriends as she led him toward The Cat. "You have a very slender frame."

"You might have warned me."

"You would have said no."

He couldn't argue with that.

Belphagor stared at himself in the mirror in his room at The Cat. Anzhela had introduced him to Masha as "Beatrix," though it was obvious that Masha knew precisely who he was. Little business was being done at the moment, since most of their clientele had been spooked by the threat of supernal surveillance, but Beatrix was given a cover story anyway; Anzhela had offered her a place at The Cat because the girls on the street didn't feel safe.

He was alternately fascinated and repulsed by the glamour. It was extraordinarily disconcerting to be without his penis, even if it was only an illusion. Belphagor hurriedly slipped into the chemise and gown Anzhela had provided. At least he wasn't expected to wear a corset. But he'd had to shave his legs and underarms as was the fashion of the day for a working demoness.

Taking patrons or not, Beatrix would be expected to keep up appearances, and the gown was designed for the overheated air in the common parlor, sleeveless and off the shoulder, with a hem well above the ankles. He drew the line, however, at exposing his breasts.

Anzhela's glamour had given him muddy blue eyes and a fair complexion, with chestnut hair piled in loose curls upon his head—an angel's bastard if he'd ever seen one. The effect reminded him of someone he'd once known in the world of Man. Long ago. In his brief days there before the fall of tsarist Russia, he'd met a prince with a fetish for wearing women's clothing. With such a beautiful face, the prince's purely mundane glamour had been so convincing that Belphagor had never guessed his identity until he'd revealed it to him.

He hadn't thought of the prince in years. The events that had followed their brief acquaintance were so painful as to have almost obliterated his memory completely. Belphagor's fingertip lingered on his lips as he applied a bit of rouge to them. *Milyy mal'chik.* The words echoed over years piled like the bones of forgotten grand dukes and duchesses, princes and tsars—murdered Romanovs in a mass grave of old memories. Belphagor hadn't cared about any of them then but one prince who'd escaped.

Milyy mal'chik. Words from the lips of a Russian prince. Belphagor hadn't heard them spoken in almost a century. But he'd said them to Vasily just a few days ago, not even remembering where he'd heard them. *Sweet boy.* Anzhela believed Vasily would forgive Belphagor any transgression. Belphagor wasn't so sure. But he was prepared to do anything to earn that forgiveness.

It occurred to him he'd never sought forgiveness from anyone in his life. It wasn't the way he lived. He did what was necessary, shared what was mutually fulfilling, and moved on when what remained was not. Life in Raqia—and in the world of Man—had taught him that it was every demon for himself. He'd never expected to need someone else.

Anzhela returned from her errand to Elysium with good news. Phaleg had received her message, and he'd agreed to come to The Cat to meet with Beatrix that evening. Of the few patrons still frequenting the brothels, angelic officers were enjoying their position as privileged guests. No one dared turn them away for fear of being shut down for good. And if they didn't feel like paying the usual sum, no one dared argue with them either.

Phaleg arrived with the same friends Belphagor had serviced on their first encounter. He'd hoped to simply get Phaleg alone, but it seemed that if one of the group showed an interest in anything, the others had to have it too. It was a good thing Beatrix had gone to the trouble of shaving.

The quiet one was far more certain of himself in this environment, and Belphagor had to endure being felt up and fingered while satisfying the first two orally. The service was no different than what he'd offered as a male, but there was a striking difference in the degree of entitlement Beatrix's patrons displayed, and the dismissive and proprietary way in which they treated her body.

Phaleg at last persuaded his comrades that he wished to negotiate with Beatrix for a private performance. Having gotten their rocks off already, they reclined with their drinks and—with a string of shockingly matter-of-fact obscenities, describing Beatrix's attributes as significantly less than the sum of their parts—sent him off with his prize to a private compartment.

Belphagor closed the door on the corner closet and tucked his manhandled breasts back into his dress. "Charming friends you have."

Phaleg blushed. "Sorry. I wish I could say they were in rare form." He shook his head, marveling at Belphagor's appearance. "So that's really you?"

Belphagor lifted his brow, letting the light from the ensconced candle on the wall glint dangerously off metal. His tattoos were gone, of course, but the little steel bar at his eyebrow remained.

"Would you like to be certain it's really me?" Before Phaleg could respond, he'd twisted a blond curl at the angel's temple in his fist and spun him down to the floor on his knees. "Turn and face the door." His tone was no less menacing for the higher octave, and Phaleg shuffled about on his knees, instantly compliant. Not nearly as gratifying as Vasily's defiance.

Belphagor crouched behind him and unbuttoned the angel's pants, prying them, with his long woolen underwear, down to the floor. The angel's cock was already bobbing against the door.

"I thought about fucking you while you faced the window looking out over the Demon Market on our last encounter, but I was already spent. And alas, I find myself temporarily without my cock." He undressed the angel while he spoke, taking the jacket and shirt and tossing them aside.

Phaleg trembled. "What are you going to do?"

"*I'm* not going to do a thing. You're going to fuck yourself." Belphagor fished in the drawer of the little three-legged table in the corner of the closet and sifted through the artificial phalluses stashed there for the purpose. He chose one made of rose quartz marble and generously proportioned. Belphagor scooped some lard from the pot beneath the table and slathered it over the head.

Phaleg was still silently facing the door, having been given no further orders. He really was a natural.

Belphagor slid the base of the phallus across the floor behind the angel. "Give me your hand," he ordered.

The angel obeyed, and Belphagor wrapped the soft palm around the phallus, closing his fist around Phaleg's fingers and squeezing until Phaleg gave a little wince of discomfort. It was nothing compared to the discomfort he was about to experience.

Belphagor removed his hand and stood. "Now sit."

"Sit?" Phaleg's voice was slightly tremulous.

Belphagor enunciated carefully. "*Sit* on the item you are holding."

The angel lowered his bare ass to the tip of the cold, greased marble with an endearing little gasp, pressed against it but no farther.

"Sit *all* the way. I want your ass on the floor."

"On the . . . floor?"

"Don't be obtuse. It's unbecoming." Belphagor waited, arms folded, while the angel continued to hesitate. "You either do as you're told, or get up and leave. Do you want to leave?"

"No, *ser*."

"It's '*Nyet, ser*.'" He snapped his fingers sharply. "Sit."

Phaleg, startled, dropped his weight onto the phallus, and with a whimper and a groan, he forced himself open with the marble head and slid to the ground. It took him a bit of time, and Belphagor allowed it. A little patience was worth seeing the rosy marble slowly swallowed up by the even rosier asshole.

Once his cheeks were firmly pressed to the floor, Phaleg rested his head against the door, mouth open and panting.

Belphagor heard soft whispering. "What's that, boy? Speak up."

Phaleg's voice quavered. "I said, 'Heaven help me.'"

Belphagor chuckled. "Heaven can't help you now." He leaned a hip against the wall of the closet, feeling a phantom hard-on beneath his skirt. The angel's prick had flagged, but Belphagor's next words made it rally. "Do you want to come with that lovely hard prick up your angelic ass?"

"*Da, ser,*" Phaleg breathed, fingers poised near his cock.

"That's a good boy. You may touch yourself. But not until you've ridden that cock." He pushed the pot of lard up beside the angel with his toe. "Grease up if you need to."

Phaleg wisely took more lubricant, wrapping one slick hand around the base of the cock inside him, and moaning, he began to draw himself up and down the length.

"Such a good boy." Belphagor rubbed at his phantom erection. "Can you get close to Duke Elyon?"

Phaleg's thighs shuddered as he rode the marble rod faster. "Oh fuck," he whispered. "Please, *ser.*"

"Just answer my questions. Is Elyon at the palace?"

Phaleg nodded, moaning.

"And can you get close to him? Get yourself assigned to some detail that will put you at his side?"

"*Da, ser.*" Phaleg groaned as the friction he was generating warmed the grease and began to facilitate more rapid movement.

"Good boy. You may hold your pretty cock."

Phaleg obeyed without missing a beat of his cheeks against the floor.

"And you'll report to me on his actions and do as I ask of you?"

Phaleg lowered his head and closed his eyes in defeat, pausing his motions. "*Da, ser.* I'll do anything you ask of me."

"Of course you will. Now make yourself come."

Phaleg yanked on his slick cock desperately, groaning loudly as he fucked himself, his whole body trembling with pleasure, fear, and an edge of agony until he brought himself to climax, the pearly white spunk splattering his abs.

He wept softly as he quivered with little aftershocks, and Belphagor crouched and wrapped his arms around the angel.

"I've got you, boy. You did well."

"You said you wouldn't ask more of me," Phaleg moaned against him.

"I'm sorry." Belphagor kissed the top of his head. "I'm a bit of a bastard."

Phaleg laughed weakly, his body completely slack against Belphagor as if he were bereft of will and strength. "It really is you."

Phaleg emerged from the closet after they'd agreed on a plan to meet regularly at The Cat for his reports, Belphagor with his hair tangled and his gown missing its laces, and a bit of Phaleg's spunk smeared on his exposed breast for good measure. Phaleg's companions cheered and made him down the rest of their bottle of ale in celebration.

The formerly quiet angel belched inelegantly. "You got both ends?"

"And then some," Phaleg boasted with a wink at Belphagor. "She won't soon forget me. Will you, Beatrix?"

Belphagor rubbed his ass through his dress. "Not even if I wanted to, sweetmeat."

"See that you don't. I expect you to be available for me whenever I stop by."

"With open legs, sweetmeat."

"That's a good girl." Phaleg slapped him on the ass, and Belphagor raised his eyebrow. The angel had to know that was going to cost him. Phaleg's wink said he did.

When Belphagor went back to his room to clean up, he gargled with a bit of water and spat into his basin to get the taste of Phaleg's friends out of his mouth. Now that he knew how they treated women, having swallowed them felt vile.

Anzhela poked her head in to check on him. "I didn't intervene because I was sure you knew what you were doing, but I didn't care for those three. If business was normal right now, I'd bar them from The Cat."

"Phaleg's a good man," he said. "A bit between a rock and a hard place with his comrades, afraid to rock the boat. As for the other two, I quite agree with you. As soon as you and Masha have the freedom to run things as you see fit again, I'd ban them for life."

Anzhela studied him with curiosity. "You handled them quite well. I didn't realize you were a professional."

"I've never worn a dress to do it before." He grinned and straightened his sleeves on his shoulders. "But, yes, I've done a fair amount of entertaining in my time."

As she turned to leave him to his privacy, Anzhela raised her brows at the sight of the marble phallus he'd left beside his washbasin to dry. "I must say, you're very resourceful. Even when you don't have sleeves, you have something up your sleeve."

Belphagor grinned. "They don't call me the Prince of Tricks for nothing, sweetheart."

As he lay in bed that night, reviewing the encounter with Phaleg in his head, he realized he had no idea how to masturbate in this glamour. Did women masturbate? He thought they must. He was a bit too alarmed by his appearance to examine anything closely. He lay in the dark, idly fingering the periphery of the borrowed sex, and forgot himself after a bit, picturing Phaleg taking that stiff marble prick as his first penetration.

The angel was probably lying in his own bed reliving it—and probably more than a bit tender in his nether region. Belphagor imagined Phaleg unavoidably reminded of what he'd allowed Belphagor to make him do, how he'd be moving gingerly for days and how every ache would probably make him hard as he pictured himself being humiliated by a demon in a dress. How many times might Phaleg come as he pleasured himself at the memory? Belphagor would possess him through that vulnerable, ecstatic moment for the rest of his life.

He felt an unexpected rush of blood to his borrowed parts, and his eyes opened in surprise as his glamoured body shook with pleasure that seemed to involve all of his cells, though it was clearly concentrated at the apex of his sex. Then it seemed as if every cell in his body ejaculated at once, and a gush of fluid shot out between his legs. He had to clamp his hand over his mouth to stifle a loud moan.

Belphagor moved over on the bed when the sensation had passed, staring at the puddle he'd left. *Holy shit.* No one had told him anything about this. He found himself giggling as he rolled over toward the wall and sighed in satisfaction.

And then he sighed with a distinct lack of satisfaction at the absence of Vasily to hold. Phaleg's unquestioning obedience had been thrilling, but it wasn't the same as his angry, sweet, beloved boy.

CHAPTER THIRTEEN

Vasily stood at the window of the guest room watching the sullen sun rise in a gray Moscow sky. He wore his *tapochki* and the warm dressing gown Belphagor had bought him, one of several garments in the shopping bag that he hadn't gotten to before Belphagor left. It was soft and thick, and maybe had been meant with someone cooler than himself in mind, but it had been purchased—or purloined—with love.

He refused to believe Belphagor didn't love him. The bastard might want him to believe it, might never admit it, might have stabbed him in the gut and kicked the knife for good measure . . .

Vasily touched his fingers to the jewelry fixed to the side of his neck to reassure himself. Belphagor couldn't have said those hateful things and meant them—not when he'd given him this at the same time. *"Will you keep the gift? Will you be my sweet boy always?"* This piece of metal in his flesh said Belphagor had been thinking far into his future, with Vasily in it.

That he'd done this after going off and fucking a whole pile of angels to spite Vasily for defying him—and that he'd done it knowing Vasily was being held against his will by Duke Elyon at the time—was hard for him to reconcile.

No, it wasn't hard to reconcile. It was fucking unforgiveable. The angry hiss of breath through his teeth melted the frost on the outside of the window. Belphagor hadn't just gone out and fucked someone else. He'd fucked angels, because Vasily had let angels buy him. And he'd done it for facets in some kind of twisted mockery of Vasily, as if to say, *What, this? This delicious angel cock jammed down my throat? This doesn't count, because I'm getting paid, same as you.*

Never mind that Vasily had nothing but what he earned from his livelihood unless he let Belphagor keep him like a pampered whore. Belphagor claimed Vasily didn't belong to him that way, yet he begrudged him his own income and his autonomy.

Not that autonomy was what he wanted, exactly. He wanted to belong to Belphagor, and he didn't care if that meant Belphagor could tell him what to do or what to wear or whom to fuck. He just wanted it to mean that Belphagor was *his*. He wanted Belphagor to desire him and not some skinny, pretty thing like Lev. And not some golden-haired angel. *Phaleg.* Belphagor had said that name in a way that meant he was more than a revenge fuck.

His hand closed over the spiked piercing. He ought to tear it from his skin and toss it out the window into the fucking snow. He toyed with one of the spikes. They screwed on. He could twist it off and do it.

The thought of the empty holes it would leave in his neck made his gut ache like another turn of the knife that wouldn't go away.

"Fuck you, Belphagor," he growled, but his hand dropped from the jewelry.

Phaleg returned to The Cat the following night. Thankfully, he came alone. Since the place was currently empty, Belphagor took him back to his room. The slight wince as Phaleg sat on the bed put a smile on Belphagor's face.

Phaleg shook his head while Belphagor perched sideways on the chair at the vanity, his chin on his arms over the chair back. "I can't get over this— What did you call it? Your disguise?"

"A glamour. It's a little alarming, to tell you the truth."

"How long does it last?"

"This one is potent. I have to take an antidote to return myself to my true form." Belphagor cleared his throat. "So I take it you have something to report?"

"Yes, sorry. Of course." Phaleg looked embarrassed, as if he'd been expecting that humiliation and ejaculation were now a given part of their interactions, a prelude to any information he divulged.

Belphagor supposed he couldn't blame him for the assumption. "Duke Elyon, as you may know, is presently residing at the Winter Palace while the principality recuperates. I managed to get myself assigned to the principality's protective detail. Not directly reporting to Elyon but possibly closer to him than those who are, given his constant communications with Principality Helison."

Belphagor nodded thoughtfully. "That may prove more advantageous. Will you have any access to the principality himself? Out of Elyon's presence?"

"I'm sure I could arrange it from time to time. I don't want to draw attention to myself by making any additional requests. If you wouldn't mind, I'd like to know what your plan is. I will not be a party to treason."

This last declaration seemed a bit contrived. Phaleg had already seen that Belphagor's intentions weren't treasonous. And it was clear that Elyon's and the Union of Liberation's were. It seemed Phaleg's feelings—or his ego—had been wounded by the impersonal tone of their meeting.

Belphagor regarded him a moment, unsmiling. "What treason do you imagine I might involve you in, Phaleg?"

"Well . . ." The angel reddened. "If you're seeking access to privileged communications between the principality and his staff . . ." His voice trailed off under Belphagor's steely gaze.

"Privileged? You come to me, a demon who has debased you in the most thorough manner possible, with concerns about privilege? I would venture to say, Lieutenant Phaleg, that in the grossest technical terms, you have already committed treason by consorting with a suspected assassin. And it has been *my* privilege to extract whatever promises of aid from you that I desire, merely by offering or withholding sexual favors that cater to your perversion, of which you are clearly ashamed."

The color drained from Phaleg's face, and he swallowed audibly.

"I would also venture to say that if I were the sort to wish harm to the principality, and you were fully aware of it, you would still do precisely as I bid you, just for a chance to be defiled once more. Is that not fair to say?"

Phaleg looked as if he might be sick if Belphagor continued. Sweat dotted his pale complexion.

"I asked you a question, boy. Perhaps you'd do better to answer on your knees."

Phaleg slid into a kneeling position on the floor before the bed, all too eager to follow direction. "*Da, ser,*" he answered miserably.

"*Da, ser.*" Belphagor shook his head. "While I must admit that your blind, groveling compliance is immensely arousing, it seems somewhat self-serving at the same time. You're using me as an excuse to commit what Men in the terrestrial sphere would call 'sin.' 'Transgression,' perhaps, might be a term you relate to. You've abdicated all responsibility for your actions with the most terrestrial—and pathetic—of excuses: the devil made me do it."

Phaleg shook his head, patches of red now marring the sickly pale Belphagor had reduced him to. "No, sir."

"*Nyet, ser,*" Belphagor instructed.

"*Nyet, ser.* I take full responsibility for my actions."

"I'm pleased to hear it." Belphagor reached between his thighs to adjust a cock that wasn't there and made a sound of exasperation. "If I had access to my cock at this moment, Lieutenant Phaleg, rest assured, you would be speared upon it, by one end or the other."

Phaleg let out a small moan.

"You've contradicted yourself quite a bit, Phaleg. Answer me truthfully. Do you wish to do my bidding, no matter how terrible, for the promise of how I might use you, or are you a man of principal, loyal to the supernal crown over the urges of your own cock?"

Phaleg opened his mouth, his face twisting with conflict. "I . . . Please . . ."

Belphagor took a coarse horsehair brush from the cosmetics tray on the vanity and struck the back of the chair with a loud clap. "Answer me!"

"I don't know!" Phaleg gasped, clutching his knees. "Both!"

Belphagor brushed the bristles over his cheek. "Pray tell, boy, how can that be?"

Phaleg was shaking with anxiety. "Because I don't believe you'll bid me to harm the principality."

"But I might."

Tears spilled over Phaleg's cheeks. "Heaven help me," he whispered once more, as if imploring the earthly god. "Please don't."

Belphagor smiled. "There, now. Honesty. That wasn't so hard, was it? Come." He snapped his fingers, and Phaleg scrambled to the side of the chair. Belphagor lifted Phaleg's chin. "You trust me."

"*Da, ser*," he gasped.

"But only to a degree. That's all right. You're sick with conflict because you don't know what you can be made to do. You fear you won't be able to resist me if I turn on you, that you'll be willing to betray everything you believe if only to know what it is to be thoroughly owned by a demon. Men might call you possessed."

Phaleg nodded, weeping.

Belphagor stroked the damp cheek. "I promise you I will never ask anything of you that you cannot give without harming yourself. The gift of your obedience means a great deal to me. I have no wish to break such a good and beautiful boy."

Phaleg choked back a sob and melted against Belphagor, head against his thigh. "I don't know how you've done this to me," he said mournfully.

Belphagor brushed the golden hair away from the damp eyes and kissed the angel's temple. "That's all right, dear boy. No one ever does."

Phaleg reported to him on a somewhat irregular basis. It would have begun to seem suspicious had he spent every evening in Beatrix's company, and his evenings, at any rate, were not always free.

Belphagor, in the meantime, was growing weary of being Beatrix, but the glamour had come dearly, and there was no sense in squandering it and taking the antidote simply because he was tired of his part. There was also the danger of being seen and reported in his true form. He could neither afford to be apprehended nor to jeopardize Masha and Anzhela's livelihood. Masha had agreed to harbor him only with Anzhela's persuasion.

Once or twice, Beatrix was asked for by angelic patrons who had heard of her skills from Phaleg's companions. Belphagor had to attend them to keep up appearances, but he insisted on providing only manual and oral pleasure.

It had been longer than he could remember since he'd been a virgin, and he wasn't about to surrender Beatrix's virtue, artificial construct though it might be, to a group of entitled angel punks. As a consequence, Beatrix began to develop a reputation as a superb cocktease, and Belphagor was offered increasing sums of facets to put out.

Beatrix's fame, whether for good or ill, drew Duke Elyon himself to The Cat. On a rare occasion of absence from the principality's side, Elyon brought his entourage to the Demon District and requested Beatrix's attentions.

The group was smartly dressed—not in uniform this time, but in the latest fashion of the day, which included coattails and top hats. A party, apparently, was being thrown in the Left Bank in Elyon's honor. Among the revelers was Phaleg, similarly attired. Belphagor suffered a pang of memory at his unexpected likeness to a long-dead Russian prince.

The duke had no intention of staying at The Cat, but intrigued by Beatrix, he'd come to request her attendance at his villa affair. After discussion with Masha and Anzhela, Belphagor chose to go against their advice. The option of refusing the wishes of Duke Elyon, at any rate, was not a wise one. Belphagor had to trust that Phaleg would have his back—so to speak.

He'd never required the protection of another man before. At least not since he'd grown to manhood in a Russian prison and learned to fight. He was certain he retained his quickness and cunning in that area even as Beatrix, but his physical strength was noticeably lessened by the glamour. Nature, he decided, had dealt women a rather shit deal in that department.

Belphagor opted to play coy with Elyon, enjoying his banquet and soaking up the flattery he was laying on thick, but keeping him at arm's length, all the while pumping him for information.

"Tell me, Your Grace," he asked over the trifle after dinner. "Is it true you threw yourself on His Supernal Majesty? I heard you took the knife from that wild firespirit demon after he'd wounded the principality, that he kept slashing at you while you protected his intended target."

Elyon raised his brow. "The tale seems to be growing a life of its own, but it was I who saw the brute go in for the kill and defended His Supernal Majesty."

At the other end of the table, Phaleg choked on a bit of trifle. So Elyon was now taking credit for Vasily's initial capture, though it had been Phaleg who'd stepped in. Belphagor had hoped the rumor he'd invented on the spot would coax the duke to brag about his part, though he hadn't expected him to take the bait so eagerly.

Duke Elyon leaned toward Belphagor and rolled up his sleeve. "Though the brute did manage to slash my arm before I apprehended him." He held out his forearm to show off the supposed stripes he'd earned. They were ridiculously shallow marks he'd obviously given himself.

Belphagor stroked his soft hand over the wounds as if they were impressive. "Goodness. The principality owes you his life. But what happened to the assassin?"

Elyon left his arm where it was for Beatrix to fawn over. "Surely you've heard all the details, living in Raqia."

"We've heard so many things, I don't know what to believe. Poor Sefira dead by his hand and Tabris in irons." Belphagor shook his head and drew his hand back into his lap. "There can't be any truth that they were involved. We were very close, and I would have known if they were mixed up in anything untoward. The Cat is loyal to the House of Arkhangel'sk. And Arcadia, of course."

"Odd that you were so close and yet I never saw you at The Cat before tonight."

"I was in the Southern Lands recuperating from a spell of poor health until recently. I came back when I heard the news." In addition to the balmy beaches at the southern tip of Heaven, the Southern Lands was a euphemism for the world of Man. Belphagor left it open to interpretation as to which he meant.

"Nothing serious, I hope?" Elyon chose to ignore the tantalizing bit of information, or perhaps had never heard the term.

Belphagor leaned close to him and whispered loudly, "An ailment of the trade. Though you sweet angelic types have exceptional hygiene, our demonic patrons sometimes bring back unwanted travelers from jaunts in the terrestrial sphere."

The duke looked puzzled. "Travelers?"

Belphagor raised his voice to a stage whisper. "Bugs." The rest of the table burst into bawdy laughter. "That's why I've been taking some precautions lately, to make sure everything's cleared up."

Elyon's face went from blank with confusion to pink with embarrassment as he finally caught on. He moved less than subtly toward the other side of his chair.

"Nothing wrong with my pipes and lungs, of course." Belphagor stuck out his tongue and opened wide as if to show the duke, earning more laughter from the rest of the table. "You can ask anyone here. Most of them have had the pleasure. Some deeper than others." He winked at Phaleg, who tried to busy himself with his trifle, but his companions slapped him on the back and made vulgar comments about the length of his cock and Belphagor's lack of a gag reflex.

"Don't worry, Your Grace." One of them lifted his tankard of mead. "We've given her plenty of protein for her health. Everything's clean as a whistle all the way down."

When they'd retired to the parlor, the rowdier angels began to expect their due from Beatrix, and Phaleg came to Belphagor's rescue, suggesting they make a game of it, letting Beatrix choose the winner of a round of "Yea or Nay."

The idea of a game was inspired, but Belphagor had another in mind. "Have any of you ever played wingcasting?"

Elyon had, of course, along with the toughs he'd brought to The Brimstone. Phaleg and his companions, along with several others, pleaded ignorance. Belphagor was pleased to enlighten them.

"We can play strip wingcasting to make it easier," he offered. "No facets will have to change hands." The angels who'd played, assuming Beatrix would be easy to beat, were all for this idea, and the others were happy to go along either way.

For the first few hands, Belphagor played sloppily, drinking a gin fizz and feigning tipsiness. By the time his opponents had gotten the hang of things, he was in his petticoat and chemise, with one stocking off and the other fallen at his ankle with the loss of both garters.

And then he began to play in earnest, and angels were losing their shirts quite literally.

Phaleg he plundered with particular enthusiasm, reducing him to long underwear and boots before the end of the fourth hand. Those who lost everything were forced to endure Beatrix's handjobs while the game continued. No one complained. Phaleg was first among them. Belphagor proposed a chance for the defeated to win back pieces of clothing with each hand the others played if they could endure manual stimulation without reaching completion. A slight smile tugged at the corner of Phaleg's mouth as he sat on a cushion beside Belphagor and submitted to the challenge.

Nearly all the others succumbed swiftly and without complaint while Phaleg began to win back clothing piece by piece. Belphagor was pleased that the angel had made such progress with so little training.

Angels panted and groaned, spurting into Belphagor's hands, while Elyon and Belphagor, along with two other diehards, played on mostly clothed. Belphagor abandoned Phaleg's cock every other hand, making him wait while he finished off two others in between playing his cards, and then started again on him. The angel was dripping sweat despite the cold air seeping through the windowpanes, but he earned back everything except his shirt and jacket before long.

Belphagor defeated the two players flanking Elyon and welcomed them to his sides, giving them extra attention with his mouth periodically as a reward for having lasted so long at the game—and of course resulting in their total, blissful defeat. Now it was Belphagor and Elyon.

Masturbating Phaleg slowly while the angel groaned beside him, Belphagor smiled at Elyon, who sat stroking himself as he played, having lost all but his underwear. The duke was determined to win but distracted by his own efforts and by his fascination with Phaleg's stamina. At last he made a fatal error and accepted his defeat, dropping his drawers and standing up to come around the table to Belphagor's side.

Belphagor reached his hand up with a smile, but Elyon shook his head.

"I think I've earned a turn in that creamy throat of yours. I am, after all, the guest of honor."

Belphagor struggled to keep the smile on his face and not resort to violence with the angel who'd taken his boy and still threatened his life. "Of course, Your Grace. As soon as Phaleg finishes. Or perhaps the two of you would like to go head-to-head in competition to see who breaks first. The winner gets to finish in my creamy throat."

The duke frowned, but Belphagor had appealed to his ego, and he clearly believed poor Phaleg, red and stiff, couldn't last much longer.

The other angels gathered around with their after-dinner drinks and cigars—habits normally reserved for the peasant class but all the rage currently among the Left Bank ton—to watch the jerk-off.

Standing on either side of him, Elyon and Phaleg groaned with pleasure as Belphagor worked them, grinning at one another periodically as each came close to coming and then regained control. Belphagor steeled himself to add a bit of tongue to the mix in order to avoid a jealous tantrum when the duke lost. He'd get his fair share of pleasure before he was done, though it was pleasure he didn't deserve.

Sliding to the edge of his seat, Belphagor dipped his head and sucked Phaleg's smooth balls into his mouth in turn. Phaleg moaned and shook, nearly at his limit. He tormented the angel a bit longer and then turned to the duke. As his tongue drew in one downy globe and he closed his lips around it, Duke Elyon cried out and grabbed Belphagor by the shoulder in surprise as he spent himself against Belphagor's cheek.

When the duke had finished, he shook Phaleg's hand and stepped aside gallantly. "You've earned it," he said with rueful admiration.

Phaleg straddled the chair and slid himself gratefully into Belphagor's mouth and began to thrust vigorously, though, to his credit, he glanced at Belphagor and waited for the discreet nod of permission before he let loose with a shout of relief and gave it all to him.

Belphagor wiped his mouth with the back of his hand and grinned after Phaleg stumbled a bit weakly and pulled out. "Well, boys," he said gazing up at Phaleg, "I have to say the pleasure has been all mine." Sucking off Phaleg after his quiet obedience in plain view of all his comrades had been more than worth the unpleasant bit of contact with the duke.

The duke was oblivious, already tucking himself away and pulling on his pants. "Surely you're not leaving so early, Beatrix? Come lie by the fire with us and get warmed up before you have to face that dreadful cold." He reclined on a luxurious pile of cushions near the hearth as he spoke, patting one next to him.

Belphagor bit his lip coquettishly. "It's awfully late, but that does look tempting." He rose and went to the hearth, curling up beside Elyon, and held a hand out to Phaleg and the angels who'd lasted longest. "Come on, cuddle up. If any of you boys want to play with each other a bit, I don't mind at all. I know how young men's tastes run, and I can see some of you are prepared to go again already, though you've quite worn me out."

Several of the angels took the offer, drawing up more cushions and gathering around in pairs and threesomes. Those who were bored with the direction the party had taken thanked the duke for his hospitality, congratulated him on his success, and let themselves out.

Belphagor watched with pleasure as angels stroked and sucked each other, happy to see Phaleg bury his head in a young angel's lap and enjoy what a few weeks ago would have mortified him. With Duke Elyon's obvious preference for the company of men, the atmosphere was far more open and relaxed than it had been on that first evening with Phaleg's friends—who had been the first to leave tonight.

"You're everything they say you are," Elyon murmured, sleepy with contentment. "And more."

"You flatter me, Your Grace. I'm only making due with the assets I have available to me while I'm on the mend."

"I'd be hard-pressed to find another whore as enthusiastic about cock as you obviously are, my dear." Elyon yawned and closed his eyes with one arm draped around him. "Consider my supernal account to be at your disposal as compensation for your excellent entertainment. Whatever you want, it's yours."

Belphagor hesitated, stroking the duke's arm. "There is one thing, but I'm afraid you'll be angry if I ask."

"Nonsense. What could you possibly ask for that would anger me?"

"It's my friend, Tabi. She's no anarchist, I swear to you. Even if Sefira got mixed up in something, Tabris doesn't have a devious bone in her body."

Elyon opened his eyes and narrowed them at him. "Just what is it you're asking?"

"Couldn't you see fit to spare her?"

Elyon's arm tightened around him. "She was there in the assassin's room with the body. She was no innocent bystander."

"Forgive me, sir, but she was! You saw that firespirit with her and Sefira yourself. Did it seem they'd ever met him before that night?"

Elyon considered. "I suppose not. But how would you know about that? You weren't at The Cat."

"It's all the talk there. No one can believe that sweet brute is a killer. But the madam told me how Tabi ran off in tears when a message came that Sefira's body was at The Brimstone. She only wanted to see her sister one more time."

"Sister?"

"Tabi is Sefi's baby sister, and she only came to work at The Cat because she had nowhere to go when their mother passed. Please, Your Grace. Have a heart and advise the principality to set her free. She doesn't know anything." Belphagor crossed his bosom-covered heart. "I swear on my life."

The duke propped himself up on one elbow and gave Belphagor a piercing stare. "It will be on your life if I find you're lying." He tucked his hand into Belphagor's bodice and stroked one pert breast with a sigh, kneading the nipple. "Though I confess I've had my suspicions that your friend was simply a victim of circumstance. She's done nothing but cry since they brought her in."

"I'd be so grateful, Your Grace." Belphagor leaned into his touch. "I can promise you the best fuck of your life as soon as I'm feeling myself."

Elyon leered. "I will take you up on that, dear Beatrix. You suck cock better than most of the rentboys I've known. I'm eager to find out if you take it up the ass half as well."

Belphagor smiled, burying the urge to strangle Elyon where he lay, and wiggled his feminine posterior provocatively. "It's my specialty, Your Grace. You'll think you're fucking a boy."

Phaleg walked Belphagor back to The Cat in the early hours before dawn, when the duke had gotten up to prepare for his morning meeting with the principality.

"I hate this." Belphagor glared at his escort as they crossed the bridge. "I hate that women need this. We're all bastards, the lot of us."

Phaleg feigned offense. "I hardly think I'm a bastard, dear Beatrix, as I am gallantly escorting you to your house of ill repute to protect your dubious virtue."

"And it's much appreciated, I'm sure, good sir." Belphagor gave him a mock curtsy. He tightened his grip on Phaleg's arm. "I think it's only fair to warn you, however, that your ass is going to pay for that 'dear Beatrix' and for your aspersions against her virtue. Though you were an exceptionally good boy this evening." He could sense Phaleg blushing beside him in the dark. "Does that bother you? To be called a boy?"

"Not . . . entirely." Phaleg was quiet for a moment. "You call your demon your boy."

Belphagor glanced up at the angel warily. "Are you jealous of him?"

"I'm only trying to understand what . . ." Phaleg's voice trailed off as if he was struggling to vocalize his thoughts.

"What you are to me?" They'd arrived at The Cat, and Belphagor stopped and turned to face him. "You are a source of great pleasure and pride."

"And nothing more?"

Belphagor sighed. "I won't deny that I feel affection for you. More than affection," he amended as the angel's face fell. "You are very dear to me. We've shared something extremely intimate that I would venture to say you will never share with anyone else. Not quite as you have with me. I will always own your fall from angelic grace and be the author of your surrender to your true desires. But you're an angel, and I'm a demon. There can never be anything more than a play of power between us. It's the nature of the eternal music of the spheres."

Phaleg nodded, silent.

"As you said," Belphagor added gently, "Vasily is my boy. He's . . . I'm . . ." It was his turn to grasp for words. Except it wasn't words that were failing him. He was failing the words. "I love him," he admitted at last, slightly horrified and immensely relieved at the same time to have finally said it.

Unexpectedly, Phaleg looked relieved as well. "I'm glad you said so. I think it makes it easier to understand what's between us, knowing that. To answer your question, no, I'm not jealous—but I am envious. Your demon is a very lucky . . . boy."

Belphagor shook his head. "*I'm* lucky. In fact, I'll be lucky if he'll still have me after the lies I told him when I left him." He sighed and shrugged deeper into his fur-lined coat in a disturbingly feminine gesture, as if his body was becoming used to being in this illusory form. "I'm a complete bastard."

Phaleg smiled. "I have a suspicion that may be what makes you so irresistible."

An inelegant snort escaped him as he reached for the door. "Well, that goes without saying."

When Phaleg had taken his leave with a gentlemanly bow and a kiss of Belphagor's hand, Belphagor went up to bed, exhausted from the evening's escapades.

He'd forgotten the promise he'd extracted from Duke Elyon and woke disoriented at the loud knock on his door some hours later, unable to recall for a few moments how he'd gotten in this bed, and that he was Beatrix. The piss that splattered around the chamber pot as he stood over it sans penis brought it all back to him.

Someone pounded on the door once more. "Beatrix, are you awake?" It was Anzhela, sounding rather anxious.

Belphagor pulled on his dressing gown and hurried to turn the key in the lock and let her in. "What is it? Has something happened?"

"It's Tabris," she said, holding the door wide for him as if ushering him out. "She showed up outside in the snow without a coat and in her bare feet. I think she'd walked all the way from Elysium. She won't speak."

Belphagor hurried with her to Masha's rooms, where Tabris sat motionless beside the madam except for a slight tremble that seemed to possess her uncontrollably. Her eyes were unfocused, and she paid no attention to their entrance.

"Tabris." Belphagor approached her. "Are you all right?" It was an idiotic question given her nearly catatonic state.

"She hasn't said a word." Masha set a hand lightly on Tabris's shoulder but pulled it quickly back when Tabris arched and screamed as if she'd burned her. Despite the odd reaction, Tabris continued to stare blankly.

Belphagor crouched in front of her. "Tabris, it's Belphagor. I know I don't look myself. I've taken a glamour. I'm the one who found Ouestucati. Vasily and I found her. You remember?"

"Ouestucati," Tabris moaned, and her staring eyes began to leak. Belphagor put a hand out toward her knee, and she recoiled.

"Are you in pain?" he asked. "Did someone hurt you?"

"Opha—" Her breath drew in sharply, and her voice rose in pitch with the second syllable before she paused and gasped out almost inaudibly, "—nim."

"The Ophanim." He cast a troubled glance at Masha. "I've been told their touch is very unpleasant, like fire ants crawling over the skin."

Masha nodded. "We saw them take her away when she was arrested at The Brimstone. She screamed without cease as they led her to the bridge."

Tabris's tremor began to intensify as tears poured silently down her cheeks.

"Perhaps we should put her to bed and let her get some rest," Belphagor suggested.

Masha nodded and coaxed Tabris to lie down in the high, canopied featherbed that was far more luxurious than any the girls had. They couldn't get her to move to turn down the covers, so Belphagor picked up a knitted blanket from the foot of the bed and laid it over her without touching. The three of them stepped into the hallway, and Masha closed the door.

"She wouldn't let me examine her," said Masha. "We warmed up her feet as best as we could while she shrieked at any contact. I don't see any signs of physical damage—as well as I can check without touching her—but she's obviously been traumatized."

"I suspect they tortured her," said Belphagor quietly. "If their touch is as unpleasant as I've heard reported, they wouldn't have had to do much but maintain continual contact while they interrogated her. I've heard of demons who've gone mad from the same."

Masha shook her head angrily. "They had no right. She's done nothing. Though I can't understand why they suddenly decided to let her go. No one even knows how she got here."

"I got her released," said Belphagor. Both Masha and Anzhela gaped at him. "I didn't think he'd do it so quickly—I wasn't even sure he'd do it at all, honestly—but I managed to extract a favor from Duke Elyon."

Unexpectedly, Masha threw her plump arms around him and gave him a startlingly strong hug. "I don't know how to thank you." She wiped at her eyes when she released him, and Anzhela produced a handkerchief for her, which she took gratefully. "You didn't have to do that for her."

"On the contrary," he objected. "I owed it to her. She and Ouestucati would never have been at that party if it weren't for me."

"My girls make their own decisions. They chose to go with you. You couldn't have known how it would turn out."

"I underestimated the duke." He didn't like to admit it. He'd taken the angel for a bit of a dandy, letting Elyon's persona fool him into thinking he was relatively harmless. It was a mistake that would have wiped him out at the wingcasting table. Instead, it had cost a woman her life, and he wasn't about to let himself off the hook for it. "I'm very glad to have been able to do what little I could for Tabris. I wish I could have done it sooner."

"We'll take care of her," said Anzhela. "She's one of ours."

Masha nodded. "She'll have a home here as long as The Cat stands." Her forehead wrinkled with worry. "Whether she can work again or not."

"I'm glad to hear it. I'd also like to contribute to her care. When I have access to my funds at The Brimstone, I'll have ample facets to get her anything she needs."

Masha studied him. "Do you really think you can bring this Elyon down and exonerate the Fallen in the attack on the principality?" She obviously hadn't expected much of him before and was now reevaluating his potential value to her in light of Tabris's release.

"I not only think it, I'll do it." Securing the ties on his dressing gown as he spoke, he pulled them tight with a decisive yank. "There isn't a demon or angel in the Heavens who can best me when I've marked him, and Elyon tried to take my boy from me. He is marked."

He didn't add that he had no idea *how* he was going to do it. He never did at the start of a game, but inspiration would strike. Or perhaps it *had* struck . . . in the person of Phaleg. Belphagor had promised he wouldn't ask him to commit treason. But that didn't mean he wouldn't ask him to pretend to commit treason.

CHAPTER FOURTEEN

Vasily was going mad cooped up in the apartment with Lev and Dmitri. Things had managed not to be too awkward between them after the intimacy they'd shared. There was a certain point at which intimacy with a stranger dissolved the barrier of "stranger" itself through the sheer knowledge of one another's most private parts—in every sense of the term. But they had nothing in common. Belphagor had been the lubricant between them, easing the bits that didn't fit precisely; without him, Lev and Dmitri, to put it plainly, bored Vasily.

Lev surprised him, however, by inviting him one evening to the *kinoteatr*. This was a term Vasily had never heard before. The *theater* part of the word, he grasped, but "kino" meant nothing to him. Lev wanted to be mysterious about it.

"It's like television," he said. "But only in the way that a political pamphlet is like a book."

Vasily had no idea what Lev meant by this. He'd never read a book. Perhaps there was something in the collective sum of pages bound together he didn't know about. But he'd found television to be the most amazing invention he'd seen yet in the world of Man. Given his boredom, he was happy enough to get out of the house, so he agreed.

The damp, chilly air was a welcome change from the apartment. He'd never done well with being indoors for too long at a time. He'd slept in alleyways under the stars and the elements for most of his life until Belphagor had given him a home.

Vasily ignored the little jab of the knife.

Despite the abysmal temperature, he was more than adequately dressed in the garments Belphagor had gotten for him. He'd worn the black turtleneck with his new coat, an ivory scarf wrapped around his neck because it was there, and a pair of dark-gray pants that had extra pockets down the sides as if for holding tools. He'd forgone the knitted gloves.

"Do you think he's coming back?" The question escaped his mouth as he trudged through the snow beside Lev. He hadn't intended to say it aloud.

Lev glanced up at him from under a thick fur hat. "Of course he's coming back. He can't live without you." He sounded a bit surprised.

"Belphagor did just fine living without me when I was locked in Duke Elyon's ice box for two days." He growled the words, thinking of all the sex Belphagor had managed to have—with *angels*—the instant he'd been free of Vasily.

Had he been biding his time all this past year, being celibate out of his stubborn insistence that Vasily was too young for him, or had he simply been finding ways to go out and fuck whomever he pleased the entire while? Despite the cold biting at Vasily's cheeks, they felt hot.

"To hear him tell it," said Lev, "he spent the whole forty-eight hours without sleep, doing everything he could to find you."

Vasily made a derisive noise. "When did he tell you this version of his 'escapades'?"

"Right after you arrived, while you were sick."

"Well, he certainly managed to make the most of those forty-eight hours. I'm sure you and Dmitri were listening outside the door when he shared the details with me."

"That was pretty harsh," Lev agreed. "But it seemed to me that he was trying to make you angry on purpose."

Vasily let out a rough bark of laughter. "He lives to make me angry on purpose. I swear it's the only way he can get hard."

Lev smirked. "You mean to tell me he goads you to anger as a matter of course—and then he wants to fuck."

Vasily frowned at the way he was making it sound. "Well . . . yes, fuck me or beat me." He couldn't help but smile a bit. "Or beat me and then fuck me."

Lev was eyeing him strangely. "I'm going to assume from the way you're smiling you're not talking about battery here."

"Battery?"

"Beating you up. Punching you."

"No, nothing like that." Vasily flicked his eyes toward Lev's briefly. "Discipline."

"Ah." The skinny Grigori shivered beneath his coat, but it didn't seem to be one of coldness. "So, to reiterate, Belphagor riles you up routinely as foreplay."

Vasily opened his mouth to argue the point and then closed it. He tried to think of a time Belphagor had been deliberately cruel when it hadn't turned out that he'd been provoking Vasily's rage because it made them both hot.

"Anyway," said Lev, "I don't think that was what he was doing this time. I think he was trying to make you so angry at him that you wouldn't want to go with him."

Vasily narrowed his eyes at the other demon. "You think he was playing me?"

Lev gave him a significant look. *Playing.* Of course he'd been playing him. He was the damned Prince of Tricks. Vasily shook his head angrily, trying to get Belphagor out of it. He wasn't going to be played with from an entire sphere away.

The *kinoteatr* turned out to be a theater with a great white screen where the stage ought to be, on which a film was projected larger than life. Vasily stared up at the moving images in awe.

The American film on the television had been as wonderful as its name, but to see a story come to life in such dimensions—with the sounds of the fictional world all around him as if he were inside it himself, and an audience beside him who gripped their seats with sharp breaths and wept silently at the same moments he did—was an experience unlike any other. If this was what it was to read a book, he wanted to open them all.

He hadn't understood all the words, but the visuals needed little to convey the story. In a disconcerting bit of synchronicity, the film, *Assassin of the Tsar*, was about a man who believed he was the reincarnation of Tsar Nikolai II's killer—the equivalent, Vasily gathered, of the principality of the Celestial Empire. The depiction of the tsar, a small, gentle man with a beard and sad eyes, was remarkably like the angel he'd seen on the platform at Council Square.

Vasily had soon forgotten the peculiar similarities, however, immersed in the heartbreaking tale that detailed the events leading up to the killings and ended with the violent death of not only the tsar but also his wife and children and their servants. He couldn't get them out of his head as he and Lev walked back through the winter night to the apartment.

"What were those weapons the killers used?" Despite his attempt to suppress his element, Vasily's breath made softly glowing vapor in the air in front of him when he spoke.

"Guns." Lev stuffed his hands into his pockets. "They're horribly efficient."

Vasily agreed. There were things about this world he was enchanted by and others that made even his firespirit blood run cold. If Duke Elyon had been able to procure such a weapon in Heaven, there was no question that Principality Helison would be dead and Vasily hanged for it. Though he'd be hanged for it anyway if Belphagor's mission didn't succeed.

That night, he lay staring at the ceiling, replaying what Lev had said about Belphagor provoking him to get him to stay in the world of Man. Even if he was right—and he probably was—there were still the angels Belphagor had fucked. Angels he was no doubt fucking this very minute. Which meant that Belphagor desired someone other than him. That Belphagor gave to someone else the things he'd only recently begun to give to Vasily. Just as he'd wanted to fuck Lev from the moment they'd arrived. Had Belphagor ever really wanted him as anything other than an object of fetish?

Vasily tried not to roll over onto the knife sticking out of him.

He didn't understand Belphagor. He didn't want to understand. He wanted Belphagor to understand him. He wished the knife and the bloody wound weren't invisible. He almost wished he'd never fallen in love with Belphagor. Because Belphagor wasn't in love with him. He was convinced of that now. Belphagor was infatuated. And maybe had grown less infatuated as soon as he'd finally given in to his desire. How long would it be before the infatuation simply burned out?

The jewelry in his neck tugged against the pillow as he turned his head. *Shit.* He'd forgotten about the piercing. His brain was racing like a mad train from one station to the next, and he wished he could shut it off. He wasn't going to have any peace until he had it out with Belphagor and either made him take out the knife or finish him off.

Belphagor sat with Tabris, who'd finally slept after hours of unresponsive trembling and weeping. He wasn't sure where Masha had spent last night—maybe in his room—but he'd slept in a chair by the bed, having volunteered to keep an eye on the demoness so Masha and Anzhela could get some rest.

Tabris stirred beside him and opened her eyes, fixing them on him.

Belphagor resisted the urge to take her hand. "Good morning, Tabris."

She sat up and pulled the blanket he'd draped over her around her shoulders. "Have they arrested you too?" He was relieved to hear her speaking, though her voice shook like an elderly demon's.

"No, sweetheart. You're at The Cat. You've been released."

"The Cat." Tabris seemed to think about the name a long time, as though her cognitive functions might be impaired. "Who are you?"

"My name's Beatrix." He figured it was best not to overwhelm her with information. "I'm new here."

The door opened a crack, and Anzhela peered in. "You have a— Oh! Tabris, you're awake." She came in and sat on the bed. "We're all so pleased to have you home. How are you feeling?"

Tabris paused a moment before answering. "I'm . . . a bit dizzy."

"You must be hungry. I'll have Cook make you some lunch."

"I'll fetch it," said Belphagor, getting up.

Anzhela nodded to him. "Oh, and you have a client."

"A client?" He frowned with annoyance. "This early?"

"It's three in the afternoon." Anzhela smiled. "You're not a morning person, are you? It's your angel boyfriend, Phaleg."

Belphagor paused at the door and glared. "He's not my boyfriend, for Heaven's sake."

She seemed awfully amused with herself. "Whatever you say."

"I'm with Vasily," he snapped, directing his anger with himself at her.

"Vasily?" Tabris perked up. "You know Vasily? The fire demon?"

"Yes, sweetheart." He came back toward the bed. "You probably don't remember when I told you last night who I—"

"Those horrible angels." Tabris shuddered, her voice rising in pitch. "I told them I didn't know where he was. They wouldn't believe me."

It occurred to him that telling her he was Belphagor would give the Ophanim something to extract from her if they came again. Perhaps it was better to leave it at Beatrix.

He gave Anzhela a pointed look. "I can't imagine how they thought any of us would know anything about that revolution business. Thank goodness you finally convinced them. All of Heaven's gone mad right now. Accusing demons who've done nothing, arresting innocent working girls." As a surrogate for her hand, he touched the edge of the bed. "Well, I'll be on my way. Don't want to keep my client waiting." He nodded to Anzhela as he headed out. "I'll tell Cook to fix something."

Phaleg was the only patron in the parlor when Belphagor had dressed and gone out to greet him. He rose and doffed his cap, giving Belphagor a cordial bow. "Miss Beatrix. I've come with an invitation from the court."

"The court?" Belphagor gaped.

"Duke Elyon requests your presence at a salon this Friday evening. It's an informal event."

"You have to be joking."

The angel shrugged. "His exact words were, 'If that demoness bint were cleaned up, she'd pass for a common angel. Take care of it for me and have her here for my salon.' So I guess I'm to have you made over. I think the first order of business is to take that bit of metal out of your brow."

"The hell I will. And I have no intention of spending another evening with that arrogant ass of an angel."

Phaleg played with the brim of his cap. "It might be the solution to your . . . dilemma."

Belphagor sighed. "Come back to my room where we can speak in private."

"Is that a euphemism for something?" Phaleg asked playfully as he followed Belphagor out.

Belphagor laughed without humor. "No, it is not." He ushered the angel into his room and closed the door, turning on Phaleg with anger. "I am not your boyfriend. You will not come here and take liberties with me. If I wish to take them with *you*, that is at my discretion."

Phaleg blinked, visibly smarting at the rebuke. "I was only trying to keep up appearances."

Belphagor let his breath out slowly and ran his fingers through the hair at his scalp. "Sorry. That was uncalled for." He sat on the bed with a sigh. "I guess I'm angry with myself."

"For what?"

"For trying to distract myself from missing my boy by indulging in your degradation." He rubbed his temples. "It's an addicting thing, having a grown man willing to grovel at my feet, humiliating himself for my pleasure."

Phaleg crossed his arms over his chest in a protective gesture. "It wasn't merely for *your* pleasure. You think rather highly of yourself."

"That wasn't what I meant. I'm trying to explain how . . . how even seeing you there, sulking, makes me want to bring you to your knees and order you to crawl to me naked." He tried not to meet Phaleg's eyes directly at the little gasp of breath that had escaped him. It would only tempt him more. "And to have one of the Host so eager to debase himself for me—I've had angels before; you're not unique in that. But you are unique in your devotion. Which I can't deny is something I crave."

"So what's wrong with that?" Phaleg's voice was harsh with desire.

"What's wrong is that I'm using you."

Phaleg allowed himself a slight smile. "Isn't that the idea?"

"Your body, certainly." Belphagor smiled as well. "Your emotions, no. Because I miss *him*, I'm taking from *you*. Does that seem fair to you?"

Phaleg took a breath as if he was short of it. "I haven't asked you to be fair. Nor do I ask anything of you now, though I'm sure you can see how merely speaking of it has affected me." He blushed, shifting his stance and holding his cap in front of him to cover his erection. "If you never make use of me again, I'll be content in the memory of the occasions you have. But until the day I die, I will be a willing participant in anything you ask of me. If that's to leave . . ." He sighed and dropped his hands to his sides. "I can do that too."

"Come sit with me." Belphagor moved over as if to make room on the bed, but when Phaleg approached him, he stopped the angel and pushed him to the floor to kneel at his feet. With his hand on the angel's cheek, he spoke kindly. "I believe you may be the best-behaved boy I've ever had the pleasure to possess."

"Your Vasily—"

Belphagor cut him off with a laugh. "My Vasily is an ill-tempered, rebellious, and maddening thing of beauty. The first time I met him, he tried to steal from me, and I gave him a thrashing to teach him a lesson. He never learned it. And he never left." He discounted the two occasions on which Vasily had gone off on his own to spite him.

Phaleg looked surprised. "You let him get away with disobedience?"

"Oh, he never gets away with it." Belphagor gave him a dark smile. "He pays dearly for it, which I begin to suspect is half the reason he does it. Of course, he rails against every act of discipline, as if he's being sorely misused—all the while with an erection between his legs you could hammer a nail with. There's nothing more delightful than bringing him to a smoldering fury and then punishing him for it, waiting for the moment he finally lets go and surrenders to what he wanted all along." He winked. "There's a lot of weeping involved."

Belphagor twisted his fingers in the angel's hair and yanked for good measure. "But don't get any ideas. I want only one naughty boy. My heart couldn't take another."

Phaleg looked up at him, nodding seriously.

"Now." Belphagor relaxed his grip. "What was it you wanted to tell me about the solution to my dilemma?"

"Well, I was thinking if you got close to the duke, letting him pass you off as a common angel, and then threatened to reveal yourself as a . . . a working demoness, you could perhaps blackmail him into making some kind of declaration of Vasily's innocence. You persuaded him to release the prostitute, did you not?"

"I did. And I *could* try to blackmail him—and find myself in an alley with a broken neck."

"I wouldn't let him do it." Phaleg's vehemence was charming.

Belphagor gave him a wan smile. "I'm not some damsel in distress to be rescued, Lieutenant. Regardless, I'm afraid any resistance would be rather ineffective against a Cherub that can apparently materialize and dematerialize at will." He stroked Phaleg's hair absently. "Perhaps if I were to trick Elyon into revealing his part in the Council Square rebellion in the presence of someone else . . ." While sitting up with the traumatized Tabris, he'd thought about how best to use Phaleg's position in the principality's detail to his advantage. "I need you to do something for me."

"Anything, *ser*."

Belphagor cupped his chin with affection. "It won't be easy. Remember when I said I wouldn't ask you to commit treason?"

The angel's pupil's constricted with alarm.

"I will keep my word," he assured him. "But I must ask you to find an opportunity to put yourself in a position to do harm to the principality."

"But I . . ." Phaleg's face twisted with anguish. "Please . . ."

"You will not harm him. You will only let him believe for a brief time that you intend to."

The angel gazed up at him, his pale face even whiter. "I don't understand."

"I can only assume that he would not go with you willingly if you asked him to spy upon the angel he believes saved his life. If, however, you persuaded him that you were a revolutionary and meant him harm, he might go with you at knifepoint."

Phaleg shook his head. "He has two Seraphim who guard him at all times."

"Even in his own chambers?"

"They stand outside the doors."

"Is no one allowed inside but the principality?"

"Well . . . no, he lets people enter to have audience with him."

"So that is when you would spin your convincing tale of anarchism. Within the enclosure of his private chambers, with the Seraphim outside and not privy to what is happening inside, you could find some reason to get him to go with you to Elyon's rooms without alerting the Seraphim to the danger. It would have to be very convincing. Like a threat on the little grand duchesses' lives."

Phaleg looked horrified. "They're only children!"

"You aren't going to harm them," Belphagor reminded him. "You won't be anywhere near them. They'll know nothing of the threat. But you'll convince the principality that you have them somewhere or have put them in danger somehow."

The angel looked sick to his stomach. "It won't matter that it isn't true. I'll be hanged. The threat itself is treason."

"Even in the interest of exposing the true traitor within his palace?"

"I don't . . ." The angel's skin was dotted with sweat, and his breathing was rapid. He'd lost his erection. "I don't know. I don't know." He was shaking his head and weeping, though he didn't seem aware of it. Belphagor had gone too far.

He slid from the mattress and gathered Phaleg into his arms. "It's all right. I won't ask you to do it. I'm sorry."

Phaleg had begun to weep in earnest. "I don't want to fail you."

"I know you don't. I'm sorry. It's all right, Phaleg. I asked too much." The angel was just loyal enough that he'd ruin himself on Belphagor's orders. Belphagor couldn't allow that. "We'll think of another way. It was only an idea."

"I'll do what you ask me," Phaleg gasped, huddled in his arms. "I'll do anything you ask me."

"I know. That's why it was wrong of me." He kissed the top of his head. "Please don't feel you've failed me, Phaleg."

The angel was still distraught. Belphagor had to change his tactics. Being kind wasn't going to bring Phaleg's focus back where it needed to be.

He pushed Phaleg away and stood. "I'll be the one to tell you if you've failed me, do you understand me?"

Phaleg nodded up at him, hollow-eyed. It was a gesture, not an answer.

Belphagor turned him roughly toward the bed. "Up on your knees. Unlace. Now."

Phaleg scrambled upright. Facing the bed where Belphagor had thrust him, he swiftly unlaced his pants. Deflated with self-doubt a moment ago, he was now hard as a crystal facet.

"What's making you hard, boy?"

"*Ser?*"

"Were there too many words in that sentence?"

Phaleg's face went pink. "*Nyet, ser.*"

"So, what is making you hard?"

His answer was barely audible. "Doing what you tell me to, *ser.*"

Belphagor nodded. "And that is what pleases me. I decide whether you've been a good boy—and how to deal with you when you have not. You have abdicated all judgment about such matters, as you've abdicated your will to resist me. I own your will, your judgment and your pleasure, and I will work them as I wish, until you've lost all sensibility."

"*Da, ser.*"

"So. Do you get to decide whether your actions please me?"

"*Nyet, ser.*"

"You will please me best by maintaining your integrity as an officer in the Supernal Army. You're of no use to me as a fallen soldier—literally or figuratively. Since you are far more familiar than I with what is required of an officer, it is your duty to tell me when I have asked something of you which will compromise that."

"*Da, ser.*"

"Turn around."

Phaleg straightened and turned about on his knees, his erection standing at attention between them.

"Lace up your pants."

"*Ser?*"

"Do you question me?"

The angel's face fell. "*Nyet, ser.*" He dutifully laced himself up, trapping the unassuaged erection inside the elkskin.

"Here's what you're going to do for me, boy. I will accept Duke Elyon's invitation, and you will see that the principality hears of my reputation at The Cat. Find an excuse for the principality to summon me for private questioning, and I will put my proposal to him myself, suggesting that he indulge me in facilitating the entrapment of the angel responsible for the attempt on his life. Will you do this for me?"

"*Da, ser.*"

Belphagor observed the angel groveling before him, begging to be used. It would certainly not be the demeanor of his Vasily in a similar position. Vasily would be glaring fire at him, his body tense and hard with defiance, his face full of temporary hatred, fueling Belphagor's own fury . . . and desire.

He felt the ache of the cleats against his chest, marks that had faded a bit externally, though beneath the surface, his ribs were still horribly bruised. Those bruises reminded him of the words he'd said to Vasily when they'd parted, letting him believe he'd abandoned him as punishment for Vasily's own infidelity.

"Go home, Phaleg."

Phaleg got to his feet, his expression crestfallen. "I'm sorry, *ser*—"

"Have I said I'm displeased with you?" Belphagor snapped.

"*Nyet, ser.*"

"I've told you to stop making such assumptions, and here we are back at the beginning. *That* displeases me."

Phaleg reddened. "*Da, ser.*"

"Go home and be a good boy, and I will see you tomorrow for my 'makeover.'"

Phaleg nodded and went to the door.

"And Phaleg."

The angel paused and looked back.

"When you get home, kneel on your kitchen table with your pants around your ankles and make yourself come."

The angel's cheeks went red. "*Da, ser,*" he answered roughly.

The corner of Belphagor's mouth turned up in a dark smile. "And repeat that while you do it, so you remember who owns your pleasure."

When Phaleg had gone, Belphagor pleasured himself in the manner to which he'd become accustomed of late, picturing the angel's cock spurting over his hand as he perched naked on his table. He knew Phaleg would do as he'd been bidden, to the letter. It was incredibly arousing to know this with certainty, but it wasn't what he needed.

A small part of him rebelled at the idea of needing anyone as he did Vasily, but he'd been hopelessly enslaved since the night they'd met, and there was nothing he could do about it. And the rest of him was eternally grateful.

Phaleg returned as bidden the following morning to call on Beatrix, and the two of them went out together, ignoring the good-natured teasing from the others girls at The Cat. The angel turned out to be well-versed in women's fashions, which Belphagor found intriguing. After a few hours in the Left Bank, they were armed with a conservative but playful gown with a peekaboo décolletage, a host of absurd undergarments, a fancy hooded cloak with a matching fur muff, and an expensive pair of button-up kidskin shoes.

Belphagor tried to pay for the purchases with his stipend from Masha and Anzhela, but Phaleg insisted that the duke had provided generously for Beatrix. Belphagor wondered just what the duke would believe he was owed for the price.

Phaleg nodded with approval as Belphagor tried the garments on all together back at The Cat, with some assistance from Anzhela with the abominable corset. "You'll be the envy of every woman there."

"I always am." Belphagor smirked and then winced as he tried to take a normal breath.

Phaleg presented him with a string of pearls, and Belphagor ignored Anzhela's snicker as she let herself out while Phaleg put them on him.

"I have to get back." Phaleg kissed Belphagor's hand without the slightest sense of irony. "But I'll come to fetch you for the salon on Friday evening."

"I'll be waiting." Belphagor stroked the pearls. "And afterward, I may show you how to make better use of these." Phaleg looked puzzled. Belphagor twisted them around his finger. "They can increase the intensity of orgasm . . . when they're being pulled out of you."

Phaleg went red to his pale roots, bowed, and took his leave.

On the appointed evening, Phaleg arrived smartly attired in his emerald dress uniform, and Beatrix, with her hair done in an elegant upsweep by Anzhela, accompanied him in her new garments and pearls to the supernal carriage awaiting them outside The Cat. Phaleg, Belphagor noted, was pointedly avoiding glancing anywhere near the string of pearls.

"You remember what I've asked you to do?" Belphagor murmured as they rode toward Elysium in comfort.

"*Da, ser*," the angel replied. "I won't let you down."

Belphagor squeezed Phaleg's gloved hand with his own. "And you won't let yourself down, either, dear boy. There's no need to do anything that goes against your conscience. All I require is an audience." He realized this last word was ambiguous, but it wasn't safe to make himself clearer in case the driver was listening, so he had to trust that Phaleg knew he meant an audience with the principality.

At the palace, Phaleg escorted him to where Duke Elyon's salon was already in progress in the green-marble-decorated Malachite Room. As Beatrix was announced, Elyon glanced up from the arm of the chair he was perched on next to a young male angel of fine form. Phaleg had presented her as the Lady Beatrix Astelovna of Arcadia.

"Ah, my dear Lady Beatrix. I was afraid you weren't coming." Elyon rose to greet him, giving him a nod of approval as he took Belphagor's hand and took in the elegant dress before he brought the gloved hand to his lips. "Your presence brightens the room."

Belphagor glanced about at the sparkling prisms of reflected flame—from the pendalogues and pendants adorning the massive chandeliers to the many gilded surfaces—dancing like tiny firespirits. "I can't imagine how you'd notice such a thing, Duke Elyon." He pulled back his hand coquettishly. "This room is positively dazzling as it is. I've never seen such grandeur. I must say I feel a bit out of my element."

"Nonsense," said Elyon, and murmured against his ear, "You're just not used to wearing so many clothes."

"Is that what feels different?" Belphagor winked while picturing himself kneeing Elyon in the groin. "At any rate, it's all quite impressive. I had no idea you were among the supernal favorites."

"Indeed?" Elyon beamed. "The principality himself has appointed me his lord chancellor while he recovers from his recent misfortune.

It was I who caught the demon brute assassin, after all." His story was growing more favorable to himself with each recitation.

"And lost him," said Belphagor.

Elyon's eyes darkened. "It was, in fact, your friend Phaleg who lost him, if you must know." He glanced up with a sneer aimed in Phaleg's direction, but the angel was nowhere to be seen. "He claims he was beset by demons in the commotion."

"But where were you?" Belphagor couldn't resist asking and had to stifle a chuckle at the answer he provided in his head in Elyon's pompous voice. *Pinned under the fiery foot of a Seraph, my dear Beatrix, squealing like a stuck pig.*

"Defending the principality," Elyon snapped. "Now why am I boring you with this tale when you've not yet had a drink?" He clutched Belphagor's elbow with unnecessary roughness to steer him toward a servant bearing a tray of sparkling nepenthe and plucked a flute from the tray to place it Belphagor's other hand. "Your disposition seems rather the worse for your outward trappings, my dear," he murmured as Belphagor took a sip, trying not to draw attention to himself. He gave Beatrix a swift, derisive visual inventory. "How ironic that you're so much more agreeable when your tits are in a man's mouth where they belong."

It took everything Belphagor had not to throw the nepenthe in the duke's face and pummel the living hell out of him right there on the shiny marble floor. "How ironic that when you're among your civilized society you behave like an uncouth swine." No longer caring if he drew attention or not, he yanked his elbow from Elyon's grasp and turned on his heel to find someone else to mingle with until Phaleg returned—hopefully to escort him to a secret meeting with the principality.

He stepped toward a pair of the angels he'd brought to a happy climax at the duke's villa and opened his mouth to utter some banal pleasantry, but Elyon had swiftly stepped up behind him and slipped a firm arm around his waist.

"Gentlemen," he said pointedly, as if to remind Beatrix that she was not one of their peers. "You remember the lovely Lady Beatrix?"

One of the angels took Belphagor's hand to kiss it, giving him an appreciative appraisal. "You look rather different this evening."

"Most likely the lack of a cock in her mouth." Elyon's tone was just low enough not to carry beyond their group. Even these angels of his intimate circle had the good graces to look a bit horrified by the duke's crudeness.

Belphagor felt his face go hot. He hadn't blushed since he was a boy flirting with a set of equally offensive Malakim in the world of Man. This wasn't mere embarrassment. This was unique to the power dynamic between the duke and a demoness. Except it wasn't about Beatrix's station. It was about her sex. This was shaming and putting a woman in her place. For once, he found himself completely without a comeback, paralyzed by the power of that simple and pernicious exchange.

Before anyone broke the shameful silence, a dazzling light burst over the glittering surfaces of the room. Two Seraphim had entered from one of the adjoining concert hall doors, which could only mean one thing.

They parted to make way for the principality to enter.

CHAPTER
FIFTEEN

Sneaking out of the flat while Dmitri and Lev were at work had been a simple matter. Finding his way to the train station and getting himself tickets to the right destination had been quite another.

Vasily had eventually lucked upon one of the people Belphagor called "Night Travelers"—humans who spoke angelic and acted as liaisons between their race and the various groups of terrestrial Fallen.

The boy looked like any street demon in Raqia, and he'd evidently taken one look at Vasily and pegged him for demonic. And a lost tourist. For a fee, he helped Vasily buy the tickets and told him which train he was to board and when. Vasily had to trust that the boy wasn't fleecing him—and if he was, there was little he could do about it; Belphagor had left him a billfold of paper rubles for expenses, but he hadn't specified their worth.

Soon he was on his way to the world's Far East, watching the frozen terrain as it sped by. He hadn't had much opportunity on the initial trip to sit and look out the window. Belphagor had been busy tormenting him.

The memory depressed him. It had been like a honeymoon period, groping and being groped, sucking and being sucked, fucking—well, being fucked, anyway—for days on end, and being utterly under Belphagor's control. He'd been livid the entire time, literally as well as figuratively, and it had been bliss.

His anger at Belphagor now for entirely different reasons nevertheless put him into a similar state. Alone for the moment in the four-person compartment in which he'd purchased one seat, he quickly got himself off. Despite his melancholy, there was something surreal and wonderful about watching the stunning landscape of crystalline ice hurtle past along the mountainside as firespirit heat boiled out of him without any need for him to temper it.

And then he was there, at the stop where they'd departed for Moscow: Sludyanka. He wasn't as lucky with the timing this trip and had to spend the night in a little inn before embarking on the last leg of the journey to the tunnel where he would climb back to Heaven.

The grandmotherly *babushka* who rented him the room had treated him with such kindness and generosity, insisting that he join her and her son for a humble dinner of beetroot soup and potatoes—a meal he could honestly say was one of the best he'd ever had—that he felt a sad, sweet sense of nostalgia already for this world before he'd left it.

He wanted to be home in Raqia with Belphagor. He was relieved to be returning to the familiarity and comforts he knew, regardless of what came of it, but terrestrial magic had taken hold of him just as Belphagor had said. Though he hadn't had a chance yet to experience his wings, he understood now what Belphagor had been trying to tell him. He knew why the Fallen fell.

After the assembled guests had lapsed into shocked silence and given him the obligatory obeisance, Principality Helison Alimielovich strode through the parlor toward Duke Elyon. Phaleg accompanied the principality at his side but a step behind, evidently as his non-seraphic personal guard.

"Your Supernal Majesty." Elyon's complexion looked as though he'd been exsanguinated when he straightened from a trembling bow. Belphagor tried to copy the other ladies in attendance, hoping he'd made a passable curtsy. Court etiquette wasn't something he'd ever had to learn, and certainly not what was expected of a woman.

"I hope you don't mind my intruding on your little gathering." It was difficult to tell from Helison's placid demeanor whether he'd delivered this with sincerity or with the most deadpan supernal sarcasm.

Elyon evidently couldn't tell either. "I hope I haven't overstepped my authority, Your Supernal Majesty. I took it upon myself to stimulate a bit of thoughtful discourse among the younger members of the peerage. I hadn't thought it worth bothering you with in your convalescence." He paused, waiting awkwardly for a response, and hurried on when none seemed forthcoming. "Should you be on your feet, Supernal Majesty? I thought the doctor's orders were to stay abed for another week or two. You don't want to risk re-aggravating the internal bleeding now that it's under control."

"Nonsense. The circulation can only be hindered by remaining stationary."

Belphagor decided the principality's demeanor of gentle civility was sincere. He'd faced enough hypocrisy over the card tables to recognize it.

"I've not met your lovely companion," Helison prompted, and Elyon's previously white face flushed with red.

"Forgive me, Supernal Majesty. May I present Lady Beatrix Astelovna of Arcadia."

Belphagor genuflected again, hoping this was the expected behavior, and Helison lifted his hand slightly with a patient smile to indicate Belphagor ought to have offered his own. He remedied the misstep swiftly. With a sort of tight bow—as though toward a partner in dance—the principality gave the gloved hand the most chaste and respectful touch of his lips, so unlike the others who had greeted Beatrix.

"I'm very pleased to make your acquaintance, Lady Beatrix. Have you known our duke long?"

"Lady Beatrix is my mother's cousin," Elyon supplied before Belphagor had to come up with something. "She's in Elysium studying music in preparation to apply to the Hermitage of Celestial Contemplation."

Belphagor nearly choked on an intake of breath and covered it with a dainty cough. The HCC was the equivalent of a nunnery in the world of Man. In Heaven, there was no religion but the admiration of Heaven itself. Women of breeding who had no prospects—those who had little to offer either in the way of physical attributes or material wealth—committed themselves to the contemplation of Heaven's majesty among the celestial "sisterhood." It was the closest thing in Heaven to what the world of Man imagined went on here.

Helison arched his brow. "Indeed? What instrument do you play, Lady Beatrix?"

"The one-handed horn," Belphagor managed to say with a completely straight face. The two angels he'd played simultaneously were mysteriously overcome with coughing fits at the same moment.

"I've not heard of that," said Helison politely. "Perhaps you'll play for Us sometime while you're in Elysium."

"It would be my pleasure, Your Supernal Majesty." Belphagor dropped a little curtsy. Beside him, the duke's fists were clenched tightly at his sides.

Helison turned to Elyon. "Would you mind if I stole Lady Beatrix away from you for a moment? I'd be delighted to speak with her a bit longer about her aspirations to the hermitage. I find the calling fascinating." Elyon's mouth dropped open, and all he managed was a mute nod as the principality offered Belphagor his arm. "Have you had a chance to see the Winter Garden?" Helison asked. "It's an absolute marvel."

"I have not, Your Supernal Majesty."

"Then you must." He turned Belphagor toward a small door and led him through an intimate dining room and across the rotunda to a terraced atrium lit by an assortment of hanging lamps of delicately painted glass. Phaleg followed them through the door and closed it behind himself, waiting at attention.

Overhead, the ceiling was composed of glass panes that would let in the sunlight during the day, the supporting spans painted with intricate vines and flowers to match the ivy-covered walls and arches. On every ledge and step, among miniature evergreens from the northern mountains of Aravoth, an array of southern flowering trees and succulents had been artfully arranged in urns and pots.

"These lovely little bushes are called poets' jasmine." Helison paused before one with apparent interest. "From the coastal lands."

Belphagor leaned down to sniff the fragrant bloom the principality cupped for him.

"I understand you have information about the demon assassin." The principality's voice was suddenly firm and sharp with authority.

Belphagor straightened slowly and met his gaze. It was level with his own, which surprised him, as he rarely met a man of his own stature. "Yes, Your Supernal Majesty. Although you've been misled about the involvement of the demons."

Helison released Belphagor's arm and crossed both of his over his chest. "How so?"

"The assassination attempt was a plot to discredit the Fallen community and was carried out by angels. The same angels who organized against you that evening in the square."

Helison cocked an eyebrow. "This 'Union of Liberation'?"

"Then you know of it."

"I have heard rumors of it since my inauspicious coronation. I am not entirely unaware of what my princedom thinks of me, nor am I fool enough to allow such treasonous talk to go unchecked. Angels suspected of involvement have been quietly dealt with."

Belphagor made an effort not to glance Phaleg's way. "What if I were able to provide you with the name of someone in the highest echelon of the union? Perhaps the very highest."

"I would be quite interested indeed in such information."

"Interested enough to offer a reward?"

Helison stared him down. "You tread on dangerous ground, Lady Beatrix." He frowned and then gave him a sharp nod. "Name your price."

"My price isn't facets or property, Your Supernal Majesty. It's the freedom of an innocent demon."

"What demon do We have in Our custody?"

"He isn't in your custody. He's on the run. He was framed as your would-be assassin."

The principality's arm shot out, and Belphagor thought for an instant he was going to strike him, but Helison gripped his arm above the elbow and stepped in close. "My guard will run you through before you can draw your blade."

"I have no blade, Your Supernal Majesty. You have nothing at all to fear from me. What I'm telling you is the absolute truth."

"You expect me to believe you're in league with the demon who attacked me and yet insist he was framed. I felt his knife in my back!"

"It was an angel who stabbed you. The demon was there under duress to take the fall. He'd been coerced into coming to the square by a threat of violence against a young woman of his acquaintance. He was unarmed and agreed to make himself visible as the obvious target in exchange for her life. The agitators killed her anyway."

"What proof do you have of these allegations?"

Belphagor sighed. "I have no proof, Your Supernal Majesty. Only my word. But I can give you the name, and I can offer myself as bait to lure the guilty party into giving you the proof of his crimes with his own tongue."

"You're no angel," the principality realized with a scowl.

"No, sire, I am not."

"Then the Lady Beatrix—you're impersonating her. What's become of her?"

"There is no Lady Beatrix," said Belphagor. "I was presented to you as such despite my benefactor being well acquainted with my occupation in the oldest profession. And that fact ought to lend credence to the validity of the name I'm about to give you."

Helison's grip softened on his arm. "What is the name?"

"Will I receive my reward? I believe you're a man of your word and will stand by it if you give it now."

The principality let go of him and paced along the border of the container garden with his hands clasped behind his back. "If you can supply a confession from this angel in the presence of my agent . . ." He paused and sighed. "I will grant a pardon to the demon."

"A pardon implies a crime. He's guilty of none."

"Absolution, then!" The principality spun toward him with exasperation. "The charges against him will be dropped."

"Thank you, sire." Belphagor inclined his head in gratitude, suppressing a joyous grin at the tremendous relief those words provided. "The angel who organized the attempt upon your life and the rebellion against your throne is Duke Elyon of the House of Arcadia."

Helison closed his eyes and breathed in deeply. "You will find it difficult to convince me of that." Despite his words, he didn't seem altogether surprised to hear the name. "Why threaten my life only to cry assassin and leap to my aid?"

"Whether or not the assassination attempt was successful was immaterial to his plan. His goal was to appear as your champion. Had you died of your injury, the Union of Liberation would have rallied around him as a hero for capturing the principality's perceived killer—whom Duke Elyon intended to kill as well, as soon as the deed was done."

Helison turned. "And how would a Fallen strumpet know of such a plot in such great detail?"

Belphagor smiled, not taking offense. "A Fallen strumpet is in a position to learn a great many things from the men who frequent her bed. Such men often like to brag of their exploits—both in and out of the brothel."

Phaleg cast him a quick look, as if wondering whether he counted among the sort of men Belphagor was disparaging.

"A Fallen strumpet is also practiced in telling lies," said Helison, though his frown said he was having more difficulty trying not to believe Belphagor than otherwise. His doubts seemed to make him angry. "If you're telling me false . . ." He shook his head. "I could have you arrested and hanged before the night is up for making such allegations against an angel of supernal blood."

"Your Supernal Majesty." Phaleg stepped away from the door, and Helison turned toward him in surprise. "I can corroborate what Beatrix is saying." The angel drew his sword, making both Helison and Belphagor stiffen with alarm, but he held it out hilt-first to the principality and bowed on one knee. "I surrender myself to your justice, sire. I am now and until my death your true and faithful servant, but I was a member of the Union of Liberation until late and was privy to all the lady is telling you."

Belphagor couldn't have been more shocked. Phaleg had been so frightened of being perceived as a traitor, and now here he was admitting to being one before the principality himself.

Helison took the sword, staring down at the angel. "Those are treasonous words."

Phaleg hung his head. "Yes, sire."

"And you are in league with this courtesan?"

"I am. And I would stake my life upon her word, Your Supernal Majesty."

The principality stroked his beard as he gripped the sword and pondered Phaleg's bowed form. "I had thought to make you my agent in this matter, Lieutenant Phaleg. But there's no point in sending you to obtain proof against Duke Elyon if you've conspired with this demoness against him. I cannot trust you in this."

Phaleg said nothing, and Belphagor could sense the shame emanating from him for having disappointed his principality.

"Your Supernal Majesty—"

Helison held up his hand to silence Belphagor and continued his fretful contemplation. At last he sighed and held the sword out, point-down, to Phaleg, who glanced up in surprise to take it. "I cannot trust you in this matter, but I feel I must trust you in all else. To have made such an admission to me cannot have been easy. You know well what the penalty for treason is, and I would have been within my rights to take your head where you knelt. Stand," he added with a note of irritation as Phaleg gazed up at him.

The angel swiftly obeyed and stood at attention once more, the sword crossed over his chest. The corner of Belphagor's mouth twitched. Such a well-trained soldier.

Helison inclined his head toward Belphagor. "I shall, however, have to give your proposal some additional thought. Right now, I believe I've overtaxed my circulation after all and will have to retire." He gave Belphagor a polite half bow as if Beatrix were a lady of the peerage and turned toward the far side of the garden that opened onto the rotunda, moving with an obvious limp.

Phaleg started after him. "Your Supernal Majesty—the Seraphim."

"Let them go to the devil," Helison snapped, a clear indication that he was in greater pain than he let on.

"I'll inform the Seraphim that His Supernal Majesty has retired." Belphagor rested a reassuring hand on Phaleg's shoulder.

Phaleg glanced back at him. "Be careful." He hurried after the principality.

When Belphagor returned to the Malachite Room, all eyes were on him. Elyon, in particular, eyed him intently. As he closed the door with no one following, the Seraphim stepped forward, the large, fiery frames moving more swiftly than Belphagor had anticipated.

He managed not to flinch. "His Supernal Majesty asked that I convey to you that he was feeling winded and has retired to his rooms."

One of the Seraphim intercepted him with two great strides. "Not acceptable." The Seraph's voice reverberated like iron struck upon iron by a giant hand. Every angel in the parlor clutched his head.

Before Belphagor could respond, the Seraph had grabbed him by the throat and lifted him off his feet. The glowing creature wasn't exactly burning like the fire he appeared to be composed of, but the searing heat was a close second.

To his surprise, Elyon came to his defense. "Let her down," he demanded. "Your mandate is to protect the principality, not assault his guests!"

The Seraph turned and glared at him—an impressive thing, coming from a being of elemental fire—and released Belphagor at the same moment so that he stumbled and nearly fell, caught by Elyon at his side. "We will protect the principality against all threats."

Elyon pressed his fingers to his temple against the horrid sound of the Seraph's voice. "Then by all means, find out whether he's in danger!"

The Seraph turned to the door and threw it wide, revealing the empty room.

Belphagor pulled himself together. "As I said, he's retired to his rooms. Lieutenant Phaleg has accompanied him."

"I suggest you hightail it to the principality's quarters." Elyon's voice conveyed an authority that suggested he'd become used to giving the supernal guard orders. "Lady Beatrix could hardly have done away with them both in the last five minutes and disposed of the bodies."

The Seraphim swept past them through the dining room into the rotunda, their bright forms radiating light as they surged down the hall.

"Well, that was unexpected." Elyon addressed the gathering, trying to laugh off the tension, his arm still around Belphagor's waist. "Another drink for the Lady Beatrix."

The servant making the rounds with the tray of nepenthe flutes responded instantly, appearing at the duke's side. Elyon handed a glass to Belphagor. "I knew having you here wouldn't make for a dull evening," he murmured as Belphagor drank a bit more than a sip. "What did you and the principality have to talk about?"

"One-handed horns," said Belphagor.

"Very funny." Elyon took the glass from his hand and set it down on one of the green-marble-topped tables. "Why don't we take a walk? I'll show you the principality's library. It's quite impressive." Without waiting for agreement, he turned Belphagor about toward the open door through which the Seraphim had just departed. They passed through the stately rotunda and into a more intimate room, where the walls were lined with bookshelves and decorated in rich tones of rosewood and leather.

Elyon closed the door and pushed Belphagor back against it. "What the hell are you up to?"

"I'm sure I don't know what you mean, my lord."

"Oh, now you play at deference." Elyon placed his fingers against the red marks from the Seraph's hot hand at Belphagor's throat and closed them around it. "What information were you giving the principality?"

Only the knowledge that he needed Elyon to exonerate Vasily kept him from blowing his cover and taking the duke down a peg. He might not possess the same physical strength as when he was himself, but he was certain his technique was unimpaired. "If you must know, Your Grace, he recognized me from The Cat."

This was evidently not the answer Elyon had expected. "The Cat?" His grip loosened. "You're telling me the principality of All the Heavens visits a demon whorehouse?"

"He has the same needs as any man. In truth, I've only seen him there once, and he certainly didn't advertise his identity. The girls took him for a rich aristocrat, but we had no idea how true that was." Belphagor placed his gloved hand over Elyon's and firmly removed it from his throat. "We'd never seen the principality, of course. How would we know what he looked like?"

Elyon's expression was calculating, as if he were examining this revelation from all angles. "When was this?"

"Oh, at least three or four years ago, now. Perhaps five. I was a fresh young thing at the time."

Elyon gave him a dubious look, and Belphagor took exception to his doubt on Beatrix's behalf. "Perhaps five . . . so he might not yet have married."

Belphagor shrugged. "He didn't divulge that information to me, at any rate. He wasn't my client, but I did entertain him a bit in the parlor while he was relaxing afterward with a pipe. He tucked a pair of huge, perfect facets into my corset. That's a thing you don't forget." Belphagor fluffed his breasts and grinned. "He said they were an 'homage to the perfection of the pair above 'em.'"

"And he remembered you?"

Belphagor gave him a mock pout, hands on hips. "Everyone remembers me, my lord."

Behind Elyon, on the second level of the library, Belphagor noted a series of cabinets that could easily conceal a grown angel, and he filed the information away. This room might be the perfect place to entrap the duke—if Belphagor ever received another invitation to the palace. "The principality wanted my assurance that I'd not come to blackmail him. I told him it was the furthest thing from my mind. Of course, I'm afraid he's now aware that you brought a whore to the palace and passed her off as your cousin. I don't think he was amused."

"One that he knew." Elyon smirked. "I doubt he's going to make a fuss about it." The duke straightened his bow tie. "Well, you've certainly proved the most interesting guest my little salon could have had, my dear Beatrix. Now it's time for you to earn your supper." His hands moved down his coat, unbuttoning to the waist. "On your knees, dear. I haven't got all day." He snapped his fingers and pointed at the floor before he began to unlace.

Belphagor tried to contain his fury. It wouldn't do to lose all the ground he'd just made. But he'd be damned if he was going to get on his knees before the son of a succubus and let him use his mouth. The suggestion dredged up memories he didn't care to revisit. His hands clenched tightly at his sides. "I've not yet had any supper." He managed to deliver the words in a lightly mocking tone and give the duke a smile.

"Supper or no supper, the nepenthe you drank alone is more than you're worth." Elyon paused at his laces in irritation as Belphagor continued to stand before him. "What do you think you're doing?"

Before Belphagor could answer, the door from the rotunda opened and Phaleg entered. "Pardon me, Your Grace. I hate to interrupt, but His Supernal Majesty has asked that I escort Beatrix off the premises."

Elyon scowled without turning his head. "Well, it can wait five minutes. She has business to attend to first."

"The principality has asked to see you."

Elyon grimaced and swore, lacing up with reluctance. "Take her, then." He gave Belphagor a pointed look as he buttoned his coat and went to the door. "We'll settle accounts another time."

After hours of climbing and doubling back repeatedly, during which he was sure he'd gone past it half a dozen times, Vasily had finally found the trap door beneath Belphagor's room at The Brimstone. With relief, he searched for a latch or a handle but found only a smooth surface. When he pounded his fist against it, the door didn't budge.

"Son of a bitch." Vasily hammered at it with both hands, but it was no use. Belphagor had magically charmed it. There was no getting in from this side without whatever magic he'd used to do it. The only way in was for someone inside to open it. He wasn't sure the pounding would be audible in the celestial realm, or if Belphagor would be there to hear it, but Vasily wasn't about to go all the way back to Moscow now, so he kept up a steady rhythm, pounding with one fist in a succession of beats, then pausing a minute and starting again.

He'd fallen asleep at some point—it was impossible to gauge the passage of time within the staircase—and when he woke, he sat up and gave it another heavy bang, expecting more nothing in response, only to have the door fly upward away from his fist. Leaning his weight on his forward foot, he nearly fell inside but caught himself with a hand on the rim before he bashed his head against it.

"Bel—" His query was cut short when Tabris's face appeared in the light above the hole, looking as shocked to see him as he was to see her.

"You!" she cried. "Where is she? What have you done with Ouesti?"

He blinked at her. "Westy?" Then he remembered the odd name Belphagor had told him. "Tabris . . ." He climbed up into the room beside her and sat on the edge of the opening. "Ouestucati is dead."

"I'm not a fool!" An odd shiver followed the outburst, like an irrepressible tic. "She was here. You brought her here. I came to see. The revealing spell . . ." She waved a hand vaguely toward the trapdoor. Some spell designed to reveal magical charms must have shown it to her, though what she'd meant to reveal, he couldn't fathom. Perhaps Sefira's spirit?

Her eyes looked at once wild and glassy, and her garments were unkempt as if she'd slept in them, perhaps several times in a row. He wasn't quite sure what to do in the face of her peculiar behavior. Was she in denial about her sister's death, or was she demanding to see the body after all this time?

"Did you speak to Belphagor?" he asked. "Is he here?" Tabris stared at him blankly. "The dark-haired demon with the ink on his skin. He took you to Duke Elyon's villa that night." He didn't want to elaborate about what night in case she truly didn't understand her sister was gone.

Tabris startled him by reaching out and touching the spiked adornment at his neck. "Did they do that to you?"

"Who?"

A shudder went through her, and she pulled her hand back. "The Ophan— Ophanim. '*Give us the demon*,'" she said in an odd voice and then seemed to answer herself. "I don't know where he is! I swear it!" She scrambled to her feet, another shudder racking her.

"Tabris—"

"You!" she cried again, pointing at him. "You're the assassin!" She fled the room, and Vasily stared after her, not knowing what to do. He couldn't very well charge out into The Brimstone in pursuit; he was a wanted demon.

After closing the door, he sealed the trapdoor and covered it with the rug. The room didn't look as if anyone had been here in days, though someone had obviously tossed things about when Sefira's body was collected and Tabris was arrested. He collected the tin cup Belphagor used for his shaving lather from the floor and sat on the bed, turning it in his hands. Belphagor hadn't been here at all. Or if he had, he'd been apprehended himself as soon as he'd arrived.

The doorknob rattled, and he jumped. Was it Tabris again, or had the Ophanim come? Before he could decide what to do, the door opened. He was sure he'd locked it.

A chestnut-haired demoness stared at him as if she knew him. "*Mal'chik*," she breathed. "What are you doing here?"

Vasily stood, outraged. "How dare you call me 'boy'! And what the hell are *you* doing in *my* room?"

The demoness closed the door. "Vasya, it's me. I took a glamour." She crossed the room and put her hand on his arm. "It's Belphagor."

He pulled away, scrutinizing her. It couldn't be. "Then where are your tattoos?"

"They're glamoured away. *Everything's* glamoured away." She made a wry face, flicking her gray-blue eyes downward for an instant.

Tilting his head as he tried to comprehend how this could be Belphagor, he felt the tug of the spike at his neck. She had no metal bar in her eyebrow. "Belphagor has a piercing. You can't glamour that away."

She sighed. "But I can take it out, you stubborn boy. Look here. You can see the holes in my skin." The demoness rose up on her toes—a very un-Belphagor-like motion—and pinched the flesh at the corner of her eyebrow. Vasily leaned forward and squinted. The holes were there. The unfamiliar mouth curved into a familiar expression, a half smile, along with a twinkle in the eyes that said she was up to no good. "You see? It's me." She reached a hand up to his face and stroked it down his cheek to his neck, resting on the spikes of the barbell. "It's your Beli. Now what the hell are you doing here?"

Vasily's heart skipped at the casually delivered phrase: *your Beli*. The intimate name that Belphagor professed to be embarrassed by, and the possessive that turned everything he'd been thinking on its head. With three short syllables, Belphagor had utterly disarmed him.

"I asked you a question." The tone of the feminine voice had the same steely authority that turned his legs to jelly.

"You're a bastard," he managed weakly. He cursed himself for falling apart within seconds of confronting Belphagor. He'd been rehearsing his words for days: how he planned to demand that

Belphagor tell him once and for all if he wanted him, if he meant to be with him always as he'd implied with the piercing of his flesh, or if all of this was only another game for Belphagor to win, Vasily just a prize that amused him when he was in the mood to use him.

"That's your answer?" The hand at the side of his neck tightened and moved to the back. "I'm a bastard? That's why you've defied me and endangered us both when I'm on the verge of clearing your name?"

Vasily tried to hold on to his defiance. "Exactly what are you doing running about Heaven like—like *that* that could possibly clear my name? Fucking more angels?"

The blue eyes narrowed with anger, but a sound from the corridor interrupted the brewing storm. "Beatrix, are you in there?" The loud whisper accompanied a sharp rap on the door.

Belphagor-turned-demoness opened the door to an alarmingly handsome supernal soldier Vasily had seen before. "Phaleg? What's going on? How did you know I was here?"

"They told me at The Cat you'd gone in search of Tabris, and Tabris has . . ." The angel's voice trailed off as he focused on Vasily before darting his eyes toward the glamoured Belphagor once more. It was a look Vasily was intimately familiar with.

The blood heated in his veins like molten ore. This was the angel Belphagor had been fucking. But there was an easy intimacy in their body language, in that deferential look. Vasily's lungs burned, as if he'd sucked in a backdraft. They'd been doing more than just fucking.

"Tabris has what, Phaleg? What did she do?"

Phaleg swallowed. "She's turned him in."

With the blood pounding in his ears, it took Vasily a moment to understand the words. The soft "Damn it" from "Beatrix," however, was unmistakable.

"I can stall my men," said Phaleg. "They're out front questioning some of the patrons. Do you have a back exit?"

Vasily stepped toward him, a feral growl rising in his throat. "I don't need your damned help."

The demoness grabbed him by the sleeve, turning him toward the door. "Don't be an ass about this, *mal'chik.*"

Vasily yanked his sleeve from her grasp with a wide swing of his arm, and his fist clipped an unexpectedly soft cheek. As she reeled back with her hand to her face, the angel steadied her in his arms. Vasily gaped at the two, not sure whether to be horrified at himself for hitting a woman, disgusted with Belphagor for behaving suddenly fragile, or livid at the sight of Phaleg as Belphagor's protector.

The superheated air in his lungs nearly choked him. "Go to fucking hell, the both of you!" He whirled about to take his chances with the Supernal Army.

CHAPTER SIXTEEN

Belphagor pulled the collar of his long fur coat close in front of him against the newly falling snow as he watched the troop of angels lead Vasily away toward the bridge in irons. They'd wrestled him to the ground outside The Brimstone after he'd barreled his way through the gaming room instead of trying to do the discreet thing and duck out the back.

Belphagor should have said to hell with it and let Phaleg know about the portal. Vasily could have been safely hidden there if he'd just opened it up and told him to wait beneath the room until the principality's men gave up and moved on. Though given the way he was acting, he probably wouldn't have set a foot below on Belphagor's orders either.

"I'll try to make sure they keep the Ophanim away from him," said Phaleg beside him.

"I need you to get me into the palace again."

"The palace? They'll be keeping him in the Conciliary."

"Not to get him out," said Belphagor. "To get Elyon alone in the library while the principality conceals himself in the gallery to listen to his confession."

Phaleg turned to look at him. "Are you sure that's wise after what happened last night?"

"You think I can't handle Elyon?"

"Oh, I'm sure you can handle him. I'm just not sure I want him to handle you."

"Phaleg, I've told you I'm not your damned damsel in distress. You may be unaware of the rest of my reputation as the Prince of Tricks, but I am quite well-versed in delivering beatings to grown men—with or without their consent."

"Belphagor may be, but Beatrix has soft, smooth knuckles and rounded, tender flesh, and is outweighed by the rather fit—and younger—duke by a good fifty pounds." Phaleg reached up and touched the tender spot on his cheek, and Belphagor winced and slapped his hand away. "Have you ever bruised like this before? Would you have thought twice about taking your Vasily down to his knees with one hand if he'd decked you in your true form?"

Belphagor shivered and glared. "Goddamn it."

Phaleg wrinkled his brow. "Is that peasant tongue?"

"No, it's extreme frustration. *Bog chert vozmi* would be what you call peasant tongue. And technically, it's Russian, a language from the world of Man."

"You've really been there." He shook his head in wonder.

"Can you get me in or can't you?"

Phaleg sighed. "I'll see what I can do. I'd better catch up with my men so I can keep an eye on him."

"Thank you," said Belphagor. "For giving a damn about him."

Phaleg seemed surprised. "Of course." He hurried after the party dragging the loud, angry demon to Elysium.

Back at The Cat, Belphagor found Tabris in the parlor weeping in Anzhela's arms.

"She found the assassin." Anzhela shared a look with him over Tabris's head, and Belphagor nodded.

"They can't touch me again?" Tabris implored Anzhela. "I gave them the demon."

"No, Tabi. They can't touch you. You're safe here."

Belphagor sat beside them and put a hand on Tabris's back, softly stroking, and for once she didn't shudder or pull away. "He knows you had to, Tabris. He understands. It's okay." Tabris cried harder, evidence that this was indeed what tormented her. What the hell had those Ophanim done to the poor girl? He smoothed her hair, and the three of them sat huddled in sisterly comfort—a strange, instinctive behavior that had come to him, evidently, along with his borrowed hormones.

Phaleg sent word the following day that the principality was amenable to his plan, but he was at a loss as to how they might lure the duke into the trap since Beatrix had been escorted off the premises on the principality's orders.

It wasn't as if she could reasonably appear for a social visit. Belphagor would have to appeal to the duke's wounded pride at having been called out by the principality on his indiscretion. Not only would his ego be vulnerable after the dressing down, but he would want to take his anger out on Beatrix for putting him in such a position—for Beatrix would clearly be the one to whom he assigned the blame.

After Belphagor came up with his plan, he waited for Phaleg's next visit to tell him of it rather than risk discovery should his message be intercepted. It was several days before Phaleg made an appearance at The Cat, and Belphagor was on edge. The angel had assured him that the principality wouldn't rush Vasily's execution, knowing that his innocence might be proven, but Belphagor couldn't help wondering how his boy was being treated.

When Phaleg was announced, Belphagor had him ushered back to his private room. He paced angrily as Phaleg sat on his bed. "You might have sent word before now."

"I did send word. Did you not get my message the morning following the arrest?"

"Yes, I got it, but it's been nearly a week since. You've told me nothing of Vasily's present state. Am I just to take it on faith that he's not being tortured?"

"I'm sorry; I thought it would be dangerous to send communications specifically about him. He's being treated with civility. No Ophanim interrogations. I promised you I'd make certain of it."

Belphagor clenched a fist in his own hair to avoid taking it out on Phaleg. Civility from angels to a demon, especially one believed to be an anarchist assassin, strained credulity. If only Vasily had listened to Belphagor and stayed away. Knowing he was sitting in some dank hole believing the worst of Belphagor—not to mention that the worst was mostly true—was eating at him like an ulcer.

Belphagor calmed his rising anxiety with some deep breaths. "How is the principality's health?"

"His health?" Phaleg gave him a puzzled look. "He's recovering."

"He needs to be seen to be in decline. Let Elyon believe the principality is too weak to be on his feet. Keep Elyon from seeing him. Rumors of a persistent fever and wasting would be even better. The less he fears the principality, the more likely he is to take chances."

Phaleg nodded. "I think I can get him to agree to that."

"We have to move as quickly as we can. I can't leave Vasily hanging." He grimaced. "Bad choice of words."

"And what move do you intend to make?"

"I plan to appeal to Elyon's desire for revenge against me for making him look a fool in front of his sovereign. I was cocky that evening. He won't have forgotten it. He'll want his pound of flesh."

Phaleg looked alarmed. "Pound of flesh?"

"It's from an earthly tale. He'll want to take it out on me to make himself feel in control."

"Belphagor—"

"Don't start with your misplaced chivalry," Belphagor snapped. "I'm warning you, Phaleg."

The angel gazed up at him, troubled. "You're angry with me. I only meant to look out for you. The duke is a dangerous man, and he'll be even more dangerous if he feels cornered."

"I am angry with you." Belphagor stopped his agitated pacing. "I'm sorry. I'm doing it again. Projecting my anger at myself onto you."

"Why are you angry at yourself?"

"Because I'm not omnipotent," he said with a harsh laugh. "Because I've hurt Vasily. And because I'm acutely aware of my privilege as a male demon and how arrogant I've been to think all Fallen were equally oppressed."

"Privilege?"

"You wouldn't think so, would you? But to realize how much I've taken for granted—that I can go anywhere I like, do anything I please, and take a man down for giving me lip or a bad look . . ." He shook his head. "All without fear of repercussion—or of harm to myself for no reason at all. You try wearing a woman's skin for a month and let me know how much you like yourself, Phaleg. I dare you."

Belphagor laughed as he realized his anger had brought him to the point of tears. "And this! It's maddening. Do you think women want to break down in tears when they're mad as hell? To top it all off, my damned breasts hurt like the dickens."

Phaleg's face went a bit pink, and he gave Belphagor an uncomfortable smile. "A *month*. Belphagor, you're—"

"Oh, for the love of hell, no!" Belphagor's eyes went wide. "Do you think . . .?" He shuddered. "I have to get out of this body. Let's get this done. Persuade the principality to take a quick turn for the worse. I'll sneak into the palace myself and let the duke apprehend me, and I'll get him into the library at the appointed time. Your job will be to get the principality there beforehand and conceal him in the gallery."

"Sneak in? How do you mean to do that? There are two hundred Ophanim surrounding the palace at all times."

Belphagor smirked. "I'm an airspirit, my angel."

Phaleg's flush deepened. "*Your* angel."

"You haven't forgotten that I own you." Belphagor stepped in front of him at the edge of the bed, forcing him to look up.

"*Nyet, ser.*" The angel's voice was gratifyingly unsteady.

"You are a very, *very* good boy." Belphagor ran his thumb over the angel's bottom lip. "You have no idea what I'd give to have possession of all my . . . faculties . . . right now." He smiled and gave the angel's lip a firm press at the center with his thumb and held it there. "I'd fuck you senseless." He ignored his conscience that said he wouldn't do any such thing.

A weak moan escaped the angel that he didn't seem conscious of, a cross between desire and fear.

"Prove yourself to me." He prodded the angel's lip into a pout, stroking against the moist rim. "Put everything in place as I've asked by this Friday night, just after dusk."

Phaleg nodded breathlessly. "*Da, ser.*"

"And you are not to interfere with my dealings with the duke. Do I make myself clear?"

Phaleg nodded again, his lips pressed tightly together. Whether it was to hold in a retort or to keep another moaning sigh from escaping, Belphagor wasn't sure.

Using information Phaleg had provided on where Duke Elyon was quartered, Belphagor targeted the northwest wing of the Winter Palace. It overlooked a walled garden where the Supernal Guard was lacking, the concentration of Ophanim being at the entrances on the square and the boulevard facing the Neba—a river whose name so closely matched its earthly counterpart, it left no question that someone involved in the establishment of one city had intimately known the other.

There was no public entrance on this side, but a discreetly recessed door led from the supernal rooms to the garden—locked securely, of course, but that was immaterial. Climbing over the wall in a dress was going to be the hard part.

He settled on tucking the skirts of his gown and crinoline into his petticoat, modesty be damned; his intent, after all, was not to be seen. Belphagor rolled his eyes at himself that modesty had suddenly become something that registered in his consciousness. Not to mention the awkward conversation he'd been forced to have with Anzhela when it turned out he had indeed taken on every physical characteristic of his temporary womanhood.

"*Bozhe moi.*" He gritted his teeth, trying to block the traumatic memory. When this was over, Vasily was going to get the thrashing of his life for having put him through this.

The thought of Vasily brought his concentration back to the task at hand. Belphagor scrambled up using the mortar between the stones and gripped the top of the wall. Swinging one petticoated leg over and then the other, he dropped soundlessly among the hedges and made his way through the little maze to the door.

After picking the lock with a hairpin, he let himself in and changed into the chambermaid's uniform Phaleg had pilfered for him.

The rooms at the top of the stairs on this corner of the palace were mostly the supernal family's private quarters, and the duke had been given the suite closest to the library. Hopefully, Phaleg had succeeded in his part.

Belphagor slipped inside the duke's receiving room, where Elyon had his back to the open bedroom door, giving his boot a quick spit polish, and took a provocative pose against the doorframe. The stark astonishment on Elyon's face when he straightened and turned was priceless.

"Beatrix?" He stepped toward Belphagor with a scowl, closing the door after a quick, nervous glance into the receiving room. "What the devil are you doing here?"

"We had unfinished business, did we not?" He batted his eyelashes.

"The last thing I need right now is the principality getting wind of your presence in my room!" Elyon grabbed Belphagor's wrist. "How the hell did you get in here?"

"Don't be cross. I have a friend who works as a chambermaid." He smoothed his free hand down the bodice of his dress. "What do you think? Do I look the part?"

"You've gone too far, whore."

Belphagor managed a pout. "I wanted to make it up to you for how things turned out at the salon. I thought surely you'd be eager to make use of my services." He stroked his finger over Elyon's crisp dinner vest and trailed it down, giving him a wink. "Haven't you a knob that needs polishing, milord?"

Elyon grasped the other wrist, pulling Belphagor harshly against him. "If you've come to service me, I expect to be fully satisfied." He pressed his hips against Belphagor's for emphasis, letting him feel his rising erection. "I trust your little problem has cleared up?"

"It has, but regretfully I'm temporarily indisposed in that direction."

"Well, fortunately for me, I intend to give it to you in the jacksie as we discussed." He turned Belphagor about and pushed him against the door as if he meant to do it standing.

Belphagor bit down his instinct to fight and giggled instead. "My, but you're eager, Your Grace. Don't you think your valet is bound to come looking for you shortly for dinner?"

Elyon paused with his hands pressing firmly against Belphagor's sides. "I suppose you have a point."

"Isn't the library just next door? There wouldn't be anyone in there at dinnertime, and no one would think to look for you there." Belphagor turned his head and gave him a sly glance. "I rather fancied the idea of being bent over His Supernal Majesty's desk. Would serve him right to have a demoness in heat on top of his personal business, and him none the wiser."

The gleam in Elyon's eyes said Belphagor had wagered perfectly. "The principality isn't well," he said as if calculating the risk. "He certainly won't be using it." He loosened his grip on Belphagor and slipped his arm around the corseted waist, pulling him intimately to his side. "You're a wicked little thing, aren't you, Beatrix? I never would have guessed."

And you haven't; not by a longshot, mudak.

Elyon led him to the library, taking a quick glance around before locking the other entrances and slipping the key into his pocket. Without another word, he turned Belphagor about and pushed him onto the principality's broad walnut writing desk, fumbling at the army of lacings up the back of the long apron connecting the straps to the sash that had given Belphagor no end of grief. "How the devil do I get at you in this thing?"

Belphagor laughed and pushed him away, straightening to work at the laces himself, and putting his back to the desk. "I'm surprised at you, my lord. Haven't you ever buggered a chambermaid before?"

Elyon smirked. "Generally, I stick to groomsmen and stable boys. Nothing like a quick go in the hay."

"But it's such a bitch getting the straw out of your crack." Belphagor released the first of the straps, which were actually buttoned in place after lacing. "Much nicer to have the run of the palace. What becomes of you if the principality succumbs to his injury?"

Elyon stepped close and wrapped his arms around Belphagor to free the second strap at the back. "As you know, he has no heir."

"You don't mean . . . Am I about to be buggered by the future principality of All the Heavens?"

Elyon untied the sash and dropped the apron, working the buttons down from Belphagor's nape. "Not officially. Not yet."

"But you're actually in line for the throne?"

"As I said, not officially." Elyon reached the base of the spine on the tight-waisted dress and turned Belphagor around again to manage the rest. "Officially, Grand Duke Lebes Alimielovich and his son Kae are next in line. Unofficially, there are some who feel a change to the old guard is in order." The last button came away as he hitched the skirt up and laid it open. Belphagor shivered at the sudden breeze as Elyon yanked the petticoat down.

"You truly do have the ass of a boy, my dear Beatrix." Elyon paused to admire it.

Belphagor stilled a shudder of revulsion as the duke stroked his finger down the center. He hoped to hell the principality was really in the gallery. "I suppose I should give it back, then."

Elyon laughed and moved to unbutton his dress pants.

"The old guard—so the Union of Liberation really means to overthrow the supernacy."

"Where the hell did you hear that?" Elyon grabbed him by the hair and yanked Belphagor's head about, his eyes like flint. "Someone's put you up to this, you dirty little bint."

"No one's put me up to anything." He gritted his teeth as Elyon twisted the hair at his nape.

"Then how do you know of the Union of Liberation?" His eyes narrowed in fury. "It's that damned Phaleg! I knew he seemed too eager about fucking a succubus."

"I suppose he ought to be murdering them, like you."

Elyon yanked Belphagor around to face him. "What the hell are you talking about?"

"My friend Sefi. She overheard your plan to stage an assassination attempt, and you had her killed." Elyon backhanded him, and Belphagor heard a noise from the gallery as he stumbled against the desk. He had to act fast to get a definitive confession. "Don't bother to deny it. The demon you framed for the attack on the principality told me everything."

"That simpleton," Elyon sneered. "He's about to swing from the gallows. And you're going to swing beside him."

"And I suppose you think the rest of the Supernal Army will rally around you and your mutineers the moment the principality's dead."

Elyon gripped him by the throat and slammed him onto the desk. Belphagor couldn't make a sound. He clawed at the duke's arm and tried to free his legs from the tangle of petticoat and crinoline so he could kick the duke in the groin. Elyon was equally silent in choking the air out of him, both hands wrapped around Belphagor's throat and thumbs pressed to his windpipe.

Bright spots exploded in Belphagor's vision like a burst of Russian Victory Day pyrotechnics. His lungs convulsed, and his grip on Elyon's hands weakened. Giving up on fighting Elyon, he felt around the desk for something—anything—to use as a weapon before he blacked out.

His fingers closed around the edge of a marble inkwell stand, but the angle was too awkward for him to get hold of it. The inkwell itself wouldn't budge, mounted in the marble. He scrabbled for the metal pen, but it rolled away from him.

At the same moment, one boot tore free of the crinoline, and he rammed his heel against the inside of Elyon's knee, but with the thickness in his head and the burning in his lungs, the amount of force he was able to muster was inadequate.

As Belphagor began to lose consciousness, Elyon gave him a violent jolt and brought his face close. "Go to hell where you belong, whore. You won't be here to see the Heaven I'll rule when the House of Arkhangel'sk is overthrown."

A cabinet above banged open just as Belphagor's hand closed around a brass letter opener in a depression in the inkwell stand. He seized it with all his remaining strength and jammed it into the side of Elyon's neck. The last thing he heard was Elyon's howl accompanied by a sharp command from the gentle principality as the room swam away.

"Belphagor. *Beatrix*." Someone slapped his cheek.

The groan it dragged out of Belphagor made him choke and gasp against the pain in his throat. The rasping cough this provoked became retching, and someone turned his head to the side. He heaved unproductively, sending a fiery stab through his lungs.

The struggle with Elyon returned to him, and he swung out instinctively against the person kneeling over him.

"Beatrix, it's Lieutenant Phaleg." The angel grabbed his swinging fist. "Thank the Heavens. You're alive."

For a moment, he saw double, and then his vision cleared. He found not only Phaleg but the principality of All the Heavens staring down at him in concern. Phaleg helped him stand, stepping quickly behind him to right his clothing while the principality politely turned his back.

"We owe you a great debt, madam." The principality clasped his hands behind him as he spoke without turning.

"The only reward I require is the demon." Belphagor brushed Phaleg's hands away when he continued to fuss with the apron laces after the buttons had been done up. "I'm presentable, Your Supernal Majesty." He put a hand to his throat at the hoarseness of his voice. Touching the bruises turned out to be ill advised.

The principality turned, frowning in concern. "And We wish to express Our dismay that you were placed in harm's way to reveal a deception within Our own ranks to which We were blinded." He stepped toward Belphagor and placed a hand lightly on his shoulder. "Are you all right, dear girl?"

Belphagor nodded. "Yes, Your Supernal Majesty." Damn, that was a bitch of a mouthful. He swallowed and regretted it.

The principality's eyes were kind. "No need to speak." He steered Belphagor gently to the leather couch by the fireplace. "You must rest here until you've recovered your strength. A physician will be along presently. When he's tended to you and you feel up to it, a carriage will be arranged, and Lieutenant Phaleg will see that you're delivered safely to your home." He patted Belphagor's hand as Belphagor sank onto the cushion. "Rest assured, your demon friend will be released as promised."

The principality pressed Belphagor's fingers with gratitude and let himself out. The brief glow of Seraphim lit the room from the corridor before he closed the door.

"I don't need a physician," Belphagor told Phaleg, who was hovering over him. "What happened to that bastard Elyon?"

"The Ophanim carted him off howling like a five-year-old. You missed his carotid by an inch."

"My aim was a bit off."

"I'm so sorry." Phaleg dropped to one knee. "We couldn't tell what was happening for a moment, and I was waiting for Elyon to fully implicate himself before I opened the cabinet."

"You were here?"

Phaleg nodded. "I concealed myself with the principality, suspecting the duke might prove dangerous when caught out. I had no idea how dangerous." His blue eyes were anxious. "Please forgive me."

"There's nothing to forgive. You did just as I asked." He took Phaleg's hand and squeezed it in lieu of further talking.

While Phaleg fetched Beatrix's customary clothing from the stairwell, Belphagor submitted reluctantly to examination by the supernal physician. The elderly looking angel—putting him somewhere north of two hundred years—pronounced Belphagor "a very lucky girl" and gave him an analgesic powder to mix into a glass of water, but Belphagor didn't want to stay a moment longer. He'd had enough of being Beatrix, and he wanted to get back to take the restorative elixir. And to be with his boy.

When Belphagor arrived back at The Cat and took the analgesic, it turned out to be a powerful sedative as well. He passed out before getting to the elixir and didn't wake until late the next morning.

When he did, Vasily was at his side.

"Beli." He handed Belphagor a glass of water when he sat up, shaking his head as he watched him drink it with care. "That *is* you, isn't it?"

"It is, indeed, *mal'chik*."

"You scared me so damned much." Vasily laid his fingers gently beside the bruises at his neck. His rough growl rivaled the hoarseness of Belphagor's voice. "That . . . *angel* of yours came to tell me what happened as I was being released." There was still bitter anger in his eyes.

"Vasya, I owe you an apology." He sighed. "A great many, I suppose."

"Forget it. It doesn't matter."

"Of course it matters. The things I said to you before I left— I needed you angry enough not to try to come with me. Nothing I did was out of spite."

"I know that." Vasily looked down at his lap. "Lev told me."

"Lev? I didn't say anything to him about it."

"Well, he seems to get you pretty well. Better than I do." More bitterness.

"It was never my intention to hurt you."

Vasily jumped to his feet. "I can't do this."

"Do . . . what?" Belphagor gazed up at the hurt in the hazel eyes, his pulse stuttering with alarm. Had he screwed up this badly? "You mean . . . be with me?"

"*Be* with you?" Vasily's mouth parted in surprise, his brow wrinkling with consternation. "I— Aren't you dumping me?"

"What the *hell*, Vasya?" Belphagor swung his legs over the side of the bed, encumbered by the gown he still wore, and yanked it from around his calves as he stood to stare Vasily down. The spiked adornment he'd given Vasily caught the light, and Belphagor put his palm against it as he clutched the back of the firespirit's neck.

"What do you think I gave you this for?" He pressed hard against the spikes, jamming them into Vasily's skin until he flinched. "Did you listen to a word I said? This is *always*, do you hear me? So you either take it out and walk away now, or you deal with my arrogance and stupidity and let me atone for my fool mistakes. Or have you forgotten our agreement? That you chose to take my punishment when I screwed up?"

Belphagor gave him a dark half smile. "If you imagined I wasn't likely to—and frequently—then you need to get to know me better, boy. I might screw up for the sheer joy of the consequence."

Vasily bit his lip—a gesture that made Belphagor want to sink his own teeth into it—and blinked his eyes, bright with moisture that was either anticipation or a prelude to tears. Or both. "Beli . . . could you . . . Are you going to stay like that?"

Belphagor looked down at his cleavage. "Why? Would you like me better this way?"

Vasily's eyes widened. "*Bozhe moi, nyet.*"

With a laugh, Belphagor went to the bureau and pulled the stopper out of the elixir meant to restore him to himself. "Here goes nothing." He threw it back like a shot of vodka, gratified to see his own tattooed hand as he set the vial down, then smoothed the dress over nonexistent cleavage and turned to Vasily with a raised eyebrow. "Better?"

"Infinitely."

"*Khorosho.*" He grabbed Vasily by the locks. "So why the hell are you not on your knees?" Belphagor twisted his grip and took him down, relishing the feel of his own musculature. He stepped behind Vasily and crouched, one fist still in his hair and the other hand sliding over Vasily's chest and abs toward his crotch. "Let me explain something to you, *mal'chik*," he murmured at his ear. "*Moi mal'chik. Milyy mal'chik.*" My boy. Sweet boy. He let his tongue linger over the syllables.

Vasily shivered.

"I have never in all my years had someone I couldn't face life without. Until you. So despite those years, despite my experience with any number of methods of physical congress and mutual power play, despite the fact that I can seduce a man with a look and bring any man to his knees with a single motion, I am a complete novice when it comes to being in love."

Vasily's shoulders twitched only slightly, but Belphagor knew him well enough to recognize that he was silently weeping.

"Don't cry, sweet boy," he whispered. "*Ya tebya lyublyu.* Of course I love you." He leaned over Vasily's shoulder and stroked his hand down the still-hesitant erection. "I'm sorry I couldn't say it before. To be honest, it frightened me—frightens me still, a bit. And for my fear and my failing, there will be a severe penalty." The hesitancy was gone, and Vasily's ample cock rose hard against Belphagor's palm. "Ah, that's my *mal'chik.*"

Belphagor let go of Vasily's hair and pressed his lips to the warm neck, running one hand down the front of his shirt and releasing the buttons as he stroked the hard shaft with the other.

Freeing the last button, he slipped the shirt from Vasily's shoulders. "I've treated you so poorly, in fact, even failing to recognize that I'd hurt you, that it may take me a day or two to administer all the correction necessary."

Vasily let out a soft groan of anticipation while Belphagor slipped his belt from its buckle and unbuttoned Vasily's fly, letting the gorgeous cock spring free of restraint. He caressed it, running his thumb around the rim and over the slit, making the hot firespirit breath escape Vasily faster. While Vasily knelt, waiting, Belphagor discarded his feminine undergarments, double-checking that all his parts were his own—and that none of them were bleeding—and came around to the front.

He lifted his skirt. "Open your mouth."

Vasily looked up, the heat of his element beginning to spark in his eyes. God, Belphagor loved that moment: the undeniable evidence that his boy desired him coupled with the kindling of his defiance, as if his body's enthusiasm were a betrayal that incensed him.

"You're going to keep that dress on?"

Belphagor had to struggle to keep a straight face at this unexpected question. "You have a problem sucking the cock of a demon in a dress?"

Vasily shrugged. "*Nyet, ser.*"

"Good boy." He grabbed the hair at Vasily's forehead. "Then shut your mouth and suck it."

The flame in Vasily's eyes fully erupted at the asperity, and he sneered. "Which do you want me to do? Shut my mouth or suck it?"

Belphagor yanked his head back. "I'm sure you can figure out a way to do both." He pressed roughly against Vasily's mouth and forced himself in while flames of fury danced in his boy's eyes. Despite his resistance, Vasily closed his lips around him and took him in deep, keeping his eyes on Belphagor to let him know he was still angry, even if he couldn't resist reveling in the pleasure of the act.

There was something especially thrilling about watching his erection disappear into Vasily's mouth over the hem of a lady's dress. There were erotic possibilities to cross-dressing he'd never considered, as it wasn't a particular predilection of his. Not only was it a defiant act in its own right, it added an unexpected element of dominance.

His long-ago Russian lover had surprised him by posing as a woman, whose advances Belphagor had tried to evade, until an encounter in a coat closet had revealed his hidden erection. It had been the best fuck of Belphagor's life. Until he'd met Vasily.

Vasily had closed his eyes, humming with enjoyment around Belphagor's cock as though he'd forgotten he was being punished. Belphagor withdrew abruptly, and Vasily's eyes opened, indignant for an instant until he saw the expression in Belphagor's. His parted lips glistened with moisture.

Belphagor pondered his options, torn between wanting to give Vasily a thorough chastisement and badly wanting to fuck him. He supposed there would be time for all sorts of chastisement. His boy wasn't going anywhere.

He hopped onto the bed with his legs crossed at the ankles, his cock exposed where the crinoline caught on it and his hands clasped behind his head as he leaned against the headboard. "The oil is on the bureau." He cast a halfhearted nod toward it as if he were bored.

Vasily's eyes narrowed at the assumption he'd obey without a command, but he rose and collected it anyway. Belphagor flicked his eyes toward his hard-on. Vasily stood stock-still for several seconds, his chest rising with indignant breath, before blowing the warm air out, uncorking the bottle of almond oil, and baptizing the erection liberally. He slammed the bottle down on the nightstand and waited for further instruction in a most unsubmissive manner, his own erection practically dominating the room.

"Drop your pants."

Vasily yanked the jeans over his thighs and started to pull his boot through one leg, but Belphagor stopped him. "I didn't tell you to take them off. Up on the bed."

Steam practically escaped with the firespirit's sigh. "You want me to leave them around my ankles?"

"Did I tell you to speak, boy?"

Vasily glared. "*Nyet, ser.*" He climbed awkwardly onto the bed, clearly furious at the hindrance of the fabric around his boots.

Belphagor had to silently count to ten to keep from gathering his beautiful, angry boy into his arms. "Well? I'm sure you know where you belong in this scenario."

The glow of elemental fire in Vasily's eyes was at full flame as he crawled forward and straddled Belphagor's hips. He swore under his breath as he tried to maneuver, at last having to lean forward on hands and knees to sit back on Belphagor's waiting cock. He'd dribbled so much oil over it that he slid down with an unceremonious grunt of surprise, and his cheeks went red. Notably, his own erection didn't waver. Belphagor lifted an eyebrow as Vasily waited, apparently, for him to do the work.

"Are you just going to lie there?" Vasily's rough voice nearly squeaked with astonishment.

"You know, Vasya, every time you speak out of turn, I make a mental note of it. The list of things for which you'll need future correction is growing quite long."

Face blazing with anger and humiliation, Vasily dug his fingers into the bedspread and began to ride up and down Belphagor's length.

Belphagor groaned with pleasure. "That's a good boy," he praised Vasily, as if he were a dog. "A little faster. Come on, now. Don't be so easy on yourself."

As Vasily began to drive himself against Belphagor's pelvis with furious force, Belphagor tipped the bottle of oil into his palm and slid his hand down Vasily's neglected cock. Vasily's own motions drove the slick flesh in and out of his grasp, and the firespirit began to moan.

The leather thong slipped from Vasily's hair, locks tumbling over his face as he let his head hang over Belphagor's chest. His moaning reached a fever pitch until at last he jerked back, flipped the hair out of his face, and let out a low, guttural groan.

Hot firespirit spunk shot up the front of the dress and splattered the side of Belphagor's mouth. It was slightly hotter than it ought to be—if he'd been swallowing Vasily, it would have stung, but as it was, it was like a spurt of hot wax that only made him harder with the rush of it.

Belphagor sat up and pulled Vasily forward, giving the hot spunk back to him with a penetrating kiss as he rose onto his knees and fucked him hard with the dress spread magnificently about them. Vasily wrapped his arms around him, moaning softly as Belphagor had his way.

Undone by Vasily's sounds and the kindling scent of his skin, Belphagor turned Vasily's head to the side, clamped his mouth over the piercing that marked Vasily as his, and buried a loud growl of pleasure against his skin as he burst inside him.

When Belphagor's body relaxed, he lay back and let Vasily fall against him, sweating and exhausted and almost purring with pleasure.

"Damn, I love you," Belphagor gasped into the tangle of his locks.

"*Ya lyublyu tebya, tozhe*, Beli," Vasily sighed against his chest. "I love you too."

When they'd cleaned up later and Belphagor had changed back into his own clothes, they came out to find a box had been delivered for

Beatrix. Bemused, Belphagor untied the string and paper and opened it. To his surprise, the box contained a small fortune in facets. A note bearing the supernal seal lay atop the sparkling gems. The principality had wished to thank him again and to reward him more formally.

He shook his head and looked up to see Tabris standing in the entrance to the parlor. Her stance was defeated, and she looked lost. He couldn't imagine her going on without Ouestucati, at any occupation.

"I believe this is for you, sweetheart." He held the box out to her. "Restitution from the Supernal House of Arkhangel'sk for your loss."

Tabris took the box and stared at it, weeping. "I can't take this. Masha told me what you did for me, and for your boy, after I—"

"It's yours," he said firmly. He thanked Masha and Anzhela for their hospitality, put his arm around Vasily, and headed home.

CHAPTER
SEVENTEEN

Belphagor was clearly feeling his oats this morning.

"You know, I still haven't decided what to do to you for showing up in Heaven and almost spoiling my game." He rocked back on the rear legs of the chair, observing Vasily with a self-satisfied smirk from across the room.

Vasily wanted to smack it off of him. Though it was a relief to see him looking more like himself. He'd put the metal bar back into his eyebrow and changed into less earthly clothing. But the black silk shirt with the lace cuffs that Vasily found irresistible on him clearly showed the ring of bruises around his neck.

Vasily picked at the surface of the bureau he was leaning against. "He nearly killed you, didn't he? Because of me."

Belphagor set the front legs of the chair on the ground. "I had things under control, *mal'chik*."

"'Under control'? If it weren't for that angel of yours, he *would* have killed you."

"Stop calling him 'that angel of mine.' In point of fact, I stabbed the bastard in the neck with a letter opener and put him out of commission before Phaleg ever managed to come to my aid. I don't suppose he mentioned that?"

"And you were unconscious before they got the door open, and they weren't sure you were breathing for a whole minute. Yes, he told me. And he's in love with you."

"What?" Belphagor blanched. "He said that?"

"He didn't have to. I could see it. I could hear it."

Belphagor looked troubled but not guilty. "Well, it's one-sided, I promise you. We've been intimate. I won't deny that." He chewed on the edge of his thumb. "I may have let things get a little out of hand."

Vasily tried to ignore the twist of steel in his gut.

"It may sound like bullshit, Vasya, but I got carried away with Phaleg because I missed you. That wasn't fair to him, and it wasn't fair to you. All I can say is that I'm an idiot and I'm sorry." His eyes searched Vasily's. "Come here. Come close to me."

"Is that an order?"

"It's a plea, *mal'chik*. I need you."

Vasily pushed away from the bureau and came to stand before him, and Belphagor pulled him onto his lap.

"I'm not used to needing anyone. You've slain me. You're *Svyatoy Georgiy*, and I'm your dragon."

"I'm who?"

"Shut up and let me be your dragon." Belphagor nuzzled at his neck, and the tightness in Vasily's stomach faded, as the blood it apparently required to maintain such angst had gone elsewhere. He'd almost forgotten the nagging feeling until someone knocked on the door.

"Phaleg." Belphagor stared in dismay when he opened the door. He'd wanted to do this privately with the angel, to thank him for all he'd done and to reassure him he would always have a special place in Belphagor's memories. But also to tell him in no uncertain terms that their lovely interlude was over. And maybe to discipline him once more as a parting sentiment—let him know he was still a good boy. He cringed inwardly at the self-indulgent thought.

"I see you're back to yourself. It suits you." Phaleg gave him a sad smile. "I didn't mean to intrude. I just wanted to make sure you were all right."

"Thank you. I wouldn't be if it weren't for you."

Phaleg shrugged. "I also wanted you to know that Duke Elyon will be hanged in Council Square tomorrow, along with half a dozen members of the Union of Liberation." He grimaced. "I didn't give up the names. I suppose Elyon must have wanted to take a few angels down with him."

Belphagor sighed. "Not surprising. I can't say I'll be glad to see a man hanged, even that one. But I doubt the Heavens will miss him."

Phaleg nodded and squared his shoulders. "Well . . . it's been an honor to know you." He hesitated, glancing behind Belphagor, and added in a quiet voice, "Goodbye, *ser*." He turned to go, but Belphagor stopped him.

"Phaleg, wait. Please come in. I'd like to speak with you a moment."

The angel's gaze darted toward Vasily once more, but when Belphagor moved aside and held the door open, Phaleg stepped in. He nodded to Vasily, looking intensely uncomfortable. Vasily, in turn, looked as if Belphagor had stabbed him.

Belphagor regarded them: one fiery, defiant demon who could take the harshest physical discipline, yet was easily injured with a word, and one proper, tightly controlled angel who could be reduced to the most extreme debasement in an instant, eager to please. An idea was forming that was almost too marvelous to work.

"Could you wait here? I need to have a word with Vasily in the hall." He looked at Vasily, silently asking him to trust him and come, though he feared the firespirit might explode at any second.

Vasily gave him a tight nod and went with him, avoiding Belphagor's eyes as he shut the door. "I'll go down to the market. I'm sure we're out of everything."

"*Mal'chik*." Belphagor waited until Vasily raised his head. "I don't want you to go anywhere."

Vasily's jaw was set tight. "You obviously need a moment with him. You can't very well let him walk away with that sad little 'Goodbye, *ser*.' You owe him something, though it makes me feel like I'm bleeding inside to say it."

"*Mal'chik*." Belphagor's sharp tone stopped Vasily's tongue. He put his hand on Vasily's cheek. "How would you feel about fucking an angel?"

It seemed to take a minute for the words to register before Vasily's eyes went wide. He opened his mouth but only made an odd sound in the back of his throat, like he'd choked on his own tongue.

Belphagor suppressed a smile. "It's true that I owe him something. But what he wants from me I can't give him. I can, however, offer him a chance to experience the utter debasement he craves—a reward that is simultaneously punishment. And it would please me immensely to see that gorgeous cock of yours buried in an angel's ass giving it the pounding it deserves."

He stroked his thumb over Vasily's bottom lip while more strangled noises came out of the firespirit as if he'd lost the capacity for speech. "It was just an idle whim. Never mind. I suppose it was a foolish one after all. Of course it's not your cup of tea."

"N— I . . ." Vasily blinked at him, and Belphagor could see the bulge of the aforementioned gorgeous cock in his pants, apparently awakened by the mention. "Unh," Vasily coughed.

Belphagor tilted his head. "Was that an answer in the affirmative after all?" The smile was gaining on him despite his best efforts as Vasily's speechlessness grew increasingly endearing. "You can nod if it's easier."

Vasily swallowed and nodded.

Belphagor's mouth curved upward just a touch. "There's a good boy. Give me a moment to inform him what's about to happen to him—and give him a chance to flee," he added with a wink. Belphagor stepped back into the room and closed the door.

Phaleg rose from the edge of the stool by the basin stand, his hat in his hand. "I'm sorry. I shouldn't have come."

"Do you wish to please me?"

Phaleg paused, looking puzzled. "I'm sorry?"

"It's a simple question."

The angel lowered his eyes. "You know I do. *Da, ser.*"

Belphagor approached him and took the hat from his hand, set it on the stool, and lifted the angel's chin. "You are without question the best behaved boy who has ever knelt before me. You've done all that I've asked you and more. You've accepted that I've toyed with you for my own selfish reasons while I love another, though it causes you sorrow."

"Belphagor—"

Without warning, Belphagor slapped him, and the angel stared, stunned. "You don't speak when I'm speaking to you, and you do not address me with such familiarity. I've hurt you, and not in ways that I intended. You deserve better, and more than I can offer you. But what I can offer is to share my most precious possession with you before we part, to show you how deeply you've moved me with your devotion. After today, we'll return to our worlds, but right now, you can get down on your hands and knees and beg me to let you take the sweetest demon cock in the Heavens up your ass while I watch, and remember it for a lifetime."

It was now—understandably—Phaleg's turn to be speechless.

Belphagor stroked the back of his hand against the angry mark he'd left on the angel's cheek. "Understand, this isn't an order. You don't have to say yes. I won't be angry, and you won't have disappointed me. We can just say our goodbyes—"

"*Da, ser*," Phaleg burst out, the rest of his face blushing to match the mark. "Please. *Da, ser.*"

Belphagor smiled. "I want you to promise me something, Phaleg."

"Anything, *ser.*"

"That you'll find someone among your kind who will give you what you need and who'll appreciate the extraordinary gifts you have to offer. I assure you, I'm not unique in my desires. You find someone who will make you crawl to him and love you for it."

Phaleg nodded silently, and Belphagor gave him the lightest of kisses, their lips barely touching, before turning to the door and opening it. He was half-afraid Vasily would have thought better of it and taken off, but he stood where Belphagor had left him, his eyes still a bit huge as if he couldn't quite believe what was about to happen. When he entered, both demon and angel blushed scarlet as their eyes met.

"Phaleg," said Belphagor, "I imagine you'll want to take off your clothes. I have a feeling this is going to get messy." He held out his arm like a valet.

The angel trembled, unbuttoning his coat and laying it over Belphagor's arm, then made swift work of undressing, giving everything to Belphagor. He stood vulnerable and naked between the fully clothed demons, apparently too scared to be aroused.

Belphagor sat on the bed. "On the ground, boy." He noted Vasily's jaw tightening at the word. "Come to me."

Phaleg got down on hands and knees and crawled to him, his eyes searching Belphagor's.

Belphagor lifted his chin. "He's not likely to be gentle, you understand. If at any time you need it to stop—for whatever reason: if it's too much for you or you've changed your mind—you say, '*pozhaluista.*' That means 'please.' Can you repeat that?"

The angel managed a close approximation.

Belphagor nodded. "Good boy." He looked up at Vasily's face, a canvas of conflicting emotion. Belphagor tossed him the bottle of almond oil from the nightstand, and Vasily caught it smoothly. "Whenever you're ready, *moi mal'chik*. And don't forget to—"

At an irritated glare from Vasily, he aborted the admonition for the firespirit to temper his element. Phaleg had begun to tremble from head to toe, and Belphagor put his hand on the angel's shoulder.

"Might I suggest, *mal'chik*, that you fucking get to it, before the poor boy dies of fright."

The sharp rebuke did the trick. Vasily yanked open the buttons of his fly and let out his eager cock, making it slick with oil. Too tall to do it crouching, he dropped to his knees, dug his fingers into the angel's left buttock to brace himself, and guided himself in.

Phaleg made a sharp sound as he was entered, and Belphagor snapped his fingers to get the angel to focus on him. "Relax. Breathe in deep. Now let it out slowly, and push back gently against him with your breath. There you go. That's it."

Phaleg's eyes were wide with effort, lips unconsciously parted, as Vasily pressed onward with an excited growl. He began to thrust, slowly at first while the angel groaned, and then picking up speed. The room was silent except for the steady slapping of skin against skin and Phaleg's soft vocalizations.

"Does that feel good, *mal'chik*?"

"*Da, ser,*" Vasily grunted, though he looked like he was concentrating rather too hard to be enjoying it.

He clucked his tongue and shook his head. "You might have a concern for Phaleg's pleasure. I see he's reacting positively to your attentions."

Vasily glared but reached his hand around to grasp the angel's half-erect cock. He began to stroke, and Phaleg responded swiftly, stiffening under Vasily's tight grip. The moans he was making were no longer tentative, growing stronger as his breathing quickened, and Vasily's enjoyment began to seem more genuine.

He relaxed his left hand to smooth it across the angel's ass, and then slid it up Phaleg's spine to twist his fingers in the golden hair. Phaleg was definitely responding now, arching as Vasily tugged his head back, eyes closing, the moans coming in a steady, melodic staccato.

Belphagor slipped off the bed and crouched next to Vasily to whisper in his ear. "I'd like to have his mouth, but if you say no, I'll stay out of it."

Vasily looked him in the eyes, his own glowing dangerously. "Do it," he growled.

With Phaleg's eyes still closed as he abandoned himself to his pleasure, Belphagor slipped quietly back onto the bed and unlaced his leather breeches. When he pressed his hardness against Phaleg's lips, the angel's eyes opened in surprise.

"You're getting a little loud, boy. I thought I'd shut you up."

Phaleg opened his mouth eagerly and took him in. Belphagor groaned with relief, having been going just a bit mad watching and having none. He'd never been good at self-denial. Phaleg moaned with enthusiasm around him, clearly enjoying having his mouth full.

Belphagor looked at Vasily and unbuttoned his shirt, revealing himself slowly, knowing it excited him and that Belphagor's steady motion in Phaleg's mouth with no hands for balance would excite him further. He wasn't wrong.

When Belphagor slipped the shirt off, Vasily leaned against Phaleg with a groan of surprise as he saw the new decorations Belphagor hadn't shown him yet. Steel rings pierced both of his nipples.

"*Bozhe moi*," Vasily breathed. "When did you— Ohhh, *fuck*!" He drove himself hard against the angel and yanked on his hair with a low roar of pleasure through gritted teeth. The vigorous motion caused Phaleg to climax an instant later, both of them groaning in unison as Phaleg shuddered beneath him, his ejaculate shooting upward at his own chest.

Pleased, Belphagor leaned forward and knitted his fingers through Vasily's in the angel's soft hair, thrust swiftly against Phaleg's moaning throat, and let out a triumphant shout as he spilled into him.

Phaleg swallowed without hesitation, with a final moaning crescendo of satisfaction.

As Belphagor finished and pulled out, the angel looked up at him, eyes bright and eager for validation. Belphagor cupped his cheek. "You've been an extraordinarily good boy. Both of you have," he added, looking up at Vasily, whose cheeks reddened a bit, as if after everything they'd shared, being called *boy* in front of Phaleg embarrassed him.

Vasily eased himself out of the angel and buttoned up. Phaleg went a bit limp against Belphagor's knees as the demon let him go, as though Vasily's efforts had been the only thing holding him up.

Belphagor pushed him back onto his heels and grinned at the trail of spunk that rose all the way to the angel's chin. "Told you it might get messy." He stroked his fingers through it and put them in Phaleg's mouth to suck them clean. While Phaleg knelt gazing up at him, Belphagor took the angel's shirt from the foot of the bed and put it around his shoulders, helping him slip his arms into the sleeves. Phaleg took this as his cue and rose to put on the rest of his uniform.

"Thank you," he murmured as he put on his cap. Skin slightly flushed, he glanced at Vasily standing against the bureau with folded arms. "Thank you, both."

"Don't mention it," said Vasily gruffly. Though he'd fucked the angel and obviously enjoyed it, he clearly wasn't about to give him or Belphagor an inch.

Phaleg gave Belphagor a sharp bob of his head as if bowing to a superior and went to the door. "It was a memorable first time." He paused with his hand on the knob and looked back at Belphagor. "All of it."

"You remember what I said," Belphagor admonished as he rose to see him out. "You find that angel. He's out there." He kissed Phaleg's cheek. "Thank you for everything you've given me, dear boy. I won't forget any of it either."

When he turned around after shutting the door, instead of glaring at him, Vasily was staring at him oddly. "What did he mean by first time? First time with two demons?"

"No, *mal'chik*. First time getting fucked." He crossed the room and kissed the stunned Vasily rather less chastely than he'd kissed the angel, pulling his head down to Belphagor's level with a fist in his hair and tasting every smoky-flavored inch of his mouth. He raised a wicked eyebrow with a smirk when he released him. "You're welcome."

Belphagor declined to attend the public hanging, and Vasily was glad of it. The politics of Heaven were of no concern to demons, and Raqia soon forgot about the extravagance and excesses of the Left Bank, leaving the bohemian set to entertain itself. Back at The Brimstone, Belphagor was still teaching him to "read" people at the wingcasting table but not letting him play.

"You'd lose my entire purse in five minutes with that fiery scowl of yours. Patience, boy."

Vasily was restless. Their room seemed unbearably small, though he'd never noticed it before. *Raqia* seemed small. Even Heaven. Yet he had nothing to be unhappy about. Belphagor loved him. Belphagor was *his*, and he'd given up that sweet piece of angel ass without complaint.

Perhaps it was all the excitement of being a fugitive that had mixed Vasily up, as though he expected drama and intrigue around every corner. It was foolish. He didn't want drama and intrigue, and he didn't want to be in that state he'd been in: loving Belphagor desperately, waiting for the other shoe to drop at any moment, waiting to be abandoned. He wanted *this*. Vasily stroked the spikes of the piercing at his neck. And yet, he wanted something . . . more.

He lost his temper at the wingcasting table when Belphagor played his game of ignoring him just to try to rile him. He was riled all right. He felt like he was going to jump right out of his skin. Belphagor sent him to their room and played out the rest of the game before joining him there.

From the doorway, Belphagor watched him silently fuming on the edge of the bed. "Are you unhappy with me here?"

Vasily's head jerked up at the worried tone. "No! No, Beli, I'm sorry. I didn't mean to make you think I was unhappy. I don't know what's wrong with me." He ran his fingers over the locks that were settling into a smooth sheaf. "I've never been so happy." Incongruously, he frowned. "I know I sound absurd."

Belphagor came and knelt beside him, something he never did, crossing his arms on Vasily's lap and resting his chin on his hands. "Sweet boy. *Moi milyy mal'chik.* I think you need to hear the bells ring."

"The bells?" Vasily stared down at him, baffled and somewhat discomfited by the reversal of their customary positions.

Belphagor glanced up with mischief in his eyes. "What do you say we take a little fall?"

Leningrad looked like a winter fairyland, trees sparkling with a glaze of snow, and little lights lining the bare branches along the Neva. *St. Petersburg*, Belphagor had to remind himself. Times changed rapidly in the world of Man.

They walked down Nevsky Prospekt at dusk after arriving by train at *Moskovskiy Vokzal*. Vasily stared with wonder when they reached *Dvortsevaya Ploshchad*, uncannily similar to Palace Square in Elysium with its earthly copy of the celestial Winter Palace.

"How?" he breathed.

Belphagor shrugged. "Who knows? Perhaps the Malakim influenced Peter the Great when he established the city." He gave Vasily a sly sidelong look. "Or perhaps Heaven is merely a lovely dream we've been having."

Vasily snorted. "Not *all* lovely."

"But you are, sweet boy. That's all I see."

Vasily blushed and ducked his head, and Belphagor itched to kiss him. He'd have to watch himself. They'd already been called unsavory names by a drunk who'd pegged them instantly as "the wrong sort" when they'd emerged onto the surface from the train. Although he'd seemed uncertain whether he objected to their perceived perversion or ethnicity, lobbing a racist slur at them before draining the bottle of cheap vodka in his hand and lobbing it as well. He'd missed by a mile. Surprisingly, they'd blended in more in Moscow. Here, they seemed to stand out, rough and unusual against the refined architecture and gilded spires.

Another passerby had snarled "*Khuysos!*" when they'd taken a detour along the Fontanka River to see the beautifully sculpted Horse Tamers that decorated the four corners of the Anichkov Bridge. Of course, that might have been because Belphagor had leaned too close to Vasily, whispering against his skin, "This wild, untamable beast rearing up on his hind legs reminds me of you."

"I suppose you're the naked man holding the bridle, then," Vasily had said with a laugh.

Belphagor had raised his eyebrow and replied, "Was that in question?"

As they got closer to the palace, Vasily asked why so many commoners were wandering about on the grounds. "They don't let them just walk in?" he exclaimed as he saw a group head through the gates.

Belphagor smiled. "They do, and we can, if you want. It's a museum now. The tsars are long gone."

Vasily did, and for a handful of rubles, they bought tickets and spent the rest of the afternoon wandering through the opulent rooms. Belphagor had a chance to see the stark similarity of the interior to the wing he'd seen as Beatrix. He'd visited the Hermitage before, but it had been years, and he'd forgotten. There was the Malachite Room, impossibly identical. He half expected Principality Helison to walk into the room flanked by shimmering Seraphim.

When the museum closed and the dour docents kicked them out, they strolled along the embankment beside the frozen Neva, even more dreamlike under the night sky with its garland of lights, as though tiny flames winked in the dormant trees.

Vasily paused and gazed across the river when they passed the forbidding edifice of Kresty Prison. "What's that building?"

"A place you never want to see the inside of." Belphagor hurried him along. He hadn't brought Vasily here to see the ugliness of the world of Man but to marvel at its beauty. But there was something more breathtaking than all the terrestrial marvels themselves, and it was within them.

Without explaining where they were going, he booked them on another train into the dark night, where Vasily promptly fell asleep against his shoulder. Belphagor eased him down onto his lap and stroked his locks as the train rushed onward.

They arrived at Vladimir, east of Moscow, early in the morning. Belphagor had chosen the town on a whim, remembering the pretty Uspensky Cathedral from when he'd passed through it once working his game on passengers on the train. With a little shared vodka and cards, he'd managed to make his way across the continent accruing stacks of rubles more than once. He calculated that they'd arrive at their destination a few minutes before Russian Orthodox matins.

Vasily followed sleepily from the train. "What are we doing here?" He yawned. "*Where* are we doing here?"

"In Vladimir," said Belphagor. "Going to church."

"Come again?"

"I told you about churches, the places where the faithful beseech God in Heaven."

"Yes, I remember," said Vasily dryly. "I'm just wondering why a couple of Raqia demons are going to one."

"We're not going in," said Belphagor, being deliberately mysterious.

They arrived in front of the white edifice topped with five golden cupolas and a central spire, looking aethereal in the gray predawn light among the snow. No one was about. Another advantage of going a bit out of the way for the experience. Belphagor slipped his arm around Vasily's waist.

Vasily jumped at the touch, already attuned to the dangers of this world. "What if someone sees us?"

"I doubt anyone's out this early. And if they are, they'll see something else in a moment that will make them forget."

The firespirit heat kept him warm while they waited, though he had to stamp his feet from time to time. And then it began: the tolling of the bells. For nearly 70 years, they'd been silent.

Vasily pulled closer to Belphagor with a start as it commenced and gazed up at the towers ringing with sound. It was both joyful and mournful in a way Belphagor couldn't explain, except that if he had a soul, the bells spoke to it. Even when he'd been most down on his luck—and he'd been down as far as anyone in any sphere could go— they'd given him a strange hope, though they belonged to a faith impossible for him to believe in.

Belphagor kissed Vasily's warm neck as the ringing finally died down.

"Did we come here for the bells?" Vasily whispered, caught by the magic of their spell.

"Every time a bell rings," said Belphagor.

Vasily tilted his head. "What's that from? It sounds familiar."

"The American movie, *It's A Wonderful Life*."

"Oh, right!" Vasily grinned. "Every time a bell rings, an angel gets his wings." He laughed. "I guess a ton of them must have just sprouted." Belphagor merely smiled at him. It took Vasily a few moments before it finally dawned on him. "You mean— Are we going to? Am *I*?"

Belphagor unbuttoned Vasily's coat and removed it, then took his shirt as well. The firespirit hardly shivered. "You are, my dear boy. I'll hold these for you in case the heat is too intense."

"The heat?"

"Your fire, *mal'chik*." He pulled Vasily's head down for a soft kiss. "Let it build inside you, like it does when I've pissed you off." He cupped the rough beard on either side of Vasily's face between his hands. "Suppose I told you to drop to your knees and service me right here in front of anyone who might walk by?"

Vasily pulled back with a jerk. "I am *not* sucking your cock in a churchyard in the world of Man!"

Belphagor lifted an eyebrow. "Well, now you've issued me a challenge, *mal'chik*. But let's keep that for sometime later. Right now, concentrate on how you're going to feel when that happens. Imagine an angelic soldier or two standing by watching."

Vasily's eyes were sparking. "I don't like this. What are you doing?" The edges of his skin had begun to dance already with a scattering of ruby flame, like filaments of plasma against the inner surface of a glass orb.

"Maybe I'll have you work me up until I'm ready to peel down the pants of one of the angels and bend him over your back while you're on your hands and knees and take him—"

"Fuck *you*!" Vasily roared, and then he jerked his shoulder blades back with a grimace of surprise, turning like a dog chasing its tail as he tried to see what was tearing at his flesh.

Belphagor took a wide step back—wisely, it turned out. Ruby flame erupted from Vasily's shoulders like molten metal and shot out toward the sides, the "feathers" of the span gleaming with shades of scarlet and vermillion.

They were wings of elemental fire, as solid and well defined as the wings of any bird yet their fire ever moving within the shape as though trapped in liquid amber.

"Fuck *me*," Vasily gasped in wonder as he let them fully unfurl. Belphagor smirked, thinking that was precisely what he wanted to do at the moment. Across the snowy yard, the cupolas glittered with Vasily's light.

"Perhaps I ought to have chosen something a little *more* out of the way," he conceded, glancing about. "But no matter. Done is done." Vasily's chest was rising and falling as he stood in a state of temporary shock. Belphagor stepped up carefully to run his hands over Vasily's shoulders toward the new limbs, and shook his head. "My lovely boy. You're simply stunning." He stroked Vasily's cheek. "Are you going to try them out?"

"Try them out? I can fly?"

Belphagor laughed softly. "What did you think they were for, dear boy? Just relax and let yourself rise. Your wings will do the rest."

Vasily stretched his wings and took a deep breath, and then gasped as his feet came off the ground. In an instant, he was off and surging into the glow of dawn, soaring over Vladimir. If anyone saw, Belphagor supposed they'd mistake him for sunrise. Their radiance was similar.

Vasily spun and dipped and rushed upward again, heading off into the distance to where Belphagor lost sight of him for a moment, nervously waiting, and then, like a flash of sun over the horizon, he glided down, landed gently, and shrugged his shoulders back, instinctively putting his wings away to where mere Men wouldn't see them. His face was alight with pure wonder, no radiance needed.

Belphagor gave him back his clothes and helped him into them, and neither spoke while he buttoned him up with care. He kissed him once more as Vasily stood silent, not giving a damn if anyone saw. Vasily engulfed him in his warm arms, lifting him off the ground a bit and making Belphagor laugh.

"That'll cost you," he said as Vasily set him down, though he couldn't do it with a stern face. "And your refusal at what you thought I was ordering you to do—that'll cost you dear."

Vasily grinned. "I don't care, Beli. Do what you like to me. It was worth it."

Dear Reader,

Thank you for reading Jane Kindred's *Prince of Tricks*!

We know your time is precious and you have many, many entertainment options, so it means a lot that you've chosen to spend your time reading. We really hope you enjoyed it.

We'd be honored if you'd consider posting a review—good or bad—on sites like **Amazon, Barnes & Noble, Kobo, Goodreads, Twitter, Facebook, Tumblr,** and your blog or website. We'd also be honored if you told your friends and family about this book. Word of mouth is a book's lifeblood!

For more information on upcoming releases, author interviews, blog tours, contests, giveaways, and more, please sign up for our weekly, spam-free newsletter and visit us around the web:

Newsletter: riptidepublishing.com/newsletter
Twitter: twitter.com/RiptideBooks
Facebook: facebook.com/RiptidePublishing
Goodreads: tinyurl.com/RiptideOnGoodreads
Tumblr: riptidepublishing.tumblr.com

Thank you so much for Reading the Rainbow!

RiptidePublishing.com

ALSO BY
JANE KINDRED

ABOUT THE AUTHOR

Jane Kindred is the author of the Harlequin Nocturne series Sisters in Sin and of the epic fantasy series The House of Arkhangel'sk and Looking Glass Gods. She spent her formative years in the desert Southwest ruining her eyes reading romance novels in the sun and watching Star Trek marathons in the dark. She now writes to the sound of San Francisco foghorns while her spoiled cat, Sophie, blinks at her from her fancy bed at the end of the mattress like Baby Yoda having just eaten a Frog Lady's egg.

You can find Jane on Twitter @JaneKindred, on her cleverly named Facebook page, JaneKindred, or via her website, at the unsurprising address of www.janekindred.com.